# THE PRINCESS AND THE SINGLE DAD

JESSICA GILMORE

# HIS MAJESTY'S FORBIDDEN FLING

SUSAN MEIER

MILLS & BOON

First published in Great Britain 2022
by Mills & Boon, an imprint of HarperCollins*Publishers* Ltd,
1 London Bridge Street, London, SE1 9GF

www.harpercollins.co.uk

HarperCollins*Publishers*
1st Floor, Watermarque Building,
Ringsend Road, Dublin 4, Ireland

The Princess and the Single Dad © 2022 Jessica Gilmore

His Majesty's Forbidden Fling © 2022 Linda Susan Meier

ISBN: 978-0-263-30221-9

07/22

MIX
Paper from
responsible sources
FSC
www.fsc.org
FSC® C007454

Incorrigible lover of a happy-ever-after, **Jessica Gilmore** is lucky enough to work for one of London's best known theatres. Married with one daughter, one fluffy dog and two dog-loathing cats, she can usually be found with her nose in a book. Jessica writes emotional romance with a hint of humour, a splash of sunshine, delicious food—and equally delicious heroes!

**Susan Meier** is the author of over fifty books for Mills & Boon. *The Tycoon's Secret Daughter* was a Romance Writers of America RITA® Award finalist, and *Nanny for the Millionaire's Twins* won the Book Buyers Best Award and was a finalist in the National Readers' Choice Awards. She is married and has three children. One of eleven children herself, she loves to write about the complexity of families and totally believes in the power of love.

Llyfrgelloedd Caerdyd
www.caerdydd.gov.uk/llyfrgelloed
Cardiff Libraries
www.cardiff.gov.uk/libraries

**Also by Jessica Gilmore**

*Indonesian Date with the Single Dad*
*Christmas with His Cinderella*

**The Princess Sister Swap miniseries**

*Cinderella and the Vicomte*


**Also by Susan Meier**

*Tuscan Summer with the Billionaire*
*The Billionaire's Island Reunion*
*The Single Dad's Italian Invitation*
*Reunited Under the Mistletoe*


Discover more at millsandboon.co.uk.

# THE PRINCESS AND THE SINGLE DAD

JESSICA GILMORE

MILLS & BOON

This book is for everyone who has been able to escape from the trials of the last couple of years through reading romance.

Here's to escapism and brighter days.

# CHAPTER ONE

JACK TRELOAR SAT back in the rather uncomfortable stone seat and surveyed his fellow audience members. No surprises here. The audience was exactly what he had expected, people from the village and the surrounding towns, mostly friends and family of the cast, together with a smattering of tourists. An easily pleased, uncritical, warm audience predisposed to be supportive of the amateur production.

Everything he wanted to change.

Although he had to admit to being pleasantly surprised by the performance itself. Yes, it was amateurish, yes, the costumes were clearly home-made, and the backdrops and props owed more to enthusiasm than skill, but some of the acting was really good, good enough to transport him—momentarily—from noticing the chill of the stone seat and the laboured scene changes. Juliet was especially good, although that was no real surprise. After all, Clem Beaumont was a professional, one who, in Jack's opinion, should go back to finding proper paid work and spend less time poking her nose into his business.

At least what he *hoped* would be his business if he could just win round the very community sitting here to his vision. He allowed his gaze to wander around the auditorium once again. This place was a gem, an open-air amphitheatre, stone seats rising up from a semi-circular stage, the sea visible beyond creating a truly atmospheric backdrop as the early June sky began to tinge pink, the sun sinking at last.

At least, it should be a gem. But right now it was more unpolished diamond than jewel in the village crown. Ticket-buyers for the pitifully few shows put on here headed in through a plain reception area where, instead of a bar and restaurant, volunteers sold lukewarm white wine and cans of beer from a trestle table. There was nowhere to mingle, to enjoy an interval drink, to soak up the atmosphere. But the potential was here for anyone with half an eye—and Jack had that eye. He could turn this theatre and Polhallow into a *destination*. A place people flocked to not just for the sea, beautiful as it was, or for the scenery or any of the other reasons that made the Cornish village such an attractive place to holiday, but for the theatre, just as people visited St Ives for art or Padstow for food. Jack had done his research; the stage was big enough to tempt the major touring companies, and the venue could host bands as well as musicals and plays. He could put Polhallow on the map.

But to say that the local community didn't share his vision would be putting it mildly; you'd think he was planning on tearing the whole thing down and replacing it with some kind of concrete monstrosity rather than trying to bring jobs and prosperity to the village outside the crucial summer season. He'd even guaranteed that the local schools, dance troupes and amateur companies could still use the theatre—so why couldn't the village see that everyone would benefit? Probably because he was the one behind the scheme. Clearly it didn't matter how rich and successful he was, the people of Polhallow would only ever see him as the town tearaway.

Well, they would learn to look again. Polhallow was the right place to raise his daughters— fresh air, outdoor pursuits and less of the monied hedonism that characterised their affluent London neighbourhood. If he had to win the townsfolk round to smooth his daughters' path then that was what he would do. Not that he would mind seeing respect, no matter how grudging, in the eyes of everyone who had doubted or judged him in the past.

Jack had intended to leave at the interval but, despite himself, he found himself getting caught up in the tragedy unfolding on the stage, even though he knew all too well where teen melodrama could lead. The play was brought to life by Clem's charisma and skill and the rest of the cast rose to meet her, some of them achieving what Jack suspected were hitherto unexpected heights. By the time Juliet collapsed on her lover's tomb and the final epilogue was spoken, Jack was shocked to feel the prickling of tears in his eyes. He looked around hurriedly, hoping nobody had seen the weakness. He needn't have worried, because although his presence had attracted a few stares and pointed comments when he'd arrived, most people were too absorbed in the play to give him more than a second glance and were now applauding the cast with gusto.

The woman sitting next to Jack was no exception. She was on her feet clapping and whooping as if she had been watching the Royal Shakespeare Company, tears trickling down her cheeks, visible despite her huge sunglasses, her shouts of 'Bravo! Bravo!' ringing out. She sat back down, removing her sunglasses to quickly wipe away the tears, and caught Jack's amused gaze with a slightly self-deprecating shrug.

'Wasn't that amazing?' She spoke English fluently and with no real discernible accent but there was a trace of something he couldn't place, almost Spanish, or southern French.

'It wasn't what I expected,' Jack said diplomatically. Amazing was maybe pushing it, but he couldn't deny the play hadn't been the car crash he had been expecting.

'Clem is so talented, I had no idea.' The woman continued clapping again enthusiastically and bouncing to her feet as the lead actress came forward. There was a definite similarity between the smiling actress and his neighbour, both had long dark curls and a similar slant to their high cheek-boned oval faces with long-lashed hazel eyes above full mouths. A sense of recognition tugged at him.

'Have we met?' Jack asked.

She shook her head, replacing the sunglasses firmly. 'I don't think so, I'm not from around here. I'm a cousin of Clem's.'

'That explains the resemblance,' he said, and she smiled but with a hint of nervousness that surely his innocuous comment couldn't have provoked.

'Are you staying here long?'

'No.' She slumped very slightly, her tone dejected. 'I have to get back; you know how it is. Duty calls, but I wish I could stay. There is something so special about Polhallow, don't you think? I would love to spend more time here.'

'I know what you mean. I just moved back from London, and I can't believe it's taken me so long.' It was definitely the right idea to move his family back to Cornwall. London felt too big, too dirty, too dangerous for his girls. He wanted them to grow up with beaches to play on and with sea air filling their lungs.

Of course, their childhood was very different to his, thanks to the big clifftop house, the swimming pool and treehouse, the playroom filled with everything their hearts desired. Jack knew the dangers of spoiling his girls, but he also knew what it was like to go without, and it was hard not to be indulgent when they'd lost their mother at such a tender age. He wanted to give them everything he had never had—including a name that was respected. His fortune and success impressed some people, but to far too many he was still that wild Treloar boy.

The cast had taken their final bow and moved off the stage and the audience around them began to move. 'It was nice meeting you.' He held out a hand. 'I'm Jack Treloar. Have a good rest of your visit and do pass my congratulations on to Clem. She's quite something.'

The woman hesitated before taking his hand. As his hand closed round her soft, cool fingers a tingle shot up his arm, unexpected and potent, and it was all he could do not to drop her hand; it had been a long time since he'd had such a powerful physical reaction to a woman, not since Lily. Sometimes he thought that part of him had been buried with his wife.

'Rosy,' she said after a brief pause. 'My friends call me Rosy.' A flower name. His chest squeezed. His wife had insisted on flower names for their daughters, to mirror hers.

'Nice to meet you, Rosy. If you find yourself making a longer stay than expected, look me up. I'd love to buy you a drink.'

Rosy looked as astonished by his offer as he felt having made it. He had been a married man since he was just eighteen thanks to an unplanned pregnancy, widowed for just two years. Jack couldn't remember the last time he'd asked a woman out. Dimples flashed in her cheeks, adding an elfin charm to her undeniable beauty.

'That's a very kind offer, Jack. Maybe one day I'll be able to take you up on it.' She nodded towards the exit. 'I need to go. Enjoy the rest of your evening.'

Jack watched the slim, graceful woman make her way out and a wry smile twisted his mouth. The first time in years he'd been tempted to make a move on a woman, and she couldn't get out of there fast enough.

*Nice job, Treloar.*

He watched her for another couple of seconds before making his own way out of the theatre, acknowledging the few who acknowledged him but not stopping to join any of the chattering groups. He wouldn't be welcome anyway. Besides, he was keen to get home and check in on his sleeping girls, to drop a kiss on their foreheads and whisper his daily affirmation that he was here, and they were safe.

Glancing towards the exit Rosy had disappeared through, he headed in the opposite direction towards home. He was unlikely to see her again and that was a good thing. He didn't have time to date. His family came first, his business second and restoring his name third. That was his choice and he stood by it.

But part of him was still disappointed that they

wouldn't have time for that drink before Clem's mysterious cousin disappeared again.

Arrosa Artega, soon to be the Crown Princess of Asturia, made it back to the little clifftop cottage where Clem lived before her half-sister and let herself in with the key she valued far more than any of her heirloom jewels. Henri, her ever-present driver and bodyguard, manoeuvred the bulky hamper she'd brought with her into the house before returning to guard the outside while Arrosa poured herself a glass of wine and curled up on the sofa in the sitting room waiting for Clem to return.

Maybe it was foolishness to risk exposing Clem's identity for such a fleeting visit, but Arrosa hadn't seen her sister in so long. She'd wanted to see her sister act, true, but she was also in a real tangle and Clem was the person who always helped her see straight.

As she sipped the wine she looked around the cosy room with its filled bookshelves and colourful paintings, Gus, the latest in a string of rescue cats, asleep on the window seat. This cottage always felt like home to her, far more than the luxurious château in which she had been raised, and she would always be grateful to Clem's mother for letting her be part of the family, even if Arrosa's—and Clem's—father, Zorien, had deceived the French woman about who he was, and then paid her off to keep Clem's existence a secret. The room was filled with Simone Beaumont's eclectic taste, reflecting her larger-than-life personality, and Arrosa's heart ached with grief for the woman who had been a second mother to her, remembering the summers she had spent here and Simone's warm wisdom and affection.

She was still lost in memory when she heard the sounds of Clem's return and jumped up to embrace her before standing back to examine her closely, drinking in the sister she barely saw.

'It's not that I'm not happy to see you, Rosy, but what on earth are you doing here?' Clem asked as Arrosa handed her a glass of wine.

'Apart from watching my sister play Juliet? Clem, you were brilliant.'

'You've never come to see me act before.'

Guilt hit her hard as she curled back up on the sofa. 'I wish I had. Clem, I'm so sorry I didn't come to Simone's funeral. I loved her so much, but...'

'That's okay, she would have understood. And you sent such beautiful flowers.'

'But you're my sister, I should have been there for you.'

'It's hard for you to get away. I know that.'

It was, but that was no real excuse, not when Clem needed her. 'It was easier when we were children,' she said wistfully. 'Especially when I was at school and could spend my exeat weekends here as well as some of the holidays.' It had been eight long years since she had last spent time here in Polhallow as plain Rosy, Clem's French cousin. In her memory every day had been sunny and filled with laughter and happiness. The joy of being just Rosy, not a princess.

Clem came and sat next to her, squeezing her hand. 'Fess up, why are you here, apart from coming to see me as Juliet? Don't think I'm not pleased to see you, but I know you and impulsive isn't in your schedule. Is everything okay?'

Arrosa took a swig of wine and summoned up the

courage to say the words she had barely dared to think, memories of her conversation with Akil Ortiz echoing through her mind. 'I'm not sure.' She paused and glanced at her sister. 'I think I just asked someone to marry me.'

'You *think* or you did? Are congratulations in order? Who is the lucky man?' She could hear the worry in Clem's voice and tried not to wince.

'Akil. He's the Vicomte d'Ortiz, a rising star of the opposition. His father, the Duc d'Ortiz, was one of Papa's most vocal critics. Our families have been enemies for generations, you know how Asturians can be, but Akil and I are friends of a sort. We have a lot in common. Family honour and expectations and that kind of thing.'

'Friends of a sort? You're not even dating? Besides, what do you mean, you *think* you asked him to marry you?'

Feeling suddenly overwhelmingly weary, Arrosa tried to find the words to explain how helpful Akil had been in unifying the opposition parties behind the new inheritance law that was due to be ratified at the end of the summer. A law that would change the course of her already restricted life, undoing the primogeniture laws and making her the official heir to the throne.

'Clem, everyone—my parents, my advisers, the newspapers—have been pushing me to marry,' she went on, taking another sip of her wine as her stomach knotted with apprehension about the weeks and months and years ahead. 'To start thinking about an heir of my own. And the country will see me as more settled, more mature if I am married. I don't like being rushed, but I see the sense in it. The problem is, not only am I single but I don't see that changing. On the rare occasion I meet someone I like, the whole princess thing scares them off. Queen-to-be is going to make that a hundred times worse.' She sighed. 'I like Akil and he understands the court and my world and we have similar ambitions for Asturia… We were talking about what I wanted to achieve as the heir and realised how aligned our goals were, and I suddenly thought, well, he's the right age, single, understands my world. I could do a lot worse.' But even as she said the words, she could hear how hollow they were, how defeatist. She wasn't quite twenty-seven yet. Did she really want to settle, no matter how sensible her choice? Looking at Clem's expression, she knew her sister was thinking the same thing.

'Rosy, I think this is something you need to take some time and think about.' Clem was obviously picking her words with care. 'Really think about. You need a break. Stay here for a few weeks, Rosy. You know the Cornish air does you good.'

Closing her eyes, Arrosa imagined waking up to the Cornish sun, long walks on the beach and carefree days. 'I'd love to, but I'm heading back tonight.' It had been hard enough concealing her movements for this one evening, any longer would be too dangerous.

'Tonight? Oh, Rosy. You said yourself that you have no meetings.'

'I don't, but the speculation if I'm not seen, even from a distance, could be damaging this close to the ratification. I didn't go anywhere for a couple of weeks when I had flu last year and, according to the tabloids, I was having a facelift, had joined a cult and eloped with a soldier.' She tried for a laugh, but she knew it was unconvincing and could see Clem's face crease with concern. 'I know it's silly and I shouldn't care, but it's not just that I don't want any rumours circulating at home—eventually the press would find me and then they'd start wondering who *you* are and that's the last thing you need. It's safest for you if we're not seen together, Clem.'

How she hated the subterfuge and lies, wished she and Clem could be sisters openly, but she had spent eight years being the target of press interest and speculation. There was no way she was subjecting her sister to that intrusion.

'*If* they find you. After all, why would they look for you here?' Clem paused, a thoughtful expression crossing her face. 'I could go back to Asturia in your place.'

*What* had she just said? Arrosa couldn't have heard her sister correctly. But Clem had a determined air that Arrosa recognised all too well, one that usually preceded a piece of mischief.

'You're serious? Clem, no one would *ever* think you were me.'

'Up close, no. But in the back of a car, hair all neat like yours, in your clothes, with those big sunglasses you wear? Why wouldn't they? People see what they expect to see. We're the same build and height, the same colouring. And I'm an actress, I can walk like you, hold myself like you. You could have the summer here and I'll spend it in Asturia making sure the press gets enough glimpses to think you're busy preparing for the ratification and leaving you free to get some serious relaxation. I talk about my cousin all the time. No one here will think anything of it if we say I've got a job and you're cat-sitting. The only unbelievable part will be that I've been cast in anything. I'll have to claim I ended up on the cutting room floor.'

'That's the craziest thing I've ever heard. We'd never get away with it.' But how she wished they could.

'If you lived in the main castle or had dozens of servants then I agree, it would be impossible...'

'But I have my own cottage in the grounds of the Palais d'Artega,' Arrosa said slowly, the idea beginning to take shape. It was crazy and impossible, but she couldn't help imagining how it might work. 'People do come in to clean, but not when I'm around. Only Marie is there regularly, but of course she and Henri would need to know if there was any chance of this succeeding...'

*Was* there a chance? Clem was right, she had no appointments, no duties, no meetings for the next six weeks. No one was expecting to see her so who would know she wasn't actually there if Clem posed as her a couple of times a week in the back of a car? For a moment she allowed herself to visualise it, waking up to freedom, walks in public with no one taking any notice of her. But then reality inserted itself into her dreams. 'But it would be lonely, Clem. You'd have to be careful that no maids, no gardeners, no staff at all saw you. Some are new but some have been at the Palais since I was a baby. What would you do with yourself?'

'I'll make sure the press see Henri drive me around dressed as you, of course, but in between I'll wear my own clothes, let my hair go back to natural wildness and explore Asturia incognito. I've always wanted to go but somehow I never have. It would be a chance for me to see our father too. It'd be easier for him to spend time with me if I'm living at yours. No one would question him visiting you.'

Arrosa took another sip of wine and sat back. Clem no longer sounded speculative or concerned—she sounded hopeful. Arrosa knew how much her sister longed for a real relationship with their father, more so since she'd lost her mother. Zorien was a politician and diplomat first, a family man second and Arrosa wasn't sure he would ever be what Clem wanted him to be, but her sister deserved the chance to find that out for herself. A few weeks living in Asturia, able to visit Zorien openly, might give her that opportunity.

Another objection occurred to her. 'But what's the point of me being here if you aren't?' Most of the joy of being in Cornwall was being with Clem.

'Well, Gus needs feeding for a start. The sea needs swimming in, scones need eating, beaches need walking on, and you need time to be you, not the Crown Princess and future Queen. This gives you that time. And I need a change of scene too. I've been putting off making plans for my future, just existing for too long. Maybe some time away will give me some much-needed perspective. You'd be doing me a favour.'

'Sure, *I'd* be doing *you* the favour.' Arrosa shook her head affectionately at Clem.

'We'll do each other a favour. We both need some time away from our lives, so why not swap for a while? Your mother's not at home, is she?'

'No, she's spending the summer on Ischia on a retreat.'

'Then we're safe. We could do this. Your call, Rosy. What will it be? Six weeks of avoiding Akil, ducking away from the press and worrying yourself into a shadow, or all the cream teas you can eat and a summer lazing on the beach?'

'We must be mad to even consider this would work.' But she couldn't deny she was tempted.

'It's easy enough to swap back if we need to,' Clem pointed out. Arrosa stared at her for another minute, unable to deny how sorely tempted she was. Not just tempted, she needed this, more than she wanted to admit. Why not agree and see what happened?

'You're right. Let's give it a week and see where we are. Thank you, Clem. Cornwall is just what I need, and I think maybe Asturia is where you need to be as well. To a change of scenery.' She held up her glass and Clem clinked it with hers.

'To the princess swap.'

# CHAPTER TWO

IT TOOK ARROSA several moments to realise where she was the next morning. So many nights she'd dreamt she was back in the Cornish cottage, it was almost a shock to find herself there in actuality and not just in her imagination. The cosy bedroom was exactly the same as it had been the last time she had slept here. It never failed to touch her that Simone and Clem had kept a room just for her. The imposing château in which she had been raised had never felt like home the way the cottage did, and even though at twenty-one she'd moved out to a villa in the estate grounds, when she thought of home she thought of here.

The walls were the same sea green she'd picked at fifteen, the curtains and bedspread the ones she'd chosen at the same time. The dressing table still held some out-of-date cosmetics and the hairbrush she'd left here eight years ago and the small built-in wardrobe was filled with her clothes, most of which still fitted despite being bought for a teen. She'd rifled through it nostalgically the night before, searching for pyjamas. Some of the clothes were a little out of date and some not suitable for a woman in her mid-twenties, but nobody would be photographing her here; there was no need to be the fashionable designer Princess who graced countless magazine covers. Here she could just be Rosy in a pair of shorts and bikini top. Besides, there was always Clem's room to raid if she needed anything more.

It wasn't just her room that had been preserved in time. Clem had left home at eighteen to go to drama school and her room, which had been redecorated the same time as Arrosa's, was still decorated in the grey and white with orange accents theme she'd chosen back then. As for Simone's room… A lump filled Arrosa's throat as she stood at the doorway. There was no trace of the sickroom it had become. Rather it was as if Simone would walk in at any time to pick up one of the chic scarves with which she would transform her deceptively simple clothes. Her jewellery hung from pegs on the wall, her bed heaped high with cushions, the window seat overlooking the sea dressed with her favourite cashmere throw. It was impossible to believe that she wouldn't be coming back.

It took Arrosa a couple of hours to get herself together and dressed, padding around the cottage as she reacquainted herself with every nook and cranny. She took coffee, fruit and yogurt outside to breakfast in the pretty cottage garden before donning some of her old denim shorts, teaming them with a bright pink vest top, tucking her curls into a ponytail and adding some sunglasses as she readied herself to leave the house.

Walking down the road, weaving in and out of crowds of tourists, browsing shop windows felt like a five-star luxury experience. Nobody was watching her, nobody was judging her, she didn't need to watch her facial expressions or ensure that every hair was in place. Almost unconsciously her stride lengthened, her pace got jauntier as she breathed in the fresh sea air and drank in the scenery. She was almost lost to her surroundings as she stepped into the road, only to stop with a shock as a car screeched to a halt, a heavy hand on the horn alerting her to the fact she had nearly got herself run over. Of course, they drove on the left here. Holding up her hands in apology, Arrosa stepped back, only to halt in surprise as she recognised the irate driver at the wheel. It was the man who'd spoken to her yesterday, Jack something. The one she'd told she wouldn't be sticking around, the one who had asked her out for a drink. Recognition mingled with interest and a pull deep down she barely recognised, a flare of attraction as she took in the broad shoulders, sensual mouth and hooded eyes.

Arrosa sensed the moment he recognised her in return, his expression changing from annoyed to momentary surprise to inscrutable. She flushed, realising that he must think that she'd lied to him to get out of the offered drink. To her surprise she felt a need to explain, to tell him that she had been tempted, surprisingly tempted, to accept, that she really hadn't expected to be here this morning. But as she stood there, hands outstretched in both apology and almost a plea to be heard, he nodded curtly before accelerating away.

'*Dammit,*' she muttered. But then again, what did it matter? It wasn't as if she'd see him again. But some of the jauntiness left her step as she continued her walk, looking out for traffic a little more carefully.

Attraction was almost a foreign feeling to her. She'd spent so long schooling her emotions to be the perfect princess, the perfect diplomat, that her own personal preferences were almost indiscernible even to her. It had been a long time since she'd had such an instinctive reaction to someone. It was nice in a way to know that she still could feel an instant attraction.

Remembering Clem's instructions to swim and eat, Arrosa popped into the bakery to buy some fresh scones, and then into the delicatessen to add jam, cream and strawberries to her bag, promising herself a jog, swim or both before she tucked in to the delicacies. As she left the deli she bumped into Clem's friend Sally who she'd known as a teen and, after explaining Clem's sudden absence and her own appearance, was delighted to be asked to come along to the pub on Saturday and invited to see the latest in a superhero series at the cinema with Sally and her daughter in a few days' time. The cinema usually meant formal premieres complete with red carpets and receptions and uncomfortable corseted ballgowns. The prospect of a normal seat with popcorn and company she'd chosen was enticing and she accepted with alacrity, promising to let Sally know about the evening drink as well.

Returning to the cottage with her bag bulging with local delicacies, Arrosa started to put them away, pausing to look at remembered plates and mugs, blinking back tears as she saw the jars of jams and chutneys labelled in Simone's exuberant script. She'd just started to chop up some salad for lunch when her phone pinged with a message and she picked it up, expecting to see Clem's name, only for embarrassment to surge through her when she saw Akil's name on the screen. Embarrassment and guilt; she couldn't believe she'd just run away from the awkward situation she'd put them both in. With no little trepidation she opened the message.

Arrosa, I'm at your house with Clem. Let me know everything is all right.

Biting her lip, she reread it. So much for her confidence that nobody would come seeking her and discover their subterfuge. Here they were, less than twenty-four hours after Clem had suggested swapping, and they'd already been found out. Did this mean that she would need to return home? With a heavy heart she tapped out a returning message.

Everything is absolutely fine. I just needed some space. You can trust Clem with anything.

Reading one of Simone's adored vintage crime books with lunch cleared her head somewhat, as did a run followed by a refreshing swim, and by the time she sat back down in the garden to catch the late afternoon sun, Gus at her feet, with a fresh cup of tea and her book some of the anxiety had faded. There was no need for Akil to tell anybody that Clem was in Asturia instead of Arrosa and she knew he was no gossip, that was one of the reasons she trusted him. But she couldn't help but be relieved when her phone rang and Clem's name lit up the screen.

'How's it going?' her sister asked.

'I've had a run, a swim and I've got a week's worth of calories waiting for me in the form of cream and buttered scones so I'm absolutely fine. I'm more worried about you. What happened with Akil?'

'He came to see you. It was all slightly mortifying. I couldn't pretend that I didn't know about your not-quite-a-proposal as he mistook me for you at a distance and by the time he realised I wasn't you he'd already mentioned it. In the end I didn't really have a choice, I had to tell him who I am. But don't worry, our secret's safe.'

Arrosa sat back, trying to decipher Clem's tone. There was a suppressed emotion she couldn't quite identify, a strange kind of self-consciousness, almost excitement, in her sister's voice. What *exactly* had she and Akil talked about?

'What did you think of him?'

'I liked him. I liked him a lot. Obviously, he's handsome, and he's clearly successful, but there's a lot more to him than that. You could do a lot worse, Arrosa.' Clem paused. 'But that's by the by. Being able to do worse is not enough. I still think you need more, you of all people, with the path you have to tread. You need a real partner, someone who loves you and will always put you first. And I told him so.'

Arrosa could just imagine it. Her sister was always forthright. 'What did he say?'

'He agreed that you both had a lot of thinking to do. But I'm going to say to you what I said to him: I can see why on paper you're a good match. You can trust him; he knows your world. But I think that if you focus on that rather than what's in your hearts then there'll be trouble down the line. You both deserve more than something second-best.'

Arrosa's eyebrows shot up. *Both* deserve more? It sounded as if Clem and Akil had had quite the chat. It also sounded as if Akil had made quite the impact on Clem. Interesting. But it was also reassuring to know that someone cared enough about her to be so blunt, to put her interests first. She might feel alone far too often, but she always had her sister.

'Look, Clem,' she said reluctantly. 'My assumption that nobody would come and visit me, that we could pull this off with no one the wiser, was obviously completely wrong. It's been one day and already you've had to explain who you are to someone. I feel better already, just having the chance to walk down the road without anybody knowing who I was is the tonic I needed. It gave me the space to untangle my head a little.' She blew out a deep breath and stared out at the sea in the distance, trying to crystallise her thoughts, rationalise her relief at being away, that odd jolt of attraction that reminded her that she was a woman as well as a princess.

'I think you're probably right,' she said slowly, feeling her way through her tangled thoughts. 'I suggested marriage to Akil out of fear and panic and they're not the right reasons for marriage. Who knows what the future holds? It'd be silly of me to close down any chance of a meaningful relationship just because I'm a little bit scared. So, job done, I feel better and I'm ready to call Akil and apologise for putting him in such an awkward situation. With all that in mind, maybe we should swap back.' She closed her eyes as she made the offer. It was the last thing she wanted, this tantalising hint of freedom to be lost before she'd really had a chance to enjoy it.

'You must be crazy,' Clem said emphatically. 'Unless you've gone around proposing marriage to several other suitable men, I can't see anyone else just turning up at a guarded palace without an invitation. Akil was clearly a special case. And no way is twenty-four hours enough time for you to be completely rested. And *I'm* not ready yet either. I've not seen our father and I've hardly started exploring. One trip to one beach and one lunch of clams, delicious as they were, isn't exactly the exploring I'd intended.'

'Which beach did you go to?'

'I'm not sure.' Self-consciousness entered Clem's voice. 'Akil took me out for lunch and for a walk.'

'That was nice of him.' The two had clearly hit it off. Arrosa wasn't sure what that meant but she resolved to clear the air—and clear up the situation—with Akil as soon as possible.

'Yes, it was. Look, Rosy, let's carry on for a little bit longer and see where we are. But I'm glad you're feeling better and I'm glad you've decided not to marry Akil. I really liked him and if you were in love with him would welcome him as a brother-in-law…' There was a tinge of reservation in her voice that Arrosa noted. Yup, Akil clearly had made *quite* the impression on Clem. 'But as you're not I really think it's for the best. And it's also for the best that you get a good long rest.'

'You're sure?' Relief flooded through Arrosa as she double-checked. It had been the right thing to offer to switch back but she didn't want to, not yet. If possible, she wanted the full six weeks. She wanted more scones, several trips to the cinema, to walk down the street every single day relishing her anonymity.

'I'm sure. Now, go eat that scone and don't forget to send me a picture of Gus so I know you're remembering to feed him. Love you.'

'I love you too.' Arrosa ended the call and placed her phone back on the table, thinking about the next call she needed to make, and sooner rather than later. She might have more time but, before she could really enjoy it, she needed to clear things up with Akil. Not just for her own sake but for her sister's. The things

Clem hadn't said were more telling than the things she had, and that self- consciousness in her voice was new.

Maybe she should suggest that Akil take Clem out for more sightseeing?

As for herself, if she saw Jack again she would apologise and offer to buy him a drink. It was the least she could do after misleading him, after all.

'Daddy, please come bodyboarding with us.' Clover tugged at Jack's hand and his phone nearly fell from his grasp, his email half drafted.

'Careful,' he said as he returned his attention to it. 'I need to finish this first. Why don't you carry on with your sandcastle?' He reread the carefully crafted words and added another line. It was time to pull in the big guns, get an external agency to advise on the comms strategy before his theatre plans were washed away by public disapproval.

'I finished my castle. Look, Daddy.'

The plaintive note in her voice tugged at his heart and Jack looked up to see Clover's disappointed expression, the familiar heavy feeling of guilt pressing down on him. He'd never really appreciated it before it had happened to him, the ever-present feeling of not being enough, not doing enough, that accompanied being a single parent. Not for the first time, and he knew not for the last, Jack wished he could go back in time and change all the careless things he'd said to his mother, the times he'd shown his own disappointment when he'd known full well that she was doing her best.

And that was all that anybody could ask, that he did his best. Which meant in this case heading into a crowded sea on a hot June weekend. 'Go on then,' he said, and Clover's bright smile was all the reward he needed. That was the thing about being six, tears turned to smiles in an instant. 'What about you, Tansy?' But he wasn't surprised when his eldest daughter shook her head, the long silky blonde hair and pointed chin so reminiscent of her mother it sometimes hurt to look at her, a reminder of his failures.

'I'll keep an eye on our things,' she said. 'Besides, I've got my reading list to finish.'

Jack touched her hair. 'You've been reading all morning. Come with us, your sister would love it.' But Tansy shook her head and returned to her book with a martyred air that was as worrying as it was irritating.

She'd always been a serious child, too serious her mother had said, with a sense of responsibility that seemed to negate her ability to just let go and have fun. But since Lily's death those traits had become more pronounced, a line of worry too often on her brow, a line wrong on an eleven-year-old girl. He caressed her hair again, telling himself not to mind as she shrugged him off with an exaggerated sigh.

'I'm *working*, Dad.'

'Okay, but you know where we are if you change your mind.' Jack looked back at the small erect figure, still worrying, as Clover pulled him into the cold waves. That was the thing about Cornwall. No matter how hot the outside temperature—and today was practically Mediterranean—the sea was always bracing. Clover didn't seem to notice as she hopped over waves, chattering on about her recent surfing lesson and how close she'd been to standing up. Some of the worry lifted as he listened. This was what he had brought them back here for, this kind of outdoor life, and the pink in her cheeks and happiness babbling through Clover's voice was all the affirmation he needed. Tansy would settle in soon enough.

As Jack and Clover waded in, waiting for the right wave to bodyboard into, he became aware of a slight figure standing further along, waist deep in the water. There was something about her that snagged his attention, the poised, graceful way she stood, almost regally, despite the surf pushing and pulling her. Jack noted dark wavy hair piled high, tendrils curling around a long neck, sunglasses shading high cheekbones. It was the woman from the theatre, the one he'd almost run into the other day. Rosy.

She wasn't moving, just standing still and letting the waves crash over her, but there was something about the way she looked up at the sky, the way she held her hands out that symbolised freedom. She looked as if she had been relieved of a huge burden and was taking this moment to celebrate with the elements. His mouth twisted wryly at the thought. It wasn't like him to be so fanciful, let alone weave stories around complete strangers—besides, she had told him that she wasn't staying around, she'd clearly wanted to let him down gently. He'd obviously imagined the strange instant connection that had seemed to sizzle between them.

As he stood and stared, Rosy turned slowly and her eyes locked on his for a breathless moment, a half-smile lingering on her full mouth before she held up one hand in a half wave. Jack nodded in return and then returned his attention to his daughter, trying his best to put the woman—Rosy—out of his mind.

The rest of the afternoon wasn't the success he'd hoped for when he'd suggested a beach day. It was hot, very hot, and the beach was crowded with the tourists who flocked to Polhallow during the summer months. As the day went on the noise on the beach grew, the sea crammed with swimmers and surfers, and Clover got first sand and then saltwater in her eyes. No sooner was that resolved than she started to cry because she was too hot, and then because she was hungry. Tansy read steadfastly on, pausing only to tend to her sister as if she were her mother, pulling first wet wipes and then suntan cream out of her bag.

'You can trust me to pack for us,' Jack said, half amused, half put out as his eldest daughter raised disbelieving eyebrows.

'Remember last time?' she said. 'You didn't remember Clover's juice.'

'That was different, I didn't expect it to be so hot last time.' And there it was again, that insidious feeling of guilt. He'd been back in Cornwall for over two months and this was only the second time he'd brought his girls to the beach—and the truth was he wouldn't be here now if the nanny hadn't broken her foot and returned to her parents for a few weeks. His daughters only had one parent. Providing for them wasn't enough, he had to make sure he met their emotional needs as well. He needed to play with them more—and somehow get Tansy to relax and trust him to have things under control.

Finally, he packed up their things, promising Clover an ice cream as they wended their way through the families, couples and groups of friends picnicking and lazing on the beach until they reached the beach café. A queue was snaking its way along the path and after a quick look at Clover's mutinous face Jack knew he would be there for some time. There was no way she was going any further without the promised ice cream and no amount of money or infamy would help him jump the queue. Forget the theatre, maybe he should buy an ice cream shop instead. He tried not to huff, jiggle impatiently or check his phone as they waited. Instead, he scanned the queue and, with that same feeling of almost inevitable recognition, clocked Rosy near the front.

Her hair was still tied up and she wore a long pink sundress over her bikini, a bag thrown over her shoulder, and yet she looked as cool and elegant as if she were in the middle of Paris, not on a hot sandy beach. As if aware of his gaze, she turned and looked at him, at Clover hopping from foot to foot and Tansy, who was sighing again as if Jack had conjured up the queue to annoy her, and waved, saying loudly and deliberately, 'Jack. *Jack*, I'm here!'

Both girls looked up at him in surprise. 'Who's that, Daddy?' Clover asked.

Jack squeezed her hand. 'Possibly the answer to our prayers. Just play along girls.'

Tansy said nothing but gave him a suspicious glance as Jack waved back and said extra heartily, 'There you are! I didn't see you, Rosy. Come on, girls. Let's tell Rosy what we want.' Nobody seemed to question the ruse as they joined Rosy at the front of the queue.

'Thank you,' Jack muttered with heartfelt gratitude and Rosy smiled radiantly, filling him with a warmth the situation hardly warranted. 'You've saved me from a long wait, which is no fun with overtired children.'

'It's no bother at all,' she said. 'Least I can do after stepping out in front of you the other day. I've been wanting to apologise. What can I get you—and, more importantly, what do the girls want?'

After some discussion, Clover decided on chocolate and Tansy vanilla with sprinkles.

'And you?' Rosy asked Jack.

He shrugged. 'I wasn't going to...'

'Daddy likes cherry,' Clover said, and Rosy's smile widened.

'Got it,' she said as she stepped up to the counter. She wouldn't take any money from him for the ice creams, insisting that it was her treat, and it seemed only polite that they fell into step with her as they walked away from the café.

'That was really kind of you,' Jack said. 'I think Clover was on the verge of a meltdown. I probably kept her out too long. Tansy was right, as usual.'

'That happens a lot?'

'More and more since her mother died.'

'I'm sorry,' Rosy said, compassion in her eyes. 'That must be really hard for all of you.'

'It's been a couple of years, but there are still challenges. Right now, the nanny has broken her foot, so she's gone home to her family for a few weeks. The timing is difficult. We only moved back here recently so the girls haven't started school here yet and I have a lot to do. But I know how lucky I am to afford a nanny at all. I'll figure something out.'

'At least they have you. They're beautiful girls.'

'They take after their mother.'

Tansy and Clover had walked ahead and now they sat down on the sea wall to finish their ice creams and as Jack reached them and stopped, Rosy did too.

'Thank you for my ice cream,' Tansy said, and Clover echoed the thanks.

'You're very welcome. Actually, you did me a favour. Ice cream tastes better with company.' Rosy said.

'You decided to stay in Polhallow after all?' Jack asked, and she shot him a slightly embarrassed grin.

'I wasn't lying,' she assured him. 'I had every intention of returning home after the play, but Clem got an unexpected job offer and needed someone to watch the house and feed the cat. I realised I could actually work from here for a few weeks, so here I am.' She shrugged a little self-consciously.

'That worked well for us. We'd still be in the queue now if it wasn't for you.'

'Where do you live?' Clover asked. 'We used to live in London, but Daddy moved here. Are you from London?'

Rosy shook her head. 'No, I come from a small country called Asturia, have you heard of it? Not many people have. But I came to school here in England, so I know London well.'

'I miss school,' Clover said.

'Ah, yes, your daddy said you haven't started school here yet. Are you looking forward to it?'

'Not really, mine is miles away.' Tansy glared at Jack.

It was an old argument, and not one Jack wanted to have in front of a stranger. 'It's a great school. You'll be fine. As we moved here just after Easter, I thought they might enjoy a long summer, especially as Tansy is starting secondary school. It didn't make sense sending her somewhere new for just one term,' he explained to Rosy. 'Tansy's school is about ten miles from here, and Clover is going to one the next town over.'

'Which means that not only do we not know anyone in Polhallow now, we won't know anyone here once we're at school either,' Tansy said.

'That's not true,' Jack said. 'There are children from Polhallow who go to both your new schools. You'll be fine.' He had the money to send the girls to the best schools possible and that was exactly what he was going to do.

'It can be tough to meet people when you move,' Rosy said sympathetically. 'But I know a little girl about your age,' she said to Clover. 'I'm going to the cinema with her and her mummy tomorrow in fact, to see that new superhero film. Do you want to come along and meet her?'

Clover's eyes widened as she turned to Jack imploringly. 'Can I, Daddy?'

'I don't know, honey.' He didn't know this woman beyond a jolt of attraction and a couple of random meetings. 'We wouldn't want to impose.'

'I'm sorry,' Rosy said, flushing. 'That was really clumsy of me. You don't even know me and here I am inviting your children out. I promise I'd take care of them. I can give you Sally's details—she's lived here all her life. Her little girl, Alice, goes to the local primary school and is Clover's age. I'm going to the cinema anyway; it really wouldn't be any trouble to take Clover as well—and Tansy if she would like to come.'

Jack hesitated. 'Sally Fletcher?'

'That's right, do you know her?'

'Only by sight. She was a few years younger than me at school, as was your cousin.' He must have seen Rosy around as a teen—but four years was a big gap at that age, and he'd left Polhallow when Sally and Clem had still been in their early teens. Still, the distant connection rooted Rosy, made her less a stranger. He looked at the girls and realised that not only was Clover looking hopeful but so was Tansy and his chest squeezed. She so seldom asked for anything. 'Are you sure it wouldn't be an imposition?'

'Not at all. In fact I haven't seen the first in the series so if the girls can bring me up to speed before the film starts, they'll be the ones doing me a favour.'

'Well, if you're sure…' The rest of the sentence was drowned out by Clover's yells of excitement and before he knew it they'd swapped numbers and Rosy made arrangements to collect the girls the following afternoon before walking off with a wave. Jack watched her retreat, admiring her elegant, graceful walk and feeling that same jolt of recognition and attraction she seemed to provoke in him every time they met. But one thing was sure, he would be checking in with Sally Fletcher tonight. Attraction or no attraction, he wasn't sending his girls out with a stranger. Their happiness and safety came first. Always.

# CHAPTER THREE

'ALICE IS REALLY nice, Daddy. Her mummy said that I can go over whenever I want. But I want her to come here and play in the treehouse. Can she, Daddy?'

Arrosa had barely had a chance to ring the doorbell before Jack had opened the door and Clover tumbled inside and onto him, babbling on excitedly about the afternoon's activities. Thank goodness she'd had such a good time; since yesterday afternoon Arrosa had asked herself several times what she'd been thinking of, volunteering to look after two complete strangers. Children at that! But once she'd collected them in Clem's small car her doubts had lessened then disappeared completely when they'd reached the cinema, where Clover and Alice had fastened onto each other like lifelong friends separated at birth, insisting on sharing their popcorn and sitting next to each other throughout the film and at the café they'd visited afterwards. However, Arrosa had been a little bit more concerned about Tansy and, despite their short acquaintance, that concern lingered.

There was something about the girl's preternatural maturity, the wrinkle of concern on her forehead, the way she watched her sister and fussed over her that made Arrosa's heart ache in recognition. She knew the signs all too well of a child who'd needed to grow up too fast, who'd shouldered responsibility beyond their years, but at least Arrosa had had summers here in Cornwall, a break from the rigid routine of her life, and her four years at boarding school to alleviate the pressure. Right now, she didn't see any sign that Tansy ever relaxed and, judging by the shadow lurking in Jack's eyes when he looked at his oldest girl, he too was worried.

At least Jack was aware; so many parents were oblivious to their children's struggles. Recognising them was the first step to solving them. Simone had taught her that and so much else that her own parents had been too busy to teach her.

Tansy followed her sister into the house, leaving Jack and Arrosa alone. Jack leaned on the door and smiled, his eyes filled with an approving warmth that seared through her. 'I'm sorry,' he said, holding the door a little bit further open. 'Where are my manners? Would you like to come in?'

She would like to, very much, but Arrosa held back. 'I'm sure you're busy,' she said. 'I'd hate to intrude.'

His eyes crinkled. 'You've given me the afternoon to work, I'm very appreciative. Please. Come in and have a coffee, it's the least I can offer in return. Are you sure they weren't too much trouble?'

'Not at all,' Arrosa assured him as she followed him into the wide two-storey hallway. She looked around with interest. She'd been impressed by the white nineteen-twenties Art Deco cube of a house with its stunning position on top of the cliffs when she'd driven up, but now she was inside she realised that the interior more than matched its outside. The house hadn't been clumsily extended or garishly modernised. Instead, it was as the architect had intended, spacious and graceful, the furniture chosen to complement the era but comfortable and obviously meant for a family to live with and use, rather than expensive antiques.

Arrosa had been brought up in a mediaeval château and spent many days in the imposing castle in the capital city where her father spent much of his time in the state apartments, and she had visited many of the heads of state around the world. She was used to money and she was used to luxury; she was used to historic and impressive buildings. Gorgeous as Jack's home was, it wasn't a palace, although money was clearly no object. But what struck her as she noted the carefully chosen art interspersed with framed children's pictures and family photos, the half open boot cupboard filled with sandals and wellies, the wicker basket stuffed with throws and cushions, was that this particular historic house was also a home. And that, as she knew all too well, was a much rarer combination.

'Nice house,' she said as she followed him into the kitchen. It was a huge room with views out towards the sea. The island in the middle held a jumble of paper, crayons and a half open book, the table by the French windows was already set for dinner. She swallowed. Jack Treloar was clearly a good father, embracing his children's clutter, not hiding it.

'We think so.' Jack leaned against the island and gestured for her to sit. 'I grew up here, in Polhallow, you know. I used to see this house and vowed one day it would be mine.' His mouth quirked into a self-deprecating grin. 'Some things should never be said out loud. That sounded like a line from a bad film. Apologies.'

'Not at all, it sounds impressive. How many people go on to achieve their dreams?' She didn't have dreams, didn't have anything to strive for. She just had duty. She envied him his purpose more than the achievement. Taking a seat at the island, she opted for a mint tea as Jack put the kettle on and took down two of the distinctive blue-striped Cornish mugs from the dresser. 'Thank you for loaning me your girls, they were great company. Alice and Clover definitely took to each other.'

Jack poured hot water into one of the mugs and handed it to her. 'That's good, they need friends. I didn't really think it through when I took them out of school after Easter. I just wanted to get them settled in before term started, give them a chance to have a long summer by the sea, to learn to surf and just enjoy being here. It's been a difficult couple of years since they lost their mother, I thought they could do with a break. But, of course, they are a little lonely. And, as you probably guessed, Tansy isn't keen on the school I chose. She wants to go to the local school.'

'That's where Clem went and where Simone taught,' Arrosa took a sip of the mint tea. 'I think it's a good one.'

'It is. But it's also the school I went to once upon a time.' He paused as he picked up his own mug. He didn't take a seat but resumed standing against the island, staring out to sea. 'I don't know if your cousin has mentioned me...'

'No, she hasn't. Besides, I don't like to gossip.' Although she *was* undeniably intrigued.

He laughed. 'Then you won't fit in around here. I've been the main topic of conversation in Polhallow for longer than I care to remember.'

'Either you have a very inflated sense of self-importance, or you really do have a reputation I should ask Clem about.'

'Probably both,' he said. 'The thing is, I don't really want my girls to know that side of my past. Not yet. I don't want them to overhear people talking about the theatre or raking up ancient history, gossiping about their mother. Besides, I've got the money, I can afford the best schools money can buy, so why shouldn't they attend them?'

Arrosa picked her words carefully, trying to dampen her interest. What past? She really *didn't* gossip but maybe she should check in with Clem. 'I don't think that my opinion matters here,' she said. 'You should do what's right for you, for your girls, not because of what anyone else says or thinks.'

His smile was rueful. 'A diplomatic answer. Forgive me, this is probably not what you expected when I asked you in for a drink. I seem to have forgotten how to do small talk—not that it was ever one of my skills.'

'I didn't have any expectations.' Arrosa picked up her mug again, glad of the distraction, but he was right. She'd expected a little bit of chitchat about the film, not this strange, intense conversation that felt almost as if they were jumping past the basics and getting straight to intimacy. But she couldn't let her guard down, not really. There was only so much that anyone could know about her. Not just because of her own need for anonymity but because Clem's identity was also at stake. Polite chitchat was all she could allow.

'Let's start again,' Jack said. 'So, what is it you do when you're not housesitting for your cousin?'

'I'm a special adviser,' she said. It was almost true.

She *did* do a lot of advising, trying to guide the politicians towards the policies she thought necessary for the development of her country. 'I work in diplomacy.'

Jack's eyebrows rose. 'Impressive. Do you offer lessons? Diplomacy is also something that doesn't come naturally to me.'

'Not to me either,' she confessed. 'I've had to learn.'

'And you can work from here, you said?'

'It's not usual, but as it's the summer I managed to make some arrangements. And I'm mostly taking the time off. It's been a long time since I was in Polhallow. I could do with a proper holiday and really get to know it again.'

'Any plans while you're here?'

'Actually, I am enjoying being plan free. I was a bit overstretched when I arrived, hence the time off. I had some tough decisions to make, so time and space is exactly what I need.'

'Personal or work?'

'Both, they get a little intermingled.' That was the understatement of the century. But at least she'd managed to step back enough to see that and to put right her misstep with Akil. She hadn't imagined the relief in his voice when she'd spoken to him a couple of days ago and suggested they stay friends and pretend her clumsy attempt at a proposal had never happened. She'd done her best to encourage him to see Clem again but hadn't heard anything since from either of them—which was either a really good sign or she'd completely misread the vibes she'd been getting from them.

'Tricky.'

She looked out at the view, as always, her anxiety abating at the sight of the sea. 'It is amazing what having the time and space to think does. Already I've made a really important decision and I feel so much better. But I really want to put work and home out of my mind and just enjoy being here—the only thing I want to worry about is the amount of clotted cream I'm consuming.'

He laughed then, warm and deep and toe-curlingly masculine. 'Yes, I'd forgotten how good food is here. London has every cuisine you can imagine but nothing tastes as good as Polhallow pastries and scones. If this carries on, I'll have to up my exercise time, which won't be easy with no nanny for the rest of the summer and all the work piling up.' He grimaced. 'Obviously, exercise is the least of my worries. This is a crucial time for the theatre renovation…' He slanted a quick glance in her direction as if waiting for a reaction. 'And my other businesses and interests need attention. But the girls can't just sit around and wait for me all day. I could try a temp agency to find a summer nanny, but they've been through so much change I don't want to risk a mismatch.'

'I could watch them sometimes,' she offered impulsively. It wasn't just that she had the time, although she did, something about Tansy still bothered her, even though she could see what a safe and loving home the girl had. She understood what it was like to feel responsibilities at a young age in a way that not many other people did. She also knew how important it was to let those responsibilities go and to have fun. Maybe she wouldn't be able to make any difference to the girl's life, but Arrosa felt an overwhelming urge to try.

It didn't hurt that she was enjoying spending time with Jack either, that she was all too aware of his every shift and movement, how the light moved across the planes of his face, the way his eyes darkened to navy when he was moved, the shape of his mouth.

'I can't ask you to do that!' But she could see he was tempted, relief clearing some of the cloud from his expression.

'You didn't. I'm not offering to be a stand-in nanny, I'm not at all qualified and I *am* on holiday. But I would be more than happy to take them around a little bit, go to the beach, organise some play dates with Sally, go to the cinema—they'd be a great excuse for catching up on all the summer releases.'

'I am really tempted...' At the word their gazes caught and locked, and she felt again that odd sense of knowing him, feeling the attraction building between them, unlike anything she'd experienced on so short an acquaintance—or even a longer acquaintance—before. 'But I'd be totally taking advantage of your good nature.'

'We could take it on a day-by-day basis. If I have free time and you need a hand then great, but I will be absolutely comfortable saying no if I have plans, and if you decide you need something more structured I won't be offended.'

'It sounds too good to be true. Look. Before you make a decision you should see them at their overtired worst. Stay for dinner and if at the end of it the offer is still open we'll discuss payment and other issues then.'

Arrosa would of course turn down the offer of payment, she had no need of money. But nobody had ever offered to pay her before. She had an allowance—a generous allowance— but it wasn't a salary. It was nice to be thought worth a wage.

She had no idea what Jack did but he was clearly well-off. It was obvious from the house and furnishings, in the way he dressed, even in a casual linen shirt and jeans, both top quality and fitting as if made for him, the linen almost—tantalisingly—translucent, the jeans clinging to narrow hips and strong, lean thighs. She swallowed, mouth dry.

'What's for dinner?'

'Lasagne. I've only got a few dishes in my repertoire and lasagne is near the top.'

'With salad and garlic bread?'

'Of course!''

'That sounds delicious. Thank you, I'd love to have dinner with you.'

But as she sat down and accepted the glass of white wine he handed her, Arrosa couldn't help wondering if she was completely mad. She should be heading out of the door as fast as she could go, not offering to babysit Jack's children. She might be inexperienced with relationships in the real world but even she could feel the chemistry sizzling between them. She was a princess, and he was a widower with two small girls. Neither should indulge in summer flirtations, no matter how tempting.

But, on the other hand, she had promised herself a summer off. A summer of being just Rosy. This was just dinner—and a dinner chaperoned by his daughters. What harm could one evening do?

As June continued the British summer started to live up to its flaky reputation. The long, hot early summer days had been replaced by intermittent rain and drizzle, interspersed with moments of blazing sunshine. It was the kind of weather that meant leaving the house without a bag packed with suntan cream, wellies, sunhats and raincoats was ill-advised. Jack was seriously considering investing in a mule to help with the baggage even a brief walk entailed. Worse, the weather made entertaining the girls even more tricky and he couldn't help but think his decision to give them an extra-long summer had been ill thought through: weeks filled with adventure and time to explore was idyllic on paper but, in reality, less than practical, especially now he was looking after them alone.

This was where being a single parent was so hard. There was nobody to sense check his ideas with. But, then again, Lily had always preferred to leave all responsibility to him. She would probably have enthusiastically supported the thought of a long summer, come up with a dozen impractical plans and whipped the girls up into a frenzy of expectation before disappearing off for a summer of house parties and social events, leaving the girls to their nanny. As for the autumn, she would have wanted Tansy away at boarding school, not at a private day school just a few towns over. After all, she'd first suggested sending her when their eldest had been barely eight. He could hear her now, those languid upper-class tones caressing and yet repelling him at the same time.

*'But darling, girls of that age are tricky. I should know!' Tinkling laugh. 'She'd be much happier with girls of her own age, don't you think?'*

No, he would have got no backup or sense checking from Lily. It had always been down to him where the girls were concerned. So why was he suddenly feeling so lonely—and second-guessing himself? Maybe it was because Tansy was entering those dangerous tween and teen years and he of all people knew how important stability was around then, especially for those whose early years had been the opposite. His childhood had, despite his mother's best endeavours, been difficult and his early teen years full of trouble and mischief; he'd come very close to getting a criminal record. But then again Lily had had everything and she had thought herself invincible, had adored the thrill of danger. That was why she had taken up with him after all—there was nothing as rebellious as dating the village bad boy. Getting pregnant and marrying him had been the ultimate rejection of all her parents' hopes for her.

Lily had loved her girls—but she'd been impulsive and heedless, and Tansy especially had been painfully aware of how mercurial her mother could be. Her death had obviously compounded Tansy's insecurity and, although she was less than enthusiastic about the move, part of his motivation for returning to Cornwall was to try and centre her somewhere less frantic and fast paced than the big city.

'Come on, girls,' he said for the twentieth time that day. The words were fast becoming his catchphrase, maybe he should get them tattooed on his forehead. As usual they had little effect as Clover dawdled behind in a world of her own, Tansy walking in the middle, looking most put upon. But, to be fair, he knew that a business meeting was not their idea of a fun afternoon out, even if it *was* in a theatre.

Of course, he could have taken Rosy up on her offer to watch them sometimes. It had clearly been genuinely meant. She seemed to like the girls and, more importantly, they clearly liked her. But he'd been reluctant to get back in touch with her after the evening they'd spent together. Not because he hadn't enjoyed it. In fact, quite the opposite. The whole evening had gone smoothly, with conversation and laughter flowing easily. She fitted in with them, almost too well, and by the end of dinner the girls were acting as if they'd known her all their lives. But they *didn't* know her. He had no real idea where she was from, what she did or how long she would stay. And the last point was crucial. Clover was predisposed to like everybody, but his eldest was a different matter and Rosy and she seemed to have connected. He hadn't heard Tansy chat so much or laugh so much or volunteer so much information in a long time. Which was why he hadn't dared ask Rosy to watch then—she was only here for the summer. He couldn't risk his girls getting too attached.

Or himself. The attraction he felt had just intensified with the time they'd spent together but he couldn't allow himself the indulgence of a fling.

'Rosy!'

Jack looked up in surprise as Clover's cry interrupted his thoughts. There, as if he'd summoned her by thought alone, was Rosy, casually dressed in jeans, a turquoise T-shirt and a long grey cardigan, but yet again something about the way she wore the simple outfit elevated it to a high fashion statement.

Rosy's face lit up. 'Hello, how are you two? I was just thinking about you.' And then, more quietly, 'Hi, Jack.'

'Hi.' For a moment they both just stood and looked at each other, Jack almost lost in her hazel eyes, a beguiling mix of green and amber, in the warmth of her smile.

'You were? Why?' Clover danced up to Rosy and tugged at her hand. 'Why were you thinking about us?'

'I had a surfing lesson this morning with Dan, and

he said that you are both naturals. Unfortunately, he didn't say the same about me. Which is very lowering because once upon a time I was not bad at all. Take my advice, girls; don't stop for years or you'll lose all your balance and skill.' She mock sighed and both girls giggled. 'Where are you off to? Somewhere fun?'

'We're going to the theatre,' Clover told her. 'Daddy has a boring meeting.'

'Boring? The theatre? Surely not. There's a stage and an auditorium, lots of fun places to discover. Do either of you like plays?'

'I do,' Tansy said. 'Drama was my best subject at school. I should have had the lead in the end of term play, but we moved.' She gulped and blinked rapidly, eyes reddening as Jack stared at her in consternation. He knew that Tansy liked acting but in his haste to leave London he hadn't even considered the end of term play which was the highlight for year six leavers. But he should have—after all, Tansy had been fixated on starring in it ever since she'd started school.

'They put on plays in the theatre and local people can be in them,' Rosy said, to Jack's relief. 'That's where my cousin Clem started and now she's a professional actress. I'm sure she'd be happy to talk to you about it and give you tips.'

'Do you really think so?'

'I know so. She's always happy to chat acting and plays—and I bet she could introduce you to the community theatre group if your dad didn't mind.'

'That would be brilliant.' All trace of tears had gone as Tansy turned to him. 'Can I, Dad?'

'It sounds good, let me look into it.' He needed to

bring the community theatre onside first. The last thing
he wanted was for Tansy to be ostracised because of him.

'Come with us to the theatre?' Clover asked Rosy
and Tansy agreed.

'Please do, it'll be a lot more fun if you're there.'

'Thanks, girls!' Jack laid a firm hand on both blonde
heads. 'I'm sure Rosy has better things to do than tag
along to my business meeting.'

But Rosy didn't take the get-out clause he'd handed
her. 'Actually, if you don't mind, I'd like to come. I
haven't looked around the theatre properly for years.
My aunt—Simone Beaumont—the theatre was her pet
project. The first time I came here to stay she spent the
whole summer writing out grant applications and organising fundraising events. When they reopened it after
the renovations the councillor who gave a speech said
that she had single-handedly saved it. They were going
to demolish it originally. Simone had many causes and
projects, but this theatre was her main passion—sometimes I wonder if that's why Clem took up drama, so
her mother could see her on this stage. Simone could
be a very busy woman. It was hard to pin her down, but
she never missed a single performance.'

Jack shot Rosy a sharp glance, but she was all inno-
cence. Maybe she had no idea of his plans. If not, if he
could show her his vision then maybe she would be able
to convince her cousin that he was on the village's side?
'In that case of course you're welcome to come along.'

In the end he found that he was relieved to have Rosy
with him as he sat down with the PR agency he was considering hiring. Investing in the theatre was so unlike
anything he had ever done before. He knew he needed
guidance. He was usually the man behind the scenes,

the angel investor being wowed not doing the wowing, listening to PR teams not recruiting them. It was important he brief the company well. But as he expanded on his vision he could see the girls and Rosy exploring, hear laughter and chatter coming from all areas before the three ended up on the stage, clearly putting on some kind of mini play, Tansy directing the other two.

Jack paused and watched the antics on stage. It was so good to see Tansy acting her age, he needed to ensure it happened more often. Maybe he should stop worrying about what would happen when Rosy left and take her up on her offer to watch his daughters. It would be good for the girls.

As for him, he might be attracted to her but that didn't mean he needed to act on it.

Finally, the meeting came to an end and after taking some photos the agency representatives left, leaving Jack alone at the top of the auditorium answering some emails. A slight sound made him look up to see Rosy making her way across the row to join him. The girls were still on stage, volubly discussing who should be standing where.

'Exhausted by artistic endeavours?'

Dimples flashed. 'I'm not the actor, that's Clem. Tansy definitely needs to meet her. That daughter of yours has got some real understanding of staging.'

'Never been tempted to do something that way yourself?'

'Not at all.' She laughed a little self- consciously. 'Acting has never been a love of mine. I was more likely to be found painting scenery than trying out for the lead. But in some ways, I guess, I do spend a lot of time acting, channelling a more confident, assertive me. Clem taught me techniques—how to stand, to project. How to breathe—that's been very useful. Simone was great too at preparing me to speak up in intimidating circumstances. She was one of the most matter-of-fact and forthright people you'll ever meet, she passed that quality onto Clem. They both taught me to focus on what's important. I owe them both a lot.'

'Sounds like being a diplomat is hard. You must be young to have so much responsibility. I think of diplomats as older—not that I've dedicated too much time to the topic,' he added hastily, although he had been thinking about it of late, since meeting her.

'I *am* young to have some of the responsibilities I do, but politics is the family business. I was raised to it. And yes, at times the focus is on me, but more what I represent, if that makes sense, rather than me as a person. That's why it can help to play a part, to take the personal out. How about you? What's today about? Planning to set up a troupe of players to stage your opus?'

'Not exactly. I'm not one for being on stage either, but I am interested in this theatre in particular.'

'In what way?'

He took a deep breath. Now was the time to make his pitch. 'I want to take out a long-term lease and carry on the restoration process to take the theatre to the next level. Make it an asset that *works* for the community, *not* take it away from the community.' He could hear his tone sharpen at the last words and her eyes widened.

'You clearly feel passionately about it,' she said.

Jack nodded grimly. 'I'm not the only one. According to the village—and your cousin—everything I want to do goes against what this theatre is for. That's what the meeting just then was about—I am going to have to hire a PR firm to untangle the web of gossip and rumours about what I am trying to do here. Because it *will* happen. The Council will lease it to me, they have to. This place is expensive to run, they're relieved to get it off their hands, for someone else to be responsible for the upkeep, but I'd rather go ahead with the backing of the village. I'm not interested in cementing my role as the bad boy outsider.'

Rosy sat back, eyebrows raised. 'Is that who you are? That's not how I would describe you. A hard-working father maybe, a mean maker of a lasagne, a man who obviously cares about his community, but not a bad boy outsider. And I'm usually a good judge of character.'

Her words warmed Jack through. Maybe he did have a chance to start again—with the incomers at least. 'People in Polhallow have long memories and the Treloars a certain reputation. I wouldn't care if it wasn't for the girls.' He stopped and thought about his words. 'That's not true. I do mind, I always have,' he admitted, surprised at his honesty, to her and to himself. 'But back then, instead of trying to prove people wrong, I went the other way, became the boy they expected me to be for a short while. But even when things changed, when *I* changed, all the local community could see was who they expected to see. And that is who many people in the village see now, no matter where I live or how I act. They hear I have plans for the theatre and assume the worst because of my name and the actions of a messed-up teen. That's not what I want for the girls. I want people to hear their name and respect them, respect their origins.'

'That seems like a laudable ambition to me,' she said softly and with her words he felt some of the brittleness within him break as if she had given him a benediction, a blessing on his plans.

'You want to hear what I have in mind?'

Rosy reached out and touched his arm, the warmth of her touch searing him. 'I'd love to.'

'Come on then.' This was a great opportunity to start to change things. Clem was influential and if her own cousin could advocate for him then his battle might be half won before it started. But as Jack began to expand on his ideas, he knew that it wasn't the village he was trying to impress—it was this one woman.

# CHAPTER FOUR

ARROSA WASN'T JUST being polite when she said she wanted to hear more, although it was Jack's allusions to his youthful reputation and motivations that piqued her interest rather than the actual means of achieving his aims. But as the tour progressed she got swept away. There was something about Jack's vision that made things come alive. She could see the theatre as he did, filled with chattering, excited people, smell the greasepaint, feel the heat of the lights. She could see the entrance opened up and welcoming, imagine the glass-fronted café overlooking the bay, picture the currently unused boxes turned into sought-after seats for special occasions. He didn't just want to restore the front of the theatre, he also had plans to refurbish the dressing rooms, currently more reminiscent of a school locker room, and create VIP areas backstage.

'I want to attract the best,' he told her as he sketched out his ideas. 'The best dance companies, opera, repertory theatre, touring musicals, even bands. When I was a kid we had to travel for any kind of culture, which for people like me meant it was completely inaccessible. When Lily and I moved to London I was intimidated by theatres and museums, I didn't think they were for the likes of me. I don't want any child within twenty miles of here to ever think that. I want this to be a destination theatre that attracts tourists all year round, but it's important that anyone and everyone who lives here has full access too—and at an affordable price. What do you think?'

Arrosa circled round, seeing the currently drab bar area through his eyes, bright and busy. 'Honestly? I love it! Your plans are completely inspiring.' She meant every word although she knew Clem was opposed to any changes to the current set-up. But surely her sister wasn't fully informed about what Jack had planned? Loyalty to Simone might make Clem stubborn but her own ambitions for the theatre weren't dissimilar to everything Jack wanted to do. 'But I can see your comms problem; I've not heard anything about any of this, just that the theatre needs saving.'

'I think I went about it all wrong, dived straight in without laying the groundwork first.' Jack was clearly frustrated. 'I'm not used to being the upfront spokesperson, I'm usually behind the scenes. I thought the plans would speak for themselves, but as soon as it became known I wanted a long lease and changes were involved rumours started. You can see why I need a PR agency to help turn things around.'

'Changing public perceptions can be a long process and it's important to remember that even if opposition feels personal it usually isn't,' she assured him. She should know. After all, it had been over eight years since realising his hoped-for son was never going to come, her father had turned his attention to amending Asturia's laws in order to make Arrosa Crown Princess and eventual Queen. They'd had to work tirelessly over those eight years to get to the point where public opinion was in favour and for all the opposition parties to agree to change the age-old laws. Eight years of Arrosa not putting a foot wrong, of treading the delicate line of not looking too eager to become Queen whilst displaying leadership and diplomacy. Eight years of only being photographed looking calm, friendly and professional.

Eight years of knowing that this was just the beginning. That her entire life had to live up to the promise of her eight year-long audition for the role.

'Daddy, I'm hungry!' Clover clambered up the stairs towards them. 'Can Rosy have dinner with us again?'

Arrosa could see Jack hesitate and tried to think of an excuse she could use to help him out as after an uncomfortable pause he nodded. 'Of course. She's very welcome if she doesn't have other plans.'

'I did defrost a chicken.' It was a rubbish excuse, and she knew it from the disappointment in Clover's face. 'But you could come to me,' Arrosa offered before she could remember all the reasons getting further entangled with the small family was a bad idea.

Jack didn't reply at once. Instead, he met her gaze as if seeking confirmation that the offer was genuine and not mere politeness. Not for the first time, Arrosa noted the wariness behind what often looked like arrogance and confidence, giving her a sense of the lonely and potentially misunderstood boy he had once been. 'If you're sure. There's a lot of us to feed.'

'I can't promise anything as magnificent as your lasagne,' she said. 'But I could cook you chicken the Asturian way with lemon and garlic, fresh salad and these little cubed potatoes covered with a special secret spicy sauce. Does that sound any good?'

Clover agreed volubly that it did and before Arrosa knew it she was being whisked back home in Jack's oversized car, despite protesting it was only a short walk away. He parked outside and she opened the little picket gate, the family following her down the path which wound through the flower-filled garden to the white cottage's front door.

'Is this your home?' Clover asked as Arrosa unlocked the front door and ushered them inside.

'No, it belongs to my cousin Clem, but it *feels* like my home. I spent lots of very happy times here.'

The cottage was very old, parts of it dating back to Elizabethan times, with a large hallway which held a cupboard for coats and shoes, a hatstand and a table flanked by small chairs. Doors on either side led into low- ceilinged square rooms, on the left the sitting room, on the other a combined library, study and dining space. This was the room where Simone had often held court, plotting out her many campaigns, the dining table more often used to paint placards than to hold food.

The kitchen ran across the whole back of the cottage, holding at one end a battered leather sofa and an ancient pine kitchen table, with wooden cabinets painted a pretty eggshell blue and worktops on the other side. Stairs led up from the kitchen to the three bedrooms and one bathroom. It was simple but, thanks to Polhallow's popularity as a holiday destination and desirability as a second home location, Rosy knew the house would sell for a small fortune—but nowhere near the amount of money Jack's stylish white cube would command.

There were colourful paintings and framed posters on every available wall space and photos on every table and shelf. Jack wandered over to examine a collection of photos on the kitchen dresser, mostly Clem in various roles. Some were of Simone, often with a placard in her hand, off to save whatever cause she was spearheading that month, but there were also photos of her as a young woman, of the chic student who had attracted a future king, of the backpacker on the deck of a boat, of the young mother with her arms around a tiny Clem. There were no pictures of Arrosa on public display, it was too dangerous in case anyone recognised her, but she knew that upstairs on Simone's bedside table a photo of Arrosa and Clem side by side had pride of place.

'Your aunt taught me at school,' Jack said after a while. 'She was always kind. Bracing, said what she thought, but kind.'

Arrosa laughed. 'Those traits run in the family; Clem is just the same.'

'In your family too?'

Arrosa thought about her father, always King first and second, father a poor third. Of her mother, whose feelings were always hidden behind a regal smile. 'They are diplomats, as you know,' she said. 'It's an innate characteristic, even at home.'

'Sounds chilly.'

Chilly. Was that the right word? Formal, yes. But not cold exactly. 'Their expectations of me are high, that's true. That's why I liked being here, where the only expectations were that Clem and I help out making placards, or working bake sales, or one unforgettable summer trying to knit squares for a peace blanket, although it turned out knitting wasn't something either of us were good at! Simone was a second mother to me.'

'You were lucky to have her,' Jack said, and she nodded.

'Lots of people felt the same way—that Simone was

like an aunt or a sister. She had a gift of drawing people in. That's part of your problem with the theatre. I think people feel that your plans might expunge what she did. It wouldn't even still be here without her, they were going to knock it down, as you know, and she spearheaded the campaign to keep it and raised the money to restore it. But, actually, I can't help thinking that she would be excited by your ideas.'

'You think?' His rather grim expression relaxed and Arrosa felt her stomach flip.

'The problem is your timing is off. Simone is so recently gone; Clem is still grieving. I think that's why she and the rest of the community group jumped straight into organising a campaign against you. Simone loved a campaign. It's a way of keeping her close, especially as they feel your plans are a threat to her legacy. You need to listen to their concerns and show them that you need their expertise and passion, want them involved, that this is an evolution not a takeover. It might help to acknowledge the original restoration campaign in all your literature and plans, name some part of it after Simone.'

Jack didn't reply at first, his face thoughtful. 'You're right of course. Thank you,' he said after a while.

'An outsider's perspective is always useful.'

'No, it's more than that. I can tell you're used to brokering deals. Treaties must fall into your hands.'

'I wouldn't quite say that.'

'You've given me a lot to think about. Thank you.' He picked up a photo of Simone standing outside the theatre, grinning widely. 'If you wouldn't mind, I'd love your input when the PR agency send me their campaign ideas. You have a real insight; your thoughts would be invaluable.'

'You're welcome.' Arrosa could feel her face flush at the unaccustomed thanks. In her job nobody ever said *well done*, there were no performance reviews, apart from tabloid headlines, newspaper articles or social media posts as likely to be sharply critical as they were to be fawning. It might be silly to feel quite so touched by a few words of praise, but she was.

It didn't take her long to rustle up dinner, setting the kitchen table with the pretty floral dinner set that Simone had bought from a car boot sale many years before and the antique pearl-handled cutlery Arrosa had given her one birthday.

'I love this house, it's like a fairy tale cottage,' Clover said as they sat round the table after dinner, an old edition of Snakes and Ladders in front of them.

'It is, isn't it? I felt very lucky to spend my summers here,' Arrosa agreed.

'What's your own home like? Did you live somewhere like this when you were little?' Tansy asked.

Arrosa paused and thought. How could she convey the difference between the small, comfortable, chic yet homey cottage and the vast palace filled with antiques and portraits of ancestors where she'd been raised without giving away anything about who she was? Of course she'd had acres of land to run and ride on, a lake to swim in, woods to build dens in, but it had all been rather lonely. Her ancestral estate might have been a more fun place to grow up if she'd had a sibling who lived with her rather than one a thousand miles away.

'Not really. I'm an only child, you see.' Every time she said that it felt like a betrayal of Clem. 'My parents are diplomats, so we always lived in houses that weren't exactly ours.'

That wasn't a lie. The family estate and the castle, where her father resided most of the time in state apartments, belonged to the country, not to Arrosa or her family. They were owned by the crown, her family were custodians not owners.

'A lot of the furniture was antique, so we had to look after it,' she continued. 'I can't complain, I've been very lucky. I've travelled a lot and I've met some important people, and I've seen many, many things that I wouldn't have if I'd lived a different life, but the truth is when I think of home this cottage is the place I see. I'm just glad I get to spend the summer here. That this is where I spent many happy childhood summers.'

Tansy shook the dice and gleefully moved her counter up a long ladder to Clover's voluble dismay. 'Polhallow is so small though. Didn't you get bored spending every summer here?'

'*Bored?* Never.' Arrosa got up to collect the cake she'd bought from Sally's family's café earlier, cutting generous slices and placing them on the table. 'Sometimes, Tansy, you have to find your own adventures. I suppose I was a little bit older than you when Clem and I started to go out by ourselves, but there was always something to do. Surfing, of course, swimming, going for ice creams, learning to sail. But simpler things too. For instance, we built our own adventure trail once in the woods outside the house and we used to camp out in the garden sometimes; one summer it was so hot I don't think we slept indoors for a month. We even tried to persuade Simone to let us build an outdoor loo and shower, but she resisted. Although I think that was more Clem than me. I was actually quite relieved to be able to go in and use a proper bath.'

'Camping! I've never been camping.' Tansy turned to her father. 'Daddy, can we get a tent? Can we sleep in the garden like Clem and Rosy did? I've always wanted to try.'

Jack reached out for his cake with a nod of thanks. 'Tansy Treloar, you have been on some incredible holidays. How many theme parks have you been to? And that amazing resort in Sardinia with five swimming pools where you got to do activities all the time. Would you really rather sleep in a tent?'

'It would be fantastic,' she said, eyes shining, and Clover joined in.

'Please, Daddy! I've always wanted to sleep in a tent too, always!'

Arrosa couldn't help but laugh. 'It's a long time since I've camped,' she said. 'And it can be amazing, but don't get carried away. It can be hard to get the balance of blankets right. One moment you're boiling hot, the next you're freezing cold, and then, of course, if you need the loo in the middle of the night you have to walk across the dew-filled field to get to it and if you forget wellies that means soggy feet. Sometimes spiders and other creepy-crawlies can find their way into the tent, but on the other hand, there is something special about sitting around a campfire and looking up at the stars and telling each other stories. Toasting marshmallows, of course.'

Oh, dear. Both girls' eyes had grown bigger and their expressions more excited, but Jack's lips were compressed. She probably shouldn't have said anything. 'But five swimming pools in Sardinia sounds pretty amazing too. And you guys have a swimming pool at your house too. If Clem and I had had a pool of our own I'm sure that would have kept us busy.'

Her attempt to backtrack obviously hadn't helped. Tansy turned to Jack, her face full of hope, her voice pleading. 'Daddy, *please* can we go camping?'

'Sorry, Tansy, but absolutely not.' He sounded adamant.

'But...'

'I said no. The subject is closed.'

Arrosa stared at Jack in surprise. He seemed like a very capable man to her. He was physically fit, and the lean muscles she was all too aware of didn't seem like gym-built bulk but rather the muscles of a man who was prepared to put his hand to anything that needed to get done. He'd been raised around here, a local boy, which meant he was likely to be outdoorsy. Surely a couple of nights in a tent wouldn't be that big a deal?

He caught her eye and she sensed that he knew what she was thinking.

'It's after six,' she said. 'Do you want a beer? You can walk back from here. And girls? How about I make you hot chocolate with marshmallows and we can take it outside and sit around the fire pit?'

The suggestion was met with approval and Arrosa got herself and Jack a beer, sending the girls out to gather some firewood from the log pile with strict instructions not to go anywhere near the matches until she was there, and showed them how to lay and light a fire properly.

'Simone got a fire pit long before it was fashionable, thanks to Clem and my obsession with being outside in all weathers,' she said as she spooned hot chocolate into mugs. She reached into the cupboard for the marshmallows. 'I'm sorry, I didn't mean to get the girls so excited.'

She dropped a handful of marshmallows into each cup and added hot water before carrying the tall mugs over to the table. 'Parenting must be hard enough without well-meaning outsiders stirring things up.'

Jack reached up and took one of the mugs from her and put it down, knowing he owed Rosy an explanation at the very least. 'Look, I'm the one who should apologise. That was a bit of an overreaction.' He winced. 'I seem to have fallen into a pattern of promising to be a better father and then messing up at the first opportunity.'

Rosy set the mug she was holding down and pulled at a chair. 'Don't be silly. I completely understand. Now I'm an adult, I'm all about the thread count and a good mattress too.'

Jack exhaled slowly. He could, he should, leave it there. Let her believe he just didn't want to rough it, that money had turned him into the kind of man who needed five-star service and all the trimmings. But he wanted her to think better of him. Needed her understanding in a way he couldn't articulate.

'It's not that. I wish it were that simple.'

She pushed a curl behind her ear. 'Jack, you don't owe me any kind of explanation. Whatever your reasons, I'm sure they're valid, but it's really none of my business.'

'As I mentioned earlier, the Treloar name isn't particularly respected around here. My father, my grandfather, even my great-great-grandfather, were petty thieves, petty criminals, lazy vagabonds all. Go through the village's history and you'll find our name over and over, mentioned for public drunkenness, begging, theft. My mother was the complete opposite. She was—is—

hardworking and no-nonsense, but she came down here on holiday and fell for my father's charms, such as they were, and stayed. I don't think it was long before she realised what a bad bargain she had made when she was left alone with me, working three jobs to try and keep food on the table and a roof over our heads.'

'She sounds like quite a woman.'

He nodded. 'She is. Not an easy woman. Life made sure of that, knocked the warmth and trust out of her early, but she is everything my father wasn't. And she did her best by me.'

'That's all any of us can ask.'

He nodded. 'She was always determined that, no matter how bad things were, we would have a holiday. Now I'm an adult I can see she needed to get away herself, leave her life behind for a few days, go somewhere where she wasn't pitied or looked down upon.'

'That's understandable.'

'Of course all we could afford was to camp. She didn't have a car so we would take the bus and carry everything. We couldn't go too far because it would be expensive, so usually we made it just over the border into Devon. And then we would find the most basic, cheapest campsite we could, set up our tent and live on baked beans and sausages, cooked over the fire, marshmallows as a treat.'

He could almost smell the sausages, hear the crackle of the fire and, despite himself, his mouth curled into a reminiscent smile. 'Looking back, those were some of the happiest times we shared. She was usually too busy to spend much time with me, but those camping weeks we were together all the time. But with such limited resources we couldn't do much other than walk, swim or hang out reading at the campsite. Probably exactly what she needed, but the older I got, the more I realised how different my holiday experience was to other kids'. One year she was getting the tent out and I told her not to bother. That I hated holidays with her. Why couldn't we go on a proper holiday like normal people?' He inhaled, the old shame filling him. 'I'll never forget the stricken expression in her eyes. She didn't say anything, just put the tent away and we never went camping again. I'd give anything to go back and change that day, give anything to help her get the tent ready.'

'Jack, I'm sure she knew you didn't mean it, not really.'

'But that's just it. I *did* mean it and she knew it. Oh, I have apologised since, many times. But I hurt her dreadfully that day, not just with words but with my contempt and carelessness, like my father before me.'

His behaviour still shamed him. The memory shamed him. As it should.

'Does she still live around here?'

'She moved to Spain a few years ago.' He'd offered her an allowance but she'd turned it down, so instead he'd funded the purchase of a beach bar and bought her a comfortable villa. 'We have a good relationship now when we see each other, but I caused her a lot of anxiety when I was younger, and I'd give anything to take it back. Sometimes it feels as if those camping holidays sum up my childhood—my mother working harder than anyone should have to do to try and supply me with the basics. Although she loves me, loved me then, she was always anxious. Partly because she was so busy, so tired, and partly because she was always looking out for traces of my father in me.'

He couldn't believe he'd revealed so much. It was hard to meet her eyes, to see the sympathy there. He'd never spoken of those days before, not even with Lily—especially not with Lily. She'd never tried to understand him, never really wanted to understand him, found the poverty of his childhood picturesque, the reality would have disgusted her. No wonder he'd preferred not to discuss his past with her. Their marriage had been based on his reliability and dependability. Lily was the one who got to be flaky, Jack the lynchpin who held them together. It was lonely, unfulfilling, but he had wanted to give the girls everything he had never had—stability, both parents in their lives—and if that meant putting his own barely articulated needs away, that was a price he had been, he was, willing to pay.

But not only did he feel that he could be honest with Rosy, he wanted to be. 'Just the thought of setting up a tent, the smell of one, it brings it all back. Not just that day, but also the helplessness of poverty.'

He could see her pause, search for the right thing to say. 'Look, tell me to butt out if you want and I promise not to be offended, but I do get where the girls are coming from. I can't pretend to understand your life. Money was never an issue in my childhood, the opposite in fact, my life has been pretty luxurious. Materially, I had more than I needed or wanted. But, on the other hand, my parents were distant, not really ones for cuddles and displays of affection. I went on plenty of holidays, mostly to exclusive villas where I had no one to play with and nothing to do. I didn't want the pool or the luxury, I wanted companionship and fun. I wanted my parents to want to spend time with me. Which is why this cottage was so special, my summers here so important. I had freedom and companionship and adventure and that meant more to me than a private jet and the fanciest hotel suite.'

'My girls get both. The luxury holidays and my attention.' He wasn't over-compensating for his lack of time with money, was he? No, he made time for them, he always had.

'I know they do. But they're still of an age where camping seems like an adventure not a budget option. So why not banish some of those demons and take the girls camping? It might be cathartic. Besides, things have moved on since you were a child.' She reached over for her tablet and opened it, typing quickly. 'What about glamping? All you need to do is turn up and everything is ready, you even get to sleep on a proper bed. Why not surprise the girls?' She passed the tablet to him. 'Look, this place is just a few miles away and you can choose between shepherd huts, yurts, bell tents and even treehouses.'

Jack took a moment to scan the website. Rosy was right, the campsite was a million miles away from the field of his youth, with promises of home-cooked meals delivered to your fully furnished accommodation, underfloor heating in the showers and private baths—to say nothing of the luxury interiors showcased. 'You might be right. Look, there's some last-minute availability this weekend. Why don't you come along too?'

The words hung in the air as Rosy stared at him motionless, her pupils dilated. Part of Jack wanted to recall the words. Hadn't he told himself to keep his distance from her? The girls were clearly getting attached and she would be gone soon. But on the other hand…

On the other hand, he liked her, and it had been so

long since he had opened up to anyone the way he had opened up to her. And she liked him, he knew it with every nerve and sinew. He knew by the way her skin flushed the colour of her name when their eyes met, by the way her breathing quickened when he was near, by the way she said his name. Maybe it was foolhardy to invite her along, but he wanted her there—and he so seldom wanted anything other than to keep his girls safe.

And who was to say that if something flared up between them that it could go nowhere? There were still several weeks of summer left. This attraction might peter out as suddenly as it had appeared, and if not? Well, Asturia wasn't that far away. If things progressed maybe they could find a way to work things out.

He grinned, deliberately lightening the atmosphere. 'Honestly, even the thought of luxury camping makes me a little nervous. It would be good to have another adult along who actually wanted to be there.'

Rosy looked down at her beer and then back up. 'I'd love to,' she said eventually, her voice bright and impersonal. 'And shall we invite Sally and her daughter along? As you know, Alice and Clover get along really well, it might be fun to have a group of us. The real camping experience.'

So she didn't want to be alone with him. Maybe he'd misread the signals, or maybe a widower with two daughters was too complicated a package for her. Either way, it was fine.

'Why not,' he said, getting to his feet and picking up the two mugs. 'I'd better deliver these before they get cold.'

She opened her mouth then closed it again. 'Yes, good idea. I promised to show them how to light a fire.'

The intimacy sparked by his confidences was gone as if it had never been and that was probably a good thing. It was certainly safer. His life was complicated enough without adding in a long-distance relationship or the fallout of a failed short-term fling.

But as he followed Rosy out to the patio where the girls awaited them, a pile of logs at their feet, Jack couldn't help wishing that this connection between them was exactly what it felt like, the start of something, and not just a glimpse of what might have been. The kind of partnership he had never dared dream of.

# CHAPTER FIVE

JACK WASN'T EXACTLY converted to camping but even he had to admit glamping was on another level.

Usually Jack enjoyed the outdoors, cooking on fires, physical exercise, the challenge of making or putting things together. It was just something about the smell of wet tents, bedrolls and sleeping bags that took him back to those nights in their small, cheap plastic tent, shifting uncomfortably on his too-thin mat, pretending to be asleep as his mother cried after a day of trying to make the best of another soggy day. For many years he'd thrown himself into every moment, pretending enthusiasm, not wanting to give her any other reason to cry until along with adolescence came the all-consuming selfishness that often accompanied that stage of life and he'd switched from pretending too much to not pretending enough.

But his girls had none of his reservations and they were more than delighted with the luxury outdoor accommodation. The spacious round bell tents they'd booked were already set up when they arrived, furnished with actual beds, the canvas floors covered with thick luxurious rugs. He'd booked a group pitch with two large tents and one smaller one. The large tents had two bedrooms, both of which easily fitted either a double bed or two large singles, complete with small bedside cabinets and a wooden rail for clothes. The front half of the tent was a large semicircle furnished with a velvet sofa, a couple of large beanbags and a low wooden table that could double as dining or coffee table. The smaller tent Rosy would sleep in didn't have a bedroom, her double bed took up one side of the tent, a loveseat and table the other. All three tents were richly decorated in deep reds, golds and oranges.

At the back of the pitch stood a covered wooden platform that held the kitchen area complete with a sink and running hot and cold water, an oven, fridge and kettle and fully stocked cupboards holding crockery, cutlery and saucepans. Centred in front of the tents but far enough away to be safe and to ensure no smoke wafted into the sleeping areas was a sunken fire pit surrounded by sofas. Four posts sat at each corner so a cover could be pulled over to shelter the sitting area in case of rain.

'This is *not* how I remember camping,' Sally said as their host gave them a tour. The girls had run off to explore the adventure playground with Tansy in charge. Jack was relieved to see that although as usual she took the responsibility seriously, she seemed less solemn, her blue eyes sparkling with excitement and a smile lighting up her thin face. 'I've stayed in holiday cottages more spartan than this.'

'It really is quite something,' Rosy agreed as she scanned the information folder the host had left them with. 'The freezer has ready meals for emergencies, and there's a takeaway menu as well. Ooh, there's also a proper woodfired pizza oven by the kitchen and they can supply dough and all the other ingredients. I vote for pizza tonight.'

The atmosphere between the three adults was comfortable but Jack could sense Rosy hanging back, leaving Sally and him to talk. He knew Sally a little, as was natural when they'd grown up in the same village, but as she was a few years younger they'd never socialised before. Watching Rosy step aside to leave them together, he couldn't help but suspect that she might be trying to set the two of them up. He could see why she might think they would hit it off—after all, they were both single parents and lived in the same place, but although he liked what he knew of Sally, he didn't feel a single atom of the attraction he felt for Rosy.

On the other hand, he could do with friends locally. Nor could he discount the fact that not only was Sally close to Clem, she was also part of the theatre campaign. Whatever Rosy's motivations in inviting Sally along, the night away gave him a great opportunity to discuss his plans with her and see if there was any thawing in opposition. She might even be prepared to be the bridge between Jack and the theatre group.

The afternoon passed quickly and before they knew it the girls were clamouring for food. Jack was more than happy to play with the professional-looking pizza oven and after a busy day of exploring the campsite, farm and beach, Rosy, Sally and the girls made far more pizza than they could all eat while Jack experimented with cooking them until he'd perfected his technique. After dinner he built up the fire and they sat around toasting marshmallows and heating up hot chocolate using the pot provided. The adults took turns telling campfire tales, careful to keep them age appropriate whilst providing the right amount of chill for the setting. Jack couldn't remember the last time he'd had such a carefree evening, or the last time he'd laughed so much as Rosy held them all captive with a comic horror story that by turns made them gasp then giggle. She might claim not to be an actress but she knew how to speak, her voice rich and curiously intimate as if she were pitching her words at everyone individually.

By the time dusk fell all three children were drowsy, even Tansy, and the novelty of sleeping in tents meant sending them to bed was surprisingly easy. They all trooped off happily to the bathing hut with Sally to clean up and put on pyjamas. Clover had begged to sleep with Alice and so Jack kissed her before she headed into the other tent, and he settled Tansy into her bed with a torch and a book.

With the children in bed and the fire starting to die down, Jack opened a bottle of wine. After they'd dissected the day, the conversation naturally turned to the theatre and Jack tried to make his pitch as neutrally as he could, not wanting Sally to feel that she was being set up. But to his relief once he—with Rosy chiming in every now and then— explained what he wanted to achieve, understanding dawned in her intelligent green eyes.

'I think,' she said as she refilled their glasses and handed around some chocolates she'd brought with her, 'that there's been a lot of miscommunication and misunderstanding here, Jack. On both sides.'

Jack couldn't help but agree. 'I dashed in all guns blazing,' he said. 'I saw an opportunity and just wanted to get started. I didn't take account of the recent history, the sense of ownership you all feel—and rightly so. No wonder people think I'm working against you, not with you. But believe me, Sally, I am tired of being seen as a lone wolf. I want the theatre to be a partnership between me and the community. I'm doing it for Polhallow, not despite of it.'

She nodded. 'What you've told me sounds really exciting, and I really think the committee will think so too when they hear it properly. Look, why don't you set up a tour? A chance for you to show us around, just as you showed Rosy around, and then we can sit down and look at the details: what a busier, professional theatre means for the local groups who rely on it, the finances, the legalities. Be honest with us and then let's see where we are.'

It was a fair offer, maybe fairer than he had expected, and Jack gratefully accepted.

'It's exciting to hear it all coming together,' Rosy said, smothering a yawn. 'But even so I can feel myself falling asleep. I think I'll turn in, that delicious-looking bed is calling to me.'

Jack tried to push away the vision of Rosy tumbling into bed, dark curls falling around her bare shoulders. So much for respecting her boundaries, he scolded himself. It was one thing to find her attractive, quite another to allow himself to indulge in fantasies. Besides, although she'd been her usual friendly self all day, there had been a touch of reserve in her manner when she was talking to him, a clear hint that she wasn't interested. A hint he needed to heed.

Rosy's decision was echoed by Sally and Jack decided to head in also and after a quick shower in the luxurious shower block with its underfloor heating and spacious tiled cubicles he pulled on a pair of tracksuit bottoms and a T-shirt and returned to his tent. He could see the glow of Tansy's torch signifying she was still reading and, looking at his watch, realised it was far too early for him to sleep. Instead, he took his laptop to the sofa and set about trying to capture all the questions Sally had asked him around the campfire, making sure he was as prepared for the pitch to the community group as possible, but as he tried to work his mind kept drifting. All he could see was Rosy's face lit by the glow of the fire, hear the echo of her infectious laugh as she told stories, her excitement as they toasted marshmallows, the interest she seemed to take in every small detail of the girls' day.

It was a shame he hadn't met her at a different time and a different place. Rosy was the kind of woman any man would want—beautiful, intelligent, warm, interesting. And what did Jack have to offer? Money? She didn't seem short of that. The truth was he had two goals: to raise his daughters and to redeem his family name. Anything and anyone else would have to be prepared to come in third. It was a lot to ask of anyone, especially a woman like Rosy. No, better he put all thoughts of dating aside until the girls settled and he was established, and he had the time and energy any relationship needed.

Besides, he knew very little about Rosy. In fact, he could count what he did know on one hand and have fingers to spare. She came from a small country he'd barely heard of; she was obviously well-connected, the kind of woman whose family had expectations for her, expectations she accepted, although he sensed she wasn't entirely happy; she was beautiful. But there was so much more to her, kindness and integrity were evident in every gesture. She was the kind of woman who saw a problem and stepped in to help, even helping a virtual stranger struggling with fractious children. But that was it. He didn't know her childhood dreams, her favourite colour. He didn't even know if she was in some kind of relationship right now.

He knew he wanted her.

The words blurred in front of his eyes and so he closed his laptop, and picked up his book, only to find he couldn't concentrate on that either. What he needed was some air. The fire was still glowing and so he grabbed his book and headed back out, picking up his wine glass as he went. But as he approached the fire a figure moved. He wasn't the only one who couldn't sleep. There, wrapped in a blanket, staring into the flames was Rosy. He paused, unsure whether to join her or not, when she turned and smiled, and he knew he was lost.

It was inevitable maybe that Jack would appear as if Arrosa's thoughts had conjured him. It had been far harder than she'd anticipated keeping her distance from him all day. It was as if she were connected to him by some invisible cord. She could sense when he glanced over at her, feel his sudden and unexpectedly sweet smile, couldn't look away from him as he worked to build the fire or make pizza or help the girls on the zipwire. She was constantly aware of him, of his wrists, the vee of his throat, the nape of his neck. Her own gaze lingered on all the exposed vulnerable places as if she was learning them by heart.

'I'm sorry,' he said. 'You probably want to be alone…'

He was giving her the perfect get-out clause and she should take it, but she'd been good all day and it had left her aching with frustration and loneliness. 'I don't have a monopoly on the fire. Join me, please.'

He waited just a second as if checking the offer was real and then sat on the sofa next to hers. 'Not sleepy?'

'Turns out not. How about you? Camping better than expected?'

'Do you think I was being foolish?'

She straightened at that and turned to him in surprise. 'Not at all! We all have our trigger points, Jack, our regrets, memories we don't want to relive. We all keep ourselves safe the best way we know how. Putting your daughters first makes you courageous, not foolish.'

'It's not like we're roughing it. Sometimes I worry that I have gone too far the other way from my childhood, that I sling money at my problems and hope they'll disappear.'

Arrosa wasn't sure what to say. Once again Jack was opening up to her, really opening up to her, an experience so far removed from the polite small talk that dominated her life. And she couldn't help but wonder if he would speak so candidly if he knew who she really was.

'Have you ever spoken to your mother about all of this? About your childhood?' Who was she to ask? She would never discuss her inner feelings with her parents, wouldn't know where to start.

'I've apologised.' His grin was tired. 'Several times. More than apologised. I was able to put money in trust for her, so she doesn't have to work if she doesn't want to. But she told me in no uncertain terms that she had no intention of sitting on her hands all day at barely fifty and suggested if I really wanted to help then I would buy her a business. She sent me the details of the beach bar the very next day. It's no vanity project either, it's thriving and she's already expanding.'

Arrosa laughed. 'She sounds kind of formidable.'

'Oh, she is. I don't think she quite trusts the money I give her is either legal or sustainable. If it's not been earned by her own two hands, or in this case my two hands, she doesn't see how it could be real.'

Arrosa had always been taught that discussing money was rude, but curiosity got the better of her. 'What exactly is it that you do? You can't be more than…what? Thirty? That's some meteoric rise from the childhood you described.'

'Meteoric?' He shrugged but she saw him smile and knew he liked the description. 'Maybe, but honestly it's not that exciting a story. I was interested in programming, and because we couldn't afford for me to have the kind of top-of-the-range computer I wanted I learned to build it for myself from odds and ends. Village gossip will tell you that between fifteen and eighteen I was creating chaos, but the reality was I spent a lot of time in the flat honing my tech skills. At sixteen I started building websites for other people and by seventeen I was already making more than my mother.'

'Impressive.' She meant it. 'But in that case why the reputation? It can't just be your name, can it?'

He blew out a long breath. 'Partly the name, partly me and partly the result of poverty. The fact is, Rosy, that when you're a kid and your clothes are shabbier than everyone else's, and you don't always do your homework because your mother works three jobs and doesn't necessarily have time to help you with your spellings then you are pigeonholed—as lazy or rebellious or whatever. It's not right and it's not fair, but that's how it can be. And when you're alone a lot and bored it's easy to find trouble, and I did.'

'You're right,' she said softly. 'It's not fair.' Things weren't necessarily better in Asturia, which was why she had spearheaded before and after school schemes. It was a drop in the ocean of what needed to be done, but every child provided with a hot breakfast, with a place to do homework was another child given a chance to succeed.

'The year I was fourteen I was already nearing six foot—I looked older and thought I acted it. I got into a bad crowd, the kind made up of rich summer boys. They were all older than me. You can imagine how cool I thought I was, with no idea that they saw me as a convenient scapegoat. They were loud and drunk and annoying all summer and I tagged along, grateful to be included. Then one of them took his father's car out when he wasn't supposed to and when the police got involved they all blamed me. Of course everybody believed the Treloar boy had been out joyriding. Luckily for me, I got a decent solicitor who pointed out quite clearly that it could have been any of us and got the charges dropped, but everyone immediately knew that I was on the same path as my father.'

Her heart ached for the lonely, misunderstood boy he had been—no wonder redeeming his name was so important to him.

'Only you weren't.'

'No. That scare brought me to my senses—I was lucky not to get a spell in juvenile detention, but worse was the disappointment in my mother's eyes. I swore then that I never wanted to make her look like that again. So over the next few years I kept my head down, programming and honing my skills until at eighteen I got an offer from a start-up to join them. The idea was that we would build apps for businesses and people with ideas in return for a share in the app. It was a bit of a gamble. For every ten apps we put our time and energy into, nine we effectively built for free, and they'd sink without a trace. But when an app made it, it really did. And after a couple of years I stopped just making a good living and started to get rich.'

'And that's what you do now?'

'Not any more. A few years back I took some of the money I had made and looked for ways to invest it in other start-ups, not just apps. An angel, they call it— again I provide the money in return for a share in the company. I started off backing a small local chain of Lebanese cafés who wanted to expand, an organic skincare brand, a tech concierge service. It's similar to the apps; there's a risk that many will fail, others may stay small-time, but the ones that succeed really succeed. I have a team now who scout small businesses with potential for me.'

Rosy leaned forward, fascinated by his drive, his tenacity, his integrity. 'And this is why the theatre means so much—you want to invest in the village?'

'And to show the people here who I am now. Make our name respected, not reviled. And to help create something I am invested in, not just give money to others. Show my girls who I am, make them proud.'

'Of course they're proud. And you should be too. You're an amazing father! How many eighteen-year-olds do what you did? You built yourself up from someone who had barely anything to someone who can afford almost anything, but more importantly to being the best father you could be. Your girls are very, very lucky to have you.'

He didn't answer for a long while. 'Money isn't everything. They don't have a mother; I couldn't give them that.'

There was a lot going on here, more than Arrosa could unpack right now. She knew, she sensed with every fibre of her being that Jack rarely, if ever, opened up like this. What was it about them that made confidences between them so easy? And yet she couldn't repay him with any semblance of truth. It wasn't fair. She couldn't allow the imbalance to tip any further.

'I'm sorry.' She stood up, summoning her best social voice, her best social smile. 'You came here for some time alone with your thoughts. I should leave you to them.'

'Don't go.'

The words were so low she thought for a moment she had imagined them, but then Jack spoke again, his voice almost a guttural growl, reaching out to take her hand. 'Don't go.'

His touch shivered through her, every nerve jumping to attention as her whole body responded to the feel of his fingers threaded through hers, her body hollowing out, an insistent sweet ache pulsing low in her stomach, in her breasts. She almost gasped at the sensation, her own fingers folding around his, anchoring her to him as sensation shot through her.

'I…' She had no idea what to say, what to do. She was all desire, all need, and all the reasons she needed to retreat had floated away, leaving her standing there staring at him helplessly, looking for answers. Jack rose to his feet in one graceful movement and looked down at her, tenderness and need stark in his eyes.

This is a bad idea, she tried to remind herself, but she couldn't remember why that mattered. Why anything mattered but the stars overhead, shining on them as if in approval, the glow of the dying fire, the sweet smell of applewood permeating the atmosphere and the fact that Jack Treloar was looking at her as if she were the moon and the stars.

She stared up at him, drinking in the sharply defined lines of his face, the slope of his cheekbones and the curve of his mouth. Her gaze lingered on his mouth, the sensual curl enticing, inviting her, and she stepped closer, as if of its own volition her hand reaching up to trace his cheekbone, the lines of his jaw.

'Jack,' she whispered, unsure whether it was a plea or a protest. His skin was rough under her fingers, his stubble grazing her as she continued her exploration, returning along his jaw and up until she reached his mouth. He was motionless, eyes dark and full of a desire she had never seen before, never evoked before, and it filled her with a power she couldn't resist as he finally, finally tilted her chin and lowered his mouth to hers.

This was no gentle exploratory kiss but a claiming on both sides that shook Arrosa through even as she matched him, moving so close she could feel his every bone and muscle hard against her. She luxuriated in him, in the owning of him as she explored him, her hands running over shoulders and back, neck and chest, touching and teasing and learning. His hands were wrapped in her hair and she welcomed the slight pull as he wound the curls around his fingers. He tasted of wine and salt, smelt of woodsmoke and something uniquely him that she recognised at a molecular level. She wanted no barriers between them, she wanted him naked and in her, fast and hard and sweet and slow and please God could it be now…

And then, as if the heavens had opened and dowsed her in reality, Arrosa stepped back, all the reasons this couldn't, shouldn't, mustn't happen spinning through her.

'I am so sorry, Jack, I can't. I mustn't.' She reached towards him for one weak moment as she whispered, 'I wish I could', before whirling around and running back to her tent.

# CHAPTER SIX

DESPITE THE EXCELLENT mattress and comfortable surroundings, Arrosa didn't manage to get any sleep that
night, reliving the kiss over and over in glorious Tech-
nicolor until she was both exhausted and frustrated,
filled with unsated desire and regret.

*What had she been thinking?*

The truth was she hadn't been thinking. Instead,
she'd allowed herself to be swept away. Turned out a
starlit sky, firelight and a handsome man were her own
personal kryptonite. Thank goodness she had come to
her senses before she'd lost even more control. At least
it was just a kiss.

But, oh, what a kiss. The kind of kiss she would remember until her dying moment. Just the thought of it
sent flames flicking through her.

It didn't help that Jack kissed in a way guaranteed
to make a girl's knees quiver. It wasn't just that he had
felt, had tasted, so good. No, the problem was the *way*
he'd kissed her. As if kissing her was exactly what he
should be doing, was born to do. And she, God help her,
had kissed him in exactly the same way.

The truth was it wasn't just a kiss. It was the culmi-
nation of a promise, a moment they'd been careering to-

wards from the very first second. A moment she should have done her best to head off, not grasping with both hands as if it was her last chance of happiness.

Only maybe it was. After all, just three weeks ago she had practically proposed to someone she had no interest at all in kissing. Had resigned herself to a love-less, lust-less future.

And now? Now she didn't know what she wanted, what to do. No, that wasn't true. She wanted to kiss Jack again. But she couldn't, not while he had no idea who or what she was. Not when her heart seemed so firmly on the line.

To her surprise—and her relief—Jack seemed to act completely normally over breakfast and if the shadows under his blue eyes were darker than usual, well, there were lots of explanations for that. Maybe she'd read him wrong, read the situation wrong. Maybe for him the kiss had been nothing more than a passing whim, he'd just been taking advantage of what was undeniably a very romantic situation. But when Sally volunteered to take the now washed and dressed girls down to see the farm animals, the look he gave Arrosa made it clear that a reckoning was due.

'Fancy a walk?' he asked so casually that if she hadn't been so attuned to him, hadn't seen the pulse beating in his throat, hadn't observed his almost preternatural stillness she might not have known the request was more of a command.

'Sure, let me just get my bag.' She took a few minutes in her tent to breathe and compose herself, before pulling on a cardigan and grabbing her bag. Neither spoke as they made their way to the clifftop path which wound steeply down to a wide pebbly cove and started to make their way across the rocky beach.

'I owe you an apology,' Jack said at last, his jaw tight. 'I misread the situation last night. I didn't mean to make you uncomfortable. Please accept my apologies. It won't happen again.'

There it was, a get-out. Arrosa could say yes, he had misread the situation and they could both pretend she hadn't touched him, hadn't explored the austere planes of his face, hadn't pulled him so tight against her she could still feel him imprinted on her.

But she wasn't a liar. 'You didn't misread the situation. I wanted to be there with you, I wanted to kiss you and I wanted you to kiss me. I was all in, Jack. You don't need to apologise.'

'Okay...' Now he looked confused. 'Was it too soon? Were we moving too fast?' His brows drew together. 'Or are you in a relationship?'

Arrosa didn't know what to say. In one way all of the reasons were true. 'Jack...' She had no idea where to go next. Her hands curled into fists as she took a deep breath. She had to be honest. He was a good man, he deserved the truth from her. 'Yes to all those reasons and no at the same time. I'm not seeing anyone romantically, but my life isn't my own, Jack. That's why I'm here in Cornwall. I'm enjoying a few weeks' freedom before I pledge myself to Asturia. I know, I have always known, that my happiness will always have to come second. And so I shouldn't have kissed you. It was selfish of me because I knew I couldn't pursue it any further, but I just wanted something that was mine, just for once.'

His expression grew even more confused. 'Do you mean you're going to become a nun?'

She laughed, although in some ways the analogy fitted. 'No, although many of my ancestors were. Convents were always a good way to deal with wayward daughters and unwanted wives. Look, Jack, my full name is Arrosa Artega…'

She waited but now he just looked blank. Her name obviously meant nothing to him.

'That's a pretty name,' he said carefully, obviously wondering where this was going.

'Thank you. But this is about more than my name. Okay.' She looked out to sea, trying to find the right words. 'What I am about to tell you can go no further, because it doesn't just affect me. It affects Clem as well. And I really want you to know that I didn't mean to mislead you, I certainly didn't mean for things to escalate between us. But they have and that means you deserve the truth. I'm not a diplomat, Jack. I'm a princess. And in a few weeks' time the laws of my country will be changed to enable me to become next in line to the throne and the next monarch.'

There, it was out, and with it a load she hadn't even known she was carrying.

Arrosa cast a quick glance in Jack's direction to try and gauge his reaction. For a moment she could have sworn she saw hurt flit over his face, only to be wiped away as if it never was as his expression became shuttered.

'I must be very slow,' he said, his voice curiously polite. 'Did you just say you're a princess?'

'I didn't mean to deceive you…' she started but he dismissed her apology with a casual wave of his hand.

'Please don't worry about it, Your Highness. Is that the right title? You'll have to forgive me; I'm not used to addressing royalty.' Each word hammered into her, and she flinched.

'Rosy is fine. Look, Jack, like I said, this isn't just my secret. It involves Clem as well and that means I can't tell you everything, but I really want to try and make you understand.'

'Honestly, there's no need. You've been slumming it with the common people, that's absolutely fine. I hope I helped you relax.' His tone was still ultra-polite, deceptively casual, but she could see by the beat of a pulse in his cheek and the tensing of his jaw that polite was the last thing Jack Treloar was feeling right now.

For a minute she toyed with the idea of turning her back on him, heading back to the campsite and gathering her things before returning to the cottage. In a few weeks' time she'd be back in Asturia and would never see him again. Besides, she didn't owe him any explanation.

But then again, that wasn't exactly true. She'd allowed herself to step into his carefully ordered life. She'd offered to look after his girls, suggested this camping trip. She'd entangled herself with him, gained his trust—and that she knew was a rarity for this proud man.

Now he thought she'd betrayed it, betrayed him, and after he'd allowed himself to be vulnerable in front of her. No wonder he was so cold. She deserved it.

They'd reached the end of the beach, only rocks ahead until the point of the headland. The nearest rock was flat and smooth and Arrosa headed to it and sat, staring out at the horizon. Jack halted a few metres away and tried to calm his tumbling thoughts, quell his instinctive anger.

How could he have been such an idiot? How could he once again have fallen for a woman who didn't have any interest in him apart from as a diversion? A momentary dabble in the real world before stepping back into her gilded life.

It hadn't taken him long after their marriage to realise that Lily had been more interested in his reputation than Jack himself. He had been supposed to be a summer rebellion, the local lord of the manor's daughter slumming it with the village bad boy. Her marriage to him, their baby, a continuation of that rebellion. She'd loved him in her own careless way, but she had never really been in love with him, he knew that now, maybe had always known it.

And now he had once again fallen for a woman who came from a different sphere, who had no long-term interest in him. He was a fool.

'Jack,' she said quietly, almost helplessly. 'Please let me explain.'

His first instinct was to refuse, to walk away, but there was something heartbreakingly vulnerable in her straight-backed posture and so instead he nodded curtly. He owed her nothing, but she could have her say.

She clasped her hands together and stared out to sea for a while, visibly searching for the words, before exhaling softly and looking up at him candidly. 'I came to Cornwall every summer as a child. It's a place that means a lot to me. It was a chance to get away from everything life in Asturia entailed. Like I said to you a few days ago, I had a very privileged but very lonely childhood. One which meant I got to stay in palaces and castles all over the world, but one where I was never allowed to be a child. I always had to be perfectly presented and perfectly behaved. Coming to Cornwall, being Rosy, not Arrosa, was the only time I was free just to be me, to even figure out who me *was*.' She blinked and he could have sworn he saw the glint of tears.

'I always knew that as a girl I couldn't inherit the throne and, apart from the innate sexism of the law, that was more than fine with me. As I got older and got to go to boarding school here in England as well as spend summers here, I could see some kind of freedom in my future. Balancing a career and royal duties is a difficult thing to do, as many minor royals have found before me, and I had no idea what that path would be for me, but I was looking forward to university and figuring it all out. It felt like I had all the time in the world. But I was wrong.' She threw him a quick anxious glance but he couldn't respond, couldn't move, frozen into place by the spell of her words.

'I spent the summer here after turning eighteen and it was golden. I don't know if that's because, when I look back, it was the last time I was truly free, or whether it really was. Clem and I were dating these guys in an intense teen kind of way and the four of us spent the summer surfing and sailing and at festivals. But then my father summoned me home and told me that the right thing to do for our family and for the country was to overturn the primogeniture law retrospectively so that I could become Crown Princess.'

He finally spoke. 'So now you're the heir to the throne?'

'Not quite yet, but soon. In Asturia, the monarch has a lot of political power. The people dislike change. I think it's partly because of where we are positioned, our history is full of war and conflict. It's taken eight years to get to the place where the overturning of the primogeniture law can be ratified. Every opposition party has agreed to support it and the country as a whole agreed in a referendum. During the eight years the change has been debated I have had to be completely perfect in appearance and word and deed. And once I become heir I will have to be even more so. It can be overwhelming at times.'

She blew out a breath. 'Clem thought I needed a break and so she persuaded me to stay here while she is in Asturia pretending to be me—and you are one of just a very small number of people who know that. Jack, if this got out not only would it destroy the public's confidence in me but for Clem the exposure would be life-changing. That I can't tell you any more about, it's not my story to tell, but I hope you see how much I trust you in revealing this much.'

'Clem is pretending to be you? Sure, you resemble each other, but you're hardly identical.' But he could feel his anger starting to thaw. She must have felt desperate to have agreed to such a risky scheme.

'That is definitely the flaw in the plan. But I'd kept my diary free this summer to help me prepare for the ratification, so Clem is being driven out every so often dressed up as me, and that's hopefully enough to keep the tabloids at bay. I've been closely followed, you see, ever since I came of age. A leave of absence would be immediately gossiped about, any kind of hint I needed a break so close to the ratification could lead to the kind of speculation I've spent the last eight years trying to avoid. It's risky, maybe too risky, but the thought of spending six weeks here, being Rosy again one last time, was irresistible. Clem had her own reasons for proposing the switch.'

She looked up at him and he could see the need for understanding, the apology in her expression and he knew her reaction was real. Lily had never cared about being understood, had never apologised to him once, no matter what. But Lily had merely been a rich man's daughter—Rosy was a princess. He had made his own money but he would never be able to create the kind of background and privilege she would need in any future partner.

'There you go, Jack. The whole story. You now know more about me than almost any other person in the world except Clem, my father and my bodyguard.'

'Your secrets are safe with me,' he said at last. 'I can promise you that.'

'Thank you. Jack, I hope you see why I had to step away last night. I couldn't allow us to continue if you didn't know who I am. I didn't want to deceive you any further. But...' She paused and her cheeks pinkened. 'I'd like us to still be friends. I have really appreciated getting to know you over the last few weeks.'

Friends? Was that even possible any more after such an incendiary kiss, after the sharing of such confidences? He'd started to fall for her, hard, and now he was grappling with the fact that she had misled him— and that there was definitely no future for them. Men like him might climb up the social ladder so far, but royalty was definitely a step too far.

Plus, he'd always sworn that if and when he started

to date, the girls came first. A relationship with no hope of going anywhere failed that test spectacularly.

But, at the same time, he couldn't just walk away. There was a loneliness to Rosy that he had never really appreciated before, a loneliness that called to him.

'I need to think about it.' He saw her face fall although she tried to hide it. 'It's a lot, Rosy. It was already a lot. You started to change things for me and for the girls in ways I hadn't expected or planned for. And although I knew you weren't planning on living here full-time, that there was no future for us, I couldn't help but wonder that if things carried on the way they'd started maybe somehow there might have been. That we could figure it all out. But now? Now there can never be anything beyond this summer. I know it sounds a little crazy, talking about the future after just a few meetings as if I was still a romantic teen. But there's a connection between us. Isn't there?'

'Yes.'

'So I need time to think this all through.'

'I'm sorry, Jack,' she said, her voice breaking slightly.

Jack wanted to hold her, to promise her that it would all be okay, but that wasn't a promise he could make so instead he simply nodded then turned and walked away.

The irony was that in every other way the camping trip was a great success. The girls seemed happier and more settled, while Jack and Sally were now, if not friends exactly, then friendly, Sally willing to set up a meeting with him and the theatre committee.

But it wasn't lost on Jack that Rosy was responsible for that success—after all, she had suggested the trip and invited Sally along. But thinking of her was like touching a sore spot. He felt hollow inside when he thought about her revelations, the knowledge that it was easier and more sensible to move on with his life without involving her any further in it.

Jack did his best to throw himself into work, but for once it didn't hold his attention the way he had always relied upon it to do. It didn't help that the girls were away; Lily's parents were staying at their Polhallow house and had asked to have their granddaughters for a few days. He had a good relationship with his in-laws now; it was a long time since they'd viewed him as the teenage boy who'd seduced away their daughter.

But with the girls away the house felt too big and too empty and although there were plenty of things he could and should be doing he couldn't seem to get going and this morning was no different. He knew he had to have the promised conversation with Rosy. The problem was, he still had no idea what to say.

It was late morning and already hot as he set out on foot, popping into the café Sally's family owned for snacks and coffees before walking up the hill to Clem's clifftop cottage.

There was no answer to his initial knock on the door, but the windows were wide open and so Jack walked around the house to the back garden, where he paused, his blood rushing at the sight of a bikini-clad Rosy stretched out on a sunbed, eyes half closed and her face upturned to the sun, a book unopened in her hand.

'Are you open to visitors?'

She started and looked up, wary at first, almost scared, and with a pang of conscience he remembered what she'd said about living under scrutiny, always having to be picture perfect. He was pretty sure that description didn't include lounging in nothing but a bikini, although she did look pretty perfect to him. His mouth dried as he took in the long lines of her body; he'd rather take this relaxed Rosy than any prim and proper princess. Not, of course, that either were his to take.

'I've brought lunch,' he said and held out the paper bag.

For a moment she didn't react, just stared at him before sitting up, her full mouth curving into a wide smile. 'Oh, well, if you brought lunch...'

'It's nothing fancy...' He was barely conscious of what he was saying, just using words to try and bridge the chasm that had sprung up between them.

'Even better.' She pushed herself up to her feet with grace and Jack couldn't tear his gaze away from her long, tanned legs, her exposed midriff, the curve of her breasts showcased by the yellow bikini top. He swallowed as the desire that had never quite subsided flared up, hot and urgent. 'I was just trying to get up the energy to fix some lunch. Shall we eat here?' She gestured to the wrought iron table he was standing next to.

'Perfect.' Jack placed the coffee and bags on the table and watched her as she walked over, pulling an oversized striped T-shirt dress on as she did so.

'Hi,' she said softly.

'Hi.' They looked at each other for a charged moment before taking their seats and Jack tore open the bags to reveal the savoury pastries, olives and marinated tomatoes and peppers he'd bought, pushing a coffee towards Rosy.

She sniffed it appreciatively. 'Flat white, no sugar?'

'I've been paying attention.'

'Thanks.' Colour rose in her cheeks as she took a sip.

Jack pushed one of the bags towards her and they ate, making polite conversation about the quality of the food, the girls' plans for the rest of the week, until the bags were empty and Rosy sat back with a satisfied sigh. 'Delicious, thank you.' She looked down at her hands. 'I'm glad you stopped by. I wasn't sure you would.'

'Neither was I,' he said honestly.

She nodded. 'I get it. My situation is a lot.'

But she *didn't* get it and Jack realised how much he wanted her to understand. 'It is, but Rosy, I've been here before.'

'Here?' Her expression was confused.

'An amusing diversion for a rich, entitled girl who fancied slumming it in the real world.' He enunciated every word. 'I have no intention of ever being that gullible again.'

Understanding and hurt flared in her eyes and he saw her swallow. 'That's not who I am, Jack.' She swallowed again and with an almost defensive toss of her head reached over and took his hand, lacing her fingers through his. 'I don't think I'm entitled, and you are more than my equal in every way. I can't tell you what this thing is between us because I don't know, but I promise that's not how I see you at all. I didn't intend any of this to happen. I shouldn't have allowed myself to get so close to the girls, to allow myself to get so close to you.' Her gaze was devastatingly candid. 'Especially once I realised how attracted I was to you.'

'And I am attracted to you, but it isn't that simple. It matters. Who you are matters.'

'Right now, I am just Rosy, enjoying the sun, and I intend to be her for another two weeks.' She let his hand drop, tilting her chin, and despite her words he could see the proud Princess in every line of her.

But he could see the woman he'd got to know and care for too. 'That's the problem. Because I don't know the Princess, but I do know Rosy. And it's Rosy I want.' He hadn't meant to admit that, but the words were out and couldn't be unsaid.

Her eyes were huge, her lips slightly parted. 'So what do we do?'

'I don't know,' he admitted, 'The sensible thing would have been not to come here at all.'

Rosy sat and looked at him for a long moment. 'Why do you think I see you as a diversion, Jack? You must know how much you have to offer any woman, even a princess. You're rich and good-looking, successful, a great father, fun to be with. Any woman would be lucky to have you.'

'I shouldn't have said that,' he admitted. 'Seeing Lily's parents today brought the past crashing back; it always does, although they mean well.'

'That's understandable. You were married for a long time.'

'You think we got a happy ever after?'

'I know it ended tragically, but raising two wonderful girls together was an achievement.'

It was one way to look at his marriage. He'd always thought of it as an endurance, not an achievement. 'Lily was complicated, which meant our marriage was complicated.'

'How so?'

How could he describe Lily? 'She was wild and beautiful and talented and capricious. She could make you feel like no one else existed or freeze you out completely and you would never know which way it would be.'

'That sounds exhausting.'

'It was.' It was only now that he could look back and see how much his marriage had drained him.

'How did you meet?'

'At the Harbour pub. We set eyes on each other and it was instant fireworks, the way it can only be when you're young and naïve and think *Romeo and Juliet* is a romance not a cautionary tale. Taking up with me was the ultimate two fingers up at her parents and their expectations for her. Her parents wanted her to join the family law firm after Oxford, she wanted to study art. I was her ultimate rebellion, son of the village petty criminal with a reputation of my own. The irony is, she was a lot wilder than me. I think actually I disappointed her in many ways.' He inhaled, thinking back to the naïve young man he'd once been, who thought that love was enough.

'We didn't intend to get pregnant, and she certainly didn't intend to marry me. I was meant to be her summer fun.' He saw Rosy wince and realised she now understood parallels he'd noticed between her situation and his past. 'I think when people gossip about back then, they imagine me whisking her off to some bedsit on the outer edges of London. Instead, I was on such a good salary that we could move to a nice area and once Tansy was born Lily went to art school, just like she wanted. She was talented, but when she left college she was more interested in partying than working and I was making more than enough for her to indulge herself. It wasn't that she didn't love the girls, she just didn't know how to be a mother and didn't care to learn; the children would be brought out at parties and then sent away with the nanny. Just as her childhood had been.'

He reached out and swigged his now cold coffee, grateful for the caffeine. 'Poor Lily, rather than scandalise her parents, in the end they were actually proud of me. Instead of a husband as wild as her, she found herself married to a man with a ridiculous work ethic who made more money than her parents could ever dream of and gave her the kind of life they wanted for her.'

'Were you ever happy?'

It was a long time since he had thought of happiness where his marriage was concerned.

'Sometimes,' he said slowly. 'At least we tried to be.' After all, he'd known her as he knew himself, understood the insecurities that led to her destructive behaviour. 'She loved the girls but motherhood bored her, so I compensated. I went to every play and dance recital, created every holiday tradition. I wanted them to have a perfect childhood. Sometimes I think that somewhere between being the best father I could and my work drive I forgot to be a husband. I didn't want Lily to feel she'd made a mistake marrying me, I didn't want her to feel trapped, the way my mother did. So I never challenged her about her behaviour, never questioned her about her drinking or the drugs I was pretty sure she was taking on a night out. She took lovers and I pretended not to know. Maybe if I'd intervened she wouldn't have ended up overdosing in a hotel room at the age of twenty-eight.'

Jack couldn't believe the words that had just tumbled out of his mouth, words he had barely dared to think before, let alone say. Words that were his truth. His shame.

But there was no condemnation on Rosy's face. No horror. 'I am so, so sorry, Jack.'

He shrugged, suddenly tired. 'It's been over two years now. Clover barely remembers her. At first, I didn't want to make any big moves, all the books say to give it a year, not to make any sudden decisions in the first wave of grief. And the girls needed their routine. But we lived in a wealthy area, and I could see how young it started. The drinking, the drugs, the dangerous and entitled behaviour. I'm not saying Cornwall doesn't have its problems, I know it does, and I know every school has its own issues. But I wanted to show them a different way before it was too late.'

Rosy reached out and took his hand again and he was glad of the warmth, the firmness of her grip. 'You are not just a good father, Jack Treloar, you are an amazing one. And I am sure Lily would be glad her girls have you looking out for them.'

'You think so?'

'I know so.'

And for the first time in a long time Jack knew so too, freed from the guilt and grief that had plagued him since Lily's death. He was doing his best and that was enough.

# CHAPTER SEVEN

ARROSA SAT STILL for a moment, absorbing everything Jack had told her. Every instinct she possessed told her that she now knew more about Jack Treloar than any other person alive. He'd gifted her his regrets and his hopes and his dreams. It was a precious, fragile gift and she knew how rare it was. Would he have entrusted her with so much if she were staying here? Was the intensity between them fast-tracked by the finite nature of their relationship, that knowledge the clock was ticking, and she was already over halfway through her time here?

And in return Jack knew most of her secrets, apart from Clem's identity. This was as intimate as she was ever likely to be with another human being. And that wasn't something she could just walk away from.

But what else could she do?

'How long are the girls with their grandparents?'

Surprise—and intrigue—flitted across his expression.

'Until Sunday at the earliest, possibly early next week, depending on how long their grandparents can cope. Losing Lily took a toll on them both, so I like to keep arrangements flexible in case the girls need to come back early.'

'And it's Thursday lunchtime now.' She glanced at her watch. 'If you include this afternoon then you have three days until the end of the weekend.'

Jack raised his eyebrows in bemused query. 'Three days to what?'

'To take a leaf out of my book and get away from it all,' she said. 'Responsibility and duty and shouldering everything yourself is all very well, but if you don't put down your burdens occasionally then you run the risk of breaking.'

'My girls are not a burden.' But, to her relief, he didn't sound angry.

Emboldened, she went on. 'No, of course not. But I don't know a single parent who isn't glad of a break every now and then. We all need to refill the well, Jack. And if your plans for the next few days are just work, work, work how are you going to do any refilling?'

'You think I'm in danger of running dry?' Now he sounded amused as well as curious.

'All I'm saying is that I do know a lot about burnout. I had no idea how close I was myself until the morning I woke up here. It was almost overwhelming, I almost left it too late. But I know now never to let myself get to that stage again.' Arrosa picked up her coffee and drained it. 'You know, I always thought my mother was selfish, disappearing off on retreat every summer without me and without my father. It always seemed an affectation to me, but I understand her better now. For forty-eight weeks of the year she's the perfect Queen. She puts all her own hopes and desires to one side and concentrates on supporting my father, supporting me, making small talk, being the consummate hostess. No wonder she needs four weeks a year when she's just herself.'

Truth was, Arrosa was a little ashamed of how judge-mental she'd been. She, of all people, knew that her parents' marriage was no fairy tale but rather a some-times brutal business arrangement, one broken before it had had a chance to flourish after Zorien had con-fessed about his love affair with Clem's mother. How could she judge her mother for taking one month a year for herself? She made a quick resolve to call her. They didn't have the sort of relationship which included cosy chats or calls to just check in, but maybe that was some-thing that could change. She might have lost her second mother, but her own mother was still alive and well and Arrosa should not take that for granted.

'So, you think I need a break?'

'Tell me you're not tempted.'

'And you will come with me on this break.'

It was not a question. Which was a good thing be-cause she didn't have an answer.

'That's not…'

But he didn't let her finish. 'Where do you want to go?'

'Jack, it was a suggestion, not a proposition.' But she couldn't deny she was tempted. Very tempted. She'd never been on a mini-break before. And just a few days ago she had resigned herself to not seeing Jack again and now he was offering her the opportunity to spend some real time with him.

She was inexperienced romantically, but she wasn't a fool. She knew what would happen if she agreed.

Her pulse sped up at the thought.

'And it was a good suggestion. I could do with a break, you're right. But I spend a lot of time alone with-out adult company. If I was going to unwind, really unwind, I might need some help.' His gaze was burning into her. 'So, any requests?'

Arrosa took a deep breath, her chest tight with anticipation. Three days away with Jack—three days and three nights. Without the girls there would be no need to worry about mixed signals and raising expectations. They were both adults and they both knew the score. Had acknowledged how they felt, knew the barriers, that there was no future for them.

Maybe it needed to happen. Maybe if she left Cornwall with this connection still simmering between them, this desire unconsummated, then she would be condemning herself to a constant *what might have been*, a refrain that might run throughout her life. And who knew? Maybe they would burn out as quickly as they'd started.

'Anywhere,' she said and saw Jack relax just a little at the tacit agreement. 'Not abroad as I can't use my passport. If I did the press would instantly be alerted.'

'How did you get here?'

'Private jet and airfield. It's an option but it would take too long to arrange.' Besides, she didn't want to involve the Court or her bodyguard, not in something as private as this.

'UK then. Probably not too far if we only have a couple of days. Besides…'

'Besides, you don't want to be too far from the girls.' She quite understood.

Anticipation buzzed through her. This was nothing Arrosa had experienced before, discussing weekend plans with a man she burned for. 'Let's just get one thing straight,' she told him. 'I know you're a man with refined tastes, but I'm a woman who is very easily impressed. Fish and chips and a decent beach are all I require. Maybe a pint in a really good pub.'

His mouth quirked into a devastating grin and the anticipation intensified. 'You don't need your own concierge service?' She shook her head. 'Chauffeured limo? Michelin stars? Personal spa?'

'None of the above. If you could manage a clear sky and some stars I'd be very grateful, and I prefer my bed to be freshly made, but otherwise anything goes.'

His gaze softened into something so tender it hurt. 'Leave it with me.'

Jack disappeared to make arrangements and Arrosa quickly tidied away the lunch things, texting Sally to see if she'd be able to feed Gus for just a couple of nights, and went upstairs to pack, singing to herself as she did, her feelings so intense she could barely concentrate. Thank goodness she could use Clem's wardrobe; her own array of tiny beach dresses, shorts and bikinis clearly wouldn't take her very far.

Clem favoured vintage cuts, bright colours, whereas Arrosa usually dressed in more subtle tones and cuts, but then again, she'd never really had a chance to figure out her own taste. Once the project to turn her into the perfect Crown Princess had commenced, a stylist had been employed to make sure that Arrosa trod the fine line between fashion and appropriateness and so although her clothes were made just for her, and although she was always completely up to the minute in terms of cut and colour, there was something depressingly interchangeable about the dresses and little jackets, tailored trousers and neat jumpers she usually wore. Looking through Clem's eclectic mix of dresses and skirts, silky little tops and jumpers was a lot of fun and, before she knew it, she had selected enough for a week away, let alone just a couple of days. But, then again, she had no idea where they were going.

Jack collected her an hour later, refusing to give her any hints, although he drove deeper into Cornwall and not away from the county until they finally reached Penzance. He continued winding his way through the town, pulling in at a car park near the docks.

'We have to leave the car here,' he said as he swung their cases out of the boot. 'They don't allow visitors' cars where we're going.'

Arrosa looked towards the dock and the ferry sign, excitement mounting. 'The Isles of Scilly? Oh, Jack! That's perfect. Clem and Simone went one spring, and their photos were amazing!'

She'd always wanted to visit the small cluster of islands at the southern tip of Britain. Famous for their microclimate and wildlife, something about the islands had always appealed to her.

'It turns out that finding something last minute for a weekend in early July isn't that easy, but luckily I know people who know people. Sure this is okay?'

'It couldn't be more okay,' she said as he took both cases and headed towards the boarding gate for the ferry.

It was a windy couple of hours on a surprisingly rough ocean, but Arrosa drank in every second, laughing as her hair escaped the coil she'd fastened it into and whipped around her face. She, Arrosa Artega, was heading off on a romantic weekend with a man she had started to care for and right now everything was perfect.

Rosy's enthusiasm was infectious. She loved everything, from the ferry journey over to St Mary's and the transfer to the smaller boat which took them to Tresco, exclaiming at the seals and dolphins they spotted in the waves. She didn't even mind the mile-long walk to the cottage Jack had managed to borrow, despite the stiff climb and her bulky case, waving away his offer of help.

'Don't treat me like a princess,' she told him.

'It's chivalry,' he protested.

'I'm quite capable, and I'm the one who overpacked.'

Finally, they reached the whitewashed cottage which sat alone on the headland. It had been cleaned and prepared for them and Jack retrieved the key from the keysafe, opening the door and standing back, allowing Rosy to precede him.

He followed her into the small but perfectly formed cottage. The ground floor was one room, kitchen, dining space and lounge combined, with floor-to-ceiling windows framing the dramatic ocean views on one end and the cliffs on either side. It was comfortably yet stylishly decorated and Rosy turned to Jack, eyes glowing.

'I love it. I can't wait to explore!'

You would never think that Rosy was a princess, used to the best of everything, Jack reflected as she exclaimed in delight, exploring every inch of the cottage, dashing from view to view, opening cupboards, examining the bookcases.

'It's not too small?'

She shook her head, her delighted smile widening even further if that was possible. 'You know, even though I moved out of the château when I was twenty-one, I still have four bedrooms in a house where no one comes to stay, and a couple of downstairs rooms I don't even use. I don't need or want a big house; cosy suits me fine.'

And that was part of what he liked about her. She wasn't influenced by how much something cost, but by what it meant.

'That's good to hear because this place is certainly bijou,' he said. 'And of course,' he added hurriedly, not wanting there to be any misunderstandings between them, 'I'll take the pull-out bed.'

There was only one bedroom, taking up the whole of the upper floor, with a luxury shower room off it—the bath was on a raised platform by the window in the bedroom so the occupant could fill it with water and the decadent-smelling bath oil and lounge comfortably, looking out to sea.

'The pull-out?'

He nodded towards the sofa. 'It turns into a bed.'

She held his gaze levelly, but he could see a trace of uncertainty in her eyes. Not, he thought, uncertainty about what she was about to say, but more uncertainty about his reaction.

'It's a big bed,' she said deliberately. 'I would say it's big enough to share.'

Jack swallowed at the hope in her gaze. It wasn't an unexpected offer. After all, this was no platonic getaway. The prospect of consummating their connection had been there since the moment he'd suggested she join him for a getaway, the moment she'd accepted. Staying in a small, isolated cottage in the middle of nowhere, a cottage made for lovers, just set those expectations more firmly. But it was the first time either of them had alluded to it out loud.

'Okay.'

Her smile was mischievous. 'I mean, you can sleep on the sofa bed if you prefer.'

'I'm sure the bed will be fine.'

Her dimples flashed. 'Good, I'm glad that's settled.'

Jack continued to watch her as she whirled around the cottage, still discovering new things to exclaim at in surprise or approval. He needed to concentrate on the here and now and deliberately, very deliberately, not think about what he was doing. Not think about the promise that hovered over them, the evening just a very few short hours away.

This trip was impulsive, frivolous, dedicated to momentary pleasure, all things Jack rarely allowed. He liked his life planned and organised and deliberate, had done ever since the day the policeman had told his fourteen-year-old self that he could be facing a lengthy spell in youth detention. The next two hours, alone in a cell waiting for his mother, afraid of the sadness and, worse, the resignation he knew he'd see on her too-worn face had changed him. He'd realised what an impulsive fool he had been, played with by older, richer boys who saw him as little more than amusement and had no compunction in using him as their scapegoat. He'd seen his future stretched out before him, full of rooms like that, spells in and out of jail, like his father had before him, leaving a trail of broken hearts and broken potential behind him. He'd vowed then and there that that would not be his destiny and everything he'd done since had been a rebuttal of the policeman's words.

The only time he'd allowed himself to step off the path he'd set himself was when he'd met Lily. That summer his future had seemed assured, his job lined up and already enough money saved to change his life. But even that hadn't derailed him. When he'd found out Lily was pregnant he'd just adjusted his plans, used the prospect of becoming a father to motivate him even more.

Now he was stepping off the path again for a very different woman. A woman who was considered and responsible, one who accepted her responsibilities and fate, who wasn't trying to outrun her destiny but to meet it with grace and acceptance.

'You look very pensive.' Rosy came to stand next to him, close but not touching. For two people away on a romantic weekend they were very careful not to touch, but he could feel the air around them tense.

'I'm just thinking what a lucky man I am,' he said, and her face softened.

'Don't you forget it.'

'It's a little late to explore the island,' Jack said. "But we have this place until Sunday, so shall we head out and get some food? There are a couple of really good restaurants; they are probably fully booked but I'm sure I could pull some strings.'

'You know, I don't want a fancy restaurant.' Rosy put a hand on his shoulder and looked up at him almost shyly. 'I wasn't kidding earlier. What I really, really want is fish and chips, maybe a beer, sitting on the beach, watching the boats go by. Does that sound really boring?'

'No,' he said slowly. 'That sounds perfect.'

Too perfect. This was a summer idyll, nothing more, but with every passing moment he knew he was falling harder for her.

'They were the best fish and chips I ever had in my entire life,' Rosy said, leaning against him with a contented sigh, and Jack agreed. The takeaway had been perfectly cooked, slightly crispy chips melting in the middle and covered with the perfect amount of salt and vinegar, delicately flaked fish in melt-in-the-mouth batter accompanied by a tart locally brewed beer with just the right amount of hops. Add in the soft sandy beach, the stunning sunset and the sea views and Jack realised he'd never enjoyed a meal more. Nor had he ever felt anything like the anticipation for what came next. Much as he wanted to drag her back to the cottage and kiss her until neither of them could speak, he also wanted to enjoy the wait a little longer.

'Fancy trying the local pub?' he asked and she agreed, exclaiming how lucky they were to find a small table by the window as he fetched the drinks, like any normal couple out on a date, making small talk about books and films and dreams.

'Have you ever thought about who you would be if you weren't you?' Jack asked after a while and Arrosa stared at him in confusion.

'If I wasn't me?'

'I'm trying to be discreet,' he said. 'You know, if you didn't have to do the job you have to do.'

'Oh.' Her face fell a little. 'It's not something I think about,' she said at last. 'It is what it is, and I can't change it so I try not to waste time wishing for something else. But I'm glad I don't have one overwhelming passion. If Clem was me, for instance, and couldn't act, then it would have destroyed her. I wasn't overjoyed about the closing down of other paths, but I accepted it. I think if I can keep some semblance of normality in my life, like living in my villa, that kind of thing, then I'll be okay.'

'That's a very healthy attitude.'

She shrugged. 'I could have said no to my dad, I

guess, but then how could I advocate for change if I didn't want to be that change? I can't run away from who I am, from my responsibilities, at least not for ever. How about you? Any unlived dreams?'

'Obviously, I was married and a father young, so like you, I suppose, I accepted responsibility then and learned not to waste time on daydreams. But the truth is my girls give my life meaning and purpose. I wouldn't want to imagine a world where they aren't my life. I guess,' he said slowly, 'what we have in common is that even if circumstances don't work out the way we thought they might, we know how to make the best of the situation we're in. That's pretty rare in my experience.'

Rosy held up her drink. 'To the cards we're dealt'.

He clinked his glass against hers but as they made the toast couldn't help wondering if they would be so philosophical when Rosy left for good.

Her gaze was fixed on his as she finished her drink. 'You know I don't want another drink here. Let's get back.'

'You sure?' he asked, and they both knew he was asking about more than the drink.

'Yes,' she said. 'I have never been surer. Let's go.'

# CHAPTER EIGHT

NEITHER SPOKE AS they walked back in the rapidly darkening dusk, anticipation colouring every step, every movement, every glance. Arrosa was attuned to Jack's every move, breath and glance. Desire swirled, hot and intense, throughout her entire body, pooling in the pit of her stomach, causing flickers of heat in every nerve, her breasts heavy and almost painful. It was like some specific kind of torture, almost painful, apprehension mingling with anticipation.

They still hadn't spoken by the time they reached the cottage and Jack once again unlocked the door and ushered her in. Arrosa swallowed nervously as she slipped off her wrap and stood slightly awkwardly in the middle of the lounge watching Jack as he closed the door behind him and moved towards her, graceful, masculine and seemingly unaffected by the nerves that now consumed her.

He reached her and paused, tilting her chin up so that he could look in her eyes. It took everything Arrosa had to meet his dark gaze.

'We don't have to do anything you don't want to,' he told her, and she loved him for it.

'But I do want to,' she said and before she could

change her mind wound her arms around his neck, bringing him closer, until once again she was kissing him the way she had wanted to since their first kiss a few days before.

Just like the kiss at the fire, there was no gentle introduction as once again the kiss ratcheted from nought to sixty without passing go. His mouth was strong and possessive, his hands sure and knowing, and even though he was only touching her back and waist, her whole body ached for more, arching towards him. She found herself tugging at his shirt, impatient to get to the skin underneath, to run her hands over the smooth muscled planes of his body, needing to know him in every way, to discover every inch, to make him hers. She dragged her mouth from his, pressing kisses along his jawline as she finally wrenched his shirt off, leaving her free to explore the skin underneath.

He hissed as her hands moved lower, now pulling at his belt. 'Rosy, we have all the time in the world.'

But they didn't! They had here and now and if they were lucky a couple more weeks and that was it. What had she been thinking of, waiting an entire month? They could have been here already; this could be one moment in a long line, not the first. She pressed even closer, holding his face between her hands as she kissed him harder, impatient for him to touch her in all the places that ached for him.

Jack didn't protest any more, kissing her back with equal intensity, finally, finally sliding his hands up her back, his clever fingers tracing every inch of skin until she was boneless with desire and only then sliding down with excruciating slowness to explore every rib before slowly, so slowly, inching back up towards her aching breasts. Arrosa moaned as his finger finally brushed against one tight nipple, arching into him as sensation engulfed her. 'Can we go upstairs?'

She felt his rumble of amusement, 'I feel like I should be sweeping you up and carrying you to the bed,' he said. 'But that spiral staircase isn't made for grand gestures. Ladies first.' She felt cold as she stepped away from him, her legs shaky as she made her way upstairs and turned to face him, all too aware of the giant bed which dominated the room.

For all her bravado, and her desperation to get past the niceties, her nerves had returned in full and her hands shook as she unzipped her dress. Jack stood near the staircase watching her, his expression unfathomable.

'What's wrong?'

'I'm a little nervous.' She tried to smile but his expression darkened.

'Rosy, I meant every word. We don't have to do anything you don't want to do. I have no expectations.'

'I know.' She bit her lip. Now it came to it, she couldn't quite find the words. 'It's just I've not done this before.'

She flushed hot at the surprise in his eyes, followed by understanding. 'I see.'

'It's a princess thing, you see,' she said hurriedly. 'I don't really date. The only people that ask me out are those that see the Princess, not the person, and that is possibly the least sexy thing I could imagine. Plus, there's always that fear in the back of my mind, if things don't work out, what if they go to the press? I couldn't bear any *My night of passion with the Princess* headlines. So there's never been anyone I've been willing to risk it for before. Not before you.'

His eyes darkened even more as he took a step closer. 'I don't see the Princess. I see the woman. I see you, Rosy. And it's you I want. But if it makes you feel better, I am just as nervous.'

'You are?' It was her turn to be surprised.

'Of course I am. For a start, you are one hell of a woman and that would make any man nervous. Secondly, now I know it's your first time I want to make it as special as I can. And thirdly, in a way it's a first time for me. You see, I've only ever slept with Lily.' Her gaze was glued to his but all she could see was candour and honesty.

'Really?'

'Really.'

'But...'

'It's a little bit like the princess thing, I suppose. When I was younger the kind of girls who were attracted to my reputation weren't the kind of girls I wanted to be with. Then I was married to Lily for ten years and, although it was an imperfect marriage, I took my marriage vows seriously. Since she died the girls come first and I haven't even considered dating. So, it's a first for me as well.'

'Then I'm the one who's honoured.'

It was as if their confidences had broken the ice. Her shyness had gone, her trepidation disappeared; all she wanted was this man now. She laughed a little breathlessly as he backed her onto the bed, luxuriating as she felt his weight upon her, as he kissed her until she could barely think any more, the last layers of clothing expertly discarded until there was nothing between them.

'Is this okay?' Jack kissed his way down her throat, one hand expertly palming her breast, and she moaned.

'Yes.'

'And this?' He drew her nipple into his mouth and she bucked as sensation flooded through her, barely able to articulate assent.

'And this? And this?'

He continued to murmur endearments, checking in as he explored her with a languid ease that left her panting and writhing until she was begging him to just please do it *now*, crying out as he finally entered her, pulling him closer, demanding more.

'Are you sure you haven't done this before,' he said many hours later as they lay tangled together. 'I must be a very good teacher.'

She laughed, raising herself onto one elbow to look down on him and kiss him. 'I didn't say I was a total novice. I'd done stuff.'

'Stuff? What stuff?'

'Do you want me to show you?'

His smile was pure wolf. 'Yes, please.'

She stayed there for a moment, drinking him in, luxuriating in his evident desire for her, for Rosy, not the Princess, and then bent her head, flicking her tongue along his chest and enjoying his intake of breath.

'As you wish.'

What happened in the Isles of Scilly was supposed to stay in the Isles of Scilly, but although they had both agreed that it would be too difficult to carry on their relationship back in Polhallow, Jack managed to find time nearly every day to sneak over to the cottage to make love to Rosy. Despite their good intentions, one weekend together had not been nearly enough time and they couldn't bring themselves to stop, not with the time till Rosy's departure ticking away faster and faster, the nights and days flying by at unbearable speed.

They were very careful not to let anyone suspect what had happened, was happening, not to show by a single glance or touch that there was anything more between them than friendship. It was hard, fiendishly hard. Jack allowed his gaze to linger on Rosy, sitting at his kitchen table helping Tansy learn her lines for a forthcoming audition. She looked like summer personified in a lemon sundress, her curls escaping from her ponytail, and it was all he could do not to kiss the tempting back of her neck. He'd had his doubts about whether Rosy should see the girls regularly with her departure so close, but he couldn't deny that she had a knack with them, especially Tansy, and as they didn't know that there was more between their father and Rosy it seemed a shame to deny them the friendship.

As Jack had hoped, the sea air and the change of routine was working miracles with his oldest daughter and she was visibly blooming before his eyes. Thanks to her surf lessons and the theatre group, she'd started to make friends and she'd also stopped second-guessing his every decision and was acting more like a sister than a mother to Clover. Their relationship seemed far more normal now for siblings, and he was surprisingly relieved to hear them bicker over everything from which film to watch to what he should make for dinner.

'That's really good, Tansy.' Rosy closed her copy of the script and smiled at his daughter. 'You're going to be a real asset to the theatre group, I can tell.'

Tansy's face lit up. 'You think?'

'I know. Don't forget I grew up with an actress. I see the same determination in you that I saw in her.' She picked up her phone. 'I need to get back. Make sure you let me know how the audition goes. Bye, Jack.'

He raised a nonchalant hand as if he hadn't got plans to spend the evening at hers once he'd dropped Tansy off at her new friend's house, a fellow aspiring actress she'd met at the theatre.

'Dad…' Tansy was watching him '… I like Rosy. I really like her.'

'We all do, she's been a good friend to us.'

'Dad, you know, it's okay if you want to start dating someone. Clover and I wouldn't mind. Not if it was someone like Rosy. You like her, don't you? I mean, *like* her like her.'

Jack stilled. His girls had idolised their elusive, fragile mother. 'Tansy…'

'Mummy's been gone for a long time now. I just wanted you to know we'd be okay if you wanted to see someone.' Her blue eyes were filled with hope and Jack's chest tightened. This was everything he'd tried to avoid.

'Rosy is great, and you're right.' He made the decision not to lie to his daughter. 'I do like her, and if things were different, who knows? But her life isn't here, kiddo. She doesn't belong in Polhallow, she has a really important job in Asturia. So, friends is all we can be and that's great. You can never have too many friends.'

'But you don't have to stay here. Couldn't you do your job in Asturia?'

'Honey, we've only just moved here. We don't want to keep moving.'

Tansy shrugged. 'I'm just saying that if you and Rosy did like each other we could move again.'

Jack searched for the right words, not wanting to quash her honesty nor raise her hopes. 'Thank you for saying that, but we have only known Rosy a few weeks. It would be far too early, even if we *were* dating, to be talking about moving. Sometimes, Tansy, the timing just isn't right, and you just have to accept that. It's part of life. What time are you due at Clara's?'

But she clearly wasn't going to drop the topic. 'Clover thinks you should get married, but that's because she wants to be a bridesmaid. It's too early to think of *that*, but I think it's silly not to at least try if you like each other. Rosy likes being with us. She looked all worried when we first met her and now she laughs all the time. I like it when we all laugh. It's fun to be in a big group.'

Guilt pierced him. He'd done his best to provide his daughters with everything they needed. More, a good education, the kind of exclusive experiences most children dreamt of. And the three of them were a tight bubble of love and laughter. But outside of that bubble there wasn't a great deal of humour or socialising. Lily had preferred the dramatic to the everyday and was so often absent, and there was no extended family of cousins and uncles and aunts. Nor did they have a large social circle. In some ways, their childhood was as solitary as his had been. As Rosy's had been.

'Tansy, I'm glad you and Clover like Rosy so much.' He searched for the right words. 'And it's good to know that you'd be okay if I started dating again. It's not a priority, but who knows what will happen? But darling, it can't be Rosy. She goes home next week.' He hated to disappoint her, but he also needed to nip this in the bud. Any prevarication and they might carry on hoping.

'Like I said, her home is far from here and we are

building lives here. Friendship is just as important as romance, Tansy. Don't forget that. Romances can flare and disappear as if they never were, but a good friend-ship lasts for ever.'

Tansy's eyes were clouded with disappointment as she nodded and ran upstairs to pack a bag for the night ahead. Jack watched her go, heart heavy. He'd done this, roused hopes in his girls he couldn't fulfil. They'd tried hard to be discreet but the connection between them was so palpable even his girls had picked up on it.

There were just a few days left. They needed to be more discreet than ever. And he needed to heed the words he'd said to Tansy because they were true. He and Rosy might not be able to have a real romance but maybe they could be friends. Hell, he had few enough of them. Maybe there would be a way of keeping her in his life, because there was no way he was ready to let her go for good.

# CHAPTER NINE

IT WAS ANOTHER beautiful afternoon. In fact, every afternoon over the last week had been beautiful. There had been something restorative about the light summer rain that had punctuated the week before, something dramatic about the sheets of rain that had cleaned the beaches and outside tables the day before that. Every type of weather seemed fresh and restorative. But today was the best afternoon of all: hot but not humid, sunny but gently, glowing not glaring. And every atom in and around Arrosa was glad to be alive.

She laughed a little self-mockingly as she shook flour into the mixing bowl and reached for the cubed butter she'd cooled earlier. She knew she was being slightly ridiculous—more than slightly—but she couldn't help it. And if this was what good sex, lots and lots of sex, did to a person then she'd clearly been missing out all those years. Those long afternoons of listening to speeches, soothing the overinflated egos of local bureaucrats and top politicians, of dress fittings and hair appointments and ribbon-cutting would have been a lot easier with this sated languor playing through her body. The radio switched to another song, one she loved, and she joined in, singing loudly as she continued to rub the butter into the flour.

Jack was coming over later, and she wanted to wow him with home-made scones as if they were a real couple, as if this was just another date, not the beginning of the end. Because the truth she was denying was that Arrosa was running out of time. Next week Clem would return and they would switch back, and she would have to say goodbye to her life here, to her friends—and to the small family who had captured her heart. How had this happened? What had started out as a flirtation had developed too quickly and too intensely. She knew Jack felt it too—the other evening he had suggested that maybe there was a way they could remain friends once she returned.

In one way she wanted to, but in another she thought it would be harder to have Jack in her life but not by her side. She spent long hours imagining introducing Jack to her life in Asturia, the girls to her pretty lakeside villa. Her imagination worked when they were in the palace grounds; it was the wider world where it failed completely. Her life was one of formality and discipline; there was little fun there for two girls still learning how to smile again after tragedy had robbed them of so much.

Any consort of hers would spend their life in the spotlight. Every word, every look and expression dissected. Jack was an intensely private man; how could she ask him to give up that privacy and allow his past to be raked over after just a couple of weeks of an idyllic summer romance? She couldn't.

So she needed to push any daydreams of the future aside to enjoy the here and now. To focus on the good part, to remember that Jack had shown her that she was capable of loving and being loved. That there was a living, breathing woman in the proper Princess.

Arrosa's hands stilled. Where had that thought come from? Capable of *love*? Attraction, of course. Desire? Liking? Yes and yes. She really, really liked him and she really, really desired him. But she couldn't have fallen in *love*, not in just five weeks.

But, then again, how could she *not* have fallen in love with Jack? Her mind ran through memories like a movie montage: Jack strolling over the beach, Clover on his shoulders, explaining the tides. Jack handing over his ice cream to Clover because she'd dropped the one she'd bought. Jack hearing Tansy's lines yet again. Jack spending many anxious moments deliberating over whether the hoodie he was buying her was too babyish or too adult or just right. Jack pacing on the stage, explaining his vision, lit up with an enthusiasm that inspired her too. Jack sitting opposite her, confiding things she instinctively knew he had never confided to anyone before. Jack holding her, touching her, kissing her, making her feel like a woman reborn.

How could she *not* love him? It was impossible. As impossible as loving him.

With a herculean effort she pushed the thought away, resuming singing and rubbing the sticky mixture, focusing fiercely on the here and now until the sound of her phone made her look up and she realised she'd missed a call. She used her voice to activate the voicemail, still humming along to the music.

'Arrosa?' And, just like that, her mood evaporated.

'Papa,' she breathed as she began to brush the mixture off her fingers. Even though he couldn't see or hear her, it was as if she could sense his disapproval down the line.

'I hope you've had a good break, Arrosa. I wish you'd been a little more discreet, but indiscretion seems to run in the family at the moment.'

Shamed heat flared up instantly. Of course he'd had her followed, she'd expected it. And yet she'd also allowed herself to forget it. Had her father's spy followed her to Tresco? Had they watched her sitting with Jack on the beach? Flirting with him in the pub? Had they seen them the day after, wrapped around each other, unable to let go of each other's hands as they explored the island? Reported on the kisses and the way they touched?

Of course they had. The thought filled her with revulsion.

'Well, it doesn't matter now, because I'm going to say to you exactly what I said to your sister. Holiday time is over, Arrosa. It's time to come home.'

Her hands dropped to her sides, still sticky and covered with the flour and butter mixture. 'No,' she said to the phone, as if it weren't a recorded message she was answering. 'It's too early, I've got another week.'

'People are beginning to talk, Arrosa. Your sister's absences from the palace with no explanation are beginning to be noticed. I need you back here doing your normal day-to-day duties to allay those suspicions. And you are allowing your personal life to become public. It just needs one person to recognise you in the background of one photo or video for the whole thing to blow sky-high. You are staying in one of the most photographed spots in the UK, the chances of you being spotted with this man you're spending all your time with are too high.'

She had nothing to say. Of course, as usual, he was right.

'Look…' and suddenly he sounded kind and that was so out of character it felt worse than his usual hectoring tones '… I allowed the charade to go ahead because I understood that you needed a break. But you had your fun, and your sister's had hers, and it's time for you both to go home. Henri will be escorting your sister to Cornwall tonight and will collect you. I'll see you tomorrow.'

The message came to an abrupt end. Mechanically, Arrosa carried on making the scones, but she couldn't have said what ingredients she added. Instead, her mind repeated the inescapable facts. Her time was up. By this evening she would be back in Asturia and that would be it, her life prescribed and small and necessary. She'd known it was coming. She'd thought she was prepared.

Her phone pinged with a couple of follow-up messages from her father, arrangements for meetings over the next few days, but she ignored them, watching the scones turn the perfect shade of brown and pulling them out of the oven. They looked and smelled delicious, but she had no appetite, no sense of achievement.

The desolation overtook her as she sank onto a chair, eyes dry and sore. She wasn't ready to go home, not yet. How could she be? She'd fallen in love and before she'd even had time to come to terms with what that meant she had to walk away.

Her phone rang again and this time after a few seconds' hesitation she picked it up, noting Akil's name on the screen. She summoned up her best princess persona.

'Akil, is everything okay?' She winced at the words. She knew Clem had grown increasingly close to Akil.

She was unlikely to be looking forward to coming home either.

His voice was grim. 'Not exactly. Have you spoken to your father?'

'Funny you should ask that. He's left me a voice-mail and a couple of messages, telling me it's time to come home.'

'He's told Clem the same thing, that her time here is up.'

'I guess we always knew it wasn't for ever,' Arrosa said, unable to keep the unhappiness from her voice.

'You certainly couldn't keep this pretence up for ever. At some point people will want to see the Princess's face. Clem needs to be able to leave the Palais without disguises and subterfuge. But that doesn't mean that things should have to go back to the way they were. Don't you agree?'

Agree? With what? 'What do you mean?'

'We're about to begin a new era here in Asturia, spearheaded by you, Arrosa. Don't you think it's time for a new start in every way?'

'Is this about Clem?'

'I love her. And I think that she loves me, but she won't stay here with me, she won't put her happiness first, because your father has told her that if anyone finds out who she is the scandal would be too much for you and she loves you too much to be a burden to you.'

Of course he had said that. *Of course* he had. Zorien Artega, the arch manipulator. 'But that's not it at all, Akil. I would love everyone to know who she is, I am so proud of her, but how could I do that to her? Clem has never been the target of the press. She's never been followed anywhere, she's never been commented on, she's never had her outfits dissected, her love life speculated on, her every expression misinterpreted until she had to learn to show no expression at all. She has a freedom that I can never have, and that freedom is the greatest gift I can give her. If anyone knew who she was, she'd lose that.'

'I think that should be her decision, don't you? Arrosa, don't you see, you're protecting her and she's protecting you and the only people losing out are the two of you?'

'And this is all altruistic on your part?'

'I don't deny that I would like her to stay in Asturia, that I would like to carry on seeing her, but this is beyond us, whatever we are. She is all alone, Arrosa. She is going back to Cornwall with no family, no one who really cares about her apart from you and me.'

Arrosa looked around the cosy cottage filled with memories. Akil was right. Clem's future had stuttered to a halt the day her mother was diagnosed. She had friends, many of them, but her family—and the man who loved her—were hundreds of miles away. 'What do you want me to do?'

'I'm going to go and see your father to tell him that I think he should come out and acknowledge her if that's what she wants. And then I am going to see if I can persuade your stubborn sister to give us a chance. I just need to know: will you back me up or not?'

Arrosa didn't hesitate. 'If that's what Clem wants, then yes. I will.'

'Thank you, that's all I needed.'

Akil rang off and Arrosa sat and stared at her phone, her heart filled with hope and happiness for her sister even as she could see no reciprocal happy-ever-after for herself. After a long time, she pulled her phone to her and typed a message to Clem.

I just want to say that whatever you do decide I have your back, always. I'm proud of you and I'm proud to have you in my life and I am happy to shout it from the rooftops to anyone and everyone if that's what you want. I love you, big sis.

The reply came back quickly.

Right back atcha!

Arrosa smiled and sent another text, this time to Akil.

Whatever Clem wants, whatever Clem decides, I will always back her.

She had no idea what would happen next, but if Clem found happiness then at least one good thing would come out of this swap. That had to be enough.

Something was wrong and Jack couldn't put his finger on what it was. Rosy looked the same as usual, delectable in a flowery maxi dress, her hair down and cascading over her shoulders. She'd set the table with freshly baked scones, fresh fruit, jam and cream, flowers from the garden in a jug in the centre.

But even so something was definitely wrong, her smile mechanical and her eyes dull as she kissed him. 'I made you scones.'

'They look delicious,' he said cautiously. 'Can I have

one?' But his appetite had gone even as he split it in two, adding cream and jam to the still-warm scone. Rosy had retreated to the sink, washing up, her hair veiling her face. 'Hey, why don't you come sit with me?'

She stayed silent and every quiet second filled him with dread until she finally turned, her face still completely expressionless. 'I have to go home, Jack.'

'I know,' he said, searching for the right words. 'I've always known.' Although he realised, with a shock, he was by no means ready. He'd known this time together was finite, and told himself that was okay, but the truth was, like a child ignoring something unpleasant, he'd not allowed himself to look forward, hoping that maybe they would mutually decide they'd had enough, that this relationship would just peter out.

But he knew that wasn't going to happen, not yet at least. Maybe not ever.

'I have to go home tonight.'

'What? Why?' Had he heard right?

'My father has summoned me. He's sending Clem home and he wants me back.'

'You're a grown woman. You can go when you're ready.'

'It's not that simple. I have responsibilities and a destiny I can't walk away from, no matter how much I may want to.'

'*Do* you want to?'

She didn't answer for a long moment, then her mouth curved into a sad reminiscent smile.

'In the pub in Tresco you asked me who I would be if I could be anybody I wanted. And I told you that I don't waste time on such thoughts, that it's a waste of energy imagining anything different. Remember?'

He nodded.

'I meant it, Jack. That's how I live my life. But over the last couple of weeks I've allowed myself to imagine a different life, imagine what it would be like to really live here. Imagine that I was free to know you, to love you.'

Love. The word hung in the air, almost physical, he could trace the lines of it.

'I think I've been doing the same thing.'

She looked at him then, and her lip trembled. 'It's a lovely dream. But I'm not Rosy, I can't be. And although I don't and won't ever regret the way you make me feel or the way I feel about you and your girls, my feelings don't change anything.' Her expression was anxious. 'You do understand, don't you?'

Of course he did. He was also a man with commitments and honour and responsibilities, and he knew how that could drive a person. If Rosy had been the kind of woman who put her own needs before those things then she wouldn't be the person he was falling for. It was that integrity he'd first noticed in her, and ironically it was that integrity that meant they could never be.

'How long do we have?'

'A few hours.'

'Right.' He sat for a moment, absorbing this change in events, the feelings coursing through him: disappointment, sadness, the sense that something rare and precious was about to slip through his fingers. But not yet. They still had a few hours. 'Then we'd better not waste them.'

Rosy's troubled expression turned confused, and Jack pushed his chair back, leaving the scone uneaten as he stood and strode over to her, taking her hands in his. 'Jack,' she half whispered, and he captured her mouth with his, urging himself to seize every moment, every sensation, every touch.

'This has been more than just a fling for me,' he said, breaking away to cup her face in his hands.

'Me too. If things were different. But these are the cards we were dealt.'

'We just need to make the best of them.'

She knew him, she understood him, and Jack knew how rare that was. Lily and he had shared passion and built a life together, but she had never understood him and, try as he might, she had eluded his understanding too.

'I wouldn't change a thing either,' she added. 'You're a wonderful father and a wonderful man, Jack. That's why I have come to care for you as much as I do. But...'

'You don't have to say anything else. We both knew that this was a one summer thing. I went into it with my eyes wide open and I wouldn't change a thing.'

'You wouldn't?'

'Well, maybe one thing. If I'd known you were leaving so soon I would have kissed you the first day I met you and not stopped.'

'That might have got awkward. People would have definitely noticed.'

'It would have been worth it.' And then he did kiss her, slow and sweet, as if they had all the time in the world, not just a few hours, breathing her in, memorising her, trying his best to show her what she meant to him without words. Rosy responded in kind, holding him close so he could feel her imprinted on him. Jack refused to think of the countdown until she had to leave, not deepening the kiss or rushing them, instinctively aware that whatever they did, whatever they said in the hours to come, this right here was the real goodbye.

Rosy filled his senses, her scent, sweet and warm and uniquely her, her taste, the sound of her breath and her occasional murmured endearments, the silk of her skin under his fingers until all he could think of was the here, the now and her.

She pulled back and looked up at him, lips swollen and expression hazy with desire. 'Let's go upstairs,' she said. 'I want you.'

'You have me,' he vowed and swung her into his arms, enjoying her surprised shriek as he carried her upstairs. 'You have me.' And he meant every word. For today at least.

# CHAPTER TEN

'MAMAN, ARE YOU OKAY?'

As usual Queen Iara was impossible to read. Arrosa's mother had perfected the art of the professional mask a long time ago and Arrosa had never seen it slip. But if she was ever going to falter then today would surely be the day because in less than half an hour the Asturian Royal Family would hold a press conference and announce Clem's existence to the world.

'I'm fine, dear. Clemence is a lovely young woman, and I am happy to be welcoming her into the family.'

'Maman, this is me; you don't have to repeat the press statement.' But they had never had a close relationship, never confided in one another and maybe that was why Arrosa had not told her mother about Jack and how much she missed him.

She'd hoped time would help but although she'd now been apart from Jack for longer than she'd known him, she still felt his absence keenly. She'd been too busy to pine but she couldn't shake the feeling that something was missing, a constant sense of loss. As a result, she'd welcomed her packed diary, preferring to work from the minute she poured her first coffee until she cleaned her teeth at night.

The ratification of the law had gone through unanimously the month before and Arrosa was now the Crown Princess and official heiress to the throne, tripling her workload and responsibilities overnight. She, her father and Clem had discussed making Clem's existence public before the ratification, but Clem had not been ready, nor had she wanted to overshadow Arrosa's big moment. Just knowing that their father was willing to acknowledge her had been enough for her then. But Clem had accepted Arrosa's invitation to stay at the villa and house share with her and, even though the press didn't have access to the estate, Clem's existence was being noticed and questions were being asked, especially as she and Akil were seen more and more in public together.

Once Clem had agreed that she was ready to face the spotlight they had just needed the Queen's agreement for today's announcement. An announcement that would change Clem's life for ever. Arrosa just hoped her sister was ready. And that her mother really was as comfortable with it all as she claimed.

'The past is about to be raked over, that's got to be difficult.'

'Your father's romance was over before we married.' The Queen's smile was serene.

'Barely. And you might not have been formally engaged when he was with Simone, but you had an understanding…'

'Arrosa. Things are different for us, you know this. I didn't love your father when I married him, and I didn't expect him to love me. We married because I knew what being the Queen would entail and I was willing to make the sacrifices necessary. I respected your father and I still do. Clem and her mother didn't change that.'

Was that true? After all, Arrosa's mother hadn't found out about Clem's existence until after she was pregnant with Arrosa and there had been no more children once she was born. Her parents had separate suites of rooms, separate beds. Had they tried for more children or had the realisation that her husband loved another poisoned their marriage, despite her mother's calm words? Once again, she wished she had the kind of relationship with her parents that would enable those questions to be answered.

She laid a hand on her mother's arm, wishing she could give her the kind of easy, warm hug Simone had doled out so easily. 'Well, I just want you to know how much I appreciate it. Thank you for making Clem welcome and agreeing to let her be part of our family in every way. It can't be easy, but it means a lot to me. I hope you know how much.'

'Her mother was very good to you, and I was always grateful for that. You bloomed in Cornwall, would come back refreshed and invigorated—and you did once again this summer. I was pleased to see you looking so well. I had been worried about you but since you returned you seem more like your old self.'

'Thank you.' Arrosa had had no idea that her mother had noticed that she was run-down. Arrosa could feel her cheeks heating as memories of the summer—of Jack—flooded her senses. 'I understand why you always needed your summer retreats now. Time away from the public eye.'

'I accepted a role with certain expectations. I can't complain when those expectations get too much, but a month away every summer ensures I never get over-whelmed by the pressures of my life. And I hope you will always make sure you have time to recharge.

'Things have changed, Arrosa, your new role is tes-tament to that. You don't have to follow the same path your father and I tread; you will be a new kind of mon-arch in a new Asturia.' Her mother looked over at Clem, who stood in the opposite corner, unusually smart in a blue dress and matching jacket, looking up at Akil with a trust and love that took Arrosa's breath away. 'Your sister's life is about to alter irrevocably but she has you and the Ortiz heir by her side. And after today she can be publicly in your life as you take on your new duties. I know you'll need that support in the years ahead.'

Was that why her mother was agreeing to stand by her husband's side when he announced the existence of a child who wasn't hers, for Arrosa's sake? Arrosa knew her mother loved her, but she was always so hands-off, the thought of her making such a personal sacrifice for her was almost overwhelming. Maybe they could have a warmer, more intimate relationship, maybe it wasn't too late.

'I know the next few weeks will be difficult for us all, especially Clem, but I have to admit I'm happy we won't have to hide any more—and you're right. Hav-ing her here in Asturia and openly part of my life will make everything easier.'

'I hope that you will find a different kind of support too, Arrosa. That you will meet a man who looks at you the way Akil Ortiz looks at your sister, who will support you the way he supports her. Being a monarch can be a lonely job but with the right people around you it doesn't have to be that way. Ah, your father is ready. It's time.'

Without a backward glance her mother glided over to Arrosa's father and laid a hand on his arm, her expression calm and inscrutable as ever. Arrosa took a deep breath as she joined her sister, falling in behind her parents and, with a reassuring squeeze of Clem's hand, the four of them made their way out to face the awaiting press.

As expected, the news of Clem's parentage made headline news across the globe. It had, Akil noted wryly, all the ingredients any good royal scandal needed: a secret love affair, an illegitimate child, a wronged wife standing by her husband's side and two beautiful young women, one a Crown Princess. Any hope that the scandal would be a twenty-four-hour wonder soon disappeared as the world's press descended on Asturia, desperate for a new angle on the story. Descended on Asturia *and* Polhallow, where the cottage was besieged by photographers despite nobody living there, Gus having accompanied Arrosa to Asturia, where he'd promptly taken up residence in her villa.

Arrosa should have foreseen that it was only a matter of time before someone put two and two together and realised that Clem's French cousin Rosy and her royal half- sister were one and the same. Sure enough, a few weeks later, just as the original scandal started to abate, the connection was made, creating a flurry of new headlines and speculation. Sally's family's café was surrounded by reporters wanting the inside scoop on her friendship with both the Princess and Clem, and worse, someone mentioned 'Rosy's' friendship with Jack to one reporter, who immediately splashed the story with suitably salacious headlines.

'Look at this.' Arrosa pushed her tablet over to Clem, her chest tight with anxiety.

'You shouldn't read this stuff, any of it,' Clem said staunchly, but her sister was pale and Arrosa felt a stab of guilt at the world she'd been catapulted into. Adverts Clem had starred in were all over social media, a love scene from a daytime TV show replayed endlessly, her headshots reproduced over and over.

'It's not about me or you. It's Jack.'

'Jack?' Clem's eyebrows shot up. 'Jack Treloar?'

Arrosa had always been able to tell her sister anything, but somehow she'd not found the words to talk about Jack. The memories were too raw, too recent to share, her own feelings so mixed up, especially when Clem and Akil were obviously falling deeper in love every day.

'Yes, we were…friendly.'

'Friendly?' Clem reached over for the tablet. 'How friendly?' She started to read out loud. '*Princess's Summer Fling with Local Bad Boy*—honestly, you babysat for him a couple of times and they turn it into some kind of torrid romance. Listen to this: *'Princess Arrosa enjoyed more than a secret Cornish getaway this summer. We can exclusively reveal that the twenty-six-year-old heir to the Asturian throne enjoyed a summer fling with local self-made millionaire Jack Treloar. Jack, thirty, was married to tragic socialite Lily Fforde-Browne, who overdosed two years ago, leaving two daughters. Now it seems the not-so-grieving widower has moved onwards and upwards. Treloar's teenage marriage to Fforde-Browne raised eyebrows amongst her friends at the time, thanks to his reputation as the town troublemaker, but Treloar put his past behind him, found-*

*ing Treloar Capital Investments and buying a mansion in London's exclusive Primrose Hill, before moving his family back to Cornwall where they live in a stunning Art Deco house, last valued at a cool three million pounds. The Princess and the rebel are reported to have sneaked away for a romantic getaway on the Isles of Scilly. "They seemed very much in love," said fellow tourist, Lucy Christie. "They couldn't keep their hands off each other."* Honestly, the things they make up!'

Arrosa couldn't answer, her cheeks hot, and Clem narrowed her eyes. 'Not made up? You and Jack Treloar? It's true? Why didn't you say anything?'

'I don't know,' she said miserably. 'I was going to but there's so much going on it just never seemed relevant.'

'Relevant? You're my sister. What hurts you hurts me. Was it serious?'

'How could it be? You know my life! Jack's so private, he would hate my world.'

'Well, that's unfortunate because right now he's right in the middle of it.'

Clem's words were bracing but her tone sympathetic as Arrosa took the tablet back and read through the article again, cringing at every word. 'So hateful, implying he's some kind of social climber—and mentioning Lily as well. I knew I should have stayed away from him. That there was only one way this could end.'

'In that case why didn't you?'

'I thought that nobody would find out. I thought I deserved the chance to grab some happiness before everything changed. Truth is, Clem, I couldn't help it. Jack's not the man in this article, he's kind and principled and…'

'And drop-dead gorgeous?' her sister helpfully supplied.

Arrosa groaned. 'So gorgeous. I have never in my life wanted anyone the way I wanted Jack. You know, at times I thought there might be something wrong with me. It was so easy to behave like the proper Princess I was expected to be, I was never truly tempted by any man, not enough to let my guard down. And then there was Jack, and it was like *boom*! I couldn't have resisted him if I'd tried—and I didn't try very hard.'

Clem reached over and took her hand. 'You're allowed to be normal, you know. You're allowed to fancy someone, to date, to have romantic getaways.'

'They make it sound so sordid and it wasn't. It was beautiful, Clem.'

'Are you still in touch?'

She shook her head. 'We said we'd try and stay friends but it was too difficult, I couldn't see how to do it. The girls didn't know who I was, although I guess they do now. And the way my life is, it was easier to make a clean break. It was meant to be easier anyway.'

'But you miss him?'

She nodded. 'I really do.'

'You know what I think?'

'I think you're about to tell me.'

'I think I am going to say to you what Akil said to me and to Zorien.' Clem still didn't call their father *Dad*, maybe she never would. 'Secrets only have power while they're secrets. Once things are out in the open, they can't be used against you. Look, I was thinking we need to help Sally out over the next couple of weeks. She's besieged by reporters; it's impacting on the café and it's scary for Alice. Let's invite her and Jack and all the kids here.'

'Here? To Asturia?'

'Here to the estate. There's plenty of space in the château itself, thanks to all those unused apartments. Your parents are never here, you don't use your rooms and there's the grounds to explore and soldiers on the gates. It's the perfect place to ride out the media interest safely. And with you and Jack in close proximity, well, who knows? At least you'd get a chance to see if there is anything real here.'

Arrosa could see the sense in everything that Clem said, and she should have thought about how to help Sally negotiate the press herself. She did have plenty of room. There were several unused guest apartments in the old medieval Artega palais—and with her villa a mile away, even though it was in the estate grounds, she and Jack wouldn't be forced into proximity. 'But if Jack comes to Asturia everyone will think we're an item and we're not.'

'Well, either we keep it a secret, fly him in quietly and hope no one sees or let them think it. Legitimise the headlines and get rid of the speculation. Seize control of the narrative. Maybe there is more there than a summer fling, maybe not. Either way, you steer the story and get some more time together.'

Arrosa bit her lip. Clem was making sense except… 'He won't come. School's started and the whole thing will be too disorientating for the girls.' Plus, she suspected he was too proud to seek shelter from her. He probably blamed her for setting this circus on him.

'Want to bet?' Clem slid her phone over. It was playing a British news channel showing helicopters circling over Jack's house, photographers at his gate. 'It's October now, nearly half-term, so they wouldn't miss more than a couple of weeks, and I can't imagine they're finding it easy to concentrate with all this going on. Call him and ask him to come. I think he'll say yes.'

'Daddy, Daddy, it's like a fairy tale.' Clover circled a suit of armour a little warily, as if unsure whether it really was inanimate or not. 'This is a real castle!'

Jack had to admit that Clover had a point. It had been late afternoon when the private plane had landed in Asturia and he had glimpsed mountains and valleys, seas and flower-filled villages as the plane had circled before landing. They had been transferred directly into a limousine before being driven through a back gate and straight to the Artega family estate. Soldiers had checked their ID at the imposing gates and then they had been driven for what felt like miles through parkland, woods and formal gardens until they'd reached the old château, graceful with its turrets and spires and carved stonework. It had been a visceral reminder that, although he might now have wealth, he and Arrosa came from worlds apart.

A housekeeper had taken them through the receiving hall and up a grand staircase to an apartment as elegant and well-appointed as any top hotel, where dinner had been served to the by now weary travellers. It hadn't taken Tansy, Clover and Alice long to recover themselves, although he suspected he'd worn an identical shell-shocked expression to Sally throughout the five courses accompanied by some excellent wine, thanks to the juxtaposition of the morning spent escaping the baying photographers and their present situation with candlelight and silver service.

Since Rosy's summer adventures had hit the headlines, it had been an intense couple of days although, to his relief, both girls, even Tansy, seemed to find the whole experience a huge adventure. He'd worried she might feel betrayed by Arrosa's secret but instead she viewed it as impossibly romantic.

It wasn't his first brush with the tabloids and gossip columns, thanks to Lily's bohemian lifestyle and tragic death, but nothing had prepared him for the shock of being in the sightline of the world's media. He could understand Rosy's need for time away now, her determination to keep her stay secret—and her insistence her life wasn't for sharing. Who would willingly put themselves in this position?

'Alice and I are meeting up with Clem this morning to explore. She says she's only walked in a quarter of the grounds at most. Imagine having a place so big you can go for a walk in your own grounds. Apparently, we can swim in the lake as well. Can you believe how warm it is for mid-October?' Sally looked a lot more relaxed this morning. Jack just wished he felt the same way. 'Do you want me to take your girls so you can work—or do you and Rosy have plans?' She sipped her coffee, a demure expression on her face as she waited for his answer.

'She's not Rosy here, she's Arrosa.' Jack poured himself more coffee and surveyed the sumptuous spread of fresh fruit, pastries, cheeses, meats and bread, but despite the tempting smells he had little appetite.

'She's the same person.'

Jack looked around at the silk curtains, the antique furniture, the high ceilings with ornate mouldings, polished wooden floors and vast amounts of gilt. This was a guest apartment—a guest apartment with four bedrooms with en suite bathrooms, a dining room, morning room, formal sitting room and snug. What were the royal apartments like if this was a guest suite? What would it do to a person to be raised amongst all this?

But she didn't live here, she had moved out at twenty-one. And Sally was right. She was still the same person. A person who he was supposedly friends with. A person he had made love to the last time he had seen her.

'If you don't mind having all three?'

'Not at all. Don't feel you have to hurry; Clem and I have a lot of catching-up to do and it will be nicer for Alice if she has friends to play with.'

The girls were delighted with the plan to spend the day exploring, swimming and visiting the stables and getting to meet Clem, who had taken on mythological status in their eyes as she was a real-life actress—Tansy—and a long-lost princess—Clover. Jack let that one stand, he wasn't up to explaining illegitimacy laws and royalty to a six-year-old, leaving him free to follow the path leading to the lake, where Rosy's house was situated. He didn't allow himself to think about how she hadn't been there to meet them, nor how formal she had sounded when she'd called and asked him if he would accompany Sally and Alice to Asturia for a few days until the interest in them died down. Nor did he want to think about how much he'd missed her over the last few months, how often he'd considered picking up the phone, only to remind himself there was no point. Now here he was, in her country, in her grounds, walking to her house.

To his surprise her cottage was charming rather than grand, a one-storey whitewashed villa by the lake, surrounded by a beautiful garden. He took a deep breath and let himself in at the gate and walked down the path.

It didn't feel as if he was calling on a princess, there were no visible guards, no servants, but he had no doubt that every step he was taking was being tracked. Before he could knock on the door it opened and there she was.

Jack had no idea why it was a shock that she looked exactly the same—what had he expected, that she would open the door in a ball dress and a crown? It might have been easier if she had because with her hair loose, wearing a green maxi dress cinched in at the waist, she looked like the Rosy he had fallen for, not the Princess he'd said goodbye to three months before.

'Hi,' he said, hovering a few steps away, not wanting to complicate things by touching her, kissing her, not trusting himself not to if he got within touching distance.

'Hi. Do you want some coffee?'

'Sure.'

'Come in then.'

The house was simply but beautifully furnished, wooden furniture polished until it glowed, colourful rugs on the floor, cushions on the grey sofas, pictures on the white walls. Everything was well made and no doubt expensive but also clearly chosen because it was wanted, not because of how much it cost, a landscape next to an abstract, hand-thrown vases next to a stack of books. The scent of coffee permeated the air as she led him through to a light-filled kitchen with French windows that led into the garden, the lake visible beyond.

'Your house is nice,' he said.

'Thank you. I always loved the Cornish house and wanted a similar vibe; I don't have Simone's eye or taste but I'm pretty happy with how it turned out.'

'It's very different to the palace.'

'Oh, dear. I had you put in the Mendoza Suite because it's the least formal, but the décor can be a bit much.'

'The *least* formal?'

'Can't you tell? The gold leaf is pretty pared back.' Her mouth was twitching as he nodded solemnly.

'I thought so.'

And with that the ice was broken and Jack found himself at the table, a coffee in his hands and a plate of pastries before him, his appetite returned, but she was careful to step around him, and he waited for her to take a pastry before he took his, both equally careful not to touch even by accident.

'I'm so sorry,' Rosy said, taking the seat opposite him. 'We realised that telling the world about Clem would send the press sniffing around Polhallow and her life there, but I hadn't really factored in my unmasking. I guess I thought I lived so quietly I'd slipped under the radar. I'm not usually that naïve. Regardless, I should have prewarned you and Sally. Planned for this in advance—to be fair, my father cautioned me that I might be recognised in retrospect and of course he was right.'

But Jack didn't blame her. 'You *did* warn me—you made it clear that getting entangled with you came with risks. As for Sally, her family have been taking full advantage. They've put tables all over the pavement and any member of the press trying to get a picture or a quote is forced to buy food. They've even introduced a Princess Afternoon Tea in your honour.'

'I'm glad someone's getting some benefit from this mess. But I am truly sorry, Jack. The attention must have been scary for the girls. Are they okay?'

'They are. And thank you for having them here. It's made the whole thing into a huge adventure.'

'But to be missing school when they were so looking forward to getting settled in.'

'All the headteachers agreed that taking the next couple of weeks off before half-term made sense, it was hard to settle with press at the school gates. They've been set work. It's fine.'

'And you? Are you okay?'

Okay? The whole experience had brought back memories of Lily's death, the most private, difficult moments chronicled in the headlines, but he knew Rosy was feeling guilty enough.

'I'm fine. If it wasn't for the girls, I would have ridden the whole thing out, but it was all a little intense for them.'

'We can make it up to them now they're here. There's loads of fun things for them to do here on the estate and Henri is a master at smuggling people out the gates. I've thought of loads of activities.' Her smile was hopeful.

Jack was sure the girls would want to do every one of them—but the fine line he and Rosy trod was already too blurred. 'I'm sure, but look, you don't have to worry about running after us, you must be far too busy. Just point us in the right direction and we'll be fine. We don't want to encourage more speculation about the two of us after all. Don't get me wrong, I'm grateful for the seamless way your guys extracted us, but the last thing we want to do is encourage any more rumours. No one knows we're here and I'd like to keep it that way. Being seen out with you would be the quickest way to heap fuel onto the fire.'

'Of course. I totally get that. But…' She hesitated, twisting a tendril of hair around her finger.

'But?'

'I can see that you want to just lie low and wait for all this to pass, but there is a good chance that your stay here will leak despite our best efforts.'

That had occurred to him, but he hadn't been able to pass up the chance to give the girls a safe place—or, if he was honest with himself, the chance to see Rosy and make sure she was okay.

'If it makes it easier, we could go somewhere else.'

'Or…' She hesitated again. 'We could give them what they want.'

'What do you mean?'

'Look, the reason everything has gone so crazy is because the press think they are cracking this huge secret. But if we take control of that secret then there's no reason for them to hound you.'

'Okay,' he said cautiously, trying to figure out exactly what she meant. 'In what way?'

'Well, we could give an interview, say we met through Clem and have been dating for a few months but wanted to keep it quiet until we knew if it was going somewhere. We are seen in public a few times then you go back to the UK and after a few weeks we say it didn't work out and we called it off. It won't stop the press interest completely, I get that, but we control the story. You know, make it all open and out there until they lose interest.'

'Just for show?'

'I guess that's something we could decide. Things ended abruptly between us. We weren't ready. I wasn't ready. I regret that.'

Much as he didn't want to, Jack knew that he had to end the conversation right now before he was tempted into doing something stupid like agreeing to her plan.

'I miss you, Rosy.'

'I miss you too.' Their gazes caught and held, and he drank her in.

'And I understand your reasoning but...' He saw her straight-backed posture sag just a little as he said *but*. 'I can't do that to the girls. They like you, Rosy. *I* like you, you know that, but I'm a grown man and I can cope with a little heartbreak. They can't.'

But how he wanted to agree. How he wanted to spend time with her as if it were still the summer, be with her openly, hold her hand and kiss her and make love to her. Because after all it was the fish and chip loving, ice cream eating, denim shorts and bikini-clad Rosy he'd fallen for. Surely spending time with the Princess in her formal world would be the cure he needed? But it was too much of a risk—and not just for his girls.

'I appreciate you giving us a place to lie low for a while and I know the girls can't wait to see you, but let's think of another way to put a stop to the rumours.'

'Of course.' Her smile was determinedly bright. 'It was just an idea. What are you thinking?'

'Well, the theatre, for example.' Inspiration hit him. 'After all, we're all connected to it. Who's to say that's not why you were in Polhallow this summer? Nobody has any proof that we *were* together, apart from a woman who thinks she saw us and a few rumours. Let the romance talk die a death but use it to do something good for Polhallow instead.'

She stared at him for a long moment, her expression unreadable before nodding. 'Yes, that makes sense.'

'Good, well, let me make some plans. Thank you for the coffee. I'd better get back.'

'Sure.'

He sat there for a moment, wishing for one moment things were different. Jack knew that he was about to turn his back on an opportunity that would never present itself again, turn down the second chance that he had been dreaming of in his heart of hearts.

'Okay. I'll see you soon. No, don't get up, I'll see myself out. Thanks for the coffee.'

As Jack shut the front door behind him he couldn't shake the image of Rosy, straight-backed again, a serene expression on her face, only a hint of a shadow in her eyes giving any hint that she wasn't completely happy with his decision. He could tell himself with perfect truth that all his reasons for saying no were to do with the girls. After all, the last couple of days had been bewildering, terrifying and out of control. They'd had to flee their home, seek sanctuary in a strange country. If this was just what the rumour of a romance between himself and a princess could do, what would any confirmation of that rumour provoke? No, better to let all the speculation die down and return to their normal life as soon as possible.

But Jack was also aware enough to know that there was more to his decision. He'd been burned before, and he couldn't risk being burned again. Of course, he absolved Rosy from having similar motives to Lily. She wasn't looking to shock anyone, to rebel against her parents and societal position, but if they were together, for whatever reasons, it would still be a mésalliance. Nobody in her world would think him a suitable consort for their Crown Princess. He had no idea about court life, he knew nothing about Asturia—until a couple of months ago he couldn't have pointed it out on the map—he didn't speak the language, didn't know the customs. If he was with Rosy, in reality or pretence, then he would be repeating the same pattern as before, be completely out of place, a scandalous object of interest.

None of Lily's friends had believed that she was seriously considering marrying him. Boys like Jack, he'd heard one of her friends say, were perfectly acceptable for messing around with—after all, everyone knew that boys with everything to prove were the best lovers—but one simply didn't marry them. He'd done everything in his power to prove every single one of them wrong and he still got a visceral sense of satisfaction when *they* now courted him, asked him to dinner parties, solicited his advice and sought his investments. But he'd never forgotten how they'd made him feel. Vowed never to be put in that situation again.

And that was why he had to walk away. Because here she wasn't Rosy, she was the Crown Princess, and girls like her simply weren't for guys like him.

# CHAPTER ELEVEN

'DID YOU SEE JACK?' Clem asked when she returned to the villa that evening. Sharing a home with her sister was something Arrosa wasn't sure she would ever take for granted. She would never not appreciate having Clem on hand to laugh with, cry with, watch meaningless television with, chat through her problems with.

It wasn't just the companionship; she was so proud of her sister it almost hurt. Clem had risen above the headlines and started to carve out her own identity here in Asturia. She was looking at university courses, still volunteering at the local hospital and was officially assisting Arrosa. She was also dipping her toes into court life and had been invited to a ball at the British Embassy in a week's time.

But, of course, the downside to having her sister so close was that she knew Arrosa better than anyone and there was no dissembling, no hiding behind her princess face.

'He turned me down.' Some of the heartbreak she didn't want to admit even to herself cracked through the armour she had donned and quickly she added, 'It's complicated. It's fine. I expected it. It's probably for the best.'

'Okay.' Clem poured them both a glass of wine and nodded towards the garden. 'It's still so warm out even if it is October. Shall we?'

With unspoken accord the sisters headed down to the lake. They shared a deep love of water, and both felt better when they were gazing into it. They sat on the comfortable chairs Arrosa kept on the jetty and Clem sniffed the wine before taking an appreciative sip.

'This is much needed; three children are a lot for a full day! But it's so nice to see Sally. I've asked her to come to the ball with me. Akil is attending, but in a work capacity, and I could do with moral support—and she could do with an evening off.'

'Sounds good. And what did you think of Tansy and Clover?' Arrosa half held her breath as she waited for her sister's reply. It really mattered that Clem liked them, she realised.

'They're nice girls, a credit to their dad. And they're both wild about you. I was a pretty poor substitute. They kept asking when they would see you.'

Arrosa stared down at her wine. 'I'm not sure that's such a good idea. Jack made it clear there's no future for us. I don't want to complicate things further.'

'I met him too, back at the château.'

Arrosa couldn't bring herself to ask what Clem thought of Jack. 'He's right, you know. If we tried to control this thing by saying we were in a relationship, by trying out being in a relationship, it would just confuse the girls, and that's the last thing they need. He wants them to have stability and I support that, I always have.'

'He's obviously a great dad. I have to admit it, I got him wrong. He's not the overbearing tycoon I expected but, from what you and Sally say and the little I've seen, he seems a surprisingly kind man. A principled man who I would guess is also clearly head over heels about you and I know you feel the same way. So what I don't understand is why you are both so sure that you have no future.'

'He doesn't want the kind of life I lead, Clem, not for him, not for his girls, and I don't blame him.'

Clem sipped her wine and sat back, her expression thoughtful. 'Rosy, is your life really so bad? I know it got a little overwhelming recently, but I would say that Asturia allows its high-profile people more privacy than many other countries, and the world's press will get bored with this story eventually. I'm not saying that if you gave it another go the first few weeks and months wouldn't be a challenge, but after that I think you could build a pretty decent life here. I should know! It's easier for me in some ways, my education included handling publicity, I know how to work the camera, speak in palatable soundbites and ensure my social media is squeaky clean and, yes, I admit I've still been overwhelmed. But there's been beauty amongst the madness and I'm seeing my way to a future, the opportunities my position gives me. That could be true for Jack as well.'

How Rosy wished her sister was right.

'But you wanted to be part of the family, Jack doesn't. He has some past experiences which make him shy away from publicity, from high profile relationships. He thinks we're better denying everything, using his investment in the theatre as a pretext for our friendship. I owe him that, Clem.'

'The theatre?'

'I haven't really had a chance to discuss it with you, but I think you will love what he has in mind, that Simone would have too. If we say that we were working together on the theatre in memory of your mother, that gives me a reason to have spent the summer in Cornwall and to have been seen with Jack. And in the end Polhallow will have the kind of theatre Simone would have been proud of. It all makes sense.'

But Arrosa knew she was trying to convince herself as well as her sister, was trying not to think about how differently she could have played the morning's conversation. Because absence really had made her heart grow fonder. The moment Jack had walked through the door her home had felt complete.

She'd known what he was thinking, could have sworn that her heart beat in time with his, and she knew that if she'd just reached out, had just touched him, that everything would be different and he would be hers, for now at least.

But she wanted him to come to her because that was where he wanted to be, not seduced into intimacy. The theatre was a worthy project. It gave them an angle. It was a memorial, and these were all good things. Just because her whole being ached with sadness and loss didn't change any of those things.

'Look,' Clem said, putting her glass down. 'Whatever you decide I will support, I hope you know that. But if having Jack in your life is what you want, and if having Jack by your side makes your difficult role an iota easier, then you should fight for that, Rosy. You have always done what's right, you always put other people first. Maybe now is the time to concentrate on you. I believe you deserve someone by your side who sees how special you are. If that person is Jack then don't let him walk away because he doesn't understand your life. Show him how he fits in. Show him that your life has magic as well as duty. I get how he feels. I didn't want to stay here as Akil's mysterious English lover. I had to figure out how I could be here as me and I found that. But I didn't find it alone—Akil helped me. You don't have to do this alone either, nor does Jack. Just promise me you'll think about it.'

Arrosa blinked, her eyes hot and heavy with tears she refused to shed. Was it simply as easy as deciding she wanted Jack in her life? How could it be?

'I'll think about it. Thank you, Clem.'

Her sister smiled affectionately. 'What are sisters for?'

Over the next ten days Arrosa did more than think. Instead of hiding away from Jack and the girls she made time in her hectic schedule to show Jack exactly what made her country so special and why she loved it so much. The girls were usually busy during her pockets of free time, once, to her amazement, with her parents, who had never been the kind to spend time with children before. She suspected Clem of making sure Jack was on his own when she was able to join him, but her sister denied the charge with an innocent look that didn't fool Arrosa one jot. But she wasn't complaining because, whatever the reason behind Tansy and Clover's busy schedule, it left her free to smuggle Jack out with her bodyguard, Henri's, help to show him the country she loved and the work that was needed to bring it properly into the twenty-first century. Just as she'd hoped, Jack was soon filled with enthusiasm and ideas for how things could be improved.

They weren't long excursions, just a few hours here and there, never a full day, although there was some time in every day, but in those moments she was the perfect blend of Arrosa and Rosy, princess and person, and she could feel herself falling harder and harder for Jack. But although he seemed to enjoy their time together, there was still a chasm between them. They didn't touch, and never alluded to any kind of future together. It was as much torture as it was joy. It was all she had.

She walked into the house late one afternoon, looking for Clem, who was getting ready for the ball at the British Embassy. She found her sister in her room, putting the last touches to her hair and make-up, a stunning red floor-length cocktail dress hanging ready.

Arrosa whistled in appreciation. 'You look amazing.'

'Thank you. It feels odd to be there as an Asturian representative.'

'You'll be brilliant.'

Clem sucked in a breath. 'I'm glad I persuaded Sally to come, she deserves some fun and I could do with the backup. How was your day?'

'Good. I spent the morning going over my speech for the day after tomorrow and in meetings then I took Jack on my favourite mountain walk. I needed the exercise. You know, even though it's still quite warm, I can feel winter in the air. Those trails will be under snow within a month.'

It had been a lovely walk but sometimes Arrosa wondered what she and Jack were doing. They seemed no further forward. If anything, they seemed to be slipping away from each other every time they spent a polite, distanced time together.

Clem swivelled round on her stool. 'It's been over a week, Rosy. Have you told Jack how you feel yet?'

'I…'

'Told him that you love him?' her sister went on remorselessly.

Arrosa stared at her and swallowed. 'Love? I…' But she'd stopped lying to herself a long time ago, she wouldn't lie to her sister. 'I've told him that I like him, Clem, he knows how much I fancy him…' *Fancy.* Such a trite word to describe the depth of longing she felt whenever he was near. 'I think we both know that it might have been love if things were different but, after all, we've not really known each other that long.'

'About as long as I've known Akil,' her sister reminded her.

There was no point quibbling or reminding Clem that she and Akil had spent far more time together because she knew it had taken just a few weeks for her sister and friend to fall firmly and irrevocably in love. To forge the kind of partnership Arrosa had only ever dreamed of.

'I can't.'

'Rosy. This last week and a half you've been lit up with happiness and I know it's not because you're finally addressing the Senate in two days' time! It's thanks to Jack, and he deserves to know the truth.'

'I've seen him every day and he's made no attempt to even touch me. He likes Asturia and he has ideas, good ones, but he hasn't offered any more than those thoughts. It's obvious he doesn't see a future here. And, even if he did, there's the girls. Who knows, maybe we can try again when they are grown up, maybe in ten years or so.' The thought was bleak indeed and her chest constricted at the thought of spending those years alone.

'In a decade? Come on, Rosy, listen to yourself.'

'Clem, you don't understand. If I told him how I feel then I am forcing him to make a choice. His marriage was hard, Lily manipulative at best, I think. It wasn't a happy marriage, Clem. She used him. I won't do that to him.'

Clem sighed. 'Rosy, have you ever thought that by not being honest with him maybe you're the one doing the manipulating? That maybe you're the one depriving him of agency. He should know how you feel. Tell him.'

Jack had enjoyed the last twelve days almost too much, and the more time he spent with Rosy, seeing Asturia through her eyes, the more he could see her hopes and dreams. More, in every project and plan he saw ways he could contribute, how he could be an integral part of her world. But still he hesitated. This was no more real life than Cornwall had been, their friendship still kept firmly under wraps.

If friendship was what this was. The air between them was still charged although there was no intimacy, but he was still more relaxed with Rosy than with anyone else, than he had ever been with another person.

There were still some intrepid photographers hanging around the Palais walls, trying to photograph every car that left the house, but Henri was an old hand at shaking off unwanted attention and some days Jack and the girls were completely free to wander around and explore with nobody giving them more than a quick half amused sideways look.

And the more he explored, the more he fell in love with the small country. He loved the crispness of the mountain air as early autumn which felt more like an English late summer softened and cooled. The actual autumn was short, with snow usually expected by December. This, of course, sent the girls into spirals of excitement and they begged to be able to stay until the snow came. Every day he had to remind himself as much as them that this was just a visit, that they were establishing their lives in Polhallow. Somehow his plans didn't feel certain as they had before, that sense of rightness that had driven the move eluding him.

And, of course, there was Rosy. His tour guide, filled with infectious excitement about her country and the plans she had to improve it. She seemed to know every hidden corner and selflessly shared them with him.

They had successfully renegotiated their relationship from lovers into friends, and that, he knew, was rare and precious. But he still felt an almost overwhelming sense of loss when he stood next to her but couldn't hold her, when he said goodbye but didn't kiss her, alone in his huge luxury bed.

'Look, Daddy!' Clover pointed at the TV. 'There's Rosy.'

He'd found a cable channel of English language children's programmes and Clover and Alice had been curled up in front of a film while he packed for an afternoon on the beach, but somehow the channel had switched to a local news one. The anchor was speaking about this historic day in the fast-paced Spanish-accented French dialect he was slowly starting to understand. This was the day Arrosa was finally presented to Parliament as the Crown Princess and heir to the throne.

Jack had learnt a lot about Asturian customs and politics over the last few days and knew that, unlike the UK, the Asturian monarch sat in the Senate, their Upper Chamber, and was very much engaged in Parliamentary procedure. When he chose, the King could deputise his heir to step in for him—and now she was officially the heir that meant Rosy, who today was taking her place as the Royal representative. Custom dictated that a new member of the Senate would need to be presented, approved and welcomed by the House before giving their first speech.

Jack knew how nervous Rosy felt. She was no stranger to politics or public speaking, but this was her first formal step into her country's political arena. It was a relief to see Akil, a prominent member of the opposition and a fellow member of the Senate, was there, looking strong and supportive, and to hear the whole chamber burst into applause as she entered.

Jack stared at the screen, his heart hammering, mouth dry. This was not Rosy, this was all Arrosa. Her hair was up in a complicated knot and she wore a calf-length blue silk dress with a short matching jacket, diamonds at her throat and in her ears, a crown perched on the top of her head. She could almost have come straight out of the fairy tales Clover adored.

'She looks beautiful,' Clover said breathlessly.

'Yes, but she looks scared too,' Tansy said.

'No, she doesn't,' Alice chimed in and Sally laid a hand on her daughter's head.

'Why do you think that, Tansy?'

Tansy studied the screen. 'Her hands are pressed together, and she bit her bottom lip just then. She does that when she's nervous, have you noticed?'

Jack *had* noticed, but he was surprised his daughter had. 'You're right,' he said. 'But she hides it well. That's very astute of you, Tansy.'

His oldest daughter tossed her hair. 'I'm an actress,' she told him. 'Studying people is what I do.'

He laughed but quickly quietened as Rosy started to speak. There was no trace of any nervousness in her voice as she spoke, her voice rich and melodious. Her father beamed proudly from behind her.

The family had plans for the day. With their time in Asturia nearing its end there was plenty they still wanted to pack in, but Jack forgot to hurry the girls up or to gather his own things together. Instead, he stood transfixed as he watched the woman he loved address the country she was born to rule.

The chasm between them had never felt bigger and yet in some ways he felt that he should and could almost step into the TV to stand beside her and support her just with his presence. Jack had been telling himself over the last twelve days that Rosy needed a man like Akil. She needed someone versed in Asturia's culture and politics, someone with a background similar to hers. But as he stood watching her speak that certainty escaped him.

Culture and nationality and birthright were all important and all things he lacked, but he did have qualities he knew she needed. He could provide her with the reassurance that she could do the immense job that lay ahead of her, he could be the person she bounced ideas off—after all, she had run every word of her speech past him, practised it on him until he could probably recite it himself in Asturian and English, could have cited her sources as she focused on education, equality and the need for a sustainable future.

But, at the same time, although they had spent a great deal of time together there was a consciousness between them that hadn't been there before. Rosy was her usual thoughtful, enthusiastic self, unfailingly courteous, great with the girls as always, funny and sweet, but he knew he wasn't imagining the distance between them, and he wasn't sure who was responsible for it. In some ways he welcomed it. After all, there was no future for them.

But the knowledge didn't feel as certain as it once had. The future he'd mapped out no longer felt so safe or so desirable. Instead it felt empty. Lonely. His girls were everything, but they would grow up and have their own lives and that was how it should be. And when they were gone what would he have? A white box on the top of a cliff, a self-made fortune and no one to share either with.

Rosy's speech was coming to an end. Her pace had quickened, her tone reaching an emotional peak before calming once again as she laid down her notes and gazed confidently into the camera, just the pink in her cheeks betraying her nervousness. There was no need as the chamber erupted into applause and a few whoops. She bowed her head respectfully to the chamber of men—and it was still all men—before retaking her seat. Jack could see her father—King Zorien—in the background, also clapping along, his face red with pride, but as he struggled to his feet the colour seemed to drain from his face and, to Jack's horror, he sank back down again, hands pressed to his chest.

Time seemed to stop as the applause stilled and all eyes focused on the clearly struggling King, the camera cutting away as Arrosa sank to her knees beside her father, fear evident on her face.

And Jack knew one thing. None of the barriers or problems or reasons to keep his distance mattered. Rosy needed him; it was as simple as that.

# CHAPTER TWELVE

ARROSA HAD NEVER spent much time in hospitals before, apart from as a royal visitor, there to cut ribbons and talk to pre-selected patients, and she was more grateful than ever for the presence of Clem and Akil. Thanks to their volunteer work, they were both well-known and familiar with the city hospital and on friendly terms with many of the staff.

Her father had been rushed to the private rooms reserved for the Royal Family and other VIP patients but, even with the comforting décor and peace, it was clear that this was a medical facility not a five-star hotel. The lingering smell was one of boiled vegetables and antiseptic, there were medical instruments evident all around and she knew that, even though she was in a plushly furnished sitting room, the tight ball of dread preventing her breathing properly was the same as that in the chests of everyone waiting in the wards and family rooms across the wider hospital.

Her father had been rushed straight into emergency surgery. Arrosa had tried to take in the words from the family liaison nurse, words like *heart* and *bypass* and *serious*, but she couldn't concentrate. Her mother had been at a prearranged event at the other side of the country. Although Arrosa knew she was sorry to have missed her speech, she hadn't wanted to let the school down, duty as important to Queen Iara as family. She had been informed about the incident straight away and was on her way back, so all Arrosa could do was pace and sit, pace and sit and let the various hot drinks cool untouched.

'Go home and rest,' Clem said, taking her hand. 'Or at least change.' Arrosa touched her hair, almost surprised to feel the cold of the platinum crown on her head. The morning's speech felt like a lifetime ago. She removed it with shaky hands, her head instantly lighter, and pulled out the hairpins keeping her hair confined in the intricate knot, pulling it back into a loose ponytail instead.

'I can't leave him.'

'Then at least try and drink something.'

And to please her sister Arrosa managed a couple of sips of coffee before her stomach tightened and she couldn't swallow any more.

She paced over to the window and stared out at the hospital grounds, the trees now turning to orange, red and yellow, seeing her sister and Akil reflected in the glass. They were sitting together on the sofa, Clem leaning into Akil, his comforting arms around her shoulders. For one brief, shameful moment she felt a pang of such pure envy it shocked her out of her stupor. Not for Clem's happiness, that was something that filled her with joy, but because she wanted something similar for herself. Because she'd been so close to having something similar, but life and obligation and cowardice had pushed it away.

At that moment the door opened and she whirled

around, expecting to see a doctor. Instead, Henri walked in, followed by the one person she realised she needed more than anyone else.

'Jack?' Had she dreamed him? But no, he felt solid enough as she ran to him, and he pulled her against him. 'You came.'

'I didn't want to intrude,' he said, looking uncharacteristically diffident, and she reached up to touch his cheek.

'You're not intruding, you never could.'

He led her to the sofa opposite Clem and Akil and pulled her down to sit next to him. 'How's your father?'

'It's not good, Jack. They rushed him straight in for bypass surgery. It's his heart.'

'I see.'

'His *heart*, Jack. It's like history repeating itself. You know his father abdicated because of *his* heart and then he died anyway, just a couple of years later. What if…?' She broke off, swallowing back almost hysterical tears. 'I can't lose him yet. I'm not ready.'

Then Jack's arms were around her, pulling her in tight, holding her, allowing her the freedom to let go, to be supported. She was dimly aware of Clem and Akil muttering something about going to get coffee and food and then she and Jack were alone and for the first time in a long time she allowed herself the luxury of tears. Once she'd started, she couldn't stop, all her fears and worries and regrets mingling with the shock and worry for her father's health and what that meant for the whole family, for her.

Arrosa had no idea how long she cried. When she finally choked back a last sob she was cradled in Jack's arms, his shirt wet through, a damp tissue clasped in her hands.

'I'm sorry. Look at your shirt,' she said, pulling back a little.

'I'm used to it,' he said, and his smile was tender. 'I have a six-year-old.'

'I didn't mean...'

He shook his head. 'Never apologise to me for having emotions, Rosy. You're allowed to be scared and upset and all that entails.'

'My father has dedicated his whole life to duty. He needs more time to live, not just be. He and Clem have only just started building a relationship. It would break her heart if anything happened to him before she really got to spend time with him.'

'And what about you?'

'Me?'

'Like I said, you're allowed to have feelings too, especially around me.'

Arrosa buried her head in his shoulder, her voice muffled when she did speak. 'I feel so selfish to be thinking of me at a time like this.'

'But?'

'Oh, Jack. My father was around my age when he had to become King, and because of that he left Clem's mother, left Clem, and married Maman, and they haven't had a happy marriage. Instead he dedicated his life to service, as did she. I know that is my future, I've come to terms with it, but I'm not ready, not yet. And...' She almost choked back the next words but she made herself keep going. 'I don't want to do it alone. I know I have Clem, but...' She couldn't quite bring herself to say the words quivering on her tongue. To say that she didn't want to do this without Jack. To tell him that having him here by her side, in her country was more than she had ever wished for, hoped for.

To tell him that she loved him.

But this wasn't the time and place.

'I'm sorry. I'm being cowardly and weak.'

Jack took her hands in his. 'Arrosa Artega, you're the bravest person I know.'

But she wasn't being brave now, was she? 'I…'

Before she could say anything else Clem and Akil arrived back with fresh hot drinks and an array of food. To her surprise, Arrosa discovered that she was a little hungry and managed half a roll and some of the coffee but the time to confide in Jack had passed. The day stretched on as the minutes slowly ticked by and there was still no news of her father.

Her mother arrived soon after Clem returned and Arrosa was both surprised and moved by the Queen's evident distress. In some ways it seemed that the events of the last few weeks had brought the royal couple closer together, which made it even more imperative that her father should make a swift and full recovery. If she had to take on more responsibility to enable that to happen then of course she would. She wanted her parents to have the time to enjoy this new understanding between them, for her father and Clem to have the time to develop a proper relationship, for her father to be able to enjoy his grandchildren when they finally came along. She was prepared to do whatever she needed to do to enable that. But she knew now that it would be easier with Jack by her side.

Clem was right. Arrosa had thought she was protecting Jack by hiding her feelings from him but, really, she was disempowering him. He deserved the chance to know how she felt and to make his own decisions.

It felt like an age before the doctor came in, removing his mask and rubbing his eyes wearily. 'I'm pleased to say that the operation went as well as could be expected,' he said. 'We're not out of the woods yet, but I'm as cautiously optimistic as I can be. His Majesty is sleeping now and although I can allow Her Majesty a few minutes at his side if she wishes, I suggest the rest of you go home, get some sleep and return to see him tomorrow.'

The Queen waved off their suggestion that they waited for her, insisting that her car and driver were waiting and she would rather be alone tonight anyway. Arrosa lingered, knowing her mother's tendency to hide behind what she thought she should do rather than what she wanted, but her mother met her gaze firmly and nodded.

'You too, Arrosa,' she said. 'You've had an exceptionally busy day. Go and get some rest.'

Her hug was warmer and more heartfelt than usual and Arrosa impulsively pressed a quick kiss to her mother's smooth cheek before allowing Henri to escort her out of the room, Jack closely behind.

Jack stayed in the car until they drew up outside Arrosa's villa, rather than asking to be dropped off at the palace. He checked in with Sally from the car, relieved when she reassured him that the girls were fine and although they were naturally worried about Arrosa and the King, who they had all met and liked, she had managed to distract them for most of the day. They were currently enjoying dinner in front of the television after an afternoon at the beach and barely mustered up the energy to shout hellos when she prompted them. Sally finished by telling him not to hurry back, and that she was happy to look after Tansy and Clover for as long as he needed her to. Jack said a few words of heartfelt gratitude before, with a nod at Henri, following Arrosa into her home. He took her bag out of her unprotesting fingers and set it on the hallway table.

'Go on,' he said. 'Go and get changed. That dress is beautiful, and you look beautiful, but it doesn't look that comfortable.'

She laughed a little shakily. 'You know, I spent the first hour we were at the hospital still wearing a crown. Isn't that ridiculous?'

'For anybody else, maybe.'

'Par for the course for me?' She made no move away, but stood looking up at him, confusion and hope in her eyes. 'He is going to be all right, isn't he, Jack?'

'The doctor seemed optimistic. That's encouraging.'

'Yes. Thank you for coming, Jack.'

'Any time.'

'Do you want a drink?' She was nervous, he realised as she whirled into the kitchen and found him a beer, grabbing one for herself, opening the back doors and ushering him outside. The evenings were chilly now but she didn't seem to feel the cold as she stood staring out at the lake.

'Jack,' she said at last, turning to him. 'When you arrived at the hospital I realised you were exactly who I needed. That you are always who I need. I can't let you go without telling you how I feel. I love you, Jack, with all my heart. I tried not to, but I can't help it.'

Jack stood there, unable to move or speak as each word sank in, warming him through, bringing him to life like soft rain on parched earth.

'I know what the papers say, and how you feel, that my world isn't yours, but I don't believe that. To me you are the knight in shining armour I didn't believe existed. A man who is kind and dependable and who understands me. A man I can trust with every thought and emotion. A man who has proved that over and over. I know you come as part of a package, and I love that too—but I also know that's why you are wary. If this life isn't for you then I will never blame you for that, but I had to tell you how I feel. I want you in my life for ever, you and the girls. I love you.'

'Oh, Rosy. I love you too. I think I have done from the moment you bought us ice cream and saved me from a full-on meltdown.' Jack inhaled, long and deep, searching for the right words. 'I wasn't going to say anything today. I thought what with the speech as well as your father you'd probably had all the emotion you could handle but, as usual, I underestimated you.'

She laughed and took a step closer. Deliberately, Jack took her undrunk beer from her hand and set it down on the garden table next to his and entwined his fingers through hers. The simple act of holding hands after so many weeks apart was like a balm to his soul.

'I told myself I had to stay away for the girls' sake,' he told her honestly. 'And there was truth in that, but I was also hiding behind them. My experience of marrying someone from a different world to me was difficult.

My marriage brought me my girls but little happiness. I had to prove myself every day, and still I knew that to the world I was an interloper. I knew if I was with you it would be a thousand times worse. A boy from my background daring to court the Crown Princess? I don't care what the papers say about me, what the Court says, but I care about you. I didn't want you put in a difficult position. I didn't want you to ever regret choosing me.'

There it was, Jack's truth, and Arrosa knew how privileged she was to hear it.

'I will never regret choosing you,' she told him, cupping his cheek and luxuriating in the rough stubble under her fingers, losing herself in the heat in his eyes. 'Never. The Court will say how clever I am to have snared a man who has made a fortune in such a short time and will wonder how we can best use your talents here, and the papers will come around, they always do. But even if they didn't, I wouldn't care. I know the truth and that's all that matters. But the girls, Jack, if we do this then you would have to be here. Would that work, would they mind?' With the headiness of the relief over her father and the knowledge that Jack loved her, the practicalities of their situation had been too easy to ignore.

'The girls love you and they love it here. There's an international school in the city with a great reputation and they have been begging to stay until the snow comes. It won't always be easy. Tansy is so nearly a teenager, there are bound to be storms ahead...'

'But if we navigate them together...'

'Then nothing is impossible.' He smiled down at her and she found herself laughing in giddy relief.

'Does that mean you'll stay?'

'It means that I will be looking for a place for me and the girls in the city...'

'But...' she interjected, and he put a finger on her lips.

'Get them settled in school and start to figure out my life here. And while I'm doing that, I want to do some old-fashioned courting. I know I could stay in the apartment where we are, and I am getting rather fond of all those ancestors of yours even if every male is brandishing a sword in a threatening manner and every woman a fan in an even scarier manner, and I am sure you would welcome us here, but Rosy, I rushed into one marriage. This time I want to take my time.'

'You do?' She completely understood—and courting did sound like fun. 'What do you have in mind?'

'The usual. Dinner, walks, theatre trips.' His voice deepened. 'Kissing, I think there should be lots of kissing.'

'Me too.'

'And touching.' Her knees weakened at the intent in his smile. 'Lots and lots of touching.'

'I could get on board with that.' They were so close now there was no space between them, her arms wound around his neck, her body pressed to his. 'What else?'

'I think I will have to show you.'

She laughed out loud as he swung her up into his arms, carrying her towards the kitchen. 'You might have to show me every day.'

'Oh, I intend to.' And then his mouth was finally on hers and Arrosa could lose herself in his kiss, his scent, the surety of his touch. With Jack by her side, she could face anything, any future, any obstacle. It was more than she had ever dared to dream of, and she couldn't have been more excited about what the future held.

# EPILOGUE

'THE THEATRE looks stunning, Jack.'

Arrosa squeezed Clem's hand gratefully. Even though her sister had become close to Jack and the girls over the last year she knew Clem still struggled with the changes to her mother's restoration work, even with the lack of facilities and comfort in the original theatre. But Jack had worked miracles and the theatre had come alive in the way he had envisioned, from comfortable backstage areas to tempt the biggest stars to Cornwall, to a café open all year round, a fancy restaurant with sea views and a beautiful bar area. The seats were still the original carved stone and open to the air, but patrons could rent or buy seat pads and the theatre sold long raincoats for the times the elements didn't cooperate.

They were here for the official opening night, a Gala in Simone's honour for the local hospice, for which they had all combined their resources to lure in some big names to perform songs, musical theatre numbers, dances and scenes from Shakespeare.

The eight of them sat in the newly created Royal Box, with an actual roof and cushioned seat, its own dining room and cloakroom. Jack had created several of these VIP areas with an eye on the hospitality market and Arrosa was grateful for the shelter even as she looked nostalgically across at the seat where she had met Jack for the first time.

'Do you wish you were performing, Clem?' Queen Iara asked. Arrosa still couldn't believe her mother had asked to attend the Gala in honour of her husband's great love, but she had insisted she wanted to get to know the town where her daughter had been so happy— and to pay homage to the woman who had loved her daughter so selflessly. She and Zorien had the seats of honour at the front and Arrosa was sure she had seen them hold hands earlier—and not for the first time.

'Part of me does,' Clem admitted, her hand straying to her stomach. Akil had not been able to keep his word to wait a year before he proposed, and the pair had married in the spring with their first child expected at Christmas. Arrosa couldn't wait to be an aunt—a hands-on acknowledged aunt who would always be part of the baby's life. 'But it is fun to be in the audience too. I'm just glad the community group still gets to use this space. Thank you, Jack.'

'The theatre wouldn't exist without the community— and I wouldn't have met Rosy either. I'm just glad we had a happier outcome than Romeo and Juliet.' Jack reached for her hand and smiled and Arrosa leaned over to kiss his cheek.

'Me too.' She looked down at her engagement ring, loving the way the rubies caught the light. Jack had stayed in Asturia and they had spent the past nine months really getting to know one another over a slow, sweet courtship which had given the girls plenty of time to adjust to their new lives in Asturia. Jack had proposed a couple of weeks ago, a year to the date they had met, with Clover and Tansy's help in a play the three had written and performed for her. Arrosa couldn't have imagined a more perfect proposal—or a more perfect ring, picked out by the girls for her.

The girls sat next to the King and Queen, bickering amicably over the programme. Over the last year Tansy had lost the last of her worried look and now had a social life to rival Arrosa's and was pursuing acting in the youth theatre in Asturia, while Clover had developed a love of horse riding, never happier than when they were at the Artega estate and she could spend the day in the stables. Both girls would be bridesmaids at the wedding in early autumn, with Clem as maid of honour.

'A toast.' Akil handed around the glasses of champagne, with elderflower cordial for the girls and Clem. 'To Simone, who I wish I had been able to meet, and her legacy.'

'To Simone,' they all chorused, even Queen Iara, while Clem held her cordial up to the sky, where the first stars were visible.

'To Mum.'

'And to Cornwall,' Arrosa added. Clem had decided to keep the cottage so her baby would get to know the village she loved so much. Jack had sold his dream home, reassuring her that his dreams had changed, but the pair could borrow the cottage whenever they wanted, with Henri always on hand to ensure their privacy was respected.

'And to the Asturians for making us so welcome,' Jack finished. 'Thank you for letting us be part of your family.'

'Thank you for letting me be part of yours,' Arrosa replied and as he leaned over to kiss her she made a mental note to never forget this feeling, surrounded by those she loved and who loved her, in a place dedicated to a woman who had helped raise her. Just a year ago Arrosa had felt completely alone, with the weight of the country on her shoulders. Now look at her, engaged, a stepmother, a soon-to-be aunt.

As the stage lights blazed to life and the show began, she sent a small prayer of thanks to the heavens. Nothing was impossible as long as she was with those she loved, and right now Arrosa Artega, Crown Princess of Asturia, knew she was the luckiest woman alive.

\* \* \* \* \*

# HIS MAJESTY'S FORBIDDEN FLING

SUSAN MEIER

MILLS & BOON

# CHAPTER ONE

KING JOZEF SOKOL settled himself in his seat in the private box at the Royal Theater of Prosperita. He did not want to be there, but his sons had arranged for him to join them for the opera and it was non-negotiable. They'd been hounding him for weeks about the fact that he was rarely seen in public anymore. Though he hated buckling under, he'd seen the true concern on their faces, and he'd decided to give in.

Once.

Just this once. There was nothing wrong with his life. Liam and Axel were simply being overly protective.

He smiled at the royal photographer and nodded to let him know he was dismissed after only one whirr of the camera. This wasn't a photo shoot. It wasn't even an opportunity for the press. It was as close as he would come to alleviating the fears of his sons that something serious was wrong with him. Particularly since they were overreacting, assuming he was depressed or worse, because he hadn't appeared in public in weeks…

Well, months—closer to a year, actually. But he didn't quibble over little things like that. He enjoyed his privacy. He enjoyed his work as ruler of a small, thriving island. His days had become a routine that guaranteed Prosperita stayed number one in the Mediterranean in terms of agricultural goods and the manufacturing and export of specialty equipment.

He sat up straighter, trying to get comfortable. He knew people in the theater's audience could turn and see glimpses of him, even with the box's lights down. Which was fine. His subjects were respectful and wouldn't react, beyond nudging their companions and discreetly pointing out that he was at the royal theater, out and about. If enough people noticed, he wouldn't have to do this again for another year or so.

He leaned into the velvet Queen Anne chair—uncomfortable things for a box designed for royalty— and made a mental note to have these chairs changed. A program sat on a silver tray atop the elbow-height table to his right. He opened it and scanned the names of the performers.

The sound of the curtain behind him sliding open rolled into the royal box. Assuming his sons were arriving, he turned and saw a tall woman with long, curly auburn hair. Dressed in a purple strapless gown that showed off milky white shoulders and a long length of shapely leg where the dress was split up the side, she walked directly to the chair beside his and sat.

His chest tightened and something weird happened to his breathing. And not because of fear—which is what his reaction should have been, given that a stranger had infiltrated the most exclusive area in the theater. His breathing had stuttered because the woman was stunning.

He shook his head to clear it. Her intrusion into the royal box without permission was against the law. Pressing the discreet button for security, he glared at her. "Who are you?"

She offered her hand to shake his. "Rowan Gray."

She said it as if he should have known her. Then he wondered where the hell his security detail was. Not because they hadn't scrambled in at his beck and call, but because she'd gotten in at all. He hadn't heard anyone talking, asking to be granted entry.

Security had let her in without as much as a question?

"How did you get in here?"

"I have ways."

His jaw dropped. "Don't be flip! This is the *royal* box. You don't get in here without an engraved invitation."

She handed him a business card. He glanced down and saw it belonged to one of his sons.

"That's engraved. It's just not an invitation." She shrugged. "But I'll remember that for next time."

She handed him another card. This one had her name on it.

He met her gaze. "Sterling, Grant, Paris?"

"Your PR firm."

He groaned. What the hell were his kids up to? Yes, they had concerns about him not getting out in public much. But this was ridiculous. "Seriously?"

"It's why the guards didn't stop me. They were informed I'd be here."

He blew his breath out on a long sigh. He would dispatch her in short order and then find his sons. "I didn't authorize you."

"Castle Admin did."

That stopped him. Castle Administration was the name used for the staff for the royals. Typically, they followed his orders. But there were times they could make decisions about things that fell under their purview. The choice of dinnerware for a state dinner. Whom to invite to a royal ball. Authorization of trips to other countries or for visits to their country. And anything they believed was necessary for the betterment of Prosperita, which sometimes gave them latitude he didn't like. This wasn't merely a family matter anymore. It had grown into something he might not be able to control.

"My sons went over my head?"

She shrugged those perfect white shoulders. "Ech. What does it matter?"

He turned to one of his guards who had finally arrived. "Tomorrow morning, I want Joaquim in my office. I have serious concerns about our security."

"Yes, Your Majesty."

He handed Rowan's two cards to her. "You're fired."

She settled into the chair. "No. Theoretically, you didn't hire me so you can't fire me. Plus, we have work to do. I'm thrilled that you decided to come out in public for this performance—"

"For my sons."

She inclined her head, causing her pretty curls to shuffle. "It's a good start, but you need to say something to the press when you leave. Just say, 'the opera was lovely,' while you're racing down the stairs before your security team escorts you into your private elevator that will take you to your limo in the parking facility on the ground floor."

"No."

Her delicate eyebrows rose. "No?"

He didn't want to make a scene by standing and

pointing at the curtain and ordering her to leave. God knew how many camera lenses from cell phones were pointed at him right now.

He tried the easy way, smiling and saying, "I didn't hire you. I don't want you. I don't need you. I'm not going to do what you say."

She laughed.

Her impertinence infuriated him, but he suddenly noticed that her shiny auburn hair cascaded down her naked back. The color set off her creamy skin, so smooth and white that it probably never saw the sun. It also accented her green eyes.

He blinked, taken aback by the fact that he even noticed her looks. Worse, his heart rate had accelerated, and his pulse had scrambled.

He'd been married for over two decades before his wife passed five years ago, and he'd never felt this overwhelming desire to stare at a woman. He'd never been sucked in by a woman's beauty. And he wouldn't be now. If his sons or the castle staff thought it was funny to throw a beautiful woman at him to see if he turned into a wimp who would melt at her feet and do what she wanted, they were crazy.

He was a king.

*Kings did not melt.*

They did what the hell they wanted.

He rose from his seat and walked out of the box, jogging down the stairs with his security detail scrambling after him. Ten steps on the edge of the almost empty lobby took him to a private elevator. He got in and rode to the ground floor, where a tunnel took him to parking accommodations for his limo.

He hated that *she* knew that.

He collapsed onto the back seat, wondering what in the hell had happened to his world—

He shook his head. What was to wonder about? He was a forty-five-year-old father whose children had come of age. That's what had happened. Liam was twenty-five and Axel was twenty-three.

It appeared they didn't like how he chose to live, and they had taken matters into their own hands. Two pups who didn't know a damned thing about real life were nosing into his?

*That* he would deal with swiftly.

Rowan watched him go with a heavy sigh, but she also had to admit she needed a moment—maybe the rest of the night—to regroup before she saw him again.

First, he was a king, and he wasn't pleased that his sons had done an end run around him and hired a PR firm. He could be her most difficult client ever.

Second, no one had told her this guy was smoking hot and had the kind of accent that could melt butter. His Mediterranean island had been under British rule for a century before it gained independence. The residents didn't merely speak English. Their dialect combined the lovely melodious tones of their natural voices with British pronunciations.

Plus, forty-five wasn't old, and his glorious head of black hair made him look thirty-five. Muscles that moved beneath his jacket showed he obviously worked out. Add a black tux with a royal sash across his chest that had real medals and he was...

*Tempting. Enticing. Intoxicating.*

Those words never crossed her mind with clients. Never. But holy everything, the man dripped sex appeal.

Needing to get home to her computer to investigate a few things before she reported back to her boss, she left the opera as inconspicuously as she had arrived, which was one of the fun things about being in PR. One minute she would be rubbing elbows with the rich and famous and the next she was walking in a warm July night to her rented sport utility vehicle. No security. No one noticing.

Though if anyone knew she'd just been with King Jozef, they'd be hounding *her* for a comment. The man hadn't spoken to the press in a year and he was handing out jobs to his sons like a monarch looking to retire, and despite how gorgeous he was, there was something brooding and haunted in his dark eyes.

Which unfortunately made him all the sexier.

She jumped in her car, admitting to herself that she didn't understand his recent withdrawal from the world. His wife had been gone for five years and from everything she'd read to prepare for this assignment, he and his queen had had a great marriage. He should have positive feelings about love and relationships and be eager to find someone.

She unexpectedly envied him. After the way her fiancé publicly humiliated her, she'd thrown herself into her work and was happy to be a successful woman who didn't need a man in her life, but some days—

She shook her head at the tiny spark of loneliness that formed in her chest. Because it was tiny. Barely discernible. And probably caused by the tingly feelings that had arisen around the handsome King. She didn't want them. Didn't trust them. She'd been the most naively trusting woman in the world until her fiancé had pulled the rug out from under her by running away with her best friend and getting married a week before *their* wedding.

Who in their right mind would even consider trusting again after publicly being made a fool?

Not her. She would never risk that kind of pain again. She had absolutely no idea how a heart expanded enough to love again, but she did know King Jozef shouldn't have the kinds of reservations she did. He was handsome, sought after, and had a stellar relationship in his past. The kind of relationship that should make him want another—

So why was he hiding? Why did he seem to prefer to be alone?

Her brain back in work mode, she called a few of her media sources in Prosperita as she drove to the small apartment Sterling, Grant, Paris had rented for her stay. She breathed a sigh of relief, when none of them knew anything about the King even having been at the theater, let alone leaving abruptly.

Maybe she'd get lucky, and no one would have noticed Jozef racing out before the opera even started.

She winced. Doubtful. Somebody always saw something. Like it or not, *she'd* been the one who caused him to do the one thing that would make his refusal to appear in public even shakier: run out like his feet were on fire.

She would check what the papers printed *before* they hit the stands and then she'd talk to her boss.

Jozef climbed the grand stairway of the silent foyer. He should have taken an elevator, but something drew him to the elegant winding stairway in the dark, quiet castle. He wasn't expecting to run into either of his sons. Most likely they were hiding. But first thing in the morning, they would be getting a sermon they would never forget. They wouldn't interfere in his life again.

The echoing expanse of the castle pressed in on him, as his quiet footfalls took him to the door at the back of the long second-floor hall that led to his quarters. He knew why the place felt so empty. He was alone. Wife gone. Children grown.

Stepping into the foyer of his apartment, he shook his head and told himself to stop being silly. So it was quiet? So he was alone?

He was a king with responsibilities, two sons, tons of friends. Hell, he was friends with the people who ruled the world. No. He *was* one of the people who ruled the world. He had nothing to be moody about.

He walked through his formal living room, the library and his home office to his bedroom suite. The second he stepped inside and saw his wife's picture on the bedside table, he knew why he was moody. He'd met a pretty woman that night and he'd reacted like a randy teenager. His breathing had all but stopped, his pulse had raced. It was a miracle he hadn't stuttered.

He sat on the bed and lifted his wife's portrait. No one wore a crown like Annalise had. She might not have been breathtaking like Rowan Gray, but she had been beautiful. She'd lit royal events. She'd made Christmas with their sons personal. She done her job with dignity and poise. Even after she'd gotten sick.

And he'd let his head be turned by somebody who was closer to his son's age than his own.

He returned the picture to its spot, telling himself he'd succumbed to biology—a racing heart and weird breathing were nothing but physiology—and went to bed.

His big, empty bed in his silent, silent world.

Up until tonight the quiet had been his sanctuary. Now suddenly it felt like a prison.

# CHAPTER TWO

THE NEXT MORNING, his phone woke him with pings for texts from his sons, who apologized because they wouldn't be at breakfast, and a text from Castle Admin that read very much like a reprimand. An astute reporter had noticed Jozef's escape the night before, and their news outlet was reporting that something had to have been wrong with the King, given the expression on his face and the way he ran out.

He rolled his eyes. First his sons, then Castle Admin and now the press were homed in on him, as if he were crazy.

Oh, he definitely would handle this today.

He dressed in black trousers and a white oxford cloth shirt and headed downstairs.

Two members of Castle Admin—Art Andino, a tall, thin man in wire frame glasses, and Mrs. Jones, an older woman who had served as his mother's assistant for decades and now was head of "continuity"—stood just outside the door to the informal dining room and followed him to the table. They stopped beside two seats on the left.

An unfamiliar man in a gray suit sat at the far end

of the table. And *she* was sitting at the chair right beside *his*.

Her glorious red-brown hair had been wound into a clumsy knot at the top of her head that allowed strands to escape and frame her face. She wore a unisex black suit with a white shirt open at the throat that somehow made her all the more feminine.

His heart jumped. All his nerve endings jingled.

He straightened his shoulders and took the power afforded him as ruler. Continuing the walk to his seat, he said, "Good morning, everyone."

Castle Admin said, "Good morning, Your Majesty."

The man in the gray suit and pretty Rowan gave him the courtesy demanded by his office and rose as they said, "Good morning, Your Majesty."

Before he got to his seat, he addressed her directly. "Why are you here? I fired you last night."

"Yes, you did, Your Majesty. But because you didn't hire me you can't fire me." She pointed at the man in the gray suit. "That's Peter Sterling, my boss."

"Perhaps I can fire him?"

Peter looked ready to faint or hyperventilate. Jozef knew he was imposing. Tall. Sturdy. With eyes that warned an adversary not to cross him.

Still, Pete said, "Actually, Your Majesty, Castle Admin hired me."

"Then maybe I should fire them?"

Mrs. Jones's eyes grew huge with fear. Stuffy Art Andino shifted from one foot to the other. Tension hung in the air.

Jozef took his seat, allowing everyone to take theirs. "And why are you here, Mrs. Jones?"

She shot him a sly look. "Moral support?"

He had to stifle a laugh. He'd known Ella Jones his entire life. If she felt he needed moral support, then shivering in their boots or not, they really were ganging up on him.

And something really was wrong.

Rowan said, "Somebody got a picture of you racing out of the theater last night and sold it to everyone. This morning's articles in all the news outlets are similar, reporting that you appear to be ill. You're thin and pale. Tired looking."

"I see." Though he wasn't pleased with the casual way she spoke to him, he suddenly understood the fuss. In the months before his wife's illness had been officially announced, she'd lost weight and had withdrawn. No wonder his subjects were sensitive to his isolation. They worried he was going down the same path his wife had, waiting until she was terminal to announce her illness.

Rowan gave him a quick once-over, the purely clinical assessment of a PR person. "Honestly, the comments baffle me. You look great to me—really great—for a guy of your age."

He balked. "I'm forty-five, not eighty-five." Still, her compliment went through him like a bolt of sexual electricity.

And finally, the reaction struck the right chord. There was no denying that he had a real, honest-to-God attraction to this woman who wanted to work for him. But in a way that was good. Knowing that what he was feeling wasn't fleeting, admitting it was real, he knew how to dismiss it.

Her boss shifted on his seat. "This doesn't have to be a big deal. The way I see it, you simply need to get out a few times in the next two months, so your subjects can see you're happy and healthy and stop the questions."

"The questions?" He turned his gaze on Mrs. Jones.

Her face flushed. "People have been questioning your sons for weeks. Every time you send one of them to an event you usually attend, the organizers and participants seek them out, ask if you're okay."

He took a long, resigned breath. He'd made the correct guess about why this was getting blown out of proportion. But that meant he had to address his subjects' concerns. Whether he needed a PR firm to do it was still up in the air.

The server arrived with Jozef's breakfast and Peter Sterling started talking again. "Your Majesty," he said, his voice dripping with respect for Jozef's position. "We believe all you need to do is go to some fundraisers. Perhaps a soccer game."

But Rowan eyed him, as if appraising him for sale at an auction. "I don't think fundraisers and soccer games are going to do it. I think he needs to go on a few dates."

*Dates?*

Gobsmacked into silence, Jozef only stared at her.

Rowan continued talking about him as if he were an inanimate object who couldn't hear or speak for himself. "Two dates. With two different women, spaced properly so no one thinks he has a new love interest, but also it won't appear he's gone off the deep end by dating so many different women he looks sleazy. We need to make him look like a normal guy, with normal…feelings."

Her candor rendered him speechless. But just when he was about to tell her to watch her step with him, everything she said fell into place in his brain, and he saw her point. His subjects deserved to have their fears relieved. More than that, though, given his abrupt and strong reaction to Rowen, he wondered if his body wasn't telling him something. Oh, he didn't want to get married again, or even settle in with one woman. But forty-five wasn't old enough to put himself out to pasture. A date every once in a while wasn't out of line.

He said, "Okay." But he wasn't letting a stranger choose his dates. He would pick the women he spent time with. "I will find two women and go out on two dates in the next four weeks."

He was about to dismiss them when the waitstaff returned with breakfast for Rowan and her boss. Mrs. Jones and Art Andino discreetly left, apparently already having eaten, but also satisfied that he'd agreed to go out in public again.

As the waitstaff left, Pete said, "It's not a good idea for you to choose your own dates." He winced. "I'm sorry if I sound disrespectful, but these first two dates—maybe even three—need to be chosen with care. You need to be seen with the right women who will project the correct image."

Annoyed that Pete hadn't simply taken him at his word the way Castle Admin had, he smiled his most kingly smile and said, "I thank you for your opinion. But I can handle this. In fact, rather than date, I can more easily clear everything up in one press conference. I won't mince words." He never did. "I'll apologize for isolating myself and I'll assure them I'm fine."

Sterling grimaced and carefully said, "I'm sorry again, but that won't work."

Rowan said, "If you hold a press conference to tell people you're fine, you'll look like you're making ex-

cuses. A guy who is fine is out in the world, doing his
job and socializing. You haven't been. A slow, steady
campaign of getting you out in public again would work
best. You're also going to have to take back a few of
the royal appearances you gave to your sons and you're
going to have to be social. Not just rubbing elbows at
state dinners. But dating. So we can avoid more articles like these—"

She pointed at the newspapers strewn across the
table.

*King races from theater.*
*Pale and drawn, King not strong enough to stay for*
*entire performance.*
*What's the castle hiding?*

Josef frowned. He never let his subjects worry or allowed the press to whip them into a frenzy. How had
he missed that suspicion was growing or that the press
was fanning the fires?

Pete rose. "Plus, you're in great hands. Rowan is old
enough to have sufficient experience with the PR end of
things and young enough that she's still in touch with
trends etc. She knows to find you someone more like
Adele than Lady Gaga."

Josef shifted his gaze to Rowan and she smiled at
him.

"She'll also choose your wardrobe and write quick,
snappy lines you can shoot at the press if they ask you
questions... And you want them to. You want to get
your message out to the public."

Holding her gaze, he realized again how young she
was, and knew there could be nothing between them.

She seemed to understand his situation better than he did. And if her boss had assigned her such a high-profile assignment, she had to be good at what she did.

If he thought of her as an assistant, not someone finding him dates, but someone arranging royal appearances of a sort, he would not merely get through this, the outings would do the job they were supposed to do. And his life could go back to normal.

He took a breath. "And what is my message?"

Pete turned to Rowan. "Rowan?"

Still holding his gaze, she said, "That you're a youthful king. Still strong. Still vital. Not merely able to lead but someone worthy of a position of prominence. Someone handsome, a good face of your country."

His heart fluttered a bit when she called him strong and vital and then handsome, but he ignored it.

"And how do you turn that into one-liners?"

"I don't. I write things like, 'Good morning, everyone, isn't it a beautiful day,' for you to say when you're walking to a limo with the woman I've chosen for you to take out. Then they'll subconsciously connect your sentiment about the day to your sentiment about your companion and they'll know you're fine."

It sounded so easy, like something that would weave into his life without much fanfare. It also sounded like a simple way to reassure his subjects without having to hold a press conference or issue a statement that *would* sound like he was making excuses.

It was the personification of actions speaking louder than words.

Pete said, "And that's it in a nutshell, Your Majesty. Now, if you'll excuse me, I have another meeting."

With that he left and Jozef was suddenly alone with

Rowan. The silent room vibrated with possibilities, as they held each other's gaze. The attraction he didn't want to feel for her tightened his chest. But he was too old for her and she had a job to do. If she did it right, he could get out of this blip of trouble without making it into a big deal.

Rowan set her napkin beside her untouched plate of food and pushed back her chair. "I'm going to get started with some research. Do you want to meet this afternoon?"

Telling himself to just do it and get it over with, he said, "Yes. I'll see you this afternoon."

Then he watched her leave. Confusing emotions rattled through him. He couldn't believe he hadn't seen how his actions would worry his subjects, but he hadn't. He also couldn't believe he was attracted to a woman closer to his sons' ages than his own. But he was.

Luckily dignity and pride came to his rescue. He would humble himself to alleviate the fears of his subjects. And he would not make things worse by salivating over a woman who was too young for him. He wouldn't disrespect his position or his late wife that way.

Rowan drove back to work, forcing her mind to go over choices of eligible women who could be potential dates for a king. There was a glamorous American actress in her forties who—like Jozef—looked no older than thirty-five. Sterling, Grant, Paris also had a client who was a princess from a neighboring country. She'd gotten a bad deal when her husband was caught cheating and divorced her. The whole world would probably love to see her on a date with a handsome man, a king no less. That would put Princess Helaina's cheating spouse in his place. And if Rowan really wanted to get bold, she could set Jozef up with a billionaire tech genius, who sometimes used Sterling, Grant, Paris's services. That would be great for *Jozef's* image. He wouldn't merely be dating a pretty woman, he'd be dating someone who was smart and savvy enough to run one of the biggest companies in the world.

Taking the elevator to the third-floor temporary office suite Sterling, Grant, Paris had rented for this job, she decided the tech genius was definitely in the running, but she had to be the second or third date. Not first. The first date had to be casual, maybe a soccer game, with the American actress. She was beautiful, smart and fun, and they could look like two friends who had connected over a mutual love of soccer. The tech genius could be second. The Princess would be third. By then the public would be accustomed to seeing Jozef out on dates again, and they'd be hoping for him and the Princess to connect for real. Maybe date long-term—

Or even get married! What a royal treat that would be for all of Europe! She could see the press coverage now. It would be magnificent.

Pride rippled through her, but it was followed by the oddest jolt of regret. She was marrying off a man she found both interesting and tempting. A good-looking man who was intelligent and in control. A guy who would clearly be fascinating on a date and amazing after the date, when they'd go back to his place and—

She shook her head to stop the roll of her imagination. What the hell was she thinking? Dear Lord. This was a client! And she was a rising star on the verge of starting her own firm. Plus, one humiliating breakup was enough to keep her away from relationships forever.

Thinking of the betrayal—not just her fiancé but her best friend—soured her stomach. She'd believed the sun rose and set on Cash. She could picture their future children. They had a house together and a mortgage. All that spelled commitment to her. All that gave her reason to trust him. And he'd tossed her away, along with her ability to trust, because her best friend had seduced him?

What a load of rubbish. The fact that he hadn't been able to resist her was just another way of saying Rowan wasn't good enough.

Not able to stay in her small West Virginia town after her great humiliation, she'd moved to New York City, where she'd gotten a job as an assistant in a public relations firm. She'd climbed the ladder with relative ease because she was a natural at finding the right thing for a client to say or do to get out of a jam. Then she was lured to Europe to work for Sterling, Grant, Paris. Five years later, she was at the top of the heap and married to her job. No one would ever hurt her again. But she'd also use her life to make sure people who had been hurt could raise their heads with dignity and grace after their own great humiliations.

She was going to help King Jozef. The way he hadn't even noticed he was in trouble was proof that he needed her, and that always touched her heart.

Plus, her success was going to be public. Her name might not be on the lips of every average citizen, but people in PR circles would see this and understand she had "the goods." People who needed assistance clearing their names or getting back into the world again would also see her work, and her name would be the one they'd think of when they needed help.

Which was why the minute the job with Jozef was done, she had to leave Sterling, Grant, Paris and strike out on her own.

It would be her opportunity to shine, and, by God, she was taking it.

As she walked through her assistant's workspace into her office, Geoffrey scrambled from his seat, following her.

"So?"

She shrugged out of her jacket. "So what?"

"Oh, my God, you met a king! *The King*. Of an entire country. How did it go?"

"Yesterday, not so well. Much better this morning." She didn't tell him that she'd gazed into the King's dark eyes—beautiful eyes made sexy by the brooding secrets behind them. She didn't tell him that for a minute she thought she'd felt something pass between them. Not only was she the worst judge of character when it came to romance, but also the guy she'd shared the moment with was a king. She was as common as they came. The thought of them being together was... wrong.

She sat on the tall-back chair behind the unusually high stack of paper on her desk. "What is all this?"

"Phone messages and emails I printed out. Everybody in Convenience, West Virginia wants you to come home for your dad's surprise birthday party."

A shiver of revulsion rippled through her. She thought of the day her fiancé had arrived at her parents' house with her best friend and they'd told her they'd gotten married, thought of her wedding gown still hanging in the closet of her old bedroom, thought of how quiet Convenience, West Virginia had sounded that night, as if everyone was walking on tiptoe, embarrassed for her.

With humiliation riding her blood, she pretended indifference. "Seriously? Why do this many people care?"

"You know your mom wants *all* her kids home for the party."

And part of her wanted to go. Her parents had visited her in New York and even traveled to Europe for her birthday last year. She missed them.

The other part liked the woman she'd become outside of her small town. She didn't want to revert to the naive twenty-two-year-old who'd been so blinded by love she hadn't seen the signs that her fiancé was cheating.

That part won. "I'll be busy with the King."

"But the party's the end of next month. Eight weeks from now. I thought this was a six-week gig?"

"It might run a little longer." Forcing her mind off Convenience and onto the assignment, she tapped her fingers against her lips. "We have to get King Jozef somewhere significant every other week for a month. Then that opens the door for us to set him up with Princess Helaina."

Geoffrey gasped. "Princess Helaina?"

She grinned, though something inside her felt weird again at setting Jozef up to fall in love with another woman. "I know. We'll be killing two birds with one stone. Get him out in public and make it look like our poor embarrassed princess has moved on from her cheating husband. Then a nice six-week relationship for them proves they're both over their troubles, and they can break up like normal people and look like healthy individuals."

She frowned at the way her scenario now had them breaking up. Still, it worked.

"You're a genius."

"No. I'm really sort of wishful thinking here. It will take us the whole month to get the public accustomed to seeing Jozef again without making a big deal out of it. If that works, we'll call dating Helaina his Phase II."

Geoffrey shook his head. "I still think it's genius. I'll leave you alone to work your magic."

He walked away and she picked up the phone. She had to get an American actress to Prosperita without it looking staged.

# CHAPTER THREE

AT THE END of the day, King Jozef strode down the marble corridor that led to his official office. Though he did most of his work in the private office in his suite, all meetings were handled here. He had about ten minutes until his sons were to arrive. Enough time to check his messages and figure out how he would tell his children to butt the hell out of his life.

He walked inside the workspace of his assistant, Nevel, who had apparently gone for the day, and plucked up the stack of yellow slips of paper, messages Nevel had taken that day.

Reading the messages, Jozef continued into the ornate office with velvet drapes, Oriental rugs and the massive mahogany desk of the original King of Prosperita that was over five hundred years old.

About to take his seat, he glanced up, and there, bolder than life, was Rowan Gray, sitting on the chair across from the big desk.

Her black suit was a bit rumpled, but her stunning green eyes were bright, shining.

Ignoring the jolt of attraction, he scowled. "Don't you ever call ahead or make appointments? Or do you just barge in everywhere?"

"I work for you now. And I'm told my business with you is top priority."

"Don't you have another client you could be annoying?"

"You're my main project, Your Majesty."

The way she said *Your Majesty* made his nerve endings crackle. He cursed in his head and once again had to admit his sons might be right. For him to be so attracted to a stranger who was all wrong for him, it must be time for him to get out into the world again.

"I've arranged an outing for you."

He closed his eyes and sighed. "Opera? Symphony? Grocery store opening?"

She laughed. "Nothing so trite."

"You want me to be the grand marshal for a parade?"

"We discussed you going on *dates*, remember?"

Of course, he remembered. Having a stranger choose women to accompany him to events reminded him of his teen years, when Castle Admin would suggest possible young ladies for him to date. It had been both embarrassing and overwhelming. That was part of why he and Annalise had asked their parents to arrange their marriage. Having the press following his every move and a stranger find him dates brought back that horrible feeling.

He settled into the tall leather-backed chair behind his desk.

"I have you meeting Julianna Abrahams at a soccer game on Friday."

His head snapped up. When Rowan talked about finding dates for him, he always pictured dowagers in orthopedic shoes. Julianna Abrahams was every man's fantasy.

One of his eyebrows quirked. "Julianna Abrahams?"

"She's pretty and smart and very funny. She was a client of mine a few years back. She owed me a favor and agreed to fly here and be your date."

His happiness nosedived. "Exactly what every man wants. For a pretty girl to think he needs a PR firm to get him dates."

"She doesn't think that. I told her I thought being with you could boost both of your images. She saw the point."

He snorted. "You didn't make me look pathetic?"

"Oh, Your Majesty. You are far from pathetic. You are extremely strong. It's simply time for us to remind everybody of that."

He felt the wave of attraction to her roll through him again and this time it was harder to ignore, but he managed.

"Plus, I'm trying to bolster your reputation, not make you look worse." She paused only a second before she added, "Julianna is great. And you like soccer."

"Football."

She winced. "Sorry. I know you guys call it football. But what we call your outing is beside the point. The point is she's perfect for you. Who knows? You might hit it off for real."

"And then you'd leave?" He'd said it sarcastically, but disappointment flooded him. How could that be when he had a date with America's Sweetheart? Just the thought of going out with Julianna Abrahams should dismiss his attraction to Rowan—

Shouldn't it?

Of course, it should!

So why hadn't it?

"I stay until your press is filled with pictures of you smiling at happy subjects."

He snorted in derision, but he looked at his watch and realized that any second his sons would be arriving for their meeting.

Needing to get rid of her, he rose from his seat. "Okay. Great. Email the particulars for the date with Julianna to my assistant Nevel in the morning." He walked around the desk and motioned for her to rise.

She gave him a puzzled look but stood up and turned to the door just as his sons entered.

Everybody stopped dead in their tracks as Liam and Axel stared at Rowan, and Jozef felt like a trapped rat. Though he had no idea why. He had legitimate business with Rowan. And they couldn't read his mind and see he was attracted to her.

Blond-haired, blue-eyed Liam recovered first. Stepping forward he offered her his hand. "I'm Liam. I hope we didn't interrupt anything."

"Ms. Gray was just leaving."

Axel, who was the image of Jozef when he was younger with his dark hair and eyes, also offered his hand to Rowan. "I'm Axel."

Jozef almost groaned when he held Rowan's hand a tad too long. The little player was going to hit on her!

"Okay. That's enough." He guided Rowan away from his sons. "I'll be waiting for the particulars once you give them to Nevel."

She said, "Okay," and he closed the door on her before she could say anything else.

Liam said, "Who is she?"

Jozef strode to his desk. "Really, you don't know the PR person I'm told you begged Castle Admin to hire?"

"I wouldn't say we begged," Axel said with a laugh, his straight shoulder-length black hair shifting as he moved.

Liam had the good graces to look sheepish. "We simply suggested that you needed to be seen in public more."

"And this is your business because…"

"Because you're not yourself. You've been giving all your events to either me or Liam," Axel said, sliding his hip onto the corner of his dad's desk. The casual way he behaved reminded Jozef of all the times he'd had the boys in his office when they were toddlers, then little boys, then teenagers. They'd thrown baseballs. Played tag. Played board games. He'd never wanted them to feel unwelcome in his office. More than that, though, he'd wanted Liam, heir to throne, to feel like this was where he belonged.

He suddenly missed those days, missed his sons as boys. He missed showing them the world with their mother. Then he missed their mother. Briefly, like a shadow crossing his soul, he felt the loss of the woman who'd helped him rule their country.

Jozef quietly said, "I'm training you to take my place."

Liam laughed. "Seriously? You think I need twenty years to learn to run a country?"

"You think you don't?"

Liam frowned. Axel relaxed negligently on the desk. As the non-heir, he didn't have a care in the world. But he liked supporting his brother. He enjoyed his royal duties. If he wasn't such a badass with women, he'd be the perfect child.

No. He wasn't a child anymore. Or even a teenager acting out because he missed his mother. He was a man.

And maybe his sons were feeling as adrift as his subjects felt because their dad had all but become a hermit.

"Why don't we do something tonight?"

Axel glanced over at him. "Us? The three of us?"

Jozef nodded.

Axel said, "Like what?"

"Why don't we go to the media room and watch a game?"

Liam sniffed. "It's probably already started."

"Who cares? Let's just go. We'll call the kitchen and have them make junk food."

They headed for the door and Jozef's world didn't exactly right itself. He still felt the pang of emptiness that always rose when he thought of Annalise. But he had spent the past year in a sort of no-man's-land. His boys had grown up and he was feeling alone.

Watching a soccer game together might be just what they all needed.

On Friday, video conferencing with her staff in Paris about other clients took most of Rowan's day. She found herself racing to the castle less than a half hour before Josef would be leaving for the soccer game and his date with Julianna.

By the time she got through the security gate and pulled up to the huge gray stone castle, his limo was already by the door he would use to exit. Grabbing the polo shirt Pete had asked her to buy to assure Jozef looked comfortable and relaxed on his date, she scrambled to the limo, showed her credentials to the driver and slid into the back seat.

Josef came out of the door, and she groaned. Wearing jeans and a white shirt with the collar open, he at least had one part of the outfit right. But he looked so out of touch with reality that she groaned again.

He approached the limo, and the driver opened the door. Not noticing her, he slid inside. When he saw her sitting right beside him, he started. "What are you doing here?"

She ignored his question and clicked her tongue. "Really? Jeans and a white shirt for a sporting event?"

"You're in a suit!"

"I know but I'm working. I'm not going to a soccer game."

"*Football* game! It's *football* here. And you *are* on your way to the game. That's where the limo is taking us."

She retrieved the bag from beside the seat and pulled out the red and blue striped shirt. "Here."

He looked at it then looked at her. "What's this?"

"Your new, more comfortable, more relaxed shirt. My boss apparently saw pictures of you from a game a couple of years ago, and he didn't like what you were wearing."

He rolled his eyes. "Well, we certainly can't have that, can we?"

"Come on. This is my job and my boss's job. The shirt might seem like a small thing, but we want you to look young and approachable. Just one of the guys going to a soccer game with a pretty girl."

He said, "It's football," but he took the shirt.

The scowl on his face told her he wasn't happy. When he didn't make a move to change shirts, she said, "Go ahead. Put it on."

"Over my shirt?"

She laughed. He was deliberately being difficult, but

she refused to take the bait. She'd handled worse clients. "Remove the shirt. And put on the casual, comfortable, shirt."

"In here? Right now?"

"Oh, come on. I'll bet you've changed in a limo before."

He frowned.

"Please?"

Something shifted in his eyes. He hesitated, looking at the shirt, then at her. With a disgruntled sigh, he dropped the striped shirt to the space between them on the limo seat, unbuttoned his white shirt and slipped it off, leaving him in his undershirt, which he yanked over his head.

Rowan plucked the polo from the seat and turned to hand it to him, but her gaze collided with his bare shoulders, chest and abdomen. Very flat abdomen. She successfully kept herself from reacting, but she couldn't deny she'd been checking him out and he'd probably seen.

As the garment went from her to him, their hands brushed and their eyes met. Electricity crackled between them. She wasn't just attracted to him. *He* was attracted to her.

Which was wrong.

For them both.

He was a client. Off-limits. And a *king*.

Plus, it was her job to get him out in public again on *dates* with other women. Following up on this thing between them would be self-sabotage.

She cleared her throat and turned away. "Hurry up! Get that shirt on. We'll be at the entry to your private tunnel to the stands in a few minutes."

He shrugged into the polo shirt, but he kept his gaze on her face as if confused. After a few seconds, he grinned like a Cheshire cat.

Damn it! She might have done her best to brush away her attraction, but he'd seen her reaction. He now knew she was attracted to him.

She could feel her face reddening and cursed herself. She wasn't a twelve-year-old girl. She shouldn't have stared when he took off his shirt. She couldn't even appear to be interested in him on any level but professional.

Hell, she wasn't *allowed* to be interested in him.

He. Was. A. Client.

# CHAPTER FOUR

THE LIMO SLID through the gates leading to the private tunnel that would take Jozef to an elevator that would stop right beside the royal box. Neither he nor Rowan spoke as they rode to the second floor. When they reached the royal box, she set her fingers on the forearm of the security guard who had moved to open the door.

"One second."

Her focus back on the job where it belonged, she straightened Jozef's collar, then bunched the loose shirt-sleeves to his elbows, making him look casual, relaxed. "Just be yourself."

"Sure," he said, but he grinned at her again.

*Men.* Even accidentally hint that you might be attracted to them, and they got all proud and goofy.

Yet another reason to keep everything professional with this guy.

"You might not believe this, Rowan. But I'm actually friends with world leaders. I've met a movie star or two. You don't have to babysit me."

She shook her head, then caught the gaze of the security guard who opened the door. Her PR instinct shot to high alert when she saw Jozef's sons standing by the wet bar, with Julianna Abrahams, chatting her up.

Liam said, "Dad! Look who's here."

Okay. The first thing she had to do was get rid of his sons. She couldn't really think of a way to do that that wouldn't alert the press something was up in the royal box—

Of course, that might work in her favor. There *was* something happening in the royal box. King Jozef had a date. She wanted the press to see that.

Before she could say or do anything, Josef walked over to Julianna and offered his hand to shake hers. "Excuse my sons. They sometimes forget their manners. It's a pleasure to meet you."

Julianna shook his hand, her blue eyes gleaming. She tucked a strand of long yellow hair behind her ear. "The pleasure is mine. Your sons are charming."

"*I'm* charming," Axel clarified, then he pointed at Liam. "He's a stuffed shirt because he's next in line to head the family business."

Julianna laughed. "Family business?"

Fully living up to his reputation as royal player, Axel shrugged. "Running the country goes from one of us to the next, down the line of succession. So, yeah. Family business."

That was about as much as Rowan intended to let Axel steal the show. "Shoo. Take your security detail and go sit in the stands. You're making this look like a family picnic instead of a date. It needs to look like a date!"

Julianna laughed. "You should listen to her," she told Axel and Liam. "She made me appear to be a saint when my ex left me." She smiled at Rowan. "Kept me from having to pay millions to a guy who'd been nothing but a sponge."

The boys grumbled, but they left.

Jozef turned to Julianna. "Shall we sit?"

"Okay." She glanced around. "But I'm not sure how anybody's going to see we're together." She looked at Rowan. "Isn't that the point of this?"

"Yes, that is the point of this," Rowan said, but Jozef interrupted her.

"Don't worry. Photographers have long-range lenses."

Rowan took a few steps back. "Yes. They do. And we don't necessarily want them homing in on me." She inched back another few steps. "In fact, it's probably time for me to leave too. I'll go find your sons. Smooth things over. And make sure they don't say anything we don't want them to say. You two just enjoy the game."

She quickly exited and asked a security guard to help her find the two Princes. As it turned out, Castle Admin had two royal boxes, the second one obscure. In case the royals really did want privacy, they had it.

But before she stepped inside the room, she turned and faced the official royal box again. The picture of Jozef laughing with Julianna popped into her head and sent the strangest feeling cascading through her.

White-hot jealousy.

She grimaced. That was ridiculous. She found the guy attractive, sure. But probably half the people in the known universe did. The guy was hot. And that accent? Who wouldn't turn to mush hearing that? She was normal. There was nothing more to it than that.

Although it did suddenly hit her that Liam and Axel

were closer to her age than their father, she didn't get those floaty, sometimes breathless feelings when they were around.

Which was another thing she refused to think about.

Jozef enjoyed his time with Julianna, who was bright and cheerful and accommodating. So unlike Rowan, who kept popping up out of nowhere, telling him what to do.

Seriously. He was a king. Her boss was smart enough to respect that. But Rowan? No. She just muscled her way into everything, insisting he do her bidding.

No one was supposed to tell him what to do. Advise? Sure. Tell him to take off his shirt and put on another, that was—

His breath stuttered.

"Are you okay?"

His gaze whipped to Julianna, who sat munching popcorn, enjoying the game.

"Yes. Sorry. Just thinking about things."

"Kingly duties?"

He was thinking about a woman he was attracted to and how she'd reacted when he took off his shirt. He was attracted to her and now he knew she was attracted to him. He'd seen that in her eyes when he'd removed his shirt.

"No. Not kingly duties. I can compartmentalize. And kingly duties are a lot like running a conglomerate. Though sometimes our parliament does get a bit pushy, I just think of them like the board of directors for a big company."

She smiled.

He waited to have a reaction to her. A twinkle of happiness. A shot of adrenaline. None came.

Disappointment fluttered up.

A week ago, none of this would have even registered in his mind. Now suddenly the whole country was worried about him, and he'd agreed with the PR firm Castle Admin had hired that letting them take the lead in getting him out socially was wise.

So here he was, on a date with Julianna Abrahams, when the woman he was attracted to was…

Off-limits. Wrong for him. Wrong for his image. Just plain wrong.

But she was also attracted to him.

The thought filled him with pleasure before it made him swallow hard.

His life would be a mess if he pursued her. Hell, she might not even want him pursuing her.

Otherwise, she would have flirted or something.

Wouldn't she?

Of course, she would have.

And that brought him back to Julianna Abrahams, sitting beside him in the royal box, watching a football game. He really was only forty-five. His wife was gone. It was time to get on with the rest of his life.

With Julianna engrossed in the game, he glanced around, wondering if this was what the next few years would be like as he either dated as a normal widower would or found a new wife—

No.

He couldn't even let his thoughts go that far. This was about dating like a normal widower.

If there was such a thing.

He pondered that for the rest of the game, then suddenly the final score was announced, and he'd missed it all.

The door opened and Rowan walked in. Her simple beige pantsuit made her look tall and slender. Her glorious red hair floated all around her. His gut clenched and his breath wanted to stutter.

He told his hormones to stop.

He had a country to think of. Not just himself. He might want to date like a normal widower, but he didn't think normal widowers dated hot thirty-year-olds.

That is…if she was even thirty years old.

He had no idea exactly how old she was. But were he to guess, it would be between twenty-eight and thirty.

Rowan said, "Axel and Liam are helping me get back to the castle, where I left my car. I'll see you tomorrow, Jozef."

The resignation that filled his brain as she walked away wasn't comforting. He had no intention of pursuing her. She'd let her attraction to him slip out that night, but she'd also immediately pulled back. Meaning, they were on the same page. They were two adults who appreciated each other, but nothing would come of it.

Saturday morning, the tabloids awaited him at the breakfast table. Two photographers had managed to get a shot of him kissing Julianna good-night—something he'd believed a necessity when they'd parted company to go to their respective limos.

Two got pictures of her racing to her car, as if trying to avoid paparazzi. Her not wanting people to see she'd had a date with a king only made it seem more real, not planned at all.

He chuckled. Julianna was better at this than she let

on. And though he was loath to admit it, Rowan had been correct. Their date the night before had been good for them both.

His sons came to breakfast to talk about meeting Julianna but it seemed like every other sentence contained a reference to Rowan.

"I think we should keep her on speed dial," Liam suggested, "for when Axel does the monumental screwup we all know he's going to do eventually."

Axel snorted. Jozef shook his head, not even dignifying that with a comment. Particularly since his sons' need for him to get out in public had started all this.

*He was considering dating again.*

*For real.*

That was, after he had three dates with women Rowan chose for him.

It would have made him a bit queasy, except he'd taken a second marriage off the table. He wasn't there yet. Dating now would be for fun.

He really hadn't had any fun in his life in a long time.

Lost in thought, he strode into his office with purposeful steps only to stop dead in his tracks.

"What are you doing here?"

Seated in the chair behind his desk, Rowan turned to face him. "We'll be debriefing the morning after every date."

"Fabulous." She looked pretty and perky and this morning her full lips looked incredibly kissable. "But that doesn't explain what you're doing in my chair."

She winced. "I thought your breakfast with your sons would last longer." She winced again. "And I wanted to see if sitting in the chair of a king would make me feel any different."

Telling his wayward thoughts to take a hike, he crossed his arms on his chest. "Did it?"

She glanced around as if confused. "Actually no."

"Do I have to count to ten to get you out or should I call security?"

She bounced out of the chair. "Sorry."

He waited until she rounded the desk, then he walked behind it and took his seat. "Second order of business, there is nothing to debrief about. The *date* was nice. Made me realize just how much I had been keeping myself at home and decide I really do want to get out more. And now I am fine. I can finish this on my own."

She chuckled and sat on the chair in front of his desk. "Funny stuff, Your Majesty. Especially since you know we're only in phase one. Your next date is with Paula Mason."

He thought for a second. "The tech genius?"

She smiled. "Yep."

His brain should have produced a picture of a blonde beauty with a brain as fast and accurate as the software she created, but it suddenly homed in on the fact that Rowan wasn't in a pantsuit. She wore a tight skirt and a floaty blouse that set off the color of her hair but was also extremely feminine.

"Speechless, right?"

He sort of was. Not because of Paula, but because he was not the kind of guy who noticed women's clothing. Sure. If someone had on a miniskirt or a bikini, he saw. He wasn't an idiot. But who the hell cared if someone's blouse complemented their hair? Well, apparently, he did, since he'd noticed.

"This date's going to go like this. Not this Friday, but next Friday afternoon, she'll come to the castle to meet with you and some of the members of your advisory council to talk business."

Confused, he frowned. "Business?"

"The future of...you know, computers and the internet and your country's place in that world, or maybe what you need for infrastructure to meet demand. Then you'll both come out of the castle dressed for an evening out. There's a gallery opening. Castle Admin arranged for you to go in an hour before the normal crowd is permitted to enter. I want the press to see her getting out of your limo in something glamorous..." She peered up at him. "You'll be in a tux. You'll spend an hour or so in the gallery, then it's back in the limo and to a restaurant for dinner."

That did not sound like fun. It sounded scripted and overscheduled...

Still, this wasn't the rest of his life. All Rowan got was three dates to show his subjects he was fine, and he should look at those dates as practice for when he started getting himself out into the world again. Better to mess up with women he wasn't really interested in than the ones he'd choose for himself.

"Okay. Fine."

"I'll be checking on your wardrobe."

He sighed. "I wear a suit for meetings, and you already said I'd be wearing a tux for the gallery opening."

"Sounds good." She snapped her leather notebook closed and rose. "We'll talk next Thursday."

He also rose. "The day before the date?"

"Yep. We can go over anything you want. Then we'll debrief Saturday morning."

And he wouldn't see her until then? No more having her pop up in his office or spin around in his office chair?

That was for the best. Actually, it was smart.

With that, she turned to go and Jozef watched her leave, surprised at the disappointment that consumed him. He sat down, prepared to work, but he couldn't. Everything felt off. Wrong somehow.

A week ago, he was a man who enjoyed his privacy. Then a gorgeous public relations woman came into his life, and he realized his subjects were worried about him. Wanting to alleviate their fears, he agreed to go out with a movie star. On that date, he realized she wasn't his cup of tea, but he was ready to get out into the world again.

To date.

He'd been content to be a solitary widower. Now suddenly, he was thinking about dating—

Attracted to Rowan—

Feeling alone in his castle quarters—

How the hell had this happened?

He threw his pen down on his desk and strode out of his stuffy, stifling office and into his assistant's workspace.

"Tell Castle Admin I'll be at the stables. I've decided to take the day to do some riding."

Nevel stood up nervously. "But you have two meetings—"

"Cancel them."

Rowan left his office completely flummoxed. The meeting had gone well, but there was something about Jozef that struck her as funny. She got the weird sensation of spiders crawling down her spine, the way she always did when a client was about to do something stupid—

But that was crazy talk. Jozef was as controlled as a guy could get. He wasn't about to do a striptease on the bar of a tavern the way one of her rock star clients had or race his motorcycle down Ventura Boulevard, taking cops on a four-mile, high-speed chase. He understood that he had to keep his reputation solid.

Still, sometimes when a PR firm came in and began planning a person's life, they could feel too controlled and rebel. As much as logic would tell the client that the PR plan was correct, they'd feel stifled…and do something stupid to wrestle back control.

And this guy was a king. The definition of *stupid* expanded exponentially for him. Rock stars and movie stars were given tons of leeway before anybody marked their actions as foolish. Josef had simply withdrawn and his subjects got nervous. God only knew what would happen if he did something that really was wrong.

The feeling of spiders using her spine as a superhighway intensified. She had to do something.

She tried calling him that afternoon, but he didn't answer his phone.

His assistant refused to give her any information about his whereabouts.

Castle Admin informed her he'd simply taken an afternoon off and there was nothing to worry about.

But years of experience with clients told her she was right. Something was up with Jozef.

She tried to picture him riding a motorcycle like a rocket down the streets of Prosperita's capital city and ended up with hives.

The more she thought about their ten minutes together that morning, the more she realized he'd definitely had the look of a guy who was going to burst, and technically this was her job: see the signs of a meltdown and prevent it.

She left her office, hopped into her SUV and raced to the castle. She got past security and two butlers but was told Jozef wasn't there.

"I'll wait," she said, nosing around the wide hallway outside his private quarters, as the butler blocked the door.

"This is highly irregular."

"You do know I'm his PR person, right? I'm supposed to look at his life, figure things out and change whatever is wrong. I can't do that if I'm on the outside looking in, can I?"

The weathered butler sighed. "No, ma'am, I suppose you can't."

"Call Castle Admin— No wait. I'll do it." She picked up her phone and hit the speed dial number for Art Andino. When he answered, she put the call on speaker. "Art, this is Rowan. I need to speak with Jozef and he's not in his quarters. I needed to talk to him ASAP. Like the second he gets home. I could wait in the sitting room for his residence, but his butler wants me to leave and come back later. And that means, I won't get to talk to him the second he gets home."

"Let her in the sitting room, Raphael," Art replied, obviously recognizing the call was on speaker.

The butler said, "Yes, sir."

He motioned for her to enter, then disappeared.

She closed the door behind her. "Thanks, Art."

Art sighed. "Just don't go beyond the sitting room... And don't touch anything."

Five minutes later, the butler was back asking if she wanted tea while she waited.

Having skipped lunch, she said, "Tea would be nice."

Then she glanced around the residence of her client and itched to get beyond the front room. She really should look for clues about what was going on with this guy.

Of all of her clients, *he* was the one who really could not afford to make a mistake.

Peering at the antiques and big portraits of former kings, all of whom looked as controlled as Jozef, she realized she could be overreacting. Jozef was accustomed to being in the public eye. He was also mature, intelligent and majestic—

Oh, boy. If she'd gotten this wrong, if he wasn't about to melt down, he would be furious with her when he came back and found her in his sitting room.

# CHAPTER FIVE

WHEN THE OBJECT of her fears finally walked into his residence, he wore a T-shirt and jeans and boots that looked like hiking boots. Tall and lean, just muscled enough to be sexy, with his dark hair disheveled, he gave new meaning to the word *masculinity*.

She struggled with a moment of pure lust, but quickly regained control. "Where have you been?"

She asked pleasantly because she didn't want to offend him, make him feel cornered or get fired.

"I wanted a break. And I took one. I think the bigger question is why are you in my private quarters?"

"Castle Admin authorized it. I went looking for you and when I couldn't find you, they allowed me to wait for you here." She paused for a second, then added, "But they didn't tell me where you were."

He snorted. "I was on a horse. Riding. Just taking a normal break."

*Oh, that accent.*

Seeing him at his most masculine and hearing that voice made her want to curl up beside him on a big bed with satin sheets.

But she knew better. Especially given that he was her *client.*

"And you felt you needed a little horse therapy because…"

He sucked in a long breath. "Because of something that's none of your business."

"Everything about you for the next six weeks is my business. It's why Castle Admin hired me and why they let me see you anytime I want. For the next six weeks, *you* are my job. Why did you feel you needed a break?"

Clearly frustrated, he stared at the ceiling, his hands planted on slim hips that looked so damned fine in blue jeans.

Finally, he glared at her. "I should kick you out, but I know you'd only be in my office tomorrow morning asking the same questions. So let me save us both some trouble. All this attention on my private life has me feeling things that I needed to deal with."

*Alleluia! Now they were getting somewhere.*

"That's perfectly normal! When someone has to call in a public relations firm, it's usually because there's an issue in their life that caused them to feel they needed help with their image. In your case, you withdrew." She smiled again. "So, what kind of things were you feeling today?"

He gaped at her. He'd spent hours riding, grooming his stallion and thinking, as he mucked the stall to continue doing physical things in the hope his antsy feeling would go away. Ultimately, he'd realized dating didn't bother him as much as the up-and-down feelings he'd been having around Rowan.

She was brash, bold and running his life, yet he wanted to kiss her. And that was the real conundrum.

She didn't see that *she* was the problem. And he wasn't about to tell her.

"Are you seriously asking me to tell you my feelings? Like you're a therapist? Good God, woman! Will you leave me with at least some semblance of dignity!"

"I'm not asking to be nosy. I'm asking because I can probably help. Odd feelings are normal when another person starts interfering in your life. No matter that I'm here to help and the things we'll do over the next few weeks will settle a few of your problems. It's still an intrusion. I've dealt with this before."

He sighed. He knew she was talking about typical frustration a person would have when a PR person started changing things, but he envisioned every one of her clients being attracted to her.

Unfortunately, that only made him feel more common, less kingly. So far out of his comfort zone, it frustrated him to hell and back. "Great."

"It *is* great because I have seen this hundreds of times and handled it a bunch of different ways. I can probably tell you how to fix it." She smiled briefly, clearly trying to reassure him. "What are you feeling?"

He shook his head. He knew she wouldn't let this go unless or until he threw her something. Plus, if he couched his issue in generic terms, maybe they could figure out a way to dismiss it.

"All right. You asked for it. On the off chance you really can help… I'm feeling an odd surge of frustration that borders on anger."

"That's good! See? Getting it out in the open like that means we can deal with it."

"Or it means you can put it in a sappy press release that garners sympathy but makes me look like a fool."

She gasped. "I wouldn't do that."

"Right." He shook his head. "You'll do what you need to do."

"I *need* for you to continue looking healthy and strong not sappy. I won't be doing anything that makes you look sappy."

"Don't placate me. No matter how much you try to pretend to be my buddy, this job is just a job to you. You'll do whatever you deem appropriate in the moment."

She stayed silent awhile, then eventually said, "Is that what this is? You don't trust me?"

"Why should I?"

"Because my reputation is on the line here every bit as much as yours is. Don't tell anyone, but I'm this close to leaving Sterling, Grant, Paris to start my own firm. If the whole world sees I made you look wimpy, I might as well go back to West Virginia and crochet scarfs and mittens for a living. It's a black mark on my résumé if your subjects stop worrying about you because I made them feel sorry for you."

A weird sense of balance settled over him. It shocked him that she'd confided one of her secrets. But in the most unexpected way it had shifted his feelings about dealing with her. Her reputation would suffer if she botched this.

Suddenly the whole deal didn't feel so one-sided.

Unfortunately, knowing that did absolutely nothing to alleviate his attraction to her. It might have even made his desire to kiss her stronger.

"You know what you need to do?"

He peered over at her in her pretty skirt and floaty blouse. "What?"

"You need to do something just for yourself."

"I did. I went horseback riding."

She shook her head and walked over to him. "No. You need to get crazy. Do something that's out of the ordinary, maybe even against the rules."

"Horseback riding wasn't on my schedule. Nevel had to cancel two meetings."

She shook her head. "Wow. If you consider that crazy, your life really is dull."

The statement went through him like a shock wave of realization. His life *was* dull. Predictable. And maybe that was at the bottom of all this confusion? He worked so hard to conform, to do everything right, that now that he'd hit a level of perfection—good kids, strong country, solid economy, not a skeleton in his closet—he'd stopped living, as a way to protect it all.

The surprise of seeing that was so strong, he almost had to sit. No wonder his subconscious was revolting. No wonder her suggestion to do something crazy unexpectedly sounded right.

He was tired of his life being dull.

"Plus, horseback riding is still kingly. You need to do something un-kingly. Something no one expects. But do it in private…"

His brow furrowed. "Somewhere no one sees?"

"Yes. Exactly. Somewhere no one can see. So no one knows. No ramifications. It's your little secret."

His gaze dropped to her lush mouth. "My secret?"

"No one has to know."

He stepped away from her, calling himself insane for the temptation flitting through his brain.

She laughed. "Come on! I know there's something in

there." She tapped his temple. "There's something you want to do." Her eyes brightened. "Do it."

Oh, hell. She could not know she was persuading him to kiss her...

Could she?

Maybe she did? He'd seen she was attracted to him. And it was just a kiss.

Plus, now that his confusion had broken and he realized he'd boxed himself into the most boring life possible, he was ready to be normal again.

To do what he wanted.

To be himself.

He caught her by the shoulders and simultaneously stepped closer as he pulled her to him. His mouth met hers quickly, not giving her a chance to protest, and a bolt of electricity matched the roar of thunder that sizzled through him.

She'd been correct.

This was exactly what he needed.

He could have stopped the kiss after a few seconds, but when her surprise wore off, she relaxed against him, and her hands slid to his shoulders.

His hands slid down her slim back and leisurely rose to her shoulders again.

Their mouths opened.

The kiss deepened.

For the next thirty seconds, pure bliss billowed through him. Then arousal rolled in. He wanted to take the kiss to the next level. He wanted it so much he almost couldn't believe the thoughts bouncing around like popcorn in his brain.

He struggled to remind himself that this was just supposed to be a kiss. A fun, quasi-rebellious thing to make him feel like himself again, but this was as far from his real self as he'd ever been, as wants and needs collided and took over.

He wrestled control back again and stepped back. With his hands still on her shoulders, he watched her pretty green eyes open and blink once.

"Was that risky enough for you?"

He made the joke only because he wasn't ready to face the things rumbling through him. His marriage to Annalise had been arranged by his parents, and though they'd had a fabulous sex life and a wonderful marriage, he'd never felt this kind of roaring, growling, hunger.

It had to be wrong.

She cleared her throat and stepped back too. "Well. Okay. I mean... I didn't expect that your risqué thing would be with me. But... Well, wow."

Desire blasted through him. It was thrilling to know she'd liked the kiss as much as he had. But in the next breath he faced a million commonsense reasons why what he'd just done was wrong.

*Wrong.*

It might have been right because it jarred him out of his apathy. But it was wrong on all other levels possible.

"I'm sorry."

She held up a hand. "Oh. No. No. Don't be sorry. I wasn't offended. I'm not exactly sure what's happening here but we can sort it out."

"I've wanted to kiss you since I met you."

Relief fluttered through her. That hadn't been a default kiss. He hadn't kissed her because she'd pushed him to do something risky and she was the only risky thing available. But that opened another door. Their mutual attraction had resulted in one hell of a kiss. For every bit as much as that filled her with bubbly joy, it was totally inappropriate.

"Okay. This is on me. I told you to do something slightly on the rebellious side and that kiss was it." Just saying that out loud stole her breath. She took a second to pull herself together. Then she realized he was perfectly calm. Talking like a sane person. He'd all but melted her bones and he barely seemed affected.

That realization worked to bring her down to earth until she remembered that for at least a couple of days, she'd been his fantasy kiss. She'd been the fantasy kiss of a *king*. A gorgeous, smart, sexy king.

*Stop that! You have a job to do. One blistering kiss isn't going to ruin it.*

Sensible King Jozef broke the silence. "But we can't do it again."

"Oh…no." She held up her hand as she sing-songed. "We absolutely can't."

"Still, it was pretty good."

"Yup." *Maybe too good.*

He laughed. "You were right. That did make me feel better."

She took a few steps backward, inching toward the door, wanting to put some distance between them. The conflicting feelings of happiness that she had been his fantasy kiss, and disappointment that he didn't want anything to do with her kept bumping into each other, creating a weird dichotomy. She should be glad he didn't want anything to do with her—

But that was some kiss.

Shoving her internal battle aside, she forced herself to do her job. "Let's look at it this way. You were struggling with the sense of being confined or hemmed in and you're not feeling that anymore."

She plucked her coat from the back of one of the chairs in his sitting room. It was one thing to properly identify what had happened. Quite another to hang out in a room with a guy who'd kissed her like Prince Charming, returned her glass slipper, then told her he didn't want her.

"I'll see you in the morning."

Still unaffected, he nodded.

She opened the door and ran into the hallway to race down the grand stairway, the drama of it keeping her Cinderella feelings alive. Her heart pounded and her knees were weak, but she pushed through the foyer and out the door. When she got into her rented SUV, she laid her head on the steering wheel.

The man could kiss.

But he didn't want to kiss her again and, technically, she was not allowed to kiss clients.

She comforted herself with the knowledge that it would never happen again and most likely they'd never talk about it. Still, thoughts of the kiss bubbled up the whole time she drove home, as she ordered takeout for her dinner and tried to watch TV.

She squeezed her eyes shut, telling herself she was crazy. She wasn't a hermit. She dated, and she always liked the people she went out with. Kissing them had been great too. But there was something different in Jozef's kiss. And in the silence of her rented apartment, she let herself admit that what she'd felt was that spark people talked about. The spark that said there was something here. A bigger, better attraction. An attraction that meant something—

The same spark she hadn't felt since cheating Cash.

That tossed a barrel of water on the fantasy that wanted to blossom in her brain. Cheating Cash from Convenience, West Virginia. *Convenience, West Virginia.* Because that's where she was from. She was a small-town girl. Sure, she fit into the rarified world in which she worked because she was a really good schmoozer, but she was still an employee. Not one of the bigwigs.

She tried to picture herself as a queen and couldn't. Tried to picture Jozef in Convenience, West Virginia meeting her parents and couldn't.

But she could picture another broken heart. The absolutely horrible humiliation of having a king publicly dump her.

That would be the real end to anything that might happen between them. They wouldn't get married. She didn't have to worry about being a queen. They'd never mesh. Their lives would never entwine.

They would part.

Maybe that's what he meant when he said they couldn't kiss again.

Maybe that's what her brain had been trying to tell her when it continually reminded her he was a client.

They were not right for each other.

Monday morning, from her temporary office nowhere near the castle, she solidified the arrangements for Jozef's date with Paula Mason. She'd already told Jozef that they wouldn't have a strategy meeting until the day before the date, so there was no reason for her to go to his office, or even call him.

They would have over a week to forget their kiss.

To let it fade into stardust and be blown away on an island breeze.

Which was exactly what needed to happen.

Hours later, she was ready to leave for the day when her cell phone rang with an unfamiliar number.

With a sigh, and a prayer it wasn't Jozef, she answered it.

# CHAPTER SIX

Jozef gathered the hard copy of a trade agreement Liam had negotiated and headed out of his office. Everything inside him burst with pride. Liam might have hated that his father had begun to train him so he could someday fill the King's shoes, but training was a good thing.

Evidenced by the excellent agreement Liam had negotiated. His son was taking to the position of leader like a fish to water. And he was about to surprise him not just with a personal visit to his office, but also an abundance of praise.

He took the back corridor that led to the offices of both of his sons. But as he passed Axel's work area, Rowan stepped out, Axel right behind her, his hand on the small of her back.

Surprise hit him like a punch in the gut. All his muscles froze.

"Hey, Dad! Rowan's just agreed to help with the fall fundraiser."

"Oh." He let his gaze meander to her. Her face registered the same kind of shock that was rolling around in his belly. Excitement at seeing her mixed with trepidation. He didn't think she'd told his son that he'd kissed her. But he had kissed her and she had kissed him back.

The memory bloomed, bringing with it the flood of longing he'd been fighting for the past thirty-six hours. It didn't seem right that he should want her so badly when anything between them was totally inappropriate.

"Pete and I decided to look at it as an extension of the services we're rendering for you."

Not knowing what else to say, he mumbled, "That sounds fine."

He should have gone. Liam's office was only twenty or thirty feet away. He should have said, *If you'll excuse me, I'm on my way to see Liam*. But he couldn't seem to move. She'd raced out after he'd kissed her. But not before relieving him of any responsibility for it. Like a good PR person, she'd taken the blame, told him their blistering kiss was nothing but his need to get rid of some of his tension and clearly let him know she hadn't been affected.

Of course, he'd tried to salvage his pride by pretending the kiss had been nothing but logical. He couldn't grouse that she'd looked at it logically too.

Like the good employee she was.

The silence stretched out and just when he might have gotten his feet to move, he noticed that her long hair tumbled over a simple T-shirt, drawing his gaze to blue jeans and boots. He swallowed. She hadn't even worn blue jeans to their soccer game. What was she doing in jeans at a meeting—

With his son?

"We don't have clients come to the temporary office we set up, so lots of times we dress down," she explained, obviously having followed his line of vision.

Her gaze lifted to his.

His bones felt like they melted.

"So I'll see you next Thursday for the meeting before your date with Paula Mason."

Axel whistled. "Paula Mason! Dad! You are so lucky."

He didn't feel lucky. Instead, a little bit of his anger from the Saturday returned. He'd never disputed his responsibilities as King. He'd never been rebellious like Axel. He was more like Liam. In fact, he and Annalise had concocted the scheme to marry each other at only eighteen because finding a love match would have been a disaster with the press watching. After they'd married, they'd fallen in love.

And that, they'd decided, was the way things should be. As friends, they'd already known they were good for each other. Marrying, having love arise out of their friendship, worked better than the passion and uncertainty of romantic love.

Technically, he did not know this woman he was so damned attracted to. If they pursued what they felt, it would be clumsy.

Sexual.

Messy, because he'd never really understand what they were doing.

The thought of it was unexpectedly titillating, so he took a step away from her. Kings could not operate on whims and wishes. "I'm on my way to see Liam. Have a good evening, Rowan. Axel, maybe you and I should watch the game again tonight."

In the meeting with Rowan the day before his date with Paula Mason, Jozef was confident and commanding.

Her normal procedure should be to explain the outing to him and ask if he had questions. That morning, he told her how things would go, then dismissed her in such a way she couldn't think of a reason to argue or stay. She returned to her office, finished her day and went home with takeout.

Though she was nervous about the date the next day, she forced her mind off Jozef and to her own future. With this assignment about half-done, it was time to consider the steps she'd be taking to start her own firm. She'd have to talk things over with Pete, of course, to get his blessing and hope he threw some overflow work her way until she had her own clientele.

But she also had some PR work to do for her new company. She'd have to create a campaign that announced that she was going out on her own. Especially in Manhattan. She'd chosen to go back to the States to make it easier for Sterling, Grant, Paris to recommend her to non-European clients.

And to get away from Jozef. The man had begun invading her dreams. She'd fallen asleep on the sofa the night after running into him outside Axel's office and dreamed of the episode just as it had happened, except everything suddenly morphed. Axel evaporated and the King didn't stutter or seem shellshocked. He'd taken her into his arms and kissed her—

She'd bounced up on the sofa, breathless and angry with herself, reminding herself they did not belong together.

Recalling the dream, she realized that was what his stiff and formal attitude that afternoon had been about. He might be attracted to her, but he wisely ignored those feelings. Cast them aside. Behaved like an adult.

She might be vacillating, but he wasn't.

The following afternoon she arrived at the castle to find all his cabinet members were already there. Slipping into the front foyer where Jozef stood congregating with twenty other men and women, she noticed he was the strong, self-assured ruler he had been at their meeting. Knowing he was fine, she worked to stay out of the way and simply let him be a strong, impressive king.

In fact, she was glad he was commanding and confident. Helping him come back into the world reflected well on her. He was becoming one of her success stories. He might have initially argued with her. He most certainly hadn't liked having her tell him what to do. But he hadn't had a big meltdown the way some of her clients did. He'd had a teeny tiny one that resulted in him kissing her.

Now he was ready to let go of whatever had been bothering him enough that he'd isolated and be the King he was.

She had done her job.

She should be proud.

She *was* proud.

But there was this niggling something in the back of her head that tried to ease out every once in a while, but it couldn't.

She'd think her hesitation or concern had something to do with Jozef, but he was great. Stronger than ever.

What the hell was it?

Finally, Paula's big, black limo pulled up in front of the castle, and she was escorted into the foyer. Wearing a slim blue pantsuit on her tall frame, she stepped forward, extending her hand to Jozef. Like Julianna Abrahams, she was blonde, but her hair was cut at the chin in a chic bob. Her mouth had lifted into a wide smile. Her blue eyes sparkled.

"It's a pleasure to meet you, Your Majesty."

Rowan's lips twisted as she tried to figure out why she always fixed him up with beautiful blue-eyed blondes. It was like she was saying she wasn't good enough. No redheads for the King. No women with lush figures.

No. That wasn't it. She'd chosen his dates with personality and impact in mind. Julianna Abrahams and Paula Mason were his level of stature.

Looks had nothing to do with it.

Satisfied with her explanation, she discreetly walked beside the assembled crowd of cabinet members and assorted executives of Paula's huge technology empire, as they made their way to a conference room.

It was like watching history in the making. His job was so serious, and he did it so well—

*That was it! That was the weird thing tickling her brain.*

His world was huge and filled with significance and consequence. That was true of all her clients in one way or another, but where movie stars and even corporate geniuses would fade into obscurity, historians would one day write about Jozef. Things he did, decisions he made, could someday change the fate of the world.

It was no wonder Castle Admin hired someone to make sure he stayed steady in the eyes of his subjects. He was important beyond the shores of his island. He was a world leader.

They reached the door to the huge conference room. Rowan would not be allowed to go beyond that point, but that was fine. She had other work to do.

Still, she couldn't stop watching him—

Jozef casually turned and caught her gaze.

She could have thought he was thanking her for doing a good job setting everything up with Paula. But the connection felt different. Personal.

Almost as if he'd wanted her to see *this* was his real world. Not the private times they'd had together when she'd bossed him and even sort of sassed him.

But the weight of who he was.

Was it a warning? Or an explanation.

The door closed behind him.

She stared at the polished wood. Memories of Convenience, West Virginia juxtaposed the scene of him with world leaders and the CEO of one of the biggest companies on earth.

She suddenly realized he was telling her that who he was made him different. Special. But also, he was a man who carried so much responsibility that he'd never be just a guy.

He was a king.

She was so common that she bought her undies at a big box store.

He'd wanted to kiss her because he found her attractive. But while she could dream about him, spin fantasies, there was no room in his life for something that would get him lambasted in the press—or, worse, in the eyes of the presidents, prime ministers and other royalty who were his peers.

Though the meeting with Paula Mason and her staff had been arranged as a way to get him seen out in public with her, Jozef made good use of the time. He picked her brilliant brain about her research and development

and asked for advice on what his country needed to do
to keep up with the times.

She was not shy about giving her opinion. A person
did not get to her level of prominence by holding back.
He not only respected that he used it to his advantage.

The trip to the gallery ended up being enjoyable and
dinner was lighthearted and fun as she told him about
growing up in upstate New York. Far away from where
Rowan had been raised, but similar in terms of mountains and forests and small-town life.

Walking to his residence, he yanked off his tie and
rolled his eyes. He knew his curiosity about the life-
styles in the different geographic regions of the United
States was fueled by his forbidden curiosity about
Rowan. But he had all that under control now.

Hadn't he been solid and all business in their meeting the day before his date? Of course he had been.
Because he'd gone back to who he was: a leader. Not
merely in charge of his own country but one of the rul-
ers who would shape the world.

The next morning, he entered his office, expecting
Nevel to tell him that Rowan was on her way over,
or that she'd scheduled an appointment with him, but
Nevel was nowhere around.

Then he remembered it was Saturday. Of course,
Nevel wasn't around. Unless specifically asked to work,
as he had been the week before, he took Saturdays and
Sundays off.

He strode into his office. Nevel might not be working
but Rowan surely would be. She said they would debrief
after every date. And he'd had a date the day before. She
wouldn't miss a chance to dig for every nitpicky detail.

Seconds later, she appeared at his door, takeout cup of coffee in hand.

He rose with a smile. "You don't have to bring your own coffee. I can have coffee here in under ten minutes."

She laughed. "I know. But I got up late, raced to dress and needed the caffeine boost as I was driving."

The normalcy of it made him laugh. Plus, she looked soft and happy in her jeans and boots, topped off by one of her fancy, floaty blouses.

He motioned to her chair. "Have a seat." Then a thought struck him. "Have you had breakfast?"

"No. I don't eat breakfast."

"Breakfast is the most important meal of the day!"

She shook her head as she approached the chair in front of his desk. "Not for me. Once I eat a carb, I want carbs for the rest of the day. I eat nothing but protein and fat until three or so. It's a tricky balance I have to maintain to keep my weight from climbing."

Again, the normalcy of the conversation, the simplicity of it, filled him with something he couldn't define or describe. He'd say it relaxed him, but it was more than that—

His chest tightened. *He was happy to see her.* No. He was happy to be alone with her. So happy, he almost felt giddy.

He drew a quiet breath, resurrecting the kingly demeanor he'd used the day before. "I'm sure you're here to get the details of my outing with Paula Mason."

She nodded, then took a sip of coffee.

"Everything was great. Paula's fabulous."

Their gazes met as her eyes filled with something that could have been disappointment. "You like her?"

He said, "Absolutely," but what he felt for Paula was so far removed from what he felt for Rowan it seemed wrong to let Rowan live with a deliberately misleading impression. He sighed. "I like her as a business associate. The woman's a genius. We had great conversations."

"Oh."

Her relief birthed corresponding relief in him. He recognized the road they were going down and stopped it before it really started. "And thanks to you, Prosperita now has a very strong ally. Someone who is willing to help us update technologically and maybe even put a satellite office here so we can keep more of our educated citizens on the island instead of having them move to Europe for work."

Pride filled her bright green eyes as her lips lifted into a smile. "That's great."

"It really is." Her surprise at his compliment reminded him that he'd barely let her know he'd appreciated everything she'd done for him. If he examined the slippery slope on which he'd been sliding before her firm stepped in, he realized he would have been a hermit in another few months.

She might not change the world the way Paula would, but in her own area of expertise, Rowan was as smart as Paula. Wearing jeans and a feminine shirt, with her hair in a bun, she also looked older than his sons. Actually, she looked like the hard worker he knew she was.

"I know I haven't been the best client, but you did a good job."

Her smile grew. "Thank you."

Wonderful warmth percolated through him. But he

caught it before it spilled over into the feelings he wasn't allowed to have.

"So that's it. Paula and I had a good time, made some deals, enjoyed each other's company."

"Okay. That one's in the books." She glanced down at her hands, then caught his gaze again. "One more date and you're free."

Her statement hung in the air. They both knew that after that date, he wouldn't see her again. In his entire life, he'd never felt what he did around her. And in a few weeks, it would be gone.

Not just her, but the chance.

Not to sleep with her. Not even to investigate the attraction. But to really be himself. To say what he wanted, knowing he wouldn't be judged. To laugh unrestrictedly. To give voice to the thoughts he sometimes had but didn't speak.

All because there was a spark of something between them. Something romantic and sexual. Something he'd always believed he didn't want suddenly tempted him.

He struggled for a witty comeback, but nothing came.

She sucked in a breath. "Actually, now that we're coming to the end of this, there are some things I have to tell you too."

The softness of her voice spoke of intimacy, trust. They'd scuffled and bantered, but they'd confided things. Been real with each other. He suddenly wondered if it hadn't been meeting her, rather than going on two random dates, that had forced him out of his doldrums.

"Watching you enter that conference room yesterday, I had a few 'aha' moments myself." She took another quick breath. "For one, I've treated you a little shabbily for someone who's a king."

He chuckled. "Really? You think so? I just thought all PR people were pushy and disrespectful. That that's how you got your work done."

She snorted. "That's basically true. Though not everybody has to get the cooperation of a king."

"Just the people looking to break out of the pack and start their own firm?"

She met his gaze. "We do have to prove ourselves."

He laughed again. He couldn't remember laughing this genuinely, this honestly, this comfortably in forever.

"Yesterday, I saw just how important you are."

Pride filled him, but it was replaced by a quick realization. He didn't have as much fun being important, as he did being himself. The truth of it froze him in place.

"I get it now. I looked at portraits along the walls of the main corridor, the people who ruled before you, and I realized this country has survived five hundred years because of your family. You're part of something huge."

"It's a blessing and a curse."

"Really?"

"Yes." He shifted on his chair, debating one more confidence and then decided it was long overdue. "For one thing, I like you. You see me as a normal person and we can have talks like this, where I get to be me. But I can't go out on a date with you because you're way younger than I am and the press would go nuts."

She studied his face for a second, then said, "Yeah. I of all people should know that."

"But I won't forget you. You helped me get over a very natural bump in the road in my life and I appreciate that."

She smiled.

The warmth of a genuine connection bubbled up in him, but the fact that he had to have a perfect life stomped it out, resurrecting the anger he'd felt the day he'd gone horseback riding.

Rowan was real, fun, honest. What he felt for her was amazing. And he wasn't allowed to feel it?

Art Andino walked into Nevel's office and, glad for the interruption of those morose thoughts, Jozef rose. "Art?" he called to the man who was glancing around Nevel's workspace as if confused. "We're back here."

Art ambled into Jozef's office with a smile. When he saw Rowan, the smile became a scowl. "I'm sorry. I don't mean to interrupt anything."

Confused about why Art would scowl at someone *he'd* hired, Jozef said, "You're not interrupting. Rowan and I were just debriefing about yesterday's date."

He glanced at Rowan, then swung his gaze back to Jozef. "My sources tell me that the date bombed."

Ah, that's why he seemed upset with Rowan. "The date didn't bomb."

"Sources say you behaved more like business acquaintances than people on a date."

"We'd just met that day."

Art peered at Rowan again. Jozef frowned, as Art's gaze skimmed Rowan's haphazard hair and casual clothes. If Mrs. Jones had been the one sent by Castle Admin, she'd be offering Rowan coffee and sharing pleasantries. Art peered at her as if she were gum on his shoe.

Because she dressed down? Because she was American?

Jozef wasn't sure, but he could see the disdain.

"Ms. Gray has done an admirable job of helping me get back into the public eye properly. You of all people shouldn't want me to behave like a starry-eyed simpleton over a woman."

Art's face soured even more.

Deciding to put the man out of his misery, Jozef said, "That's why I've chosen a plan for when I begin dating for real."

Art's gaze crawled back to Jozef. "Dating for real?"

Rowan shifted in her chair so she could speak directly to Art. "We agreed Jozef could pick his own dates after he went on three dates orchestrated by Sterling, Grant, Paris. Julianna Abrahams was a simple, happy date. Paula Mason was a more sophisticated date. I'll choose one more date." She glanced at Jozef and smiled. "Then he's on his own."

Art said, "I see."

"You and Mrs. Jones left the dining room before Rowan and her boss, Pete Sterling, laid all this out. But it makes sense."

"All this dating, Your Majesty…might not be good for your image."

He laughed and winked at Rowan. "I'm sorry, but the whole point of getting me back into the public eye was to keep me in the public eye. Ask Rowan, she'll tell you."

"If he goes back to being a hermit, your subjects will begin wondering about his health again. He needs to stay active."

Art peered at Rowan. She only smiled.

Castle Admin's employee faced Jozef, took a long, disapproving breath and bowed. "We'll talk again, Your Majesty."

He left the room and Rowan groaned. "Man, he's a grump."

"No. He's more like a stuffed shirt. Castle Admin is all about appearances and continuity."

"Continuity?"

"Yes. They work to keep things consistent from one reign to the next."

"I guess that makes sense."

"Every country must keep up with the times, but the world loves tradition and continuity. Castle Admin makes sure the subjects know that for all the ways the world changes there are other ways it stays the same."

"I saw that when looking around yesterday. I saw the castle is majestic and regal, but also historic."

His head tilted and he frowned. "Has anyone actually shown you around?"

"Not really."

"Why don't you let me give you a tour and then we can have lunch."

She shook her head. "I'm not so sure that's a good idea."

He thought she might have been concerned about Art, his horrible reaction to her, but she'd handled him easily. What they'd been discussing before Art arrived, however, wasn't as easily dismissed. "Because I mentioned that I liked you?"

She rose. "As much as I'm curious about the castle, it's my job to protect your reputation. If anyone sees you giving me a tour—"

"We'll remind them that you work for me and I'm showing you around, like a good employer."

"It will still spark rumors."

Being reminded that he couldn't even chat with a

woman who interested him sent a bolt of frustration through him. He remembered the months before he and Annalise went to their parents to arrange a marriage for them. How he couldn't even glance at a girl in his class without rumors starting.

She turned to the door. "I'll see you next week."

She raced out, as she had the night he'd kissed her, and he came to a conclusion that froze his lungs, stopped his heart. He wasn't simply fighting his attraction to her. She was fighting her attraction to him, and it was probably stronger than she'd let on.

Crazy happiness flooded him. She liked him enough that she didn't want to risk spending time with him. It was oxymoron at its finest. He wasn't supposed to be happy that she liked him. It added a layer of complication he couldn't control.

And the kingdom wanted him in control.

The *world* wanted him in control.

But *he* wanted *her*.

# CHAPTER SEVEN

RATHER THAN GO back to her rented apartment, Rowan drove to her office. Without Geoffrey at his desk, the small suite was eerily quiet. Preoccupied with her discussion with Jozef, she barely noticed as she strode inside the tiny space and plopped down on her desk chair.

After Jozef's unexpectedly honest comments that morning, she had serious second thoughts about sending him out with Princess Helaina. She pulled up her notes, all her research on the Princess, who'd been jilted by a cheating husband the year before and she studied them.

She understood Jozef well enough now to know that her original plan of him and Princess Helaina hitting it off, getting married and leaving the whole world grinning with pleasure wasn't going to happen. She'd nudged him into public life with two great women. His reaction had been to say goodbye to Julianna, happy to have met her, but not interested in continuing the relationship, and a more businesslike approach to Paula.

But he planned on continuing to date. He recognized he had to stay in the public eye. And if she was interpreting his discussion with Art Andino correctly, he wasn't looking at this as a time to fall in love. He simply wanted to keep his image intact.

Meaning, Princess Helaina might be the wrong woman to set him up with.

She sat back in her office chair, forcing herself to examine her conscience to make sure she wasn't simply thinking that because she couldn't stand the thought of him going out with a woman for real. Someone who would see him as a partner, a prospective mate.

He was commanding, powerful, sophisticated, sexy and funny. If to nobody but herself, she could easily admit she wanted him for herself. When he'd said he liked her and even admitted he'd thought about a date with her, her entire body had flushed with longing. She'd pictured them, with their walls down, laughing, having fun and rolling in twisted sheets, enjoying the electricity that always crackled between them.

But she couldn't have him.

He'd come right out and said it.

His position wouldn't allow it.

And she'd already had one guy publicly dump her. That was enough. She wasn't opening her heart again. Or even going out with someone who would cause a stir in the entire world when they stopped seeing each other.

That was why she'd declined lunch with him. The more time they spent together, the more she felt their click of attraction and remembered the spark of their first kiss. Only an idiot would blindly walk toward something she couldn't have.

Plus, she had to arrange one more date for him.

Princess Helaina seemed like the best candidate. First the movie star. Then the genius businesswoman. Now a royal. It made perfect sense.

But with Jozef indicating he would continue to date after the final date Rowan arranged—tossing himself into the dating pool like the world's most eligible bachelor—setting him up with Princess Helaina didn't feel right.

She rose from her seat and spun the laptop around so she could see it from the front of her desk, where she began pacing.

Princess Helaina was a starry-eyed dreamer. From the conversations Rowan had had with her, the thirty-something Princess *did* want a man to ride in on a white horse and save her. Her upbringing had made her something of a throwback, and needing a boost after her cheating husband, having someone rescue her seemed like a good idea.

If Rowan fixed her up with King Jozef and he treated her well, like the interesting, nice guy he was, Helaina would be smitten. Then, rather than have the happy ending the Princess longed for, she'd be sitting by the phone, waiting for a call that never came. The papers would undoubtedly make a bigger deal out of it than it needed to be. And her ex would read about it. It would be humiliating.

So, for Princess Helaina's sake, not Jozef's, Rowan would not make this date.

She walked to Geoffrey's office and prepared a cup of tea, pondering who she could get for Jozef's third date. She didn't let herself think beyond that, even though she recognized that his satisfactory outing with Paula Mason might result in him calling the software whiz when he began making his own dates. Which would be great for his image. And Paula's—

The thought upended her heart and suspended her breathing, but she shook her head and put her brain back on the task of coming up with a third date for the world's sexiest man alive—the guy she couldn't have.

Sipping her tea as she paced, she racked her brain, but no one came to mind. On her fiftieth turn from the window to pace back to the wall, she saw Art Andino standing in her doorway.

The shock of seeing him almost made her spill her tea. "Mr. Andino! What can I do for you?"

He stepped inside her office. "I need a moment with you."

She hadn't missed the way he'd been looking at her when he came into Jozef's office and found her chatting with the King. It was almost as if he could see or feel the attraction arching between her and Jozef.

If he was about to lecture her about falling for Prosperita's highest ranking royal, he could save his breath. She already knew nothing would happen there.

Heading for her side of the desk, she motioned to the chair in front of it. "Have a seat."

He gingerly stepped a little farther in the office. "I won't be long."

She placed her tea on her desk. "That's fine."

He sat on the edge of the chair and scowled. "I'm not exactly sure how to put this."

Oh, the damned fool was going to insult her. She stifled the urge to shake her head. She'd handled worse. "Just come right out and say it."

He opened his mouth to speak, but his gaze landed on her laptop screen, turned toward him because she'd been staring at it as she paced.

"Is that Princess Helaina?"

"Yes."

"She's beautiful."

Rowan smiled at the softness that came to his voice. For all his crabbiness, there was a heart in his chest. "Yes. She is."

He looked up from the laptop. "Now, that's really a woman for Jozef. The American actress?" He made a disgusted face. "She was trite and simple. Paula Mason? There would be times when she would overshadow him." He pointed at the screen. "But Princess Helaina? Raised royal. Knows protocols. She'd be a dutiful wife."

"Jozef's not talking about getting married. He's just getting back in the dating pool. And he has to take his time. Do this right."

He caught her gaze again. "You were considering her, though, weren't you?"

"Yes."

He rose. "I want her to be the third date."

"Mr. Andino... Art...this could really backfire. Not for Jozef but for Princess Helaina. He's not looking for someone and he could hurt her. Which would embarrass her—*again*."

"You underestimate the power of tradition, protocol and the comfort of being with someone who understands a life like his."

Not wanting to get into an argument, particularly since she'd already recognized that herself, Rowan said nothing.

"Do you think he isolated himself because he was being moody?" He snorted. "I've watched Jozef from the time he was a boy. I know what happened. Annalise has now been gone five years. His sons are raised. He knew it was time for him to remarry. He brooded at first because he truly loved Annalise. But I can see him coming to his senses."

Rowan frowned. "Coming to his senses?"

He tilted his head, studying her. "You think you're the only person who knows how to read people? When his sons came to me, I easily saw what was happening. I thought hiring you was only a way to wake him up. But you sent him on dates and got him ready to do what he needs to do—remarry. And a grateful nation thanks you."

"Jozef's not your puppet."

"No. But he knows how royalty works. Did he ever tell you the story of why he married Annalise?"

She shook her head.

"They were friends. They ran in the same circles. Both were expected to marry well and the pressure of that made dating miserable. Then one day, they had a conversation and realized they were each other's perfect mate. Not only did they like each other as friends, but each knew how royal life worked. So they made a deal. They would marry and have children and fulfill the responsibilities of their titles. They went to their parents and their parents arranged the marriage."

She scoffed at him. "You just said he loved her—"

"They came to love each other very much. But that wasn't a happy accident. That was two smart people knowing no one else in the world could understand the lives they were forced to live." He straightened in his chair. "I watched all that play out and I see the same signs now as when he and Annalise made their deal. He's lonely and wants someone in his life again, but he's wise enough to know he must choose from his own ilk, and he will."

He rose from his seat. "Set him up with Princess Helaina."

When Rowan didn't show up in the castle for three long days, Jozef knew something was wrong. She'd stayed away the week before his date with Paula Mason, the week after he'd kissed her. But this time he hadn't done anything to make her stay away. Yes, he'd admitted that he liked her but that had folded into normal conversation—

Or maybe not. She'd left the castle quickly, refusing the tour he offered her.

It killed him to think that he'd done something to offend her. He was on the verge of calling her to apologize when his computer pinged with an email.

It was late enough that he should have left it for morning, but when he reached to close his laptop and put it away, he saw the message was from Mrs. Jones and there was an attachment.

It was odd, but he was awaiting the arrangements for his third date from Rowan. If he'd offended her, she might have gone through channels to get in touch with him.

Angry with himself he clicked on the email, but there was nothing in it.

He frowned and glanced at the untitled attachment. Curiosity got the better of him and he opened it. Sure enough, the Sterling, Grant, Paris letterhead popped up. The missive was addressed to Montgomery Robertson, Head of Castle Administration.

Furious that she was arranging his third date through channels, he started reading. When he saw Princess Helaina's name, his frown deepened. As he read the entire text of the email, his blood began to boil and he called the livery.

The night duty driver answered. "Evening, Your Majesty. Is there somewhere you need to go tonight?"

"No. I want to use your car." He didn't often ask for

one of the drivers' vehicles to get an opportunity to go out on his own, but this was important. Infuriating. Something he had to deal with.

"Sir, I brought my old, rusty SUV."

"That's even better. I'll meet you in the garage. Have it ready."

Tired from the day, Rowen ambled to her shower, stripped and stepped under the hot spray, where she stood for twenty minutes. She had the distinct feeling she would be fired in the morning. There'd be no question about her starting her own firm. It would be a necessity. She simply wouldn't get any overflow business or recommendations from Sterling, Grant, Paris.

She got out, dried off and spent twenty minutes drying her long, thick hair, before she stepped into silky pajamas—an indulgence she believed she needed to soothe her soul—and walked into her kitchen to make herself a martini—another appropriate indulgence given the circumstances.

Before she returned to her sofa to watch TV, there was a determined knock on her door. Frowning, she confirmed the late hour on the step tracker on her wrist and walked to the door. "Who is it?"

"Open the door, Rowan. I can't be standing in your hall out in the open like this."

Shocked that Jozef was in her building, she clicked the locks and opened the door. "What are you doing here?"

He stepped inside, closing the door behind him before he said, "I have never been prouder of anyone in my entire life."

Knowing exactly what he was talking about, she winced. "How much did you hear?"

"I got a secret copy of the email you sent to the head of Castle Admin from Mrs. Jones." He laughed heartily. "Not only did you report Art for telling you how to do your job, but also you refused to set me up with Princess Helaina."

"She is pretty." She winced again. "And a catch."

"And depressed. Her husband left her and goes frolicking on the Riviera with his new girlfriend and Princess Helaina's kids. He's been making her a laughingstock for a year."

"She needs someone to give her a boost."

"So, offer your services." He shook his head. "I'll even pay for them. But setting the two of us up would have been a disaster."

"She's already a client. What you said is exactly how I interpreted the situation. Setting you two up would have been a disaster. But are *you* sure?"

"Am I sure of what?"

"That you and Princess Helaina wouldn't have hit it off?"

"Yes. I'm sure. Mostly because we want two different things."

"Really? Art was fairly certain the two of you could…you know… Make a match."

His eyes squinted. "Like get married?"

She squeezed her eyes shut. Then popped them open again to look Jozef in the eye when she made her confession. "Yes."

"Wow." He glanced around the room. "I think I need to sit."

He moved to the sofa and lowered himself to the cushion.

He looked so gobsmacked, Rowan sighed. "You can't be angry with him for that. He thinks you were isolating because you recognized that it was time to remarry, and it made you sad."

"I wasn't sad! I was moody because my sons are men. My job of raising them is done." He took a breath. "It was a perfectly normal reaction. I've heard people call it empty-nest syndrome. My children might still live in the castle, but they are adults now. I wasn't angling to get married."

The horrified way he said it made her laugh out loud, as she sat beside him on the sofa. "It is pretty funny now that you mention it."

"It is not funny."

She laughed all the harder. "Come on. Sure it is. Especially when you consider that it's grumpypants Art Andino picking your mate."

He snorted, then chuckled, then laughed with her. "Yeah. That's rich."

"Hey, maybe you were lucky. He could have chosen an old dowager."

He gave her the side eye. "That's actually what I thought you were going to do."

She gasped. "Really? You were expecting me to pick someone who wasn't suited to you?"

He shrugged. "Now that I know you, I realize you wouldn't do that. You have a great deal of integrity."

"Yeah, well, it might have cost me my job."

"I'd hire you."

She laughed. "Right."

"I would."

She glanced at him. "Then I'd be working full-time with a guy I was attracted to."

"I like that you're attracted to me."

She smiled.

He smiled.

"So you have a limo waiting outside?"

He winced. "I borrowed my driver's banged-up SUV."

Her eyes widened. "You drove?"

"I'm not helpless. Just pampered."

She laughed.

He leaned back on the sofa. "Driving here...*being here*...actually reminds me of when I was a kid, sneaking out, hanging out with all the wrong people."

"I'll bet you were a handful."

He shrugged. "The press was so bad when I was fourteen that I knew dating would be a nightmare."

"Is that why you struck a deal to marry yourself off at eighteen?"

He looked at her.

"Art spilled the beans. It's why he believed you would follow the pattern. Meet a suitable mate and get married again."

He groaned. "That guy's a real thorn in my side."

"You should fire him."

"I just might." He shook his head. "But I'll tell you this. I am scaling back Castle Admin. It's handy to have a bunch of people watching out for things like protocols and such. But they need to get out of my personal life."

She couldn't agree more. With that admission, she also realized her apartment felt different. Their interaction felt different. They weren't in the castle. There was no Castle Admin lurking behind a door. His kids wouldn't interrupt. No photographer would be aiming a high-powered lens at them. Not only had he sneaked out but also her drapes were drawn.

For the first time, they really were alone.

And she was in silky pajamas.

Confusion overwhelmed her for a second, but only a second. They might never have this kind of chance to enjoy each other's company again.

"Would you like a drink?"

She said it casually, not able to guess if he'd say yes or rise from the sofa and tell her it was time to leave. But she didn't want to miss this opportunity to have some real time with him.

# CHAPTER EIGHT

He GLANCED AT her martini glass then back at her. "I don't think one drink would hurt."

He didn't know if he was talking about one drink impairing his ability to drive home or the alcohol content of one drink making them want to rip each other's clothes off. Being alone with a woman he was ridiculously attracted to was so far out of the realm of his normal life that he didn't have a clue. But he did know he liked being here.

He liked being totally alone with her. Where no one would criticize or critique him. He could be himself again.

And her pajamas might be silky, but they were covering.

She rose and made him a martini. "This is basically all I have. One bottle of gin. One bottle of vermouth."

"Classic martini."

She handed him the glass. "I'm not much for sweet drinks. Don't offer me a chocolate martini or some fruity thing."

He laughed, wishing there would come a time he could offer her a drink. But he told himself not to waste the few minutes that he had by wishing for more.

They touched glasses then each took a sip.

"What else did you do today besides torment Castle Admin's most persnickety person?"

She laughed. "Not much. Now that I've sort of bowed out of being your matchmaker, I'll have time to help Axel the way I want to…unless I get fired when Pete goes into work tomorrow and reads that memo."

"I'll see to it that you don't."

She winced. "No. Don't do that."

"That's right. You want to start your own firm."

"Yes. But being fired isn't the optimal way to do it. Especially since I'd like to hang around and help Axel with his fundraiser."

He'd like for her to hang around and help Axel with his fundraiser too. That was three months away. He'd *love* for her to be in Prosperita for another three months.

"But I don't want you to go to bat for me. I can handle myself."

"I also like *that* about you." She was no helpless female. She was a star, who had worked for everything she had. There was something very sexy about that.

"It's kind of my trademark."

"I realized that." He swirled the liquid in his glass. "But you know what? That's about all I know about you. While you know one of the castle's best kept secrets. My wife and I were in an arranged marriage but technically we asked our parents to make the match, so everyone assumes we asked because we were in love." He met her gaze. "You know you have to keep that secret, right? Liam and Axel don't know."

She nodded.

And he knew she was as good as her word.

He also liked that about her, but they were getting

dangerously close to him liking everything about a woman he barely knew. Maybe if she'd tell him something awful about herself, he'd feel better about not being able to date her.

"I'd love to know more about you."

She curled up on her side of the sofa, tucking her legs beneath her as she sipped her drink. "Well, I left my small town in West Virginia for New York City when I was twenty-two." She paused and the expression on her face said there was more to the story, but she smiled brightly and glossed over it. "I didn't have a job, didn't know anyone and ran through most of my savings the first few months I was there.

"But I got a job and found a roommate. Then the next thing I knew I was clicking with the work. My bosses took notice, and I was promoted and soon I was handling entire campaigns. Then Sterling, Grant, Paris recruited me for a job at their main office in Paris, and I thought, why not?"

That didn't sound good. "Why not?"

"Why not move to Europe."

"Oh." The excitement in her voice made him believe she wasn't running from something, as he might have assumed from that weird pause when she started her story. More than that, though, it was clear she loved what she did and had no regrets.

From personal experience he knew she was good at it. Still, he wanted to know more. Wanted to hear the little things that made her who she was.

"Did you have a dog when you were a kid?"

She laughed. "What?"

"A dog, a cat, a gopher named Skippy?"

"A gopher named Skippy?" She laughed heartily. "You know, Your Majesty, you have an odd sense of humor."

"It's easy to get an odd sense of humor when half the known world is watching your every move."

"You have to laugh or you'll cry?"

"No. Nothing so serious. It's just plain weird."

And being with her, alone, in her apartment did not feel weird at all.

Which probably meant he should go before he started thinking this was okay.

He polished off his drink and stood up. "I must get Randal's car back to him."

"The rusty SUV?"

"That's the one."

She smiled. "I'm glad you came."

"I'm glad you shot Art Andino down when he wanted to do something incredibly stupid."

She grinned. "What can I say? I love my work."

He laughed and she walked him to the door. He stopped to grab the doorknob but the strongest urge to kiss her good-night overtook him and he turned to her. Before she could protest or even say good-night, he leaned in and brushed his lips against hers. She slid her hand to his shoulder and opened her mouth slightly so they could deepen the kiss.

He fell into it as if kissing her were as natural as breathing. He hadn't ever had an experience like this, and he couldn't believe he now missed it.

Craved it.

Really craved the heat and need tumbling through him.

He broke the kiss and looked into her eyes. "Thank you again, bravest, smartest person I know."

She snorted. "Let's not go overboard."

He turned, opened the door and left. Walking down the hall, he waited to hear her apartment door close, but he didn't hear it. He stepped into the stairwell, realizing she might have watched him leave and his heart lifted.

It was the craziest feeling to think about how much he liked her. Warm and fuzzy, but also thrumming with heart-pounding desire.

And wrong. He couldn't forget wrong.

Not wasting any time on the dark street, he raced to the rusty SUV. It was late, and the street was empty, but he didn't want to risk someone coming around a corner and seeing him.

He got behind the wheel, started the SUV and drove away, then he burst out laughing. He'd be lying if he didn't admit the risk of it was almost as much fun as seeing Rowan had been.

And seeing her had been amazing. No camera. No expectation. He had been himself.

Again.


The next day when he ran into her racing to Axel's office, late for a meeting, she stopped and said, "Good morning, Your Majesty."

"Good morning, Rowan. I'm guessing you're here to see Axel."

"Yes. Now that my work for you is done, Axel and I intend to make this year's festival the best ever."

He struggled not to stare into her eyes, as giddy happiness nearly overtook him. Having a secret, especially a secret relationship was fun—and he had to call it a relationship. They talked about real things. Truths he never spoke of with another person. She was a trusted confidante. Not just someone he desperately wanted to touch.

"I'm going that way too." He motioned toward the hall. "We can walk together."

They started down the hall. Feeling devilish, he said, "How was your night?"

She almost tripped over her own feet. "Excuse me?"

"Do anything interesting last night?"

She laughed. "I did have an unexpected visitor."

"Business or pleasure?"

She faced him. "Stop. Really." But her command was totally declawed by the laughter he saw in her eyes.

They reached Axel's office. He almost said, "I'll see you later," because it was the natural thing to say to someone when you parted company. But he wouldn't see her later. They no longer worked together. There was no reason for her to pop into his office.

Their secret relationship was over before it started.

That night, Rowan sat on her sofa and opened her laptop to review the long list of notes she and Axel had made in their protracted meeting. The kid might look like a slouch, but this project was his baby and he intended to do it right.

Evidenced by the myriad public relations tasks he'd found for Rowan.

She read them, categorized them by order, relevance and importance and then assigned deadlines.

A knock on her apartment door had her head jerking up. Setting her laptop on the sofa she called, "Who is it?"

"It's me."

*Jozef.*

She pressed her lips together to keep from laughing as she walked to the door. He stood in the hallway, dressed in the red and blue shirt he'd worn to the soccer game and holding a bottle of wine.

"I brought this. It's not a sweet fruity drink. It's one of the most expensive bottles in my collection."

"You collect wine?"

"It would be un-kingly if I didn't. I've made many connections by starting up a conversation about wine. Knowing wine, collecting special vintages is a badge of honor. You'd be surprised how many of your presidents stumble over something Europeans take for granted."

She chuckled and stepped aside so he could enter. "Is there something you need?"

"Actually, I liked last night's freedom so much I decided to repeat it."

She didn't know whether to be happy or proud of him. The more they talked casually, the more she liked it. But she had to watch herself with him. Now that his empty-nest syndrome had worked itself out, he could admit he was looking for something. Or maybe testing his newfound freedom. After last night's visit, it was clear he needed somewhere to go, and he knew where she lived.

She couldn't make anything more of it than that.

"Got the rusty SUV?"

"No. Orlando was working today. He drives a truck."

"A truck?"

"Beast of a thing. But that might have actually made my escape even better. No one is going to expect me behind the wheel of something that has mud flaps."

A laugh spilled out, as he confirmed her suspicions.

"Ah. I get it. It's like sneaking off to a friend's house before your mom tells you to do the dishes."

"Do the dishes?"

"Wash the dishes."

He nodded, but he clearly didn't understand the unmitigated needs of an American teenager who always seemed to be confronted by a sink full of dishes that held her back from escaping to hang out with her friends.

She led him into the small kitchenette, where she retrieved glasses. "You don't know what fun is until you've spent your teen years plotting to get out of chores."

He poured wine into the glasses and handed one to her. "A toast. To escapes. I'm only now seeing how much fun they are."

She motioned to her sofa, a bit saddened that his attraction seemed to be all about his newfound freedom. He followed her into the cubbyhole that was the living room of her cramped rental apartment. She set her glass on the coffee table, then removed the laptop.

They sat.

"So…" She peeked over at him. "Change the world today?"

He thought about it, and she realized he'd taken the question seriously because the things he did really did change the world.

"There's a trade agreement that's hung up."

"Are you going to sweep in and kick somebody's ass for being slow?"

"No. The plan is to let them think they're winning until shipments from Prosperita stop." He leaned in. "Let's see how they do without tropical fruit."

She laughed and he sat back, getting comfortable. In her ugly sitting area.

Silence stretched out between them. Their ability to talk had fizzled into nothing, as he sat silently beside her.

Finally, he set his wine on the table. "I probably shouldn't have come here."

Disappointment rattled through her. Her attraction was alive and well. But his had been nothing but a longing to get out of the castle. "It's fine."

"No. It's not. It's dangerous."

"You think someone's going to burst in and shoot us?"

He shook his head. "No. No one knows I'm here." He sucked in a breath. "It's dangerous because I want to do this." He slid his hand under her hair and pulled her to him for a long lingering kiss.

Happiness exploded inside her. He hadn't lost his attraction to her—

The movement of his mouth over hers blocked out anything but the desire that roared through her veins and caused her to glide her fingers through his thick, dark hair, as they both slid down on the couch.

His mouth devoured hers while his hands roamed her sides and her hands slipped from his shoulders to his hips, where they stopped suddenly.

"Don't stop."

Her breath stuttered. "I don't want to stop, but I—"

"Don't say it. Don't say you feel uncomfortable because I'm who I am. Damn it. Some nights I just want to be me."

The smidgen of anger that came through hit her right in the heart. She'd left her small town because being herself would have been living a Greek tragedy. She had the option of leaving, reinventing herself, creating a whole new life.

He didn't.

She pressed her palms to either side of his face and pulled him to her for a hot, hungry kiss. She'd wanted to be with him from the day she'd met him. It wasn't merely foolish to pretend otherwise, it would hurt him.

"We could take this back to the bedroom."

He broke away, studied her face.

"You don't think you're sexy enough that most women want to sleep with you?"

"I don't want most women. I want you."

It was the sexiest thing anyone had ever said to her. Arousal pooled in her middle. Her breath became shaky.

She kissed him again until every muscle and joint tingled with need. Then he scooped her off the sofa and carried her to the bed.

They desperately undressed each other. When they were finally flesh to flesh, her breath fluttered out. His hands roamed from her chest to her belly button, followed by his warm mouth.

She wasn't about to let him have all the fun. A bump of the heel of her hand against his shoulder knocked him off-balance enough that she could tumble him to his back. Before he could react, she levered herself up so she could kiss him, and her hands could be the ones sliding along his muscular torso.

He only let her have control for a minute or two before reversing their positions again and soon they became like two eager puppies, wrestling for control with both of them winning.

When their hearts were racing and their skin tingled

with need, he shifted them enough that he was on top of her. Looking into her eyes, he said, "You are beautiful. Too tempting to resist." Then he leaned in and kissed her again, as he joined them.

Her breath stuttered out as the amazing feeling of him filling her sent happy arousal careening through her.

# CHAPTER NINE

TANGLED UP IN the softest sheets he'd ever felt with the most beautiful, sexiest woman he'd ever met curled against him, Jozef lifted the corner of the sheet. "I don't think these came with the apartment."

Pressed against his side, she laughed and snuggled closer. "No. I bring those wherever I go. When you travel as much as I do, it's good to have something that makes you feel at home."

He agreed, but too soon trepidation began stealing his joy. He'd gotten so caught up in her that he'd let his instincts run wild, and while it was undoubtedly the most intense, incredible sexual experience he'd ever had, it also tiptoed so close to being godawful wrong that he had absolutely no idea how to handle it.

"I haven't ever done anything like this."

"Sleep with someone you work with?"

"Sleep with someone I'm not married to."

She sat up, bringing the sheet with her to cover her soft, soft skin. "Are you telling me you've only ever slept with your wife?"

He laughed, his tension easing enough that happiness began bubbling through him. "You have to realize everything I did was under scrutiny. There wasn't a place I could take a woman that wouldn't be seen."

"Wow."

He heard the surprised confusion in her voice. He knew he was an anomaly to her, which meant she also had to realize how very, very attracted he was to her to risk so much to have her. Yet, their stations in life were so vastly different that he had no idea of their endgame.

He knew the biology of why he'd taken the risk. Anytime she was within two feet, his heart stuttered and his blood pounded through his veins.

But she was younger than he was. An American. An independent workingwoman who wouldn't understand the restrictions of royal life.

She lay back down and traced her finger across his chest. "I think I'm honored." She peeked at him. "You're this great combination of intelligence and good looks that I just—" She shrugged. "I find it very sexy."

Unable to resist temptation, he rolled himself to his side and flipped her onto her back again. "You do?"

She gave him a smile that sent a shaft of lightning through him. "Yes. I do."

To hell with logic. This did not feel like the time for it. It felt like the time to indulge, be decadent with a woman who felt the same things he did.

He kissed her deeply and this time made love slowly and thoroughly. He banished the flash of conscience that told him there would be consequences to this indulgence. He let himself plunge into the depths of her sweet warmth and turned off his brain.

But when they were both out of breath lying side by side on the pillows again, it switched on. Logical fear bubbled up. Not that she'd sell her story to the tabloids.

She was too honorable to do that. But she was young. So young. And he had sons almost her age.

There really could be nothing between them.

"I've wanted to do that with you since the day I met you."

He closed his eyes and savored her words. That was what he'd liked about her the best. She'd never let him be King Jozef. He'd always been her client. A guy she was brutally honest with. Forcing him to be brutally honest with her.

And now here they were. Maybe only for this night.

This was not the time to change the way they behaved with each other.

He pushed himself up on his elbows. "I've wanted to do that since the day I met you too."

She laughed wickedly. "That means we're good. Stop overanalyzing."

"Is that what I'm doing?"

"I can almost hear the gears turning in your brain."

"Because I have responsibilities and obligations." He hated that reminding her of that was part of being honest. He took a breath, forced it out of his lungs in a long sigh. "If I were normal, I'd lay down, wrap myself around you and fall asleep until morning." He swung his legs over the side of the bed. "But I'm not normal. I rule a country."

She sat up. "I know."

He stepped into his pants. "Then you know I have to leave."

"Yes."

"And you're not offended?"

She had the good graces not to lie. "I don't know what I am. But I do realize the uniqueness of your circumstances. And if you're asking if I'm mad that you're leaving, the answer is no."

His shirt half-buttoned, he stared at her.

"I get it. Anything we have is going to be different. In fact, this night might be all we get. So, think it through, Jozef."

Her bluntness rendered him speechless.

"Before we do anything like this again, think through what you want. What we can have. What we can't. So we'll both know where we stand."

He left, jumped into the big truck and headed back to the castle, driving in through the servants' entrance.

He climbed the circular stairway for the first time in a long time not feeling alone or empty.

He knew their relationship was what he needed. He also knew their relationship was doomed.

So what did he want? What did he honestly believe they could have?

Rowan woke the next morning and stretched like a cat. Then she remembered why she was naked and unreasonably happy and she groaned. Had she really told a king he needed to think about what he wanted?

She had.

Well, that was who she was. Outspoken. Maybe a tad too bold. After her ex, no one, not even a one-night stand would surprise her.

She strode to the shower acknowledging that given their circumstances, this could only be a one-night stand. Disappointment washed over her like the hot spray, but she focused on washing her hair and getting herself ready for work.

When she arrived, Geoffrey handed her a cup of

coffee and shepherded her into her office to the video call with the Paris staff that had been already set up.

She took her seat and addressed the faces on her computer screen. "Good morning."

Everyone came to attention. A couple of years ago, she'd been dreaming of the day she'd command this much respect and have authority over the projects she was assigned. Today, she thought of Jozef and realized that, though she understood being the boss and having responsibility, it was only a fraction of the pressure he felt.

"Rowan?"

Geoffrey poked her, startling her back into the real world.

"I'm sorry. I zoned out for a minute."

They continued the call, with Rowan forcing her mind off Jozef and onto the conversations.

When they finally disconnected, Geoffrey said, "What's wrong with you today?"

"Nothing."

"Your cheeks are pink. There's a spring in your step. Did you go out last night? Maybe have a few too many drinks? That would explain the spring in your step and the loss of focus caused by a hangover."

She packed her files and notes into her briefcase. "No. I did not go out last night." But now that he'd mentioned it, she would have to be careful at the castle this afternoon. There wasn't any way she could change the color of her cheeks, but she could monitor the spring in her step.

She drove to the castle and walked through the front foyer and down the corridor, nervous, hoping she wouldn't giggle like a schoolgirl if she ran into Jozef.

She wasn't concerned for herself. She didn't want to embarrass *him*.

She'd never given any thought to the real life of a king or how his girlfriends would have to comport themselves and, to be honest, that was more than disconcerting.

But she didn't run into him, and Axel awaited her with open arms. With his hair pulled back in a low ponytail, he rose as she entered his office.

"Good morning, best helper a prince ever had."

She laughed. "You don't have to be charming anymore. I already like you."

He chuckled as he motioned for her to join him at the conference table set up in the lefthand corner of his office. He became serious when they got down to the business of creating a few press release articles about the festival that Rowan would get strategically placed into magazines and high-profile newspapers like the *New York Times*.

He read her drafts, had a good bit of input based on his knowledge of past festivals and even improved her verbiage.

She sat back with a smile. "You're a natural at this."

"Luckily," he said with a cheeky grin. "It gives me a way to look official."

She laughed as his phone buzzed with a text.

"Go ahead. Check it." She rose and stretched her back, which appreciated the movement after hours of sitting. "It's time I packed up and got back to my office anyway."

"Don't tell me you'll be working into the night."

"I do have other projects I'm supervising long-distance. I'll go back to my office to find progress reports that I need to read before my video call with staff in the morning."

"A public relations person's work is never done."

She laughed. "You don't know the half of it."

He chuckled and glanced down at his phone. "It's Nevel. Dad's assistant."

"Oh." She nonchalantly picked up some files, hoping to disguise the weird thump of her heart when he mentioned his father. The incredibly sexy guy who'd come to her apartment and swept her off her feet.

*That was a one-night stand.*

The reminder served to get her attention back on Axel, but the warm syrupy feelings that floated through her when she merely thought about Jozef stayed.

"They want me in the office." He stowed his phone in his jeans pocket. "I'll see you tomorrow."

"Tomorrow's Saturday, but I can work." She slid the long strap of her briefcase onto her arm. "Technically, you get me every afternoon until you think you're ready for the festival, then I'll disappear as easily as I came."

Walking to the door, he said, "Thank you. I think your help taking the public relations end of this festival out to the world will change the event from local entertainment to a reason for tourists to come to Prosperita."

"That's good."

"It is. I want it to be the kind of tourist attraction that travelers plan trips around. Our country is small, but we're important. Some days I think no one understands how important my dad is."

She'd thought the same thing.

This time when she thought of Jozef, it wasn't a vision of kissing him. She saw that moment when he'd led Paula Mason into his conference room. When he'd caught her gaze and reminded her of who he was. A king. A world leader.

Her breath stumbled, but she was glad for the reminder. There were not two Jozef Sokels. One she could have and one she couldn't. He was one person. A king. And she needed to remember that.

Axel stepped into Jozef's office and he frowned. "Jeans?"

Jozef's second son fell to one of the chairs in front of his desk. "They are work clothes and I was working. Rowan came by so we could make plans for the festival."

Just thinking about Rowan being in the castle had Jozef's stomach falling to the floor. He'd sneaked out the night before, gone to the apartment of a beautiful woman and slept with her. Not that he believed sleeping with her was wrong. It had been the best thing he'd done in a long time.

But he'd sneaked out—

Had begun an affair.

With someone everyone in the castle knew.

When he should have been worried, the idea suddenly struck him as funny. He'd awakened feeling energized. His mood had been all sunbeams and silliness. Not very kingly, but he'd been feeling off center for so long that the lift had been—

Wonderful.

Axel broke into his thoughts. "So why are we here?"

"Your grandmother's birthday is in slightly less than two weeks. Your grandfather wants a ball."

"He wants the staff to put together a ball in slightly less than two weeks?"

"It's not like they haven't ever done it before. My father asks for very little. We will accommodate him."

Axel gasped. "You know who we should get to help?"

Liam frowned. Jozef almost groaned.

"Rowan."

Jozef recovered quickly. "She's not a party planner. She's a public relations person and a damn good one. We don't want to diminish what she does or make her feel like she's our personal property."

Axel whined, "All right."

"Castle Admin will take care of inviting all the right people, but you each get a few guests. The usual rules apply. Think through who you want to invite because Castle Admin will be vetting them."

Liam said, "Yes, Dad. I remember."

Axel slouched down in his chair. "You know who we should invite?"

"I said you could pick anyone you want. Just be aware they will be vetted—"

"Rowan."

Jozef fought the urge to squeeze his eyes shut.

"I like her. She makes everything fun."

Liam tilted his head. "I like her too." He raised his gaze to meet Jozef's. "I wouldn't mind if she were invited."

Jozef shook his head. "Let's not get carried away. If we invite her, we also have to invite her boss and probably four or five other higher-ups in her firm, so no one is insulted." He rose to indicate his sons were dismissed. "You know nothing is simple for us. We don't want to put Rowan in an odd position at her job."

Though she was quitting, no one knew that.

Except him.

He knew one of her secrets. It both buoyed him and sent a feeling of responsibility through him.

Axel grinned. "Her bosses should thank her for getting them invited."

Liam agreed. "It's the perfect way to thank her for stepping in the way she did. You know, she fixed things without ever once making us feel like idiots."

Damn it. Jozef agreed.

He also knew if he protested too much his sons would wonder why.

# CHAPTER TEN

ELEVEN O'CLOCK THAT NIGHT, Rowan answered a knock at her door and found Jozef in her hallway. This time he wore an old baseball cap and what looked to be his oldest jeans and a shirt that could have been a dust rag.

"You really don't want anyone to recognize you, do you?"

"Actually, *you* don't want anyone to recognize me. If the press discovered I was visiting you, they'd be all over you." He paused. "But you know that."

She led him into her small sitting area. "I do."

He casually sat beside her.

"So what's up?"

"My sons are insisting you be invited to a ball we're hosting for my mother's birthday in two weeks."

She knew his parents were still alive because she'd done her homework before she took this assignment. After a mild heart attack, his father had retired so Jozef could step up and take the throne. His mother would be turning seventy.

"That's right. She'll be seventy. I guess that warrants a party."

Even as she thought that, she remembered her dad's

birthday party. The one she couldn't go to. She never returned to the place of her great humiliation.

But she suddenly wanted to. She missed her dad and her mom. And her brother and sister. She'd been gallivanting around the globe for eight years, perfectly happy. Why would she pick now to be homesick?

"My dad wants a party and Axel thinks we need to invite you to thank you for all you've done."

She brushed away the silly notion that she might be homesick and put herself back into the conversation. "There's no need to thank me. Especially for helping Axel. Not only is this a Sterling, Grant, Paris account for which you will be billed. But also, Axel is a very smart guy."

Jozef laughed. "He hides it well. Deliberately. His brother will be King, and as you know perceptions are everything for us. Liam must be seen as the smart, stable Prince."

"You think Axel's behavior is an act?"

"Oh, no. He's still a smartass, rebellious womanizer. He downplays his intelligence when Liam is around."

She laughed and struggled with the urge to kiss him. He was a king and she swore to herself she would never again forget that, but he was still a good dad.

A king. A sexy guy. A good dad.

She wasn't having trouble keeping his roles straight, but the more private talks they had the more sides she saw of him and the more she realized how much she liked him.

"Can I make you a martini?"

"You still have the gin?"

"Yes." She rose and walked to the kitchenette where she made two martinis. Handing him one, she sat beside him on the sofa. "Tell me about this ball. Do you want me to go?"

"I would love to have you there."

"Then why'd you feel the need to come and warn me I was being invited."

He glanced at his drink, glanced at her. "I thought it was a very good, very valid excuse to come and see you."

Her chest tightened. He had the most wonderful way of making her feel wanted. She supposed a sense of identity was the one thing she'd missed as she globe-trotted making other people feel special. It might also be the reason for her homesickness. In Convenience, she'd been an elementary school teacher. Everybody knew her. Everybody liked her. It was why her great humiliation had been so great.

"I thought about you all day." He shook his head. "I'm pretty sure I was also wearing a silly grin."

"My assistant told me my cheeks were pink and there was a spring in my step."

He laughed. Then sobered as he met her gaze. "Yesterday was nice."

"It was."

"I'm not sure of the protocol of one-night stands." He snickered. "I married young. I never got a chance to be a…player."

She laughed at the careful way he said, *player.*

"It's why the arrangement with Annalise made sense and why everything about you flummoxes me."

"I flummox you?"

"I only ever had these kinds of feelings for the woman I was married to. I've never been so hot for a stranger."

That made her laugh out loud. "Seriously?"

"I was just so proud of you for sticking by your guns and so impressed with your integrity in protecting Princess Helaina, and we had such a good time that night that I'd only come to your house to talk…but…" He shrugged. "I like you. The way you handled Princess Helaina was part of it."

"Thank you. You know I went through a whole crisis of conscience over it and had to very thoroughly consider why I was doing it."

"Really?"

She shook her head. "Of course! Jozef, the second I saw you my heart skipped a beat. I had to make sure I really was protecting her, not jumping on a convenient excuse, so I could keep you for myself."

He looked stunned by what she'd said and clearly couldn't find words to describe how he felt. "Are you telling me I'm irresistible?"

"No. If I'd had to, I would have resisted you…kept my distance." She looked at her hands, then back up at him. "I know nothing will come of this. We have an age difference, a class difference and two totally different career paths."

Brave suddenly, she slid her hands up his shoulders and clasped them at the back of his neck. "But we like each other. And working with Axel gives us three whole months, if we want them. If we don't make a big deal out of this, we can enjoy each other before I have to move on."

He put his hands on her waist. "You have to move on?"

"Starting my own company, remember?"

He leaned in, kissed her. "I remember. Your ambition is another of the things I like about you."

The kiss went on and on. His hands dropped to her waist and nudged her closer. She slid her arms to his shoulders again.

He unexpectedly broke the kiss. "I thought I was the one who was supposed to figure out what I wanted."

"You were."

"But you figured it all out for us."

She shrugged. "It's my job to think through personal situations. Your job is to keep the world safe and happy." She shrugged again. "But I think you would have realized we shouldn't miss this chance with each other."

"An affair sounds tawdry."

"You're using the wrong words. Let me give you the right PR spin. A match between us is impossible. But we like each other. So this space of time that we have is not tawdry. It's a gift."

He considered that. "I like your way of looking at things."

"So do I." She rose, gathering both of their martini glasses. "Let's not waste any time."

She put their glasses in the little dishwasher and when she turned, he was standing behind her. He pulled her to him and kissed her, turning them so they were pointed in the direction of the small bedroom.

Kissing and unbuttoning buttons, they made their way down the hall. Almost at the bed, he yanked off his shirt and she got rid of her jeans. She fell to the mattress with a giggle and he joined her.

He didn't ask any more questions about how she felt. She'd been clear and she knew him well enough to see that he believed her. He trusted her.

As the shimmer of desire began to take her, another level of intimacy entered their relationship. *He trusted her.* With his secrets. With his heart, even if it was only temporarily.

And whether she understood it or not, she also trusted him. She hadn't trusted anyone since Cash. Not even her parents. No one really knew what she did. Oh, they knew her job description, but she'd never told them about the people she'd met or the scrapes out of which she had to yank them. She'd told herself she kept her clients' dalliances quiet to protect them.

But really, she simply had lost her faith in humanity. Kept herself on the sidelines. Said all the right things. Did all the right things. Without letting anyone close.

Now here she was, not merely naked and being caressed by a king. She trusted him.

The idea sent a shiver of fear through her. The last person she'd trusted—the last *man* she'd trusted had all but ruined her.

Still, as his hands found her breasts and their kiss became so hungry her breath stuttered, she knew she would not let this chance pass her by.

Though their parting would probably shatter her.

More than losing Cash had.

Rowan seemed overly bright the next day when she arrived at the castle for a four o'clock meeting with Axel. Jozef "just happened" to be in the foyer when she entered, only because he wanted to see her. The way he felt about her sometimes scared him, but he remembered she was as logical as a person could be. She hadn't forced him to see their relationship would end.

She had eased him into realizing they had the gift of a few weeks together and they shouldn't waste it.

Wanting to see even a glimpse of her was part of the time he didn't want to waste.

"Good afternoon, Rowan."

She juggled her briefcase, purse and some loose files that she carried on her arm, clearly ready to work. "Good afternoon, Your Majesty."

"Here for a meeting with my son?"

"Yes. I believe we're briefing with your tourism board."

"On a Saturday?"

She shrugged. "I didn't have anything else to do. Seemed like a good time to fit it in."

"Well, the tourism board is made up of good people. They'll love you. Especially since you're helping them."

She laughed and he smiled. God help him, he could look at her all day.

But he knew he shouldn't. "I'll let you get to your meeting."

"Thank you, Your Majesty."

He turned to head up the stairs to his residence. When he reached the door, he paused. She'd be in her meeting at least two hours, which took them to six o'clock. What if he could get her to sneak up the back stairs and come to his home?

The idea appealed so much a ridiculous smile formed. There was something about seeing her among his things, in his bed, that made him outrageously happy.

He knew it was dangerous. Not that he worried some-one would see her but that she'd leave memories all through his quarters, things he'd have to fight when she left—

He'd be fine. And he wanted to spend time with her in his house. If he were clever, he could even have the kitchen prepare dinner for them.

He took out his phone and texted her.

What time do you think your meeting will end?

After only a few seconds, his phone pinged.

This might go to seven. Sorry.

No need to be sorry. I was thinking you should come to the residence after your meeting.

This response took a little longer. Not sure if she was busy and not able to text or if she was considering the ramifications of going to his apartment, he paced while he waited.

Finally, his phone pinged.

I'm not sure how sneaky I can be.

He decided her coming to his apartment was too risky.

Never mind. We'll do our usual. Except I'll bring food.

Another few minutes passed. He told himself not to pace but he couldn't help himself. He'd been at her apartment three times that week. Maybe she wanted some time away from him?

His phone pinged.

No. I'll be up when the meeting is over.

Reading her response, he breathed a sigh of relief. Then he phoned the kitchen and asked for chicken and rice, a salad and wine. Knowing they'd send enough for two, he strolled to his office and worked until ten till seven. Right on time, his dinner arrived at his apartment. The kitchen worker set his place at the table in his dining room, and when he scurried away, Jozef retrieved another place setting from the butler's pantry and set a place for Rowan.

She arrived in his residence with a smile, and he pulled her to him and kissed her hard.

"Thank you for coming."

She dropped her briefcase, purse and files to one of the chairs in the sitting room. "A few times of you sneaking out of the castle might go unnoticed, but if we're going to do this for three months, we need a strategy."

Her use of the word *sneaking* reminded him he hadn't told her to come up the back stairs. Worry lit his nerve endings, but he knew she'd probably been careful, and she hadn't mentioned anyone seeing her, so he forgot it as he escorted her to the dining room.

It wasn't until they were sitting that he noticed the brightness of her cheeks and the dullness of her eyes.

She smiled as she inhaled their dinner. "This smells delicious."

"It's one of my favorites."

He took a bite of his salad, but she sat looking at the plate as if it were a foreign object.

"Are you okay?"

She shook her head as if to rouse herself. "Yes. I'm fine."

He could see she wasn't. He rose from his seat. "You are not fine. What's wrong?"

She closed her eyes and blew out a long breath. He didn't think she was going to say anything but she finally admitted, "I have a headache. I get them sometimes."

"I'm sorry. Had I known that I wouldn't have pushed for you to come here."

"It's fine."

"Is it a migraine?"

She winced. "No. Usually it's tension."

"So why don't we skip dinner and relax in the den?"

"No. You waited for me to eat. Plus, I should eat something."

He hesitated but sat again.

He picked up his fork. She reluctantly mimicked his move.

Hoping to take her mind off her headache, he said, "What did you do today?"

"Before my meeting with Axel?"

He nodded.

"I'm back on the case for Princess Helaina."

That surprised him. "You are?"

"Yes. Remember I told you she's a client? So far, we haven't been able to do anything substantial, but I finally got an idea. This time, I'm not thinking dates. I talked her out of trying to find another romance. Given that her husband is flaunting his relationship, especially when he has their children, I thought we'd go the other way."

"Other way?"

"We're setting it up so she can take her kids to a theme park, a private US beach and a few national parks. They are going to do a few weeks of healthy, normal, parent-kid stuff."

He laughed. "I get it. You're calling him out. Making him look sleazy."

"Sort of. The aim is more to make Helaina look like a good mom. But if we make her ex look sleazy, it's a perk. Her husband is scum."

"It's my understanding she was advised against marrying him."

Her gaze lifted and met his. "It was a love match?"

He saw a hundred things in her eyes. Mostly, a connection to them. To the myriad reasons they couldn't have a real relationship even though there was clearly something between them.

"Yes. It was a love match. Not all royals shy away from them. They do happen and they do work out... sometimes."

She said, "Hmm," then glanced at her food.

She hadn't taken as much as a taste, while he'd eaten several hearty bites. He set his fork down. "Come on. You look awful. Not even well enough to drive yourself home." He rose and pulled out her chair for her. "What do you say, you go lie down."

He knew she felt worse than she was letting on when she didn't argue. He walked her back to the hall and led her into his bedroom. She stepped inside and stopped. Her gaze lit on the picture of Annalise.

She faced him. "This is your room."

"Yes."

"Your Majesty..."

"Stop with that. I sleep in your room when I'm at your apartment. I'm not putting you in a guest room."

She didn't look strong enough to argue, so he guided her to the bed, pulled her blouse over her head and ditched the cute skirt. Then he sat her down and removed her shoes.

She half laughed. "I feel like Cinderella."

"Don't worry. I'm not keeping your shoes."

She laughed again, but he pulled back the covers and lowered her to the pillow. "Try to sleep."

She nodded, her eyes closing immediately.

Worry flitted through him as he closed the door and returned to the dining room, but he told himself not to be silly. Or, worse, overprotective. Still, he didn't stop himself from checking up on her, his heart stumbling with fear every time he tucked the covers under her chin, and she didn't as much as flinch. Her shallow breathing alarmed him, but when she began tossing and turning, groaning as if she were in enormous pain, he couldn't stand by and do nothing.

He grabbed his phone and called his physician. When he realized it was Saturday night, he winced. "George, any chance you can make a house call tonight?"

"Of course, Your Majesty."

Without any further comment, the doctor disconnected the call and was at the door to Jozef's residence in fewer than fifteen minutes.

As he stepped inside the sitting room, he frowned. "You don't look sick."

"I'm not." He winced. "I'm counting on your discretion here."

George straightened as if insulted. "You do not even have to ask, Your Majesty."

He motioned for the doctor to follow him down the hall. "I had a friend who came to dinner tonight." He didn't stumble over the explanation. Technically, that was what had happened. "She told me she had a headache. But I could see in her eyes it was something more. She's been sleeping for four hours and doesn't seem any better."

They walked into the bedroom and Jozef tried not to flinch when George looked at her. With her bra straps visible above the blanket, George would know she was only wearing underwear. Still, she could have taken off her clothes herself.

That didn't explain why she was in his bed, not one of the five guest rooms. But he was a king. He didn't have to explain himself.

Using a scanning thermometer, George took her temperature. "Normal." He turned to Jozef. "Did you give her any over the counter pain relievers?"

"No. Should I have?"

"Maybe. But if she didn't take any pain meds and doesn't have a fever, she might have a simple headache."

"She said she thought it might be a tension headache."

"Any history of migraines?"

"I asked her if it was a migraine and she said no. I'm guessing if she had a history of migraines, she would have mentioned it."

He nodded.

Rowan stirred. "Jozef?"

"I'm here," he said, jumping to attention when she woke. "Are you okay?"

"Yeah." She tried to sit up, saw George and yanked

the covers to her neck again. She said, "What time is it?" but she looked at George suspiciously.

"Around midnight," Jozef said. "And this is George Montgomery. He's the royal physician. When you didn't move for hours, then started thrashing around, I worried that something was wrong."

George interrupted him. "*Is* there something wrong, Rowan?"

Rowan didn't hesitate. "I had very little sleep last night and a long day today."

"She's working with Axel," Jozef supplied.

"I just have a headache."

George nodded. "Are you feeling better now that you've slept?"

"Yes."

He snapped his bag closed. "Take some over the counter pain relievers and get some more sleep," he said and headed for the door. "You should be fine in the morning."

As the doctor left, Jozef hastily told Rowan, "Give me a minute and I'll get the pain relievers," then followed George out.

Walking to the entryway, George said, "I have a feeling anyone who works with Axel ends up with a headache."

Jozef laughed. "Axel's not that bad."

"No. He's not bad at all. But the kid's a go-getter. If he's in charge of the festival this year, he probably wants it perfect."

"He's trying to turn it into Prosperita's signature tourist event." Jozef grimaced. "And Rowan is our PR person."

"Okay. Mystery solved."

They reached the door. "I'm sorry to have bothered you, George."

"Jozef, after Annalise, I understand why you'd be jumpy."

"You don't think I overreacted?"

"Oh, you overreacted. But given your history, that's to be expected."

Jozef waited a second for a recrimination of some sort, but knew the doctor wouldn't interfere in his private business. It would be an insult to suggest he had to worry about his loyalty. "Good night, George."

"Good night, Your Majesty. And may I say one last thing?"

Jozef hesitated, but eventually he nodded.

"I understand you being jumpy about illnesses. But sometimes a horse is just horse. Don't start looking for zebras in a world of horses."

Jozef laughed, George left and Jozef closed the door behind him. When he returned to his bedroom, Rowan was asleep again. He gathered pain relievers and a glass of water on the table beside her bed, then carried one of the chairs over from the reading nook and sat to simply watch her.

He hated that he'd panicked. But he knew why he had. Not because he worried she was sick in the way his wife had been, but because he liked Rowan a lot more than he'd let her believe. When they were together, he had the sense that she was *his*. She made him laugh, treated him as if he were just a guy, gave him a comfortable space of time and place where his world was soft and easy. Fun.

What guy wouldn't fight with the belief that she was *his*. What guy wouldn't like her—a lot more than he'd let himself believe if he would panic and call a doctor over a simple headache.

Still, they were reasonable about their relationship. When Axel's project was completed, she would leave, and he would let her.

And he would find himself in a black hole of loneliness again. This time it wouldn't be from a natural phase in his life. This time, he would long for everything they'd had together. His soul would mourn.

But that was his life, a succession of him doing the right thing. There could be no question he would do the right thing by her.

And that was to let her go.

She was younger than he was, on the cusp of her life. She deserved a real relationship where she could have kids, start her company and grow it to perfection, and go on vacation without a million camera lenses pointed at her.

He would be selfish to steal all that from her.

# CHAPTER ELEVEN

She woke the next morning in Jozef's bed. When she turned, she almost bumped into him. He lay on his side, leaning on his elbow, staring down at her.

"You look better today."

She stretched lazily. "I feel better." Then the full ramifications of what had happened rolled through her and she bounced up. "Oh, my God. I slept in a castle."

"It's not a big deal. I do it all the time."

He wanted her to laugh. She refused to. "I don't! And everybody knows that! My God! My car was in your visitor parking lot all night!"

Exceedingly calm, Jozef said, "No. It wasn't. I have coconspirators in the livery, remember? They drove it to your apartment."

She took a breath and fell to her pillow. "Are they going to sneak me out this morning?"

"Yes." He rolled to his other side and got out of bed. "But after a proper breakfast. You didn't eat supper last night." Wearing sweats, he pulled a T-shirt over his head. "And by the way, if you're feeling sick, you tell me that. You don't accept invitations as if you're afraid to say no."

She licked her lips. "I wasn't *afraid* to say no. I just couldn't figure out how to say no."

He sat on the bed. "When we're alone, there is no such thing as royalty. I'm just me." He smiled. "It's one of the things I like about you. I trust that I can be myself when I'm with you. When you accept an invitation that you should refuse, it's like you break that trust."

She nodded.

He rose. "Okay! You get a shower. I'll make sure breakfast has been delivered. We'll eat and I will show you a tunnel to the livery."

She laughed. "It's like I'm a spy."

He frowned as if he couldn't understand why that made her happy.

She shook her head. "Kidding!"

"Okay," he said, then headed out of the room.

In a weird kind of way, it was nice that he hadn't made a pass at her or even kissed her. Then she realized she hadn't brushed her teeth the night before and wouldn't be able to brush them now and she held back a groan.

She rolled out of bed and made her way to the bathroom but paused in the doorway. The room was enormous. The shower was the size of half of her entire apartment in Paris. Marble floors greeted her feet. Elaborate silver and gold tilework on the wall surrounded a claw-foot soaking tub. Windows didn't have blinds or curtains. Some had lightly beveled glass for privacy. Other windows were gorgeous stained glass. The light fixture above the double vanity looked like crystal.

Undoing her bra, she glanced around. The room was lush, luxurious.

Jozef had lived this way his entire life. Accustomed to opulence, he probably didn't even notice it anymore.

She stepped into the shower. Four butt-high jets hit her, as water poured from an overhead fixture that mimicked rain. The room even filled with the sounds of a gentle storm. If she closed her eyes, she could pretend she was caught in the rain in a forest.

She dried herself with the thickest, softest towel she had ever touched.

The hair dryer she used was powerful, yet somehow almost silent. A drawer in the vanity held four unused toothbrushes and tubes of various kinds of toothpaste. She stared at it for a few seconds, but she'd stayed in enough hotels to know the variety was meant to accommodate guests. She fought the jealousy that threatened to consume her. It was none of her business if he'd slept with anyone before her or would sleep with a million women after her. Though he'd said he hadn't, it was clear he planned to.

Turning off the little voice in her head, she took a toothbrush.

When she returned to the bedroom, she found a pair of sweatpants with an oversize sweatshirt and put those on to pad to the dining room.

As she entered, she sniffed the air. "Do I smell pancakes?"

He rose and pulled out a chair for her. "And waffles, French toast and eggs Benedict." He walked back to his seat. "I didn't know what you liked so I ordered them all."

She gaped at him. "Won't they think you have a guest? Or, worse, think you're crazy?"

He batted a hand. "No. Sometimes when I can't make

up my mind, I ask them to send up this much food and the staff eats whatever I dismiss."

The way he said dismiss gave her a funny feeling. She'd just been in the biggest, prettiest bathroom she'd ever seen. A drawer in his vanity held enough kinds of toothpaste to please anyone—

She hated the crazy jealousy that rippled through her again. Worse, she hated the feeling of being the world's biggest bumpkin. "Your life is so different than mine."

"Don't let it scare you." He pointed at the warming trays. "Pancake? Waffle? French toast? All of them?"

It didn't scare her, but it did focus her thoughts, remind her of who she was and who he was and how she didn't have a right to even think about, let alone care about how he would be having guests in his quarters after she went back to Paris.

She forced a smile. "I'm hungry enough that I could take all three. But I wouldn't be able to eat that much… I think I'll opt for the eggs benedict."

"Ah, this is all about the carb thing, right?" he asked, lifting the tray to dish out some eggs for her. "You look better."

"I feel a hundred times better. And I'm sorry I flaked out on you." As she said *flaked out* she almost groaned. She was with a cultured, well-spoken man, a *king*, and she sometimes said the most ridiculous things. She straightened in her chair. "It will not happen again."

He handed her dish to her. Gold trimmed and elegant, it winked at her.

"It better not. But I've already had my say about you being honest with me. What's on your agenda for today?"

She hadn't missed how he'd changed the subject,

but that didn't stop more questions from swirling in her head.

What did he see in her?

He didn't disrespect or dismiss her. He liked her. He liked being himself with her. But holy hell they were wrong for each other.

She turned her attention to her breakfast, so he couldn't see the questions in her eyes. "I have to go back to my apartment so I can dress for work and get my butt in gear."

"The drivers can sneak you out with a minimum of fuss. Your car's already home. Once we get some food in you, we'll call them."

She finally understood her confusion and dismay. When they flirted in his office or made out in her apartment, she was in familiar territory. Here, in his house, she was seeing how he really lived. Who he really was. It was breathtakingly awesome, even as it was godawful condemning.

She did not belong with this man.

Still, she reminded herself this wasn't permanent. She'd had affairs. There were men she'd been attracted to. With her mind firmly focused on her career and her heart not wanting another bruising, she'd found that to be a satisfying way of life.

Why was she worried that she didn't belong with Jozef? She did not want another relationship. Trying to have one was what got a person hurt. Knowing this would end was what would keep her from getting in too deep. She was smart enough to handle this.

She lifted her fork. "Maybe I could come back tonight, and we could finish what we started last night."

He caught her free hand, lifted it to his lips and kissed it. "I would love that."

Her heart melted. This was why she wanted him. It was lovely to have someone so romantic in her life. Even if it was only for three months. "This time we have to be a little more careful about the arrangements."

"I will alert the livery that your SUV will be in the visitor parking lot and tell them to make sure to take it to the garage once it gets dark. Then you can sneak down the tunnel that I'll show you this morning and slip out virtually unnoticed."

"Virtually?"

"You have to go through security."

It dawned on her that there were now a lot of people in on their secret affair. His drivers. The kitchen probably suspected something was up. Now, security.

"Unless you want to spend the night?"

He smiled at her, and her heart did that funny thing where it felt like it melted and exploded at the same time, and she decided certain people knowing about them was fine. If Jozef trusted them, she trusted them.

It was all part of getting the chance to spend time with a guy who made her toes curl and her heart shimmy with joy.

This was as good as it got for her.

They ate and he dressed for the day in his dark trousers and white shirt. She made fun of him for being such a creature of habit, and he suggested that maybe she should help him pick out some clothes.

"Really?"

"Of course. They'd mostly be things I'd wear around the house or for football games, but you're right. It is a little silly to only have dress clothes for work and sweats for around the house. I should have more jeans, maybe some T-shirts."

She looped her arms around his neck. "Am I changing you?"

"I thought that's why Castle Admin brought you in."

She laughed. "They wanted me to get you out of the house, not change your wardrobe."

"We'll call that an added bonus."

He kissed her, then led her out the door. Instead of going straight, walking down the corridor that would take them to the circular stairway in the front entry, Jozef turned right. They went down a flight of stairs to another corridor that took them to a hidden door in a wall.

"This is clever."

He batted a hand. "This is overprotective security. We haven't had a threat in fifteen years."

They started down a long, well-lit corridor. "But you had one!" Curiosity overwhelmed her. "What was the threat?"

"Are you sure you want to hear this?"

"Yes! I love intrigue."

"This really was intrigue. Spy stuff. A gallery owner was arrested for selling state secrets."

Confused and a bit disappointed, she peeked at him. "A gallery owner?"

"We were never sure how he had access to the thumb drives containing documents he smuggled out behind paintings, but he was sending them out of our country."

"To?"

He shrugged. "Other galleries. Our security people caught the crew on the receiving end, and though everybody went to jail, we didn't get the people behind it. Our gallery owner was as quiet as a mouse about his part in things through all his interrogations. He had a heart attack and died in prison before his trial. So we never did find out who was passing the information to him."

"And that was it?"

"Security monitored his family and friends, but his wife left the country with their daughter, and she did nothing even mildly suspicious. All indication is he acted alone. If he had coconspirators, they fled or went underground."

"Okay. But that *incident* was kind of dull."

"It was a big deal to us and the country stealing the information on our defense systems. Believe me, we had to do some cleanup diplomacy." He chuckled. "But it was also one incident. We pride ourselves on being safe and quiet. A lot goes on behind the scenes to keep it that way."

She nodded. He stopped in front of another door. "The livery is right through here. This is as far as I go, though." He pulled her to him for a long, lingering kiss. "I'll see you tonight."

"Yeah, you will."

He laughed, then headed up the hall, but he stopped suddenly and faced her again. "Might not hurt to bring an overnight bag."

His thoughtfulness made her smile, then she sucked in a breath and pushed on the door. As soon as she entered, one of the drivers snapped to attention, opening the back door of a limo.

No one questioned her. No one asked her name. No one even looked at her too long.

She headed to the limo and slid inside. Before the

door closed, she heard one of the other drivers say, "Where's Axel? Wasn't he supposed to be here?"

All attention turned to the question of where Axel could be as the limo door closed and she almost felt forgotten…which was good. She was an employee, dressed in a too-big sweat suit, sneaking out of a castle. Let them focus on missing Axel!

That night, Jozef had dinner waiting for Rowan when she arrived twenty minutes early. She kissed him quickly. "It was the oddest thing. Axel canceled our meeting today."

He released her, inhaling her flowery scent. "It is Sunday. Maybe he decided to stop being a workaholic?"

"Maybe. But he didn't call. His assistant did."

"Oh, I'm sure he found some mischief to get into." He led her to the dining room. "His attention span has been great for this project, but I'm not surprised he took a day to play hooky."

She laughed. "I guess I'm not either."

They ate dinner, then they teased each other back to the bedroom. She'd brought an overnight duffel bag, and he carried that and slid it into the bathroom as she fell to the bed. He joined her and they laughed and played until they'd driven each other to distraction.

When they lay, sated and happy, with her running her big toe up his leg, he took a long breath and once again wondered what would happen when she left. He knew he'd be lost. He suspected she would be too.

In his silent bedroom, he realized the only things he would remember about her were the work she'd done for him and their times together. Worse, when he'd asked her to tell him about herself, she'd kept the focus on her work. He knew nothing about her past, her social life. Then there was the matter of the pause in her story. The few seconds of hesitation as if she were debating telling him something.

She had a secret and though he had no intention of ever letting their relationship become public, normal curiosity nagged him to ask.

"You know… We haven't talked a lot about you. You told me things about your job. Even how much you loved moving to Paris. But really, I don't know any more than that."

She frowned. "I'm sort of married to my job. There's not much more to tell."

"I told you I got married young, didn't even date much before marrying Annalise. But you've played your love life very close to the vest."

She laughed as she ran her toe up his leg again. "Oh…you want to hear about my old boyfriends."

He wanted to know everything. An old boyfriend was as plausible of a reason for that pause as any. "Why not?"

"Because some of my dating past is…*embarrassing.*"

Yep. There it was. The reason for her pause. "That's promising."

"I think you're hoping there's something bad in my past."

"No. I just sense you're not telling me everything."

"Are you afraid Castle Admin is going to investigate me and find something ugly…like I'm smuggling thumb drives out in paintings?"

She really wasn't one to give up information. Still, the more she hedged, the more curious he got. "No. You and I are just us. No one else involved, as they would usually be. And I'm curious about the past of the woman I'm crazy about."

She sighed, clearly reluctant. "Okay. I was engaged to a guy and a week before our wedding he ran away with my best friend…the maid of honor for our wedding…and married her."

His mouth fell open as he tried to figure out how to react to that. Her fiancé and her best friend had betrayed her? It was no wonder she didn't want to talk about it. "That's…well, it's not something I expected."

"It was humiliating. In fact, when I think about it, I actually refer to it as my Great Humiliation."

She said it lightly, but he could feel an ever so slight stiffening of her muscles, as if the embarrassment of it hadn't quite worn off yet.

"I'm sorry."

She sat up. "Just stop right there. If you're saying you're sorry you asked, I get that. But I hope you are not pitying me. It's the one thing I can't handle. My God, I actually left town a few weeks after they made their announcement because the tension was so thick in Convenience, West Virginia. Small town…big gossip? It was a mess." She sighed heavily. "I now know it was the best thing that could have happened because I went to New York, got an assistant job at a PR firm and I was a natural fit." She snorted and levered herself higher up on her elbows. "If you think about it, it's kind of funny. I found my calling because somebody dumped me."

"Sounds more like destiny fixing a mistake than you being dumped."

"No. I was dumped. It was a great humiliation that

I don't like to talk about." She paused then grinned at him. "Hint. Hint."

"Okay. I won't ask any more questions."

She said, "Good," and snuggled against him. "I should be leaving soon or I'm going to fall asleep. This bed is so damned comfortable."

She said it easily, conversationally, but he could still feel that fine stiffening of her muscles. He'd wanted to know more about her. But she didn't want to talk about it. And no wonder. He pictured her bright-eyed and eager to marry her fiancé and getting embarrassing, humiliating news. In front of her entire small town.

She wasn't as easygoing as she pretended to be. Seeing that, he worried that she might not be as casual about their relationship. More specifically, their upcoming breakup might not be as simple for her as she was pretending it would be. He'd experienced the ultimate loss when Annalise died, and he'd gotten through. He knew that even though he would mourn the loss of what he had with Rowan, he would survive.

Rowan referred to her breakup as the great humiliation. And he understood why. Would their breakup hurt her as much?

"I can almost hear your brain churning over there."

He wanted to laugh to lighten the mood but couldn't. "Rowan, I don't want to hurt you."

"You won't."

"Really? Because I've already realized that I'll miss you when this is over. Are you telling me you won't miss me?"

"Of course, I will. But we're adults. We've both had losses. Our losses are different, but we know how to recover from the hurt of something we couldn't control."

"We could have resisted each other."

She laughed. "See? There's where you're wrong. We're like a magnet and steel. If we'd resisted, we'd have spent our lives wondering what might have been. This way we know."

"I suppose."

"Don't spoil it." Her voice went soft with desperation.

He understood that too. They didn't have forever. She didn't want him to ruin the moment with what-ifs. "I won't."

But protectiveness rose in him again. He would think long and hard about what they were doing. He'd be so careful that no one would ever know what had happened between them.

If it killed him, this would be their secret forever.

So she wouldn't go through another great humiliation if the press discovered their secret...or even Castle Admin.

# CHAPTER TWELVE

THURSDAY EVENING, ROWAN and Pete rode up to the enormous gray stone castle in a limo for the birthday ball for Jozef's mother. A white-gloved man helped her out of the car, as another checked the authenticity of their invitation.

Waiting her turn in the entryway to the castle ballroom, on Pete Sterling's arm, she glanced beyond the receiving line into the enormous room filled with round tables boasting bright white linen tablecloths and centerpieces of yellow roses, Jozef's mom's favorite.

Axel, the first person in the official line, took her hand, as he looked at her strapless purple ball gown. "You look fabulous."

She laughed and introduced Pete and they moved on to Liam, but as they did, Jozef leaned forward just slightly and caught her gaze. He looked amazing in the red jacket with all the medals adorning a sash across his chest. Her heart stuttered. An intimate smile passed between them.

Liam caught her hand. "You're gorgeous, as always."

She thanked him, then laughed and introduced Pete. The next two steps took her to Jozef. Before Pete caught up to her, Jozef quietly said, "You're ravishing."

Their eyes locked and her breath stalled. "You're very dashing."

And suddenly Pete was right beside her.

Breaking their moment, Jozef said, "And you look lovely too."

Pete laughed. "I always wondered what people said in these lines."

"Now you know. We're as human as everyone else."

Pete nodded. "And you have an odd sense of humor, Your Majesty."

Relieved that Pete hadn't caught the intimacy between them, Rowan agreed.

Jozef turned to his left. "These are my parents. Their Royal Highnesses Alistair and Monique Sokol."

Both tall and elegant, the retired royals looked every inch the part. Alistair wore the same red jacket as Jozef. Monique was quietly elegant in a black lace gown, her salt-and-pepper hair swept up in a sophisticated chignon.

"Mom, Dad, these are Rowan Gray and Peter Sterling. They orchestrated my return to public life."

Jozef's father took her hand and kissed the knuckles. "Such a beautiful woman shouldn't have to work."

Monique rolled her eyes. "Don't listen to him. He thinks he's a charmer."

Rowan said, "Actually, he sounds just like Axel."

As Jozef's father shook Pete's hand, Monique leaned in and whispered, "It's where Axel gets it from."

She laughed. "His father can be fairly charming too."

Jozef's mom gave Rowan a curious once-over. "He can be. But Jozef typically reserves his charm for friends and family."

Rowan quickly said, "Working together we became friends."

The Queen said, "I see," but she continued to look at Rowan curiously.

With that, they were through the receiving line. A tall man in black trousers and a white dinner jacket asked to see their invitation again. He read it and motioned for a younger man in the same outfit to come over. The younger man led them to their table.

"They have a two-check system to make sure there are no fake invitations," Pete whispered as they were ushered to a table toward the back. After their escort seated Rowan, Pete thanked him, and the young man bowed and scurried away.

Pete sat. "We're in the cheap seats."

"You didn't think we'd be up front, did you?"

"I don't know. You seem to be pretty chummy with the whole family."

"Not the parents. This is the first I've met them. Jozef tells me they live in Paris."

Pete gaped at her. "No kidding! Not even on their own island?"

Pete didn't seem concerned by her intimate knowledge of the family, but a sharp stab of fear hit her in the chest. After her slip with the former Queen, she should be on her toes. Instead, she'd casually told Pete something only royal insiders knew. She had to be more careful, or Pete would start putting two and two together.

Another twenty minutes passed as the guests filed in and were greeted by the royals. When they finally made their way to the long table that sat on risers in order that everyone could see the royal family, Jozef walked to the podium and lifted his champagne glass.

What appeared to be two hundred waiters stepped forward and quickly poured champagne into the glasses of the guests.

"This is about as formal as we intend to get tonight."

Everyone laughed.

"A toast to my wonderful mother. A beautiful person inside and out. Happy birthday, Mother."

Everyone lifted their glasses and said, "Hear, hear." Everyone took a sip of champagne.

The Queen nodded happily and unexpectedly rose. Cleary confused, Jozef politely stepped back and gave her the podium.

"We'd agreed to no speeches tonight. We simply wanted to have a quiet party with family and friends."

Rowan glanced around at the four hundred guests as Pete mouthed, *A quiet party*?

"But now that we're here, I feel the need to say that I know I'm blessed."

An "aww" of appreciation rippled through the crowd.

"Our son has done an amazing job of leading our country and raising two sons. We could not be more proud of him and every day his sons amaze us. Our kingdom is in good hands."

Just like the day she saw Jozef going into the conference room with Paula Mason, Rowan once again saw his life, the importance of his life. This wasn't just a guy who was called "king" without any real say in government. He *was* Prosperita's government.

They ate a delicious meal, and as white-coated servers cleared the tables, the band played a song for the former King and Queen to dance in celebration of her birthday. Jozef danced with her next. Then Liam and Axel shared a song. Liam dancing with the Queen for the first half and handing his grandmother off to Axel for the second half.

Rowan sat mesmerized watching the royal family spread out and thank the crowd. She'd always believed American politicians bore a cross of a sort, having to reassure their constituents that they were the correct person for their elected positions. But a king, someone who gets his job by destiny, seemed to have a greater responsibility to prove he was the right person for the job.

Jozef did his duty well, but tonight Rowan saw the obligation of it. His only rest, his only reality was behind the closed doors of his residence—

Or, sometimes, behind the closed door of her rented apartment.

Pete pulled her out of her reverie. "Time to mingle."

She followed Pete into the crowd, the slit in the skirt of her purple gown allowing her to match his long strides. As Pete walked up to smaller groups and introduced himself, Rowan watched intently, knowing she'd have to schmooze with potential clients for her own company soon. But her gaze was frequently drawn to find Jozef. A tall man in a red jacket in a sea of black tuxedos was easy to spot. As Pete glad-handed, she watched Jozef move from group to group, pausing to dance with various women. Some older than he was, probably his mother's friends. Some younger. And some his own age, women who gazed at him with undisguised adoration.

Jealousy quivered through her. There were so many women who were better suited to him. And one day he would choose one of them. He wouldn't live alone forever. In fact, as Art Andino had suggested, his reclusiveness might have been the result of realizing he

needed to get out but simply not wanting to acknowledge that his life had to move on. Now that she'd shown
him the way, he'd find his new queen.

Maybe one of the women in attendance tonight.

The sadness of it nearly suffocated her, then Jozef
walked up to her, but addressed Pete. "If you don't
mind, Mr. Sterling, I'd like to thank Rowan for all her
hard work by dancing with her."

She smiled at the silly expression that came to Pete's
face. It took a few seconds before he realized that in a
kingdom such as Prosperita, a dance with the King was
an enormous honor.

Recovering as quickly as he could, Pete said, "Of
course."

Holding her hand about shoulder height, like a gen-
tleman, the way Rowan always pictured a prince would
escort a princess, he led her to the dance floor. She saw
the flashes of a camera and nearly froze.

"Relax. That's the royal photographer," he said, pulling her into a dance hold. "If this hits a paper, the angle
will be that I gave you the privilege of dancing with me.
Just as I told Pete."

"I probably should have curtsied or something,
right?"

"No. You were fine. And you look exquisite."

A shimmer of longing whispered through her, but
it was automatically tempered by reality. She was an
export of Convenience, West Virginia. A woman with
a bachelor's degree...nothing more special than that.
And she was dancing with a king.

"I'm not sure about that. I only own one gown. This
is it."

He pulled back. "One gown?"

"Take a close look at it. It might be purple, but it's dark and extremely simple. Most people wouldn't recognize it in a lineup. I'm a background person. Not someone who should be stealing the show. That's why I found this perfect, elegant, but not memorable dress."

He laughed. "Not memorable? Have you seen how sexy it is when your leg peeks out of that slit in the side?"

"Really? You think that's memorable?"

He twirled them around once. "You think it isn't?"

"Huh."

As she thought about that, his arm became restless on her back. "I feel like I should be allowed to pull you closer."

She looked up into his eyes. "I do too."

"But we can't."

"I know."

"You'd end up with more trouble than I would."

"I know that too."

Silence stretched between them. She half expected an apology. After all, it was his life that was hampering things. But he said nothing.

So she said nothing. What could she say? There was no answer for them except to accept their limited time together and realize they'd eventually move on.

"Tell me you'll meet me in my quarters later."

Her head tilted. "Later? Like after the ball?"

When he glanced at her, all the longing he felt was evident in his dark, brooding eyes. "Yes."

How could a woman resist those eyes?

"I'll have to ditch Pete. We came together."

He laughed. Simple and pure, it enveloped them in their own private world. "I could have him arrested."

"He liked your sense of humor, Jozef, but I don't think he'd get the joke in that."

"Too bad." He paused. "Can you get away?"

His soft, serious voice trembled over her nerve endings, promising things she loved, things she was coming to need. Their strong connection filled her soul, called to her body, and there wasn't a single piece of her DNA that could have refused him.

"There's always a way if you're committed to finding it."

"Then you'll meet me?"

Crazy wonderful feelings rolled through her. She'd never felt this way with or about anyone before. Not even Cash.

The realization nearly stopped her cold. She hadn't thought about her ex-fiancé in years, except with distaste. But tonight, she could remember their good times, remember why she'd loved him and feel nothing. No sense of loss. No humiliation.

Jozef had made her feel lovable again. Normal. Like a woman, not a woman scorned.

"I'll meet you."

Two hours later, though, she hadn't managed to sufficiently ditch Pete.

Standing with him in a foyer full of people who were talking, saying goodbyes, waiting for their names to be called for their limos, she racked her brain for an answer.

When inspiration finally struck, she faced Pete. "You know, I think I forgot something in Axel's office. I should go back and get it. You take the limo and head home. I'll call a cab."

"Nonsense," Pete said. "I'll walk to Axel's office

with you. We can get what you forgot and be back in time to get our limo."

Axel suddenly appeared at her side. "Thank you again, Rowan, for your help." He glanced at Pete then back at her. "But there are a few ideas I've had about our project. If you had a moment, we could discuss them."

She looked at him. He nudged his head toward Pete, as if he knew she was trying to ditch him.

"I could take a minute with you, Axel."

"Good." He faced Pete. "No need to worry. I'll have one of our limos take her home."

Pete smiled, as their limo was called. "I guess I'll see you in the morning then."

She nodded and he scurried off.

She pivoted to face Axel. "What are you doing?"

"Rescuing you." He turned to walk away but spun around again. "Don't take these stairs. There's another set. Make the first right, then two lefts. They're pretty deep into the castle, but you'll find them." He pointed down a corridor to his left, then he grinned. "And don't worry, we'll never speak of this."

With that, he ambled into the crowd, thanking guests, making everyone laugh.

Seizing her moment, she slid out of the press of people waiting for limos and down the deserted hall and two more hallways that were so deserted the lights had been dimmed. Then she found the other stairway. Lifting her skirt, she raced up the steps.

Walking down the hall to Jozef's quarters, she wondered how the hell she'd get inside his apartment. She envisioned herself waiting in the hall, as she had the day he'd had his miniscule version of a meltdown, but as she approached the door, it opened.

Jozef pulled her inside, closed the door and pressed a long, lingering kiss to her mouth.

"I've wanted to do that all night."

"So have I."

This man had freed her from her demons. Cash had damaged something in her soul. Jozef had fixed it. The monumental realization almost rendered her speechless. She should tell him. But the conclusion that was the most important thing to happen in her life in a decade really wasn't relevant to his life.

His jacket removed and his tie loosened, he motioned toward his sitting room. "Drink?"

"I think I maxed out on champagne." As she spoke, he poured himself a glass of bourbon and she realized she hadn't seen him with a drink in his hand at the ball, except the glass of champagne when he'd made his toast.

He sat on the sofa, and, still in her gown, she sashayed over and sat beside him.

"This is nice."

The quiet of the castle settled around them. She nestled into his side. She was so confused and appreciative that someone had finally gotten her beyond her great humiliation, that she almost felt she was having an out-of-body experience. In a kind world, she'd ride off in the sunset with the man who'd freed her.

But that couldn't happen. A sense of injustice poured through her like icy water. How could she have to walk away from someone she loved so much?

The casual thought froze her.

Dear God. She loved him.

Gazing into his eyes, she realized she couldn't tell him that her feelings had exploded, and her heart vibrated with longing that would go unfulfilled. She could see herself spending the rest of her life with him—if he weren't a king.

But he was a king.

She swallowed hard.

"What did you think of your first royal ball?"

She said, "Amazing," but the ache in her heart swelled until it grew so big she felt empty, hollow. Jozef had changed her life, but she couldn't admit that to anyone. She couldn't be publicly proud of him. She couldn't tell anyone they were in a relationship. Because they couldn't be in a real relationship. The press would poke into her past and then eat her alive when they found Cash. She might be beyond her great humiliation, but it would be fresh meat to them. The way to embarrass this wonderful, thoughtful, hardworking king would be through her.

She supposed accepting that was how she thanked him for bringing her back to life.

"A ball that took an entire castle staff two weeks to organize was just amazing?"

Forcing herself beyond the feelings shredding her, she faked a laugh and twisted so she could face him. "*Amazing* is a big word in my vocabulary." She waited a second, then she said, "Did *you* enjoy *yourself*?"

"My mother had a wonderful time. That's what we were aiming for."

She realized again how orchestrated and goal-oriented everything in his life was.

Except them. Their secret relationship might be the only part of his world that was unscripted and genuine.

Accepting that, accepting her place in his life took deeper meaning.

She was his respite. Being with her was the one time he was himself. Something he needed. If she could protect that with secrecy, then so be it.

He finished his bourbon and she reached for the zipper in the back of her dress. With a slow, steady swish, she lowered it. When she rose, the gown puddled at her feet. His eyebrows rose as she stepped out of it, but his eyes sharpened with need when—in nothing but purple bra and panties—she put her knees on either side of his thighs.

"What do we have here?"

"A little seduction because while everybody else was having fun, you were working."

He slid his hands to her bottom. "It's the job."

She leaned in, kissed him, then pulled back. "In some ways, I think being King is the opposite of a normal job. The hardest part of your position is when you're not supposed to be working, because that's your most important work. Schmoozing. Reassuring people. Making deals when people are comfortable and don't realize you are guiding them to see things your way."

"You're very observant."

She kissed him again. "And that's *my* job." It was also what she owed him for helping her get beyond Cash's betrayal. Reassurance. Security. Secrecy.

She undid her bra. Let it fall to his lap.

Their gazes met as his hands moved from her bottom to her breasts. She leaned in and kissed him. Sadness that this wouldn't last rippled through her, but she fought it. From here on out, every day, every hour, every minute they had together was precious.

His hands skimmed her back as their kiss became

steamy. Her fingers inched to the buttons of his shirt, opening them so she could remove his shirt and touch him.

When things heated to a boiling point, he rose from the sofa, taking her with him and carrying her to his bed.

With his breath coming in irregular pants, Jozef rolled to his side and fell to his pillow.

"You are amazing."

She levered herself up on her elbows. "I think we are an amazing team. You know how some people are just made to do what they do? Well, we're made to do that."

He laughed.

Beautifully pink and perfect in her nakedness, she turned on her side so their eyes could meet. "I know we've never really talked about this, but I'm sort of glad we aren't public with our relationship."

His chest tightened and disappointment flooded him, though he knew it shouldn't. They'd made the deal that their relationship would be temporary. The secrecy part was a natural spin-off of that.

"Watching you tonight, I realized that if anybody knew we were in a relationship, the press would dig so far into my past they'd find my great humiliation."

Though he knew her great humiliation had been awful for her, he now understood that she referred to it so condescendingly to diminish its power over her. Then the strangest thought hit him.

"You do realize you PR'd yourself."

"What?"

"You belittle your past by giving it a cute handle. Your great humiliation. But you could actually use your past to explain why you're such a good PR person."

"Really? You don't think that finding a way to explain my past to *your* media is wishful thinking."

Confused, he glanced at her. "That's what you got from that? That I was looking for a way to explain *your* past to *my* press?"

"I don't know. I've rolled some of this around in my head lately, and I'm just glad we aren't giving them a chance to embarrass you through me."

"That's because you always think like a PR person. My PR person. You're protecting me."

She laughed and dropped to her pillow again. "That's me. Always working."

He had been tired from the long day but being with her refreshed him. Obviously, it also relaxed him to the point that he didn't think about what he said. Because talking about her job had somehow taken them perilously close to talking about the future. And they had none.

Those odd feelings galloped through him again. Acknowledgment that what they had wasn't permanent did not make him happy—didn't relieve his mind—the way it should. This was simply supposed to be an affair. A once-in-a-lifetime romance that would revitalize their damaged souls, but end. He wasn't supposed to let his thoughts veer toward a future that could never be.

Mostly because being with him for real would change her life in ways no one should have to accommodate.

Telling himself he was thinking too hard, too much, and that wasn't what their relationship was about, he reached for her again, pulled her to him and bit her neck.

She laughed and he suddenly realized that they played like happy innocents when they made love.

There were no rules and there was no one watching, no one who cared. No one who even *knew*.

Because that was the way it had to be.

As a king, he understood that.

Now he knew she did too.

Maybe that was what her comment had been about? Her way of reassuring him that she truly understood their limits. Though, technically, she was the one who had established their limits, when she'd told him what they had would be temporary.

Strange feelings stuttered through him again.

Everything that had once reassured him suddenly angered him.

He fought back the anger, and they made love in the unreserved, fun way that defined their feelings for each other, then drifted off to sleep like two people without a care in the world.

The next morning, Jozef awoke with her in his bed. He fumbled for his phone to see the time. But hoping for it to be before dawn was only kidding himself. Light wasn't pouring in through the thick drapes, but there was a peek of it. One slim beam of condemnation.

With his parents in town, he had a breakfast obligation. Plus, the former King and Queen had free run of the castle. His dad could be in the livery. Or roaming the halls reminiscing. But he hadn't thought about breakfast or his roaming father, the night before. He'd been content having Rowan at his side and had fallen asleep like a man who didn't have a care in the world… or responsibilities.

Recognizing the gravity of this kind of slip, he bounced up. He reached over to wake her, but he stopped. Her abundant red hair lay on the pillow and cascaded to her breasts. The world was silent and she was perfection. Having her there when he woke up filled him with something he could neither define nor describe.

And whether he wanted to admit it or not, what he'd felt the night before as he tried to sort everything out was anger, mixed with sorrow that they couldn't think of the future.

Pressing his lips together to ward off emotions he didn't want and wasn't allowed to have, he tapped her shoulders. "Rowan. You have to get up."

Her eyelids lifted slowly, and he could see the very second she realized they'd spent the entire night together. They'd done it before, so it took another second for her to think it through.

Her green eyes widened in horror. "Oh, my gosh! I'm so sorry! Your parents are here. Everybody's probably in the dining room, waiting for you."

"It's not a big deal. We've handled this before," he said, sliding out of bed and into the trousers of his formalwear.

She rolled out of bed and glanced around as if confused before she winced. "My clothes are in your sitting room."

"Don't you have something in your overnight bag?"

She sighed. "No. I just have clean undies, a toothbrush, my own shampoo, that kind of stuff."

Before he could offer to get her things, she raced out of the bedroom. By the time he made it up the hall, she was fully dressed in her purple gown. She ran to the door, but he caught her hand before she could leave.

Half of him wanted to laugh at the silliness of their situation. The other half recognized this as part of who they were. Two people who weren't allowed to be together.

They looked into each other's eyes. Recognition passed between them. *They weren't allowed to be together.*

"You think your drivers will be expecting me?"

"Maybe," he said, forcing himself to dismiss dismal thoughts that they had no future. "But my parents have access to the tunnels, the private elevators and stairways. It's not a good idea for you to be walking in any of them. Get yourself to the front entrance, and I'll call downstairs and have a car waiting for you."

Lightening the mood, she said, "The rusty SUV?"

"Or maybe the truck with the mud flaps."

She laughed, as he wanted her to, so he kissed her. He kissed her because kissing her was the best feeling in the world, but also because she didn't criticize or call him out about their need for secrecy, for as much as an outsider could understand the rules and restrictions of his world, she understood.

## CHAPTER THIRTEEN

ROWAN SNEAKED DOWN the stairs and out of the castle. As if my magic, there was a limo. Laughing, she shook her head as the driver opened the back door.

She gave him her address and he drove her home—not to her office, though it was close to her start time. She might have had to sneak out of the castle in her gown, but she wouldn't wear it to work.

Because she arrived at the office late, Geoffrey met her at the door with a cup of coffee and that day's messages, added to his insatiable curiosity about the ball. She answered his questions as if she'd been nothing more than a lucky PR person who'd gotten a royal invitation and he'd seemed to accept that.

"Now that the King's mother's birthday celebration is over, we can't forget about tonight's gallery opening."

Her eyes widened.

"Oh, please. Do not tell me you forgot."

"I didn't." Because they'd ditched the idea of a third date, she'd scheduled Jozef to go to a gallery opening with his sons to keep him in the public eye. The birthday ball for his mother had overshadowed it, but the three Zokol men were to go to the gallery an hour before the official opening, so they could have the place to themselves, and then slip out to have a late dinner together.

This was not a big deal. Now that Geoffrey had reminded her, she was on top of it.

"After the protocols and security that I saw at that ball last night, a gallery opening should be a piece of cake."

"A nice way to get him out in public."

"Yes. Without a date," she said, keeping up the conversation as she strode to her desk. "It will be good to have him go out on his own. Now that he's been out, he can keep going out. And when he decides to find his own dates, they will be his to plan."

Geoffrey drew in a satisfied breath. "And his world is saved."

She laughed, but the knife twisted in her chest again. She might have been guiding him to this point, but the part of her that loved him did not like it.

She and Geoffrey spent some time working on Axel's fundraiser. He suggested they go to lunch together, but she declined. The realizations she'd had the night before, that she'd fallen in love with the guy who had all but erased her great humiliation, added to the reminder that they had no future, had soured her stomach. She needed time to—as Jozef said—PR herself. Remind herself why the life she'd been building was enough and focus on her own future.

And her future was her own company. A solid reputation. Which meant no one could find out about her and Jozef. She also couldn't mourn not having a future with him. She had to work.

Her mind fixed and Geoffrey out of the office, she investigated office space in Manhattan, thought about how much staff she would need, if any, when she opened her doors. Pondered hiring Geoffrey away from Sterling, Grant, Paris.

An hour later Geoffrey was back with a sandwich for her.

But she didn't stop working. Remembering Axel's vision of turning their charity fundraiser into something that would ultimately become a tourist destination, she mulled ideas until she thought of an angle.

She ran it by Geoffrey, who suggested they video conference with their Paris team, looking for problems, and before she knew it, it was five o'clock.

A knock on the door of the outer office had both of their heads snapping up.

"Delivery. Somebody has to sign for it."

Geoffrey waved her back down when she rose. "I'll sign."

Tired, she stretched in her desk chair.

Geoffrey returned to her office carrying a big box that looked more like a gift than a document.

"What's that?"

He shrugged. "I don't know. Why don't you open it? It's addressed to you."

The box was so big she had to stand up to slide the big red, ribbon off. She lifted the lid to find red tissue paper and a card.

Geoffrey's eyes grew huge. "What is it? Do you have a secret admirer?"

She laughed. "It's from the King."

His eyes grew even bigger.

"Remember the time I forced him to wear the red and blue striped polo shirt?"

He frowned but nodded. "Well, he wants me to wear this tonight."

"You're going to the gallery opening?"

"Apparently, he thinks I am. I did show up at his date with Julianna Abrahams. And I was in the foyer when he met Paula Mason." She let her voice drift away. "He probably does think I'll be going tonight."

Geoffrey reached for the box. "In this…" He pulled out an exquisite white gown dusted with tiny multicolored flowers and whistled. "Wow." He nudged the dress to her. "Feel how soft this material is!"

The dress was long and sleek, silky and sexy—yet an innocent white with delicate flowers.

She swallowed and slid the card to her desk. She'd read Geoffrey a simpler version of what Jozef had said, not mentioning the part about her escaping the castle that morning in the purple gown. Or the part telling her that she was beautiful and wonderful and deserved to be noticed.

"You'd better get going. Remember, the royals go into the gallery alone an hour earlier than the invited guests."

"Okay, I remember. I'll leave now."

But when she lifted the box from her desk, she knocked the card to the floor. Geoffrey bent to pick it up. His gaze rose to hers. "There's a lot more in this card than what you told me."

She licked her lips. "Yeah."

"What's going on?"

She cleared her throat. "I always wear the purple gown, everywhere I go and last night he noticed."

"At the ball?"

She winced because she didn't want to lie. "I told

him I always wear the simple gown, so I won't be noticed and sending this dress is his way of teasing me."

Geoffrey glanced down at the card again before he handed it to her, probably seeing that part about her sneaking out of the castle in the purple gown that morning. But as a faithful employee, he said, "Sure. I get it."

She sucked in a breath. "Don't make a big deal out of this. He's fifteen years older than I am, has sons closer to my age than his, and he's a king. Even if we wanted to pursue all our teasing and flirting, we couldn't."

He glanced at the card in her hands. "Sounds like you've been doing more than teasing and flirting."

"But that's all it can be."

"You're sure?"

"Yes! You know what will happen if he starts to date me. My secrets will come out."

He frowned. "*Your* secrets?"

She'd never told Geoffrey—or anyone she worked with—her story, but she could see he needed answers, and if she wanted him to keep her secret about Jozef, she had to fully take him into her confidence.

She fell to her desk chair. "I was engaged. A week before my wedding my fiancé came to my house with my best friend to tell me they'd run away and gotten married."

Geoffrey's eyes widened. "Oh, honey."

"It was ugly. I left town. But look around you. I made a great life. Unfortunately, I don't think the press will home in on the good I've done. Just my great humiliation. I wouldn't care if they dragged me through the mud, but they'd do a number on Jozef and I can't let that happen."

Geoffrey nodded. "Sure. Makes sense."

"Plus, Jozef also lost his wife, Annalise. If I'm understanding his situation correctly, she was the perfect spouse for him. If he replaces her, it will be with someone like her. He doesn't believe in romantic love, and I respect that."

Geoffrey sighed and shook his head. "Oh, honey. You're already in love."

She wanted to deny it but couldn't. She'd realized it the night before. "It's okay. I've lost at love before, remember? I don't belong with a king. And he doesn't really want me."

"He doesn't want you?" Geoffrey's face scrunched in confusion. "How do you know?"

"We sort of made a deal that this would only be temporary. I understood sneaking around in the beginning. When everything was just about fun and spending time together, I didn't need to dig any deeper. But yesterday, at the ball—" She shrugged. "I could just see that I don't fit in his world and he's known it all along."

"Or—maybe he doesn't know how to bring your relationship into the public eye. After all, you're the woman who was finding him dates last month."

She tried to laugh but it came out hollow. "You're missing what I'm telling you. He's a king through and through. A guy who knows he has to do what his country needs him to do. Meaning, if he marries, it will be to someone more suited than I am. Think about it. I was the woman finding him dates. Now I'm the woman helping him come out of his shell. I think I'm his rebound relationship. Not the woman he'll fall in love with. The woman he walks away from to find real love."

Saying it out loud made her voice quiver with pain. Geoffrey opened his arms to hug her. "Come here."

She took a step back. "I can't stand pity. It's why I left West Virginia. I don't want to be pitied. I want to be strong. *Never hurt.* Independent."

Geoffrey said, "And alone?"

"Maybe." She shook her head. "It doesn't matter. Being independent and strong and helping Jozef are more important." But in her heart, she suddenly realized that if Jozef would ask to take their relationship public, she'd risk it.

But he wouldn't. She knew he wouldn't. Because she was his rebound relationship.

It fell into place so clearly in her head that she almost couldn't believe she'd been so stupid that she didn't see it before this.

She drove her tired SUV back to her apartment, then clamored up the steps, wrestling with the big dress box, debating whether she should go to the gallery opening. Having everything about their relationship fall into place hurt so much she could barely breathe.

But she had a job to do.

Plus, she was a person who didn't want anything permanent, so temporary relationships were good. Exactly what she had needed.

What she had with Jozef was exactly what she had wanted.

Until now. Now she had no idea what she wanted.

She went inside her dingy apartment, walked back to the bathroom, stripped and let the water work its magic. After she calmed down, an unexpected thought struck her.

*What if Jozef had changed his mind too?*

*His feelings for her were always right there in his eyes. She knew he more than cared deeply for her.*

*What if he was finally acknowledging that?*

*What if sending her the dress, inviting her person-ally to the gallery opening, was his way of making their relationship public?*

He'd sent her a dress with an explicit card. He had to know there would be a possibility Geoffrey would open it—

And read the card.

A card that talked openly about their relationship.

Was this night about taking their relationship pubic?

They'd had a moment that morning, when they'd looked in each other's eyes and hated that she had to sneak out of the castle. Hated that no one, not even his family, could know what they were doing.

Maybe he'd had enough?

Still, his sons were going to the gallery opening. This couldn't be a date—

Except, his sons had begged off dinner after the gallery opening. They were thrilled to go to the gallery with their dad, part of the PR campaign to show the happy royals, but they also had their own lives.

Technically she and Jozef would be going out to dinner alone.

In public.

He had to know the press would make a big deal out of that.

She pulled her hair into a knot at the top of her head, then on whim decided to get fancy. She curled the strands that surrounded her face and dangled down her back and inserted some tiny flowers in strategic places.

She was about to get into her car to drive to the castle when she got a text saying a limo was outside her apartment.

*He'd sent a limo.*

Another thing he'd never done before.

Her suspicion that something important was happening grew, expanded into a big bubble of happiness in her chest.

For a guy who needed to keep his secrets, he was suddenly open as hell.

And he did nothing without thought, without purpose.

*This meant something.*

In her highest, sexiest shoes, she made her way down the stairs into the waiting limo.

The back seat was empty, but it wasn't even a five-minute drive to the gallery. Still, it was enough time for her to realize that sending a limo pretty much meant he'd be escorting her home.

Like a date.

The realization that he might be making the most important move of their lives washed through her. But she'd already decided she wanted this. Wanted *him*. There was nothing more to it than that. She would have to step up. Face everything that dating him for real meant.

But she wanted him enough to change her entire life.

She entered through the back door of the gallery as the royals had and made her way to the front room where they stood chatting with the proprietor, a pretty, thirty-something woman, whose smile was so bright Rowan almost laughed. The star power of the three bachelor royals was enough to make any woman giddy.

The conversation stopped as she entered. The eyes of all three of the Sokol men widened.

Axel recovered first. "You look amazing!"

She walked over. "I'll bet you say that to all the girls."

But for the first time she realized that the dress Jozef had sent might be sexy and gorgeous, but there was also a certain sophistication to it. Definitely more classy than the purple dress with the slit up the side, this could be the gown of a queen.

The thought nearly paralyzed her. She was not imagining things. He really was inching them into the public eye together.

Jozef was thunderstruck by how beautiful she looked in the gown he'd chosen. But, of course, she was young. And playful and wonderful. He couldn't imagine her looking bad in anything.

He smiled at Axel and Liam all but falling over themselves to chat with her because he knew she'd be his that night.

He'd even arranged for them to have dinner in his private quarters so she could accompany him and not have to bow out at the restaurant because it was too public.

They stayed with the gallery owner for most of their hour. Then Fiona Barns gave them the last ten minutes to go back to whatever sections had piqued their interest. Axel and Liam went toward the sculpture exhibits.

Suddenly, he and Rowan were alone. Too tempted to resist, he drew her to him and kissed her and she melted in his arms. Anticipation stole through him. They could drive to the castle, have dinner and spend the rest of the night together.

At the end of their hour, they left the gallery and walked to his limo, which was hidden in a back alley.

But despite what Jozef considered tight security, a reporter had gotten through.

"Who are you with?" the guy called, holding up his phone, which was obviously in record mode.

When Jozef tensed, Rowan shook her head, the motion telling him to stand down. "This is my job, remember?"

He nodded.

"I'm Rowan Gray, I work for Sterling, Grant, Paris. King Jozef and I were just enjoying the gallery opening."

"Sterling, Grant, Paris? That's a PR firm, right?"

"Yes!" Jozef said, not waiting for her to answer. "Rowan has been helping Axel with the fall fundraiser. She's amazingly talented."

Rowan sneaked a peak at him. He resisted the urge to smile at her, knowing that any sort of gesture like that could be blown out of proportion.

He made a joke. "If you'll excuse us, we're sharing a cab."

The driver opened the door, Rowan slid inside and Jozef followed her. Once the driver was securely behind the wheel, with the soundproof glass between his section and the passenger section, Jozef laughed.

"That was fun!"

She glanced over with a frown. "Which part?"

"Okay. I liked the gallery. But I've never bantered with a reporter."

She winced. "That was your banter?"

He laughed. "I didn't say I was good at it. But I wanted to say, Rowan and I are going back to the castle to make passionate love and eat dinner. And I didn't. I shifted the conversation to you and how good you are at what you do. You know, so when you begin your own firm people will remember you."

She stared at him, and he could see in her eyes that he'd said or done something that confused her.

Finally, she said, "We're eating dinner at the castle?"

Of all the things he'd said, he'd genuinely believed that was the least offensive, but obviously it was the one that bothered her most.

"My parents left at noon. Both the boys bailed on me. Meaning, I don't have to go to the restaurant. We can go back to my quarters and be alone."

She studied him for a few minutes, then said, "You didn't want to go to the restaurant with *me*?"

"We could have. You are my PR person." He shifted on his seat, uncomfortable, but not because of her questions. It was her seriousness that sent prickles up his spine. "We have a legitimate reason to be together." He paused. "I just wanted to be alone with you so we can be normal."

"You couldn't be normal in the restaurant?"

"I couldn't do this in the restaurant." He reached out and held her still so he could kiss her. "Or this." He ran his hands down the soft material of the sleeves of the gown. "Or this." With his hand at her nape, he deepened the kiss, awakening needs in himself that would have rendered him speechless if he hadn't already had all these feelings with her.

When he pulled back, she gazed into his eyes. "Why not? Why couldn't you do those things?"

He laughed. "Really? You know our situation."

"Yes. You're afraid of what people will think."

Her answer insulted him to his core. "I'm not *afraid* of what people will think! I'm more concerned about our privacy. You said it yourself last night. The press would be all over your past. It would be *you* who would be embarrassed."

"Yes. But the gossip and the embarrassment would die down."

He stared at her. "Really?"

"Eventually. It always does."

That confused him enough that he couldn't prevaricate. "What are you saying?"

"I'm not saying anything. But I thought things had changed between us."

The confusion that hit him was so stunning, he almost couldn't speak. "Between us? Yes. I think we feel more deeply for each other, but that doesn't change who I am or how I have to comport myself."

"Sure. I understand…" Her voice trailed off as she caught his gaze. "No. Actually, I don't. We laughed this morning as if we'd finally realized our situation didn't work. You sent me a gown and an explicit card that could have been opened by my assistant. You sent a limo for me—" Her eyes squeezed closed. "Oh, my God. I misinterpreted everything."

Numb for a few seconds, he said nothing, as he sifted through what she'd said to figure out what was going on. "You thought I'd changed my mind about our relationship being public?"

She searched his gaze and very carefully said, "Yes."

He wished he could. "My feelings are so strong for you that I wonder how I will survive when we have to part, but we both know we have to part. So why go through the drama of being seen together in public?"

She studied him again. Her serious eyes flickering enough that he knew she was thinking through something.

"Jozef, what would you say if I said I'm now wondering if we do have to part?"

His breath caught. Thoughts of waking beside her forever filled him with joy. But the reality of their life stopped them cold. She was the one who would suffer if they decided to continue their affair. Because one day it would come out. And when it did, she'd be inundated by the media.

"I'd say that you need to think carefully about what you're considering."

"Our feelings for each other are strong. We've spent enough time together to show me who you are and enough that you've seen my integrity, what I'm made of. I'm crazy about you. I thought you were crazy about me too."

He understood what she was saying because he'd thought the same things himself. Even as an urge to catch her and kiss her senseless raced through him, to agree with her and have a shot at keeping her in his life, his common sense prevailed.

He caught her hands, a silent entreaty that she should listen to what he was saying. "I *am* crazy about you. You are smart, funny, beautiful and so sexy I sometimes think I will never get enough of you."

"But you don't love me."

The need to disagree—to admit that the urgent longings that always raced through him when she was around had to be love—expanded in his chest.

But that was selfish. Oh, so selfish. No matter how much being with her allowed him to be his real self, to indulge his desires, to speak the truth, she didn't know what she was saying, the depth of trouble to which she'd open herself because she loved him.

*She loved him.*

His heart trembled, as the longing to accept her love roared through him.

*But his life would bring her nothing but misery.*

All his experience, all his breeding, poured through him like a rich, worthy wine. In that moment, he dropped his own yearnings and became a well-trained royal, who knew the realities of his life and wouldn't hurt her.

Refused to hurt her.

"Real love takes time. More time than we've spent together."

She shook her head. "I don't think so. I mean, sometimes, yes. But you and I had the thunderbolt. That flash of lightning that warned us early on that there was something special between us."

There was no way he could deny that, so he quietly said, "There is something special between us."

"But you don't think it's love."

Up to this point, he might have questioned it, but the feelings swamping him, the longings, the needs he knew would go unfulfilled for the rest of his life, told him otherwise.

Still, the ultimate love pushed him to do the right thing.

"No. I don't think it's love."

Rowan only stared at him. She couldn't understand how he didn't see what was right before him.

She shook her head. "If we don't at least explore the

emotion of it, then what's been happening between us is just sex—"

She stopped as the truth of that rumbled through her. A reality so crystal clear that everything else she wanted to say drifted away to nothing.

He really didn't love her. He liked her. They were fun together—dynamite in bed. And from the guidelines *she'd* set, there had been nothing wrong with what they had.

*She'd* been the one to stupidly let her guard down enough that she'd gotten real feelings for him that became love. She'd fallen hard enough, fast enough, that in the few hours of getting dressed that evening, she'd created a scenario that didn't exist. Seen things in his behavior that he hadn't meant.

Hell, she had been ready to give up her career—her *life*—for him.

Well, didn't she feel like a damned fool.

He softened his voice. "Rowan…"

She held up her hand. "Don't! There is nothing I hate worse than pity!" She leaned forward, tapped on the glass between them and the driver. "Stop here."

Jozef gaped at her. "What are you doing?"

"Spoiling your fun tonight, Your Majesty. Because while you were living in the moment, taking advantage of a really hot attraction, I was stupidly falling in love with you." When he tried to talk, she raised her hand a little higher. "I don't blame you. I set out the rules. I did not realize how charming you were or that I'd be willing to give up everything for you." She shook her head. "And I've got to tell you I feel more than a little stupid right now. So you not saying anything would work best for me."

The driver suddenly opened the back door. She attempted to slide out. He caught her hand.

"Please don't go. You're taking this all wrong."

She sniffed a laugh. "Actually, that's the first correct thing you've said all night. I did take this all wrong. What was happening between us. How we both thought about it. I got all that wrong. Good night, Your Majesty."

She exited and the driver quickly closed the door and returned to his seat behind the steering wheel before Jozef had fully processed what had happened. He nearly told the man to turn around, to take him to Rowan's apartment so they could fix this.

But that was the problem. They couldn't fix this.

She was younger than he was. *Too young for him.* He had sons closer to her age. She was also a career woman. His queen could not have a job outside the castle. And she was American. Outspoken. Independent.

All the things he liked about her were also things that would make her life miserable if she became his queen.

Her life would become a nightmare of vetting, gossip, constant questions from the press.

Marrying him would be far worse than her great humiliation.

Still, as his limo wove into traffic, all the feelings he'd had when she'd said she loved him poured through him. Joy and loss collided. He pictured waking up with her every morning, even as he pictured the press tearing apart her life.

And knew he'd made the right choice for *her.*

Not for himself. No. He'd miss her more than he could allow himself to ponder—

Because the hollow feelings he felt being driven to the castle door told him he would never forget her.

She was his one true love.

But he couldn't have her.

Though the gallery had only been a five-minute drive from Rowan's apartment, the walk back was much longer. At first, she raced toward her temporary home, but seeing that no one gave her a minute's concern, she slowed her pace. Eventually, she removed her high, high heels. Holding the skirt of her gown so she didn't get the hem dirty, she walked the remaining block to her apartment and then climbed the steps.

But she hadn't done a good job of protecting the soft white material from the dirty sidewalk. She'd have the gown cleaned, then return it to him.

Him.

The guy she loved who didn't love her.

Behind the closed door of her apartment, she took a long slow breath and closed her eyes. How had she let this happen?

Not just how had she let herself fall in love, but how had she fallen in love with a guy who didn't love her.

Again?

Tears pooled in her eyes and spilled over. She walked into her bedroom and fell face-first on the bed.

Oh, God. This hurt worse than her great humiliation. Because the source of *that* pain had been the embarrassment. This time, everything she felt was private. An ache of loss so deep and so pure she almost couldn't move.

She'd taken a chance, offered to give up everything for him and he'd politely refused.

A little voice whispered that she couldn't have been that wrong, couldn't have misread the signs that much. But he'd been very clear in his refusal.

He didn't want what she'd offered, and she had to face that. She needed cold, hard logic to constantly remind her that Jozef didn't love her. That even if what she felt was real, what he felt wasn't.

She stepped out of the pretty white gown, put on her pajamas and tried to sleep but couldn't. She hadn't wanted to be a queen. She hadn't wanted to be royalty. But she loved Jozef and she would have sacrificed everything for him.

How could one man twist her emotions so much that she'd be willing to do that?

Because that's what he'd done. That's what he lived. And in her crazy love for him, she wanted to share his burden.

She had absolutely no idea how to live with this pain. Losing Cash had been embarrassing but losing Jozef *hurt*.

In a rare move, she took the weekend off to get her bearings. But when she tried to work on Monday morning, her brain was mush.

Geoffrey teased and cajoled, trying to get her to talk, but she shrugged him off. When Jozef called, she froze, staring at the phone.

Geoffrey quietly said, "Are you going to get that?"

"No."

"Okay, look. I know something happened on Friday night at the gallery. Maybe he's calling to fix it."

He wasn't calling to fix it because the only way to fix it would be to say he'd changed his mind. And he hadn't. He was a man who knew his mind. If he said he didn't love her, he didn't love her.

Which meant he was being a diplomat, calling to smooth things over. To soften the blow of admitting he didn't love her. She didn't need to hear it. She didn't want his pity.

"He can't fix it."

"Do you want me to answer just in case he has a business reason for calling?"

She shook her head no, but Geoffrey answered anyway.

"Good afternoon, Your Majesty... No, I'm sorry, Rowan's not here right now... Why do I have her phone? She forgot it." At that, Geoffrey caught her gaze and gave her an apologetic look. "Yes. I'll be sure to tell her you called."

As he hung up the phone, the walls closed in on Rowan. "I don't think I can stay here."

"Good. Let's go get coffee or something."

She paced her office. "No. I mean I can't stay here in Prosperita." She combed her fingers through her hair. "Geoffrey, I'm a cliché. I fell for the handsome King. Worse, a reporter saw us together Friday night. God knows if he's checking into my past."

She stopped as a million thoughts assaulted her, the biggest one being she did not give a flying fig if the media found her past and plastered it all over the front pages of every newspaper in the world. It had no bearing on who she was right now.

"You know what? My past sucked but I. Am. Over. It. What the hell am I doing here when my dad's having a birthday party next weekend?"

"I don't know. What the hell are you doing here?

You haven't had a vacation in years. You should take one." Geoffrey laughed. "Want me to make airline reservations?"

"No. I can make them myself. And I'll call Pete and tell him I'm going home for my dad's party and to spend a few weeks visiting my family."

"Makes perfect sense to me."

She shook her head and Geoffrey rose to go into his office. The second he was out of her line of vision, she blew her breath out on a sigh. She was not being gutsy. She was emotionally exhausted. Her affair with Jozef had been the happiest time of her life and he'd rejected her. She'd been rejected by the most wonderful person she'd ever met.

Her eyes stung with tears again. She'd never get over him here in his country. She needed to go home.

# CHAPTER FOURTEEN

Jozef hung up the phone and paced behind his desk.

Because he hadn't seen hide nor hair of her all weekend, he'd called to make sure she was okay. The fact that she wouldn't take his call didn't reassure him. He hated that he'd hurt her. But he genuinely believed this was for the best.

He'd thought about everything she'd said, and longing poured through him. He wanted everything she thought they could have. But she didn't know the real price of loving him—

*Loving him.*

Remembering that she'd said she loved him filled him with a yearning so intense he wanted to throw something against a wall. But he didn't.

*He didn't.*

He never did anything he wasn't allowed to do.

Maybe if he could tell her that, she would understand and not be so hurt?

He stopped pacing his office. She had a standing appointment with Axel every afternoon. He would simply be in Axel's office when she arrived. Then, hopefully, he could explain better, make her see this wasn't her problem, but his life.

He walked to Axel's office a few minutes before her scheduled time and when he ambled through the door, Axel rose.

"Dad?"

"Just thought I'd check in with you and Rowan. See how the fundraiser is doing."

"It's great," Axel said, stepping away from the chair behind the desk and offering it to his father. "You're going to love some of Rowan's ideas."

He took the seat of command. "I'm sure I will."

"Can I have Genevieve get us coffee?"

Jozef said, "No, I'm good," just as Pete Sterling entered Axel's office.

Pete stuttered to a stop. "Your Majesty."

Jozef rose. "Mr. Sterling. Did you enjoy my mother's birthday party the other night?"

Sterling all but glowed. "It was amazing. Rowan and I have been to various events like that, but never as guests. We're sort of background people."

Jozef held back a wince. That was how he knew Rowan didn't understand what she was suggesting. She might have been with him for weeks, but she saw his life through the eyes of an observer, not a participant.

"Speaking of Rowan," Pete said, setting his briefcase on the conference table in the corner of Axel's office before he opened it. "She's taking a vacation." He laughed. "Actually, she's on her way home right now." He pulled a few files from the briefcase. "Her mom is having a seventieth birthday party for her dad next weekend, so she's going to West Virginia."

Jozef blinked. The fact that his mom and her dad were close to the same age sort of floored him, even as he realized she was returning to a very small town where she would undoubtedly run into the guy who hurt her.

To top off all of that, she was getting away from him. Really away from him. He would never see her again.

"So," Pete said, laying packets of papers on Axel's desk. "This is her rundown of how we'll be promoting the event worldwide."

"Worldwide?" Jozef asked, picking up one of the packets.

Axel grinned. "I mentioned this, remember? Rowan and I decided that with the proper promotion we could turn our festival into a yearly tourist attraction."

"Kind of like the running of the bulls," Pete said, looking up over his glasses at Jozef. "Without the bulls."

"And the running," Axel quipped. "This way we can centralize our tourism business. Give hotels and restaurants something to plug…and prepare for."

"Or something to steer travelers away from," Pete added. "Your hotels can say, we have crowds the first two weeks in October for our fall festival. If you want peace and serenity, come in the summer."

Jozef said, "Ah," as Pete and Axel beamed. He waited a beat before he asked, "And Rowan will be back to help finalize all this?"

"She asked for six weeks off. That takes us past your festival." Pete shrugged. "What can I say? She wanted time off."

Or she was preparing to leave Sterling, Grant, Paris and Pete didn't know—

Or she'd already left Sterling, Grant, Paris and Pete didn't want to mention that to a client?

Jozef couldn't ask. If she hadn't already quit, he didn't want to risk her plan to tell her current employer. If she had, what would he say? That he was glad for her?

He wasn't. Everything became confused. What they had wasn't supposed to end like this. Or this quickly. They were supposed to have until after the fall festival. Yet, she was gone. Now.

Always prepared for any contingency, he never found himself in a position of being surprised or left without a plan.

But she was gone.

And he was unprepared.

Forcing a smile, he picked up his packet of information about the festival and faced Axel. "I trust you. And from what I can see here, you are pointing us in a very good direction. I'm proud of you."

Taken aback, Axel said, "Thanks, Dad."

The expression on his son's face sent more confusion through Jozef. His son appeared genuinely surprised by the compliment.

Pete all but bowed as he left the room, and though Jozef was accustomed to people respecting his position, everything about it felt out of sync today.

He returned to his office and tried to leaf through the packet of information Axel and Rowan had put together, but his mind was all over the place. He sat staring out the window, watching as the afternoon sun dipped.

Everything was so damned quiet.

He tried to remember the sounds of his sons racing around the residence and couldn't. He tried to remember Annalise preparing for a holiday or a royal event and he couldn't.

But thoughts of Rowan walking around his home in one of his shirts made him smile. Thinking about borrowing the vehicles of his drivers caused him to laugh out loud. Sneaking to her apartment. Talking about everything and nothing. Those were etched in his brain. Those made him laugh even as they tightened his chest.

He'd finally gotten a taste of romantic love and the joy of it.

He could not believe he would never see the object of that love again, but, worse, he knew all these wonderful memories he had of her would fade with time.

It would be as if he hadn't even known her.

The love of his life and he would forget her in the morass of ruling his country.

Deep sorrow permeated his soul, something else he'd never known or felt. Losing her meant losing more than a person. A piece of himself also disappeared. A playful, happy guy he hadn't even known existed. A guy who'd been so wrapped up in his lover that being with her was his completion. He hadn't merely found his soul he'd found himself.

At eight o'clock his phone rang. Hoping it was Rowan, he grabbed it, but it was Liam. In the silence of his office, he felt himself being pulled back into the world he'd had before Rowan entered and sensed another piece of the guy she had helped him become flutter away.

In the days that followed, he tried to shift back into the life that had been granted to him by destiny, but he simply could not.

At the end of the week, Friday night, when his sons

should have had dates, they'd made plans once again to watch a movie.

This time he knew they recognized that something was off. And just like Rowan, he didn't want anybody's pity.

He didn't bother to change after work, just walked directly to the small in-castle theater. Dressed in jeans and oversize T-shirts, his sons sat laughing at a cartoon they were watching as they waited for him.

Pain pierced his heart again. He had never been happier than when he was with Rowan. He had never been himself the way he could be with her. He'd believed that Annalise—the relationship he had with Annalise—was perfect because he never let his guard down but what he'd had with Rowan far exceeded that. He'd never wanted to be stiff and formal, even if stiff and formal had kept him in good standing with his parents, Castle Admin and the media.

His heart stumbled. He wanted to be the guy he was with her. He wanted that life. Tons of happiness. Maybe more kids. An adventure.

And lots of fodder for the press? Things to criticize?

The movie started and he lowered himself to one of the reclining chairs. But he couldn't stop thinking about his life, about how different he had been with Rowan... About how happy he had been with Rowan.

Truth overshadowed his thoughts, though. He couldn't put Rowan through what would happen if they brought their relationship out in the open and ultimately married—

Could he?

No. He could not. That was why he wasn't with her now.

He glanced at Liam. He loved his sons in the most protective, parental way possible, yet he would be putting Liam through it.

The weight of his job pushed down on his shoulders and the sense that he had had enough filled him. It suddenly seemed all wrong.

He was the King. And though every citizen of his island had the right to hold him accountable for his decisions, no one had the right to monitor his private life, to criticize his choices, to hold his sons to the kinds of standards that would crush an ordinary man.

And *that's* what needed to change. Not him. Not Liam. And certainly not Rowan.

The way Castle Admin let the press rule them was the problem. He'd flirted with the idea of firing Art Andino...but what if he totally restructured Castle Admin?

The thought was so clear and so easy he couldn't speak for a minute as indescribable joy flooded him. He'd been trained to believe he had to be the person his position dictated—and he agreed to a point. He would never embarrass the Crown. But even the thought that there was another side to life, a wonderful, private, elevated side with Rowan, tempted him so much he couldn't let this stand. He had to change things.

He would change things.

And if he had to fight to change them, then he would fight...fight for *her.*

"Has either of you ever thought how you'd feel about me being in a relationship?"

Surprised, his sons glanced over at him.

Liam said, "You're not that old, Dad. You should want another relationship."

"I know, but if I get into another relationship, it will change things significantly around here."

Liam shrugged. "Axel and I are adults and very much on our own. It won't make any difference to us."

"I'm also thinking about changing how we handle the media."

Liam frowned. "The media?"

"Yes. I'm working on a plan that doesn't restrict their access but takes the teeth out of some of their criticisms. I might even have to restructure Castle Admin."

Axel laughed. "What?"

"I had this thought that if we stopped responding to media criticism and allowing Castle Admin to pander to them that they'd lose some of their power."

Axel thought about that, but Liam laughed. "I never thought of it that way, but we sort of do give them power by reacting when they point out what they perceive as flaws."

"I don't think it will be easy," Jozef said. "I think they'll fight back a bit, push us to get us to react, but I think if we stopped reacting and threatened to take away their access when they overstepped, we might be able to tame this tiger."

Liam said, "That would be great."

"You're just doing this to pave the way for your relationship," Axel said, then threw a handful of popcorn in his mouth.

Jozef said, "Maybe."

"Oh, come on, Dad," Axel said with a laugh. "You're already in a relationship."

Liam cast his father a confused look. "You are?"

Axel laughed. "You didn't see a change in him the

past few weeks?" When Liam still looked confused, Axel sighed. "When he was with the PR lady? Rowan?"

Liam grinned. "Seriously, Dad? She is…"

"She's hot is what she is," Axel said. "And incredibly smart."

Jozef squeezed his eyes shut. He didn't know whether to be embarrassed or to scold his sons for talking about him as if he weren't in the room.

"So," Axel said. "Are you going to go after her?"

"After her?" Liam frowned again. "Did she leave?"

Axel snorted. "Liam, you have to keep up or when you're King, Castle Admin will walk all over you." He glanced at his dad. "Of course, if we dismantle Castle Admin, they won't be walking over any of us."

Jozef rose. "That's the plan." He turned to Liam. "You have lots of time to learn to be observant." He faced Axel. "And you only picked up on something between me and Rowan because you worked with her."

He headed to the door. "And I *am* going after her."


After over a week in Manhattan to look at potential sites for the offices for her new PR firm, Rowan made it to West Virginia. She'd needed some time working on her plan and new life, to get herself past the misery of losing Jozef. Her heart still hurt, but she was feeling more like herself. Enough that she could finally go home.

She piled her suitcase, purse and carry-on into a rental car and drove the winding mountain roads to Convenience. Nestled in a rich, green forest, the little town hadn't changed in eight years.

She pulled her rental into the driveway of her parents' redbrick ranch house, with attached two-car garage. Yellow mums and pale pink hydrangeas bloomed in flower beds beneath the big windows on either side of the front door.

The garage door suddenly opened. Her mom raced out. A short woman whose red hair had begun to darken, she was the picture of happiness.

"Rowan! Oh, my God! You're *here*!"

She squeezed her daughter so tightly that Rowan dropped her carry-on bag and laughed. "You just saw me this spring."

Her mom pulled back, studied her face. "I know. But you're here! You're home!"

Rowan whispered. "For a very special event."

Her mom motioned for her to lower her voice even more. "He still doesn't know about the party."

"And he's also losing his hearing," Rowan reminded her mom with a laugh. "He won't hear us if we whisper."

"Whisper what?" her dad, said, strolling out of the garage. He caught Rowan in a big hug, then kissed her cheek before he released her. "I see you're back."

"For about a week," Rowan said, keeping her voice light and cheerful, as she glanced around, waiting for the emotion of her great humiliation to overtake her, but none came.

Instead, she saw the quiet street of her hometown, rows of various types of houses from Cape Cod and Craftsmen styles to ranch houses and Colonials. Some were brick, some were painted various colors, but all the yards were neat as a pin and decorated with flower gardens.

But as much as she loved this town, her parents, this house, it wasn't home anymore. A horrible sense of loneliness overtook her. Not because she missed Paris. Because she missed Jozef.

She immediately wondered what he would think of her home, her town. She tried to shove that thought out of her head, but it wouldn't leave. She wanted him to see her town, to know her, because she wanted him to love her. Leaving Prosperita had been the most difficult thing she had done because she'd known she would never see him again. He wouldn't seek her out. He *couldn't* seek her out. And she had no reason to return to his country.

What they had, those wonderful couple of weeks, was all she would get. Though she tried to be happy for having known him, the ache in her heart radiated to her entire body. She'd thought she'd loved Cash, but what she felt for Jozef made that pale in comparison.

And now she no longer had a great humiliation, she had a real broken heart.

"Come inside," her dad said, looping his meaty arm over her shoulders. "We'll get a beer."

A beer.

It had been a while since she'd had a beer. But she was home. Funny, that she had run from this town because of a broken relationship and now the only place she believed she could fix this broken heart was here. With her family.

Her sister and brother were happy to see her. Both had gotten engaged. Both insisted she had to come to their weddings. Her heart sank again. Here she was thirty, and she'd managed to fall in love with the one man who couldn't love her. While her younger siblings raced past her in making their lives, she had stagnated.

The thought flummoxed her. In the eight years since

her great humiliation, she'd believed marriage was a full stop, not a part of making a life. Odd how she didn't feel that way anymore. She finally saw love and marriage was just the beginning.

She took her dad to the diner for dinner when her mom pretended to have a headache and not be able to cook. He'd frowned, but when Rowan acted thrilled to be going to the diner for their famous chili, he relented.

Most of the people they'd run into didn't even mention Cash, and if her heart weren't so broken over losing Jozef that might have made her laugh. By the time they returned to the redbrick ranch, she was exhausted from pretending to be happy.

They walked up to the driveway and her dad put his hand on her forearm to stop her. "What's the matter, kitten? You're not yourself."

They were supposed to enter through the garage so her mom could pop on the lights, and everybody could jump up and yell surprise. This was not the time to pour her heart out to her dad. Though she longed to throw herself into his big arms and weep, have him comfort her as she cried it all out, she couldn't.

"Nothing. I'm fine."

"Oh, come on. You can't kid a kidder."

She laughed. "You always say that, but I pulled the wool over your eyes a lot when I was a kid."

He batted a hand. "I just let you think that."

"You did?"

"Yeah. A kid's gotta have some fun. I let you think you got away with things." He pointed at the garage door. "Just like I let your mom believe I hadn't figured out about the surprise party."

She sighed. "If I don't get you in that garage soon, Mom's gonna think I screwed up."

"Well, we can't have that."

"No, we can't," she agreed, catching his arm and dragging him to the garage door. She hit the button on the remote door opener her mom had given her and the two doors rose simultaneously. The lights flashed on. The fifty people in the garage jumped up and yelled, "Surprise!"

Her mom raced out and hugged her dad. Over her mom's shoulder, he winked at Rowan.

Then he turned to face the crowd with a smile. "Hey! Thanks!" He walked in and began shaking the hands of the guests standing around the two long tables filled with food. "Nice to see you. Thanks for coming. Nice to see you."

Twenty minutes later, he sat beside her on a bench along the back wall. "I turned seventy this week. It's a milestone. So it wasn't a stretch to guess your mom was planning something. If you want to surprise someone you need to have better timing."

She bumped his shoulder with her own. "Right."

She took a long breath, taking in the cooling September air.

"You're not going to tell me what's wrong?"

"Nope."

"You can't always hide from your troubles, kitten. You have to talk to someone sometime."

"I can't, Dad. I had all these wonderful plans of starting my own PR firm, then I fell in love, and nothing seems to have any meaning anymore."

"Whoa! Whoa! You fell in love?"

"With someone who doesn't love me." There. She'd said it. Her heart shredded again with the pain of loss and ridiculous longing.

"Well, he's an idiot."

"No. He's a king."

Her dad gaped at her. "What?"

"A king." She opened her arms, motioning around the garage. "And I'm about as common as they come. But there's more to it than that. Duty and responsibility. A need to have his life planned to a tee. I don't fit."

It hurt to say that too.

And she was at the end of her ability to talk about Jozef. She rose from the old bench. "You know what? I'm kind of tired. I think I'll go inside and get a shower. If the party's still going on I'll come out and say goodnight."

"Honey, I don't think you should…" Her dad's face scrunched in confusion then he rose and pointed down the street. "What is that?"

She followed the direction of his pointing finger and saw a long black limo pulling up in front of her house. Her heart stopped.

The driver emerged, walked to the back of the limo and opened the door.

Jozef stepped out.

Rowan stood frozen. Her eyes wide.

He ambled up the sidewalk and to the driveway, toward the open garage doors.

Standing over her shoulder, her dad leaned down and said, "Now, that's how you do a surprise."

She would have laughed but her mouth wouldn't

move. She couldn't breathe. Confused silence filled the garage.

Wearing the red and blue polo shirt she'd bought him for the soccer game, he entered the garage and walked up to her. "I'm sorry."

Knowing the eyes of all fifty people were on her, because the King of an entire country was in her family's *garage,* she couldn't process what he was saying. "What?"

"I came to some conclusions in the weeks after you left." His gaze held hers. "I do love you. I didn't want to say it the other day because I didn't want you to go through the media circus that would follow if we began dating."

"Oh. Okay."

He laughed. "I get the sense I surprised you so much you're speechless, and I'm not sure you're fully understanding me when what I have to say is really important."

She shook her head, forcing herself not to look at the fifty people who were staring at them and keeping her attention on Jozef.

"I talked with my sons. We're all tired of the media bullying us. We're all on board with accountability. But we really do not believe they should have any say in our private lives."

"No matter what you do, they'll push back."

"Let them. We've decided that if we don't react to the less important things, they will lose their hold on us."

She considered that. It was advice she'd given to a

client a time or two. She finally understood what was going on. He was here for advice.

She raised her chin, refusing to let any of the pain she felt seep through. After all, he saw her more as PR person and a friend than his lover. She'd answer his few questions and he'd leave.

"It could work, but at some point, once they realize what you're doing, they are going to push back. You'll have an uphill battle for a few years."

He held out his hand. "Want to fight it with me?"

The pain turned to ice. "You're here to hire me?"

"No. I'm here to ask you out on a date. A real date."

"So you can attack your media head-on?"

"No. Hopefully so that you'll remember you love me and eventually we'd get married." He rifled in his pocket. "I have a ring. I love you enough to face the gates of hell to keep you in my life. When I told you no it was because I didn't want to see you hurt. But you're a tough cookie. What we had is worth fighting for."

She stared at him. His handsome face. His once brooding eyes that sparkled with amusement.

"You love me?"

"I do."

Her dad came strolling out. "Hey. Hey. Save the 'I do's' for the wedding." He held out his hand. "I'm Rowan's dad."

Then her mom eased out and introduced herself. "I'm her mom."

Her sister came out. "Younger sister."

"I'm Fontain. Brother."

Everyone shook hands with Jozef and he handled it all with grace and dignity. He explained who he was and where he was from and all fifty people nodded as their eyes widened.

He ate a ham sandwich and drank two beers with her dad while answering a hundred questions. Then when interest in him died down. Rowan and Jozef sat on the front porch swing.

"I can't believe you're here."

Jozef glanced around. "I can't believe I'm here either." He slid his arm along the back of the swing. "But you know what? You make me want a life, a real life."

She cuddled closer, glancing down at her ring that sparkled in the porch light. "Doesn't get much more real than this."

He laughed. "I don't think you understand what a gift it is to be able to be yourself."

"I think I do now." A thought hit her and she gasped. "Where's your security?"

"Discreetly hidden." He took a breath. "Actually, when we made our plan, they told me that you can't sleep at your parents' house tonight. The detail they brought doesn't have enough men to keep guard over a house and a hotel. You have to come back to the hotel with me."

"Did you just make that up to get me to come back to your hotel and sleep with you?"

He laughed. "No. I swear. This is about security. But it does work in our favor."

She smiled at him. "Yeah. It does."

They stayed at the party another hour, then she packed a bag and they left for the hotel. They'd be back to say goodbye to her parents the next day, but she knew she was embarking on the greatest adventure of her life.

Not marrying a king—

Being married to a guy who loved her enough to change *his* world for her.

It was going to take a lot of kisses to thank him for that.

# EPILOGUE

AXEL STOOD AT the altar of Prosperita's cathedral. In full dress uniform, he, his brother, Liam, and his father looked about as official as a king and two princes could be.

Rowan Gray walked down the aisle toward them on the arm of her father. Through two years of his daughter dating the King, Rowan's dad had become accustomed to all things royal and he looked as calm and comfortable as he did in the backyard of his West Virginia home.

Axel took great pride in that. He'd not only realized his father was falling for the lovely PR person sent to set him up on dates, he'd also taken the lead when they made visits to her family's home. He was damned good at pool—as good as her father and brother—and he could now grill a mean hamburger. Not that he needed to here in Prosperita, but he prided himself on being the bridge of the family. The one who could create a way for groups to get along.

He should be in the diplomatic corps for the country. Now that his work with making the fall festival a tourist attraction was taking off like a rocket, maybe someday he would.

Rowan arrived at the altar. The sparkles of her flowing gown and veil were totally outdone by the sparkles in her eyes. Good God, she loved his dad.

Which was amazing and touching. He loved his dad too, and after seven years without Axel and Liam's mom, Jozef Sokol deserved the happiness Rowan had brought into his life. Axel loved her for that. Loved her for bringing life back to the castle. Loved her for being no one's pushover.

In fact, if he were honest, he'd have to admit he'd had a bit of a crush on her himself, if only because she'd never let Castle Admin push her around. And with her PR background the press was putty in her hands.

He laughed, then covered it with a cough in the solemn confines of the cathedral.

He took a breath and turned when his father and Liam did, letting the wedding service ebb and flow around him. He didn't like the public side of their lives. He much preferred being the bridge between the royals and whoever they were bringing into their inner circle, intentionally or not.

But he could endure the pomp and circumstance.

A motion at the back of the church caught his attention and he scowled. Damn it all anyway! The new security employee was flapping her arms about something.

The woman had no idea of decorum.

He had no problem with women serving in their security details, but he did not believe this one had been properly vetted.

Maybe this was one of those times when he should interfere? His dad had been busy. Liam was always being observed so he couldn't stick his nose somewhere that it didn't belong, but Axel could.

If there wasn't a very, very good reason for whatever she was flapping her arms about, she would be fired.

The ceremony ended. His father and Rowan walked out of the church, under the arch of swords and raced to the limo.

He and Rowan's sister, a bridesmaid, and Liam and one of Rowan's friends from Paris, another bridesmaid, walked out of the church and he forgot all about the security person.

The sun was warm, the entire country was celebrating the long-awaited wedding and Axel was so happy for his dad he could have burst.

\* \* \* \* \*

# COMING
# SOON!

We really hope you enjoyed reading this book.
If you're looking for more romance, be sure to
head to the shops when new books are
available on

## Thursday 4th
## August

To see which titles are coming soon, please visit
**millsandboon.co.uk/nextmonth**

# MILLS & BOON®

## Coming next month

### PREGNANCY SHOCK FOR THE GREEK BILLIONAIRE
### Kandy Shepherd

"I don't need a DNA test," Stefanos said.

"But I—"

"I don't believe you would lie about something so important."

She looked up at him, unable to stop her eyes from misting with tears. "Thank you Stefanos, that means a lot. I…I…can't tell you how much it means." Frantically she scrubbed at her eyes with her fists. "Not crying. I'm really not. It's just that I feel so unwell, and I'm so tired, and I'm overwhelmed and… and I'm terrified." Despite her every effort to suppress them, she burst into full on sobs.

Stefanos immediately drew her into a hug. He had broad, accommodating shoulders and he wrapped his arms around her and let her cry.

Finally, she sobbed herself out. Her breathing evened out except for the odd gulp and occasional sniffle. She stilled, wishing she could stay there forever and not have to face him after making such an exhibition of herself. It was humiliating.

That had been one of her grandmother's expressions when Claudia had lost her temper or started to cry, or as a teenager had had too much to drink. Grandma Eaton had had quite a lot to do with her and Mark's upbringing when her parents had been really busy at the pub. Apparently Claudia, as a child, had quite often made an exhibition of herself and had to be reprimanded. No wonder she'd grown up tamping down on strong emotions and determined to present the best possible view of herself to others.

Finally, she reluctantly pulled away from Stefanos, feeling like she was leaving a safe haven. She looked up at him and was relieved to see kindness, not criticism in his eyes.

"I'm sorry, I didn't mean—" she started.

"Do you remember what I said about not saying 'sorry'? You have absolutely nothing to be sorry about." He wiped a damp strand of hair away from a face in a gesture that was surprisingly tender.

"Your shirt! Oh no, there are damp patches." Ineffectually, she tried to dab them away with the sleeve of her wrap. "Luckily I wasn't wearing makeup, so no mascara stains at least."

"Just salty tears," he said, sounding more than a touch bemused. "They'll dry."

"But…but that nice linen fabric could be rumpled. Let me iron your shirt, it's the least I can do."

"There is absolutely no need to do that, Claudia."

"If you're sure, but it's no trouble and—"

"What I want you to do is tell me why you're terrified of having a baby."

*Continue reading*
PREGNANCY SHOCK FOR THE GREEK
BILLIONAIRE
Kandy Shepherd

*Available next month*
www.millsandboon.co.uk

# MILLS & BOON

## THE HEART OF ROMANCE

---

## A ROMANCE FOR EVERY READER

---

**MODERN**
Prepare to be swept off your feet by sophisticated, sexy and seductive heroes, in some of the world's most glamourous and romantic locations, where power and passion collide.

**HISTORICAL**
Escape with historical heroes from time gone by. Whether your passion is for wicked Regency Rakes, muscled Vikings or rugged Highlanders, awaken the romance of the past.

**MEDICAL**
Set your pulse racing with dedicated, delectable doctors in the high-pressure world of medicine, where emotions run high and passion, comfort and love are the best medicine.

**True Love**
Celebrate true love with tender stories of heartfelt romance, from the rush of falling in love to the joy a new baby can bring, and a focus on the emotional heart of a relationship.

**Desire**
Indulge in secrets and scandal, intense drama and plenty of sizzling hot action with powerful and passionate heroes who have it all: wealth, status, good looks…everything but the right woman.

**HEROES**
Experience all the excitement of a gripping thriller, with an intense romance at its heart. Resourceful, true-to-life women and strong, fearless men face danger and desire - a killer combination!

---

To see which titles are coming soon, please visit

## millsandboon.co.uk/nextmonth